I0667679

FROM THE MOUNTAINS TO YOU

LOST IN LOVE
BOOK 2

ZOE GRACE DOUGLAS

Copyright © 2025 by Zoe Grace Douglas

All rights reserved.

No part of this book may be reproduced in any form or by any electronic or
mechanical means, including information storage and retrieval systems,
without written permission from the author, except for the use of brief
quotations in a book review.

Cover Designed by @essasketch

Copy and Line Editing by @cassidyhudspethedits

Formatting by @kmortonedits

Chapter Mountain Image licensed from Canva Pro.

This is to little old me who was just as lost and scared to love, but hoped to get her own love story.
And to anyone else who has ever felt the same, you are not hard to love, you just needed the right person.

PLAYLIST

End of Beginning - Djo
So Long, London - Taylor Swift
Jealous - Labrinth
A House In Nebraska - Ethel Cain
You All Over Me - Taylor Swift, Maren Morris
Julia - Lauv
Now that we don't talk - Taylor Swift
We hug now - Sydney Rose
I love you, I'm sorry - Gracie Abrams
when the party's over - Billie Eilish
Tornado Warnings - Sabrina Carpenter
Say it Right - Nelly Furtado
Anchor - Novo Amor
Creatures in Heaven - Glass Animals
Spring into Summer - Lizzy McAlpine
The Alcott - The National, Taylor Swift
Love Song - Lana Del Rey
Always Been You - Shawn Mendes
Evermore - Taylor Swift
you! - LANY

CONTENT WARNINGS

This story includes depictions of sensitive topics that have been shaped, softened, or heightened for the sake of the story. Please take caution if any of the following subjects may be triggering for you. This book includes topics such as:

- Grief and the loss of a parent (in the past)
- On-page panic attacks (one scene) and a few mentions of previous panic attacks
- Injury
- Parental neglect and verbal / physical abuse (past, very ingrained in the mc's thoughts, one on page scene)
- Some mentions of alcohol and substance abuse (past, not on page)

1

DAKOTA

I can already feel the whispers of the past seeping into my bones as the wheels of the plane squeak against the tarmac, greeting me back home. It's been six years since I last breathed this air, and instead of making me feel a sense of belonging and comfort–like I'm home–it almost makes me want to bolt onto the next flight back to Melbourne.

Remembering another version of myself that was lost and naive, wanting nothing more than to experience what it was like to be in love, feels like a lifetime ago. I was hopeless, with stars in my eyes and longing in my heart while waiting for my first real bite of love. But of course, I couldn't have it that easy.

Because everything that happened that summer was so much more than I prepared for.

I was so quick to say good riddance to that time of my life, I didn't give myself any proper time to grieve and allow myself to stitch my heart back together.

When I first moved, I was mostly on autopilot, disassociating from everything I felt. I barely did anything other than eat, sleep, and go to my photography classes.

It was only ever at night that I let myself cry until I fell asleep. Only ever in the comfort of my bedroom did I let myself feel.

But trying to cope that way only made it worse. It made the wounds grow, letting them fester through the day and haunt my every night.

I never said more than four words a day to Ellie in that month—which now makes me feel like the biggest asshole after she took me in. But I felt so numb to everything.

Eventually, she had enough of my zombie act before deciding to drag me out of the house and introduce me to her friends, drinking and dancing the night away. It did have some sort of balming effect on my aching heart. But it only solved to slap a band-aid over everything for a short period. Which was all I needed to move out of the funk I was in at the time.

As the days and months passed, and I felt I had pieced some parts of myself back together, I found the courage to contact Daniel again, the guy I had met during our schoolies week in Airlie Beach.

He and Ellie became my saving graces in surviving Melbourne and returning to some semblance of normalcy without crying myself to sleep every night.

But I never really got the closure I needed. It wasn't until a year later that I realised it. When I was watching couples in the park and yearning for something they had after countless failed dates. I started therapy shortly after in hopes of healing the part of me that was holding back.

Even in those sessions with Callie, I still hesitated to open myself up all the way. Hesitating to talk about the one thing I needed to until the last minute. I think, subconsciously, I didn't want to let that part of my heart go. Like, there was still a part of me that wanted to hold onto the idea of him. Like talking about him was finally letting go of the possibility of us, even though I knew that was a ridiculous notion. I never imagined us ever finding each other again–didn't want to–but there was still a nugget of hope tucked into that little pocket of my heart where I kept him.

Finding that note while packing was like opening a floodgate to the endless river I had meticulously kept blocked in the back of my mind. The years of shoving it all deep down and being unwilling to release it finally crumbled to pieces.

I found myself scrambling for my phone to book an emergency appointment with Callie, and before I knew it, I was letting it all sink into the plush carpet of her office. Bottled emotions flooded every crevasse of the room that day. The guilt of letting it hold me back from returning home, choking me, diminishing every bit of progress I thought I made.

For the past six years, home hadn't felt like home anymore. It was a stranger. A ghost to the recesses of my mind. It was a reminder of my heartbroken teenage years, and I avoided it like the plague.

But I knew I couldn't avoid it forever.

I needed to mend that feeling, to retrace the good memories that still weaved through the streets and scrub away the ones that haunted me. I didn't want the ghost of the past holding me back from missing any more moments with my family and friends. I didn't want a phone screen between us when I told them about my day and exciting news.

Who knows, maybe returning would heal that part of me I'd been desperate for, stitching it together piece by tiny broken piece. Maybe I'd finally find the closure I needed from the start.

My phone pings with an onslaught of messages from the group chat and Dad as I turn airplane mode off, the plane slowing and preparing for unloading.

Alex and Avery have been blowing up my phone the last few days, planning for my arrival today. It's been too many months since I last saw them when they visited Melbourne, and I miss them.

Guilt hits me just as it always does, expecting them to come to see me, but never the other way around. They never minded the travel, though, and they loved Melbourne every time they came to visit. But the feeling never eased when I still refused to fly home.

I scroll through their messages, shouting their excitement to see me and reiterating final details of tonight, before clicking Dad's message from ten minutes ago.

> I just parked. Let me know when you land.

I start typing after flight attendants announce we can now exit and grab my bag from the overhead bin.

> Just landed. Can't wait to see you.

His message picks me up a little, easing the tight feeling in my chest as we slowly shuffle off the plane and into the bustling airport. I head straight toward baggage claim, weaving through the rush of people trying to get to their gates, wanting to get out quickly.

It's almost like deja vu with the tightness in my chest, identical to the way I felt before I left for Melbourne. However, instead of heartbreak and excitement for the new life I'm starting, this time it's a mix of guilt and excitement about my dad's upcoming wedding.

I've met his fiancée a few times over the years they have visited. Jenna is beautiful in every sense with tawny skin, tight, curly hair, and an air of gentleness and kindness. Their love and happiness shone through their eyes every time I saw them look at each other. It's the kind of thing I've only dreamed of having. The kind of thing I felt for a fleeting moment, barely registering when it was there until it was gone.

When Dad asked me to come home to help with the wedding preparations, I hesitated for only a minute. But only a minute was needed before he took to begging and convincing me in any way possible. The heavy guilt weighed on me that he needed to go to those lengths just to see me home and spend a bit more time together. He was my dad, and here he was, giving me reasons why I should come home three months earlier and planning things with me so I wouldn't think of reasons to leave. It shouldn't be so hard for him to see me, his only daughter. I should be there for him whenever he needed me.

I felt like the world's worst daughter. I *was* the worst daughter.

So I agreed, and now, here I am, spending the next three months in a place I'd avoided for years. In a place that feels far from the home I grew up in.

It's not long before the carousel starts to move, baggage from my flight coming in a slow cycle, and the other passengers push closer. I hang back though until I catch sight of mine. I squeeze through the crowd and grab it before making my way out of the airport.

The spring-scented wind whispers against my skin in a quiet relief, and a weird sense of nostalgia sets in. Just feeling the difference in the weather makes me want to drop to my knees and weep. It's taken a while to get used to the dry Melbourne weather since I was more acclimated to the humid air clinging to my skin. Feeling it now after so long, funnily enough, makes me miss it and my heart ache.

I stand outside the airport with my eyes closed and my head tilted toward the sky, letting it sink in. I probably look like an idiot, but I don't care. I just need a minute to come to terms with the fact that I'm finally here before finding Dad. That I was home.

I shake off the multitude of emotions before continuing on.

It doesn't take long to find him when I make my way to the line of awaiting cars in the pick-up zone. Especially not with his enormous grin and equally enormous sign with *Chickadee* scribbled in bold capital letters. Like father, like son, thinking back to when Nate had done the same on my return from Airlie Beach.

My cheeks heat, but I can't stop my excitement as I rush over to him.

"Hi, Dad."

He immediately pulls me into a bear hug as soon as I'm close enough to reach him. He's tall, dwarfing my five-nine frame when he holds me like this. But his warm embrace makes every muscle I didn't realise was tense instantly relax as I fall into it.

He mumbles into the top of my head, twisting me side to side. "Hey, Chickadee. You have no idea how happy I am that you're here. I've missed you so much."

He tightens his hold before letting me go, holding my shoulders with outstretched arms. I notice the glistening in his blue eyes, the same colour as mine, and I bite the inside of my lip to keep my own emotions at bay. It's hard not to mirror his emotions when he looks at me like this.

"I've missed you too, Dad."

He squeezes my shoulders, sniffling back the tears building in his eyes before clearing his throat.

"Come on. We'd better hit the road before people start yelling at us to move. I've already been given side glares from people driving past." He snickers before taking my suitcase from me and loading it into the boot.

Hopping into the car, he turns to look at me, eyes still shining with unshed tears as he squeezes my hand.

"You can't be this emotional already, Dad. It isn't even your wedding day," I joke.

He nudges my shoulder before shifting into drive and pulling into the traffic. "Don't bully your old man. I'm just happy to see you."

My lips twitch. "You saw me four months ago."

He shoots me a sideways glance before focusing back on the road. "It's not the same, and you know it."

Silence falls over us as I chew on his words.

I do know, and I wish I had the guts to have overcome my fear of facing being home sooner. I really did miss it here. I miss seeing Dad. I miss the familiarity and warmth it used to hold.

I never planned on moving so far away. But the moment my rose-tinted glasses shattered on the ground, I felt suffocated. I didn't know which way was up or down. I didn't know myself. Though I was never truly alone, being surrounded by my friends and family, I still felt so lonely in that moment.

But I've had six years to get over this irrational fear, and this was unavoidable.

The further we travel through the city and I see all the familiar streets and buildings, the more the echoes of memories push past my walls, dancing like ghosts in the wind as they play like scenes in a movie in my head. I remember the lazy days and the quiet nights. I remember my young, naive self with my head in the clouds and hope in my heart.

But it's not only my past creeping in; I also feel the whispers of the memories I've missed here. The moments I could only witness through a phone screen because I was too much of a coward to be here, to come home. From my friend's graduations to Nate's and Dad's proposals, I missed it all.

I always feared everyone would move on without me and leave me in the dust. But this was no one's fault but my own. Even with my move and all the dreams I'd chased, I still felt like everyone was moving faster than I could catch up. Sometimes it felt like I was still standing motionless, right where I was left broken and alone.

I may have left in the hopes of leaving the shell of who I was, but in doing that, I also left my friends and family. And because I was scared to return, I missed all their big moments.

I refuse to continue being that coward by missing Dad's wedding.

It's been a while since I've seen Dad as happy as he is now. He's never given me a reason to believe he was unhappy because he's always had a smile on his face, but it seems to radiate right off him now.

Jenna is the outgoing and adventurous type to my dad's cool and calm. They balance and challenge each other. She encourages him to explore and get out of the house, and he reminds her to take a minute to slow down and enjoy the little moments. It's sweet and sickening to watch, but I'm happy to see him find something people search their lifetimes to experience. Something I have been searching to fill since losing it.

But as Callie has said, this is a step to healing myself and finding the closure I have been desperate to seek.

At least I know I won't run into *him* while I'm here.

Only his ghost.

2

DAKOTA

I expect nothing less from Dad when confetti pops in front of me the moment I walk into the house, and my friends' smiling faces greet me as they shout, "Welcome home!" But it still shocks me. I stand there, mouth agape, taking everything in and holding back the tears threatening to escape.

A homemade banner with the same welcoming message hangs from the top of the stairs with pink and purple balloons draped down either side to the floor. A burst of laughter escapes me as I turn to Dad, the first tear trailing down my cheek, and I nudge his arm.

"You're too much," I tell him.

He tugs me into his arms, wrapping them around my head before he messes up my hair playfully. I immediately pull away from his grasp and straighten the short strands back into place, still not used to the way they fall from my fingers so quickly and how light it feels.

"You deserve it, Chook. Now, be with your friends. I'm gonna start dinner, so be ready by six."

He shoos me away and as he heads past me to the kitchen, my friends immediately swarm me.

"Oh my god. Your hair! When did you chop it off? *Why* did you chop it off?" Avery questions as she takes a stand of my hair between her fingers before letting it fall through them.

I comb my fingers through the shoulder-length strands at the back.

"I cut it probably a couple of days ago. Thought it was time for a change." I shrug, thinking back to my impulsivity after finding that note and the preceding events of the week. It just felt symbolic in the moment, and with every pass of the scissors, watching the hair fall, it made the tightness in my chest ease.

"A couple of days? Well, that was good timing. New start, new hair. It looks really good," Alex compliments.

"It suits you. Makes you look older. In a good way, though," Avery adds, before taking hold of my arm and guiding us to the couch. "Let's sit. I want to hear all about your latest project."

We all flop onto the couch before I dive into the project I just finished, which took months of travelling, multiple film reels, and countless editing hours.

Lately, contact between the three of us has been minimal due to our busy lives. It usually happens around this time of the year, but that only makes these reunions all the more bittersweet.

I normally only see them for a couple of weeks in a year when we plan our holidays together, and I've loved our meet-ups, but they always seem too short.

This time is different, though. I'm here and have three months with them, and it feels like coming back to our old roots.

They catch me up with what's been going on in their lives since our last video chat almost two months ago.

Alex is always on the go, being a flight attendant, and he tells us about all the places he's visited in the last couple of months, more so for my benefit.

Avery's a case manager working with clients suffering from homelessness and substance abuse in the community, and has been working nonstop lately. Most of her spare time is spent with Jake, and I have to push back the onslaught of questions I want to ask when she talks about how they are doing. It's a selfish thought pattern, because I want to hear all about how happy she is, but it's like my brain won't get rid of the connection between him and Reece.

Alex teases her about how they are almost always arguing and riling each other up, and the stinging in my chest increases, noticing, like every year, how much closer Avery and Alex are. With my reluctance to come home and the fact that they live together with Jake, they see more of each other than I do. I know it's my fault that I feel like an outsider because I could have been right beside them in all these memories they relay to me if only I weren't so afraid.

The front door opens, and Dad's fiancée swings in with her arms full of groceries.

Jenna beams over the box in her arms, her curls bundled up on top of her head as Dad comes rushing over to take it from her, kissing her cheek. She quietly thanks him before noticing me, and her smile widens. I stand, ready for her embrace, and she envelopes me immediately.

"It's so good to see you. Welcome home," she greets before pulling away, holding me at arm's length. Her eyes scan my face with a gentle smile as she presses a hand to my cheek before her eyes catch on my hair. "Your hair looks nice like this."

"Thank you. I'm happy to be home."

The word 'home' feels foreign to say out loud after so long.

She squeezes my shoulders, an earnest look in her eyes. "So are we, love."

I take a deep breath, emotions overloading, before letting her, Alex, and Avery know I'll be upstairs getting ready.

"Do you need help with your bags?" Alex asks from over the couch.

I shake my head. "No, I've only got two bags."

He nods before slapping Avery's hand as she reaches out to the top of his head. She frowns as they start bickering again, just like they always do, and I shake my head, leaving them to it.

I grab my bags from Dad's car and heave them up the stairs to my room.

I didn't really give much thought to my room before today, but as soon as I open the door, it's like a flashback to the summer before I left.

Although the room is practically empty without my belongings, the furniture remains the same. The walls, the bedspread, the curtains, everything just like I left it. I expected something about it to have changed. Something with Dad's touch, with him experimenting and his building expertise. But nothing is out of place.

Maybe I just hoped he would change it so I wouldn't face walking into the time loop I'm in now.

I wonder if he left it untouched in hopes I would return. My chest aches at the thought.

Memories still swim through every inch of the room, ones I have suppressed for a long time.

It's almost too much, the way they slam into me. Tears prick my eyes as I remember every laugh, smile, and kiss shared in this room. I remember the tears and heartache that made me never want to get out of bed. I remember every moment from that summer until I closed the door for the last time.

Silence stretches through the room, so much so that I begin to hear the faraway whispers of the past dance along the carpet, taunting me, gliding over my skin like a second coat, and coaxing me to join them in their misery. It's almost tempting to let it pull me under and drown myself in them, but I close my eyes and take a deep breath, blocking it all out.

I unpack a few of my clothes, hanging up a few of my dresses, before I pull out a pair of shorts and a T-shirt to put on, when my eyes catch the note I brought with me. The note I'm hoping to burn in some sacrilegious way to close that chapter in my life. I've been holding on to the strings that tethered me to that life for far too long, and now is the time to accept and move on.

I set the note on my dresser, anchoring it under a jewellery box so it doesn't fly away in the breeze.

But with the reminder of that tear-blotched piece of paper, it's like my walls slip and the memories flash back to me as if playing on a film reel.

I can almost see us lying in the sheets as he glides his fingers down my face, the morning light shining through the window as we share secret smiles in the safety of my room. I can almost feel that all-consuming feeling blooming in my chest, something that could nearly be mistaken for love. A feeling I've yearned to replace.

I swallow down the lump growing in my throat and shake myself out of the trance that had taken hold of me, rushing to get dressed, not wanting the past to consume me again.

Avery appears in the doorway, worry creasing her brows as she pushes open the door further, and I welcome the interruption.

"You okay?" she asks, eyes flicking between mine and taking in my frazzled appearance.

I'm not sure how to answer that properly. I'm okay, but then again, I feel like I was being consumed by all these bubbling emotions all at once.

It was the moments that I was seemingly happy and at peace that made me miss it all. The way he held me, kissed me, and touched me had my heart pinching at the ghost of it whispering against my skin. I haven't felt that since then, and it's made me wonder if I would ever find anything close to that again.

But this was how I was going to heal from it all. By confronting it and accepting all the feelings I didn't when I was eighteen. Like exposure therapy, facing all my fears.

So, I paste on a smile and nod. "Yeah, I'm okay. It's just been a while."

She smiles and squeezes my shoulder as she steps back. "It has. But I'm so glad you're back, even for just three months."

"And hopefully this means you'll come to visit now," Alex pipes in as he barges in and collapses on my bed.

I titter, discreetly wiping under my eyes as soon as their attention shifts off me and sit on the bed next to Alex's sprawled form. "Maybe."

"So, now that you're back in town, when are we going out? Sometime before you're swept up in all this wedding planning," Alex questions, always the first one to organise a night out together. And since they told me the other arrangement was just a ploy for them to surprise me, we needed to organise another night.

Avery hums. "Right. What about tomorrow? You won't be doing anything yet, will you? I have the day off Saturday, so it's perfect for my recovery."

My brows shoot up. "Recovery? Already prepared for a big night? That's unlike you."

She shrugs. "It's a big moment. And I need this night. It has been," she sighs heavily, "stressful at work lately. I've been struggling with one of my clients and I feel like I've been taking a lot of that on."

I smile and reach over from where she sits at the head of the bed and squeeze her hand. "Then tomorrow it is. We'll go into the city and Dad can pick us up later."

Alex nods. "Sounds like a plan."

"Alright, let's have dinner. I'm starved," Avery groans, pulling us up from bed and dragging us out the door.

I breathe a sigh of relief when the door closes behind me. Hopefully, I'll be too tired after this dinner to think about these things and crash into bed.

Alex and Avery rush down the stairs, but I take my time coming down, working on the breathing exercises Callie always works me through at the end of our sessions, relaxing the muscles in my shoulders before joining them all.

The doorbell rings as I hit the landing, so I go to answer it, peaking over to see the others talking and laughing amongst each other.

I pause at the door as I watch them for a moment, feeling like an outsider, looking at a family I've floated away from and am anxious to swim back to, but the current is drifting me further out of reach, thick with years of stubbornness.

It's a difficult feeling, one I know I'm overthinking, but I can't help feeling like an idiot for the years of pushing them away.

I shove the feeling to the back of my mind, though, opening the door and smiling at the sight of Mum standing there with her pressed-to-perfection suit and flawless makeup.

She brushes her hair behind her ear, her lips parting in a smile of her own when she sees me. She steps through the threshold and wraps me in her arms. It's comforting, and in this room, I'm reminded of a time when I dreaded being near her, how her hugs used to be robotic and forced, feeling like she only just tolerated me.

But now, with the years of getting to know each other, I felt like I had a mum again. She made the effort, even after I moved away. She came to visit me, which surprised me the first couple of times, but it was the start of our relationship. After countless lunches and dinners, talking and apologising, I realised I was more like my mother than I cared to admit. I would have detested that idea when I was younger, but now that I truly knew her, I couldn't help but admire that. I had a mix of both of my parents, and it filled a little missing piece in my heart.

She squeezes me before pulling away, cradling my face in her hands. She takes note of my hair and smiles at me again. "I knew it would look good on you."

She had placed the idea in my head last year, and while I originally declined the idea, it still stuck with me.

"Thank you, Mum." I smile and then frown. "I thought I was meeting you tomorrow for breakfast."

"That's still the plan, but your father invited me to have dinner with you all. I thought it sounded nice." She hooks her arm in mine and we start toward the kitchen.

"It does sound nice." Just like Dad to invite Mum so she was included.

When Dad spots us making our way toward them, he smiles and greets Mum. "Hi, Laura. Good that you made it. You've met Jenna?"

"Yes. Nice to meet you again. Thank you for inviting me." Mum smiles politely as Jenna wraps her arms around her.

"Of course. It's nice to see you, too," Jenna says, pulling away before grabbing a bowl of mash and bringing it over to the table.

"Wait," I hold my hand up, so lost on what's going on, "again? You guys have met?"

Mum looks at me like I'm strange for questioning this. "Yeah. I went to visit Nate at the same time they were there, probably a year ago now."

"Oh," is all I say as if it was totally normal for Mum to meet Dad's new fiancée. I guess I didn't really expect to see them all in the same room or interact so normally.

Dad starts to bring over some more bowls and pans of steak to where Jenna has started to set the table. After getting myself and Mum a glass of wine, we all sit around the dining table, chatting and eating the steak and vegetables Dad cooked.

I fill everyone in about what I have been up to in the last few months since they last saw me, and show them the Instagram page I started with the landscape photography I've been taking. It was only relatively new, with a few hundred followers. After working for magazines and commercials for the past five years, I wanted to try something new and explore some of my own creative control and freedom on the side. I could take the photos I wanted instead of being constrained to a set guideline.

They gush over the photos I posted, and I beam under their praises, wanting nothing more than their approval and for them to see where I was in life.

It's another hour before we clean up, and I say goodbye to Mum as she leaves.

Then, just as I planned, I crash as soon as my head hits the pillow, and the familiar smell of home lulls me to a peaceful sleep I haven't had since moving to Melbourne.

3

REECE

My knee bounces as I sit in the cramped seat, my arms folded over my chest to avoid touching the guy next to me, willing the plane to hurry up and take off.

It was the last seat I could get on this flight with the last-minute call I received, and it was just my luck that it would be economy. Usually, I would book first class for the extra legroom and personal space, but no tickets were left.

So, here I am, squished into a middle seat, making it hard to get comfortable with my long frame and the nonexistent space. I suck in a slow, steady breath, tamping down the frustration as I shift away from the leg pressing into mine from the guy in the window seat once again.

I need to suck it up. *For Jenna*, I repeat in my head to keep my ass glued to the seat and not bolt off the plane like it's on fire.

I was doing this all for the woman who practically raised me.

Jenna had been my babysitter since I was about seven years old until the age of twelve, when Dad thought I would be fine left alone at home. She was probably the only person to ever care about me. She was the only female figure I had in my life. With my negligent father, she was practically my *only* parental figure.

My life was so far from perfect with how unstable the household was, but the more she was around, the more I felt safe. Dad was hardly home, either working or drinking himself blind at one of the bars, and she would stay with me until he eventually came home and fell asleep. Even after the time Dad had let her go, she was always there for me.

I owed her my life for all she had done for me growing up, which is why I didn't think twice when she called me to come home early for her wedding. She said I needed to be there, and I booked flights within seconds while still on the phone discussing details.

It was a surprise when she called to tell me she was engaged. I didn't even know she was seeing someone.

She had always been closed off about her private life. I had tried to dig when I was a kid, and my curious mind got the better of me, but she was too good at side-skirting the conversation.

I'm happy for her, knowing she deserves a happy ending after all the years she's worked hard and dealt with my painful ass. And I will do anything to help her make sure that day is as special as she is.

But then she told me who her new fiancé was.

It punched me straight in the gut. It had been a while since I heard that last name, and memories of that summer after high school filtered through my mind.

God, thinking about my life when I was seventeen felt like a fever dream. I was young and so fucking stupid.

I fumbled the only other good thing to stumble into my life, all because I was scared. Scared of my dad. Scared I wasn't deserving. Scared I would lose everything and everyone important in my life. But I fucked it up anyway and lost way more than I imagined.

But maybe this is fate, putting her back on my path to fix what I had broken.

I was so fucking broken when I met her, fighting with the world on my shoulders. I'd felt everything in my life was put against me.

From the moment I was born, I was raised to know I didn't deserve a place here. That I had ripped an innocent person's life away just to be here. I was made to feel selfish and unworthy of anything good in this world. So when she whirled into my life, I instantly knew she was too good for me. Just from the sparkle in her eyes as she looked up at the sky by the river the first night we met, I knew.

But she had crawled under the hard casing of my heart, making herself home there, and suddenly, my life didn't seem so dark.

I just wanted to take something for myself. To have something worth fighting for in my life.

Maybe it was the selfish part of me, but I wanted to cling to the bit of relief for as long as I could.

And it was exhilarating.

She seemed to breathe life into me. She saw something I had been led to believe was nowhere inside me. She made me believe I was deserving of a life. Of love.

Of course, just as I was starting to believe I could step outside of the box I had been stuffed in, I was slapped back to reality. I crashed back into the doomed and bruised world that I belonged in. Then, I did what I did best: I self-sabotaged and let the only chance I would ever get at what I was beginning to know was love go.

I didn't just lose her, though. I lost two of my best friends. Liam was the first friend I ever made and I had betrayed him, going behind his back with Dakota when I knew he was still caught up in her months after their breakup. I tried to reach out a couple years ago, but I was left on read and never tried again. Never heard a single word from him. Neither has Jake or Sage. But he pops up on my social media every now and then and he has a whole life now with a wife and a kid on the way, which is fucking strange to think.

And Nate... Well, it fucking hurt to think about how I had broken his trust. 'Friend' was too simple of a word for what he was to me. He was my confidant, my brother. He was someone I didn't deserve when I used him and went behind his back. After the way we left things the last time I saw him, I didn't think it was ever possible to gain that back. And still, that might've been true but I was still going to try if given the change at the wedding.

But all my fears had come true and I could do nothing but blame myself. It was everything my dad had told me I was, that anything golden I touched would whittle and crumble away to dust in my undeserving hands.

I downward spiralled as everything in my life crumbled in front of me, barely able to scrape myself back to where I am.

This, all at the ripe beginning of my young adult years, did fucking wonders to my self-esteem and willingness to open up.

Safe to say that my relationship with my dad is null and void now. Especially after my rookie season in the MLB, I didn't need him for anything.

I was so ready to ghost him once I moved to the U.S after signing with the Arizona Havens, but minor leagues weren't easy to survive through with just a signing bonus and the minimum wage contract salary. Unfortunately, I still needed him. So, I busted my ass for four years. I put in the hard yards to earn a seat on the starting line. Extra training sessions, building my endurance, moving up the ranks from high A to triple-A, anything to improve in the game and get me to the best I can be. Because that was all I was taught to be and all I had. With baseball in my set vision and pushing out of my limits.

Then I finally got the call-up at the end of the season two years ago as a relief pitcher before eventually being promoted to starting pitcher mid-season last year. That was probably my best year of playing, having got the most strikeouts in my debut as a pitcher, and getting to play through to the division series. Although our team didn't make it through to the Wild Card series this year, the price of losing it all seemed to have paid up.

But it never seemed worth it. The only thing that came out of being called to the Majors was cutting my dad off. Because once I got that call, it was like the key had finally found the palm of my hand and I could unlock the stern chains holding me hostage under his control. I was on the phone with him straight after, telling him I never wanted to hear from him again. It was so fucking freeing, telling him exactly what I thought of him and how 'grateful' I was for his help. I didn't even wait for his response. I said what I wanted to say, hung up, and blocked him.

For my whole life, I had to endure his words shaped like daggers and his relentless expectations for me to live up to the life he dreamed for himself. Because I was the one who ruined his, it was my job to fulfil them. It wasn't so bad at the beginning because it was a dream I wanted too, but as I grew older, I began to wonder if it even was my dream or if it was because I was *told* that it was. I drove myself crazy with that question as I grew to resent the game that I used to love.

He had pushed beyond my limits when he trained me, and I lost grip of everything around me. So when the only lifeline that I thought was available to me was given, I grasped it with both hands, hoping to god that it would free me with the thousand-mile distance between us.

If only it didn't come at the cost of losing the love of my life.

But now...now I can right my wrongs.

I don't know if she's moved on since she blocked my number and every social media account. Jake was never super forthcoming as well, swearing to silence most times due to his girlfriend. All he was able to let slip was that she was happy. And I guess I should be relieved about that. I should be content with it. But I itch to know more. I want to know if she has a family or a boyfriend. My jaw clenches at the thought, but I shake my head at myself, knowing I don't have the right to feel like this. I just can't help but feel jealous of the hands that have touched her when they could have been mine. Shit, I'm even jealous of the air that wraps around her because it can hold her when I long to.

I knew from the moment I watched her walk away that I wouldn't be able to move on. Everything about her is still ingrained in my mind. I've never forgotten a single thing about her. Every intricate detail she let me discover was the exact thing that kept me sane in the U.S. I knew at the same moment as well that I didn't have a shot in hell of seeing her again which is why I clung to those memories. To the smell, the sight, the feel of her.

But, this is my second chance.

I just want to make everything right. I don't expect her to jump right back into my life and declare that she missed me or loved me like I'm ready to. I don't expect anything from her. This wedding is my chance to apologise for the eighteen-year-old boy I was, who was just confused, overwhelmed, and stuck. I have three months to prepare to see her, and I don't want to mess up the one chance I'll have to talk to her when the wedding comes.

It's been almost six years since I've seen Dakota Summers. I don't want to waste a single moment being in her presence.

4

DAKOTA

I spent the next afternoon working with Jenna on what things she wanted my help with to prepare for the wedding. She didn't know where to start with all the little things like music, invitations, flowers, and their pre-wedding parties. All her friends lived interstate and couldn't come until the week before, so she begged me to come to the rescue.

Dad and Jenna have been engaged for almost a year now, but only just decided on a date a couple of months ago. Jenna said it had to be this December before Christmas since everyone's schedule lined up perfectly, and she wanted to get married sooner rather than later. And Dad, who would do just about anything for Jenna, was not at all prepared for the amount of planning going into this wedding on such short notice.

The plus side, though, is that the amount of planning in store will get my mind off the whirling thoughts inside my head.

I was excited for the months to come and being able to help them have a beautiful wedding. They deserved the world.

But I can almost feel my head about to explode with the

amount of information Jenna's spewing and the ideas already stewing with inspiration.

I was ready for a drink.

It's been almost six months since I last had a night out with my friends, and from the drive through the city yesterday, Brisbane has changed a lot in the years I have been gone.

When Jenna locks her phone with her list, she sighs and shoots me a smile. "Thank you for doing this. I'm so happy that you're here. And hey, at least you won't be alone."

I frown. "What do you mean?"

"Oh," she tilts her head, "I must have forgotten to tell you. The boy I used to babysit—well, he's not quite a boy anymore —anyway, he agreed to come spend the next three months with me too. I haven't seen him in over a year, so I convinced him to come help with the wedding."

"Oh, okay. That's no problem. I'm excited to finally meet him."

She's only brought him up a couple of times around me, but I can tell he means a lot to her.

She chews her lip, dropping her gaze from mine for a moment before she pastes on a smile. "Yeah, it'll be good. He'll be here pretty early tomorrow, and we're going to have breakfast, just so you're aware. I know you're planning to go out with your friends tonight, so I apologise in advance if we make too much noise during your hangover."

"I'll be sure to wear ear muffs," I tell her, amusement filling my voice. I check the time and push back my chair. "Speaking of, I should probably start getting ready before they come. They'll take over my room otherwise."

"Have fun," Jenna sings.

I make my way upstairs and start with a shower, before coming back to my room and filtering through the closet and wardrobe to pick what to wear.

It's just as I slip on a light green dress that hits mid-thigh when they come barrelling into my room with overnight bags. Avery immediately pours products onto the mess of my bed, covering the clothes that were strewn on top of it with my indecision of what to wear, and now, makeup and curling wands join the clutter.

"Sure, no problem. Dump your things anywhere, I guess." I say sarcastically.

Alex narrows his eyes. "It was messy already. Don't act like it was us."

I roll my eyes, looking over to Avery when she beckons me over, clearing some clothes to make room for herself. "Come. Sit. I miss doing this."

My lips twitch as I move toward her, doing the same to make space for myself to sit on the edge of the bed.

Avery takes in my outfit and smiles. "I like this dress."

"Thank you. Daniel bought it," I reply.

Avery starts to dab on my makeup as Alex questions me.

"Oh, Daniel? How is he? Anything new you want to update us about?" He wiggles his brows.

I side-eye him as he sprawls on the other side of the mountain of belongings to meet my gaze.

They ask me this almost every year, wondering if there was something between Daniel and me.

And every year, my answer is the same. "We're just friends. As we always have been."

He sighs, flipping onto his back, almost as if he expects a better answer by talking to the ceiling than me. "I just don't understand how you've never hooked up with him," Alex queries, turning his head back to me with wide eyes. "He's hot, and do you not see how he looks at you? I mean, I've never looked at a friend that way, all soft and gooey-eyed."

I snort as Avery applies concealer under my eyes, and I look up for better access.

For the first few months after moving to Melbourne, I was

too heartbroken to even think about moving on. Daniel and I reconnected about a month after my move and, as promised, he showed me around to the good spots for coffee, picnics, and even nightlife. I told him the first time I saw him that I didn't want anything more than friends, and he told me that he didn't need anything more from me if I wasn't ready, but that if I was ever ready, then he'd be there.

He was sweet and always there for me as a shoulder to cry on—both he and Ellie were. However, there was one instance where I did try to come onto him a couple of months later during a night out while slightly tipsy and decided it was time to move on. But he turned me down, then drove me home. We never talked about that night since.

"Apart from when we made out in Airlie Beach six years ago, no."

Avery stops swiping mascara on my lashes and looks at me, head tilting.

"Have you not been with anyone since...you know?"

A hard lump forms at the bass of my throat. Even just a vague mention of him has me reacting this way. It's pathetic.

I chew my lip. "I have. There haven't been many, and never anything serious. A hundred percent of the time that I've been with someone else, I've had some alcohol to give me courage. I think if I hadn't, I'd just keep comparing and I couldn't do it."

Avery's shoulders drop, and she reaches over to squeeze my arm. "Oh, honey."

I shake my head. "It's fine. That's my goal while I'm here, though, to finally have my closure and move on. My dating life has suffered for *way* too long."

Alex cheers. "That's what I like to hear. Starting tonight. We'll be your wingman-slash-woman. It'll be great."

Avery continues with my makeup, brushing along my cheeks with blush as I side-eye him. "Now I'm a bit worried."

Alex waves off my faux concern. "You'll be fine. By the end

of the night, you'll be over him," he pauses, then leans over to nudge me with his shoulder, adding a suggestive lilt to his voice, "and hopefully, under someone else."

He winks, and I snort, before Avery snaps my attention to return to her.

I want nothing more than for it to be that easy.

Once we were ready, Dad drove us to the city, bidding us goodbye as he dropped us off in front of one club and letting us know he'll be waiting for our call.

We hopped from club to bar before we settled on a karaoke bar, cheering on the people on stage brave enough to sing in front of so many strangers. Both Alex and Avery, as promised, tried to set me up with a few men, but I might have gotten too intoxicated for anything to happen. I was just enjoying a night together with my best friends. That sounded better than anything else.

It's exactly what I needed. A night of laughter and fun with the two who have been there for me through thick and thin. Who have never let me down and picked up every single one of my calls. Never complained about my refusal to return to Brisbane. Their unwavering support and care was everything I never wanted to take for granted.

We finally call it quits at about three in the morning before Dad picks us up. We spend the drive home singing, slurring, and giggling at ourselves while he shakes his head at our antics.

Being the caring man he is, he helps drag our stumbling bodies up to my room, has us clean off our makeup, and brush our teeth like we were children again, before tucking us in, and we knock out almost immediately.

It feels like mere seconds from the moment my head hits the pillow to the time I wake again, sunlight casting straight through my window.

I reach over to click on my phone resting on the bedside table, seeing the time is only just past seven a.m. I groan, my throat feeling like sandpaper, and my head pounds against my skull. I search for a pack of Panadol in my bedside drawer, popping two and sipping on the water Dad brought in before we fell asleep.

That's when my ears perk up at the laughter and chatter from downstairs. My brows knit in confusion before I remember what Jenna told me yesterday. The boy she used to babysit is here.

I can't help the vague curiosity that rises. Or it might be the way my stomach rolls with the emptiness. Either way, I decide to go downstairs, get something in my stomach, and meet this guy.

Avery and Alex are still passed out beside me, so I slide out around them and quietly make my way out the door.

I probably look horrible, with hair all over the place, a long ratty T-shirt, and boy shorts that are just peeking out from underneath. I brush some strands back with my fingers, trying to tame what I can, but I don't have the energy to care too much at the moment. I feel like I'm barely hanging onto my stomach as it is.

But halfway down the stairs, my footsteps falter, and my breath hitches in my throat when my gaze finally lifts and I see who stands at the door.

I'm frozen, not sure what to do, where to go, or if I'm dreaming.

I have to be. There's no explanation for him to be standing in front of me right now, *here* in my house.

Maybe he's a ghost, and I'm just stuck in some kind of paralysing memory in my hungover state.

I have to still be sleeping.

God, I hope I am.

But when I pinch the skin of my outer thigh, nothing changes, and he's still here.

He can't be, can he?

He's not real.

It's. Not. Him.

But there he is, just as speechless as I am with his lips parted, looking just as I remember, only a little older, hair longer—curling over his ears and almost grazing his shoulders —and his build a little more filled, broader.

Those green eyes, though. I would know them anywhere. And they look too vivid for this not to be real.

Reece.

Reece.

Six years older, looking better than my imagination could muster.

I hate it.

5

REECE

Dakota.

Dakota.

Dakota.

That's all my mind can comprehend when I see her, physically standing in front of me instead of just being a figment of my imagination. Like a ghost of my past coming to haunt me, like it's done since the moment I lost her six years ago. However, this time, it's coming to torment me, placing her in front of me, knowing I can't just reach out and touch her. To curl my fingers over the contours of her cheek and kiss her with all the longing and desperation trying to claw its way out of my chest right now at the sight of her.

I was not expecting to be confronted with her as soon as I stepped through these doors. Jenna didn't mention she would be here, and I kind of assumed she wouldn't show until the day of the wedding.

I knew she hadn't set foot in Brisbane for the past six years. It was the one piece of information about her that Avery would throw at me any chance she could.

I couldn't help but asked about her when I was with Jake and Avery. It was my own kind of torture when Jake accidentally slipped information about her to me, but I clung to every piece of detail he did.

It wasn't enough I realise now that she's standing in front of me.

I want to ask her so many questions, all of the ones I prepared for the last few months pressing against the lump growing in my throat. I want to know how she is and reassure myself that I didn't destroy her when I left. I want to know if she's happy and doing better than she would have been if she stayed with me.

I just need to know she's okay. Even six years down the track. I need to know if she's still the girl I fell in love with and that I didn't dim her light.

With her standing in front of me, just in one glimpse of her physical appearance, the girl I once knew has changed entirely. She's a woman, more beautiful than I remember. Her ocean blue eyes that I used to drown in, the softness that used to shine through them, now has a steeliness to them. Her long blonde hair I used to tangle my fingers through, is now chopped short to her shoulders. Her slim curves now filled out a little more as she stands tall before me.

I see the ghosts of our memories like mirrors in her eyes. From the moment we met down by the river, where our souls intertwined. To when Liam introduced me to her as his girlfriend, the first time I felt heartbreak. The week in Airlie Beach. Every moment in between, before I left her broken and pleading with me to stay with her. I longed for those moments back every time I closed my eyes.

She's everything I dream of when I lie awake in bed, and everything that haunts my nightmares when I fall asleep.

It's beauty and pain combined seeing her again.

Absentmindedly, I take a step toward her. I don't even notice I do it, but I feel myself being drawn into her orbit, wanting to be closer to her.

But then she takes a retreating step back up the stairs, frowning, almost like she can read my mind.

I see it now, the guard that made her stand tall and strong, untouchable. Protecting herself and holding herself at arm's length from all that's around her. I can't help thinking that it's because of me. Because of the way I left her.

Six years between us, and I almost fell to my knees at just the mere sight of her.

Six years and she still holds my heart in a tight vice that I never thought of asking back. Never wanted to.

Six years and though I never wanted it to, everything has changed.

Because, when she finally opens her mouth, only a single word parts her lips, definitive and firm, and it reverberates straight through to my bones.

"No."

The walls I saw slightly fracture at the sight of me seal shut and almost reinforce as the muscles in her shoulders tighten.

I swallow hard, guilt rushing through me, as I watch her pull back and shut me out. I shouldn't be shocked, though. After everything, it's what I deserve. But still, that one word has me frozen, glued to the spot, and I can do nothing but watch her spin on her heels and retreat back to her room, the door slamming behind her.

I was the worst person to her when I was eighteen. I didn't know anything about love and ruined my only chance at it. Because I knew after her, there would be no one else.

All I wanted to do was protect her. From me, from my dad, from the life I was stuck in. It had been a steady funnel of grief and torture growing up. Dad made sure I suffered every day with the reminder that my mother wasn't here because of me and I didn't want her affected by that. She was a kaleidoscope of colour; she didn't fit into a world made to strip it all away.

Having grown up in an environment like that, I walked around with this dark cloud looming over my head. By default, I was made to do the same and infect anyone I touched. I tried to hide it from everyone around me, faking smiles and inserting humour into conversation to pretend all was sunshine and rainbows. But a few people knocked through that façade and saw me for who I was.

Dakota was one of them, and every day that I was with her, she pierced through the darkness and made it easier to see. She somehow painted colour in my otherwise dull world, letting me feel like there was hope for someone like me.

There were many times I'd been so in my head then, grief eating me alive, and I'd overthink every little thing. But when I was with Dakota, those voices dialled to a quiet hum, and I finally felt peace and comfort. Like I could just lay it all down and fall into her embrace, and everything would be fine.

But as usual, I destroyed everything in my wake. I lost two of my best friends. I lost the love of my life. Leaving me all alone once again, my world returned to its dull grey pallor.

After that, I was sure I was bound to be alone forever.

I was back to going through the motions of life, autopiloting and dragging myself through the mud. I put my all into baseball. It was my number one focus since there was nothing else going for me.

Truthfully, I was reluctant to even come home, sure that returning would tear what little I had of my heart to shreds.

It was as if the universe was calling to me though, screaming a message I didn't quite understand. Pulling me, dragging me, desperate to have me here.

Now, here, with one glimpse of her again, feeling her close proximity, I swear I can feel a little glimmer of colour returning.

Standing in this hallway, memories flashing in front of me, I understood now why there was such a strong pull to be here.

Because it wasn't the universe calling me, but my heart calling home.

6

DAKOTA

My mind whirls as I slam the door behind me, making Avery jolt from her sleep. If I didn't feel so frazzled, I would feel bad for waking her like this. But I can't focus on anything apart from the boy downstairs.

Her eyes snap open, blinking a few times and yawning before peering over to me. She slowly sits up, frowning at my expression. I undoubtedly look as white as a ghost. My fingers feel numb and my skin feels tingly, like just mere seconds of seeing him has jolted electricity through my veins, feeling all too hyper aware of his presence.

I'm just dreaming. It's just a dream. You're still asleep.

Though the first time didn't work, I continued to pinch myself with my hands behind my back as if it would magically work, and I would wake back in bed. But it didn't give me that relief, and I sag against the door behind me, squeezing my eyes shut.

I know I'm in denial, but I just can't believe this is happening. That everything I fear is coming true.

"You okay?" she asks in a croaky voice, wiping the sleep from her eyes.

I tilt my head up, ready to nod, but stop before shaking my head.

"I think I must be sleepwalking or something. I surely have to still be asleep because this is some sick joke," I spit out, running my fingers through my hair. A broken sort of laugh bursts from my lips. I'm sure it sounds crazy. Maybe I am going crazy.

Is it too late for me to fly back to Melbourne?

"What do you mean?"

"I mean, I just had the surprise of my life downstairs, and not the good kind." I swallow and look at her, the shock starting to fade away as I feel myself start to crumble. "Reece is here."

Her eyes widen, and then she turns to Alex before shaking his shoulder vigorously.

He mumbles and whines into the pillow he's cuddling, but doesn't wake. She tries again, whisper-yelling at him to wake up. He swears, peeking his eyes open at her. "What do you want, woman?" he grumbles.

"Wake the fuck up. We have an emergency."

He frowns and then flicks his gaze to me and back to Avery. "What do you mean?"

"Reece," I breathe his name, and Alex snaps straight up in bed.

He rubs his eyes and yawns. "I'm awake, what's happening? Why are we talking about him?"

"He's here," I repeat hoarsely.

He frowns and reels back. "What do you mean he's here? Like downstairs? Are you sure it's him? I thought he was overseas."

"Yes, I'm sure," I hiss. It's hard to miss those forest green eyes I fell in love with.

I swallow and pad over to my bed, dropping onto the edge before my legs decide to give out underneath me.

The puzzle pieces start clicking into place with the shock

subsiding, and my mind starts to question why he would be here. I huff out a laugh when realisation hits me, looking up to the ceiling before turning toward my friends as they watch me with careful gazes. "The universe must fucking hate me. The boy Jenna used to babysit, you remember?" When they nod, I continue. "It's Reece. Jenna told me he would be here this morning. It's got to be the only explanation why he's here now after six years."

Fuck. She also mentioned him staying for the next three months as well. How was I not told about this? They must have known. How could they not have?

"How was this not brought up beforehand? Your dad must know Reece. He knows what happened, doesn't he?" Alex continues peppering questions. My eyes shift to Avery briefly, who seems to be unusually quiet now, and I frown.

"I haven't told him the full story, but I mean, he noticed my full breakdown, and I know Nate told him who it was over." I'd gathered that after Dad visited the first time in Melbourne and we talked about it all.

"I can go down and beat his ass if you want? What gives him the nerve to show up here? I don't care if his nanny is marrying your dad; he should know this is forbidden territory."

While Alex rants, my attention shifts back to Avery as she frowns and taps at her phone.

I clear my throat, and her head snaps up. I narrow my eyes at her, having a sinking suspicion. "What's going on?"

She locks her phone and shakes her head. "Nothing."

I glare at her. "Who were you texting?"

I already have a hunch, but I want to hear it from her.

"No one." Her answer is immediate.

"Avery."

"Yes?"

"Bullshit."

She curses under her breath. "We're not even playing right now, you can't pull that card."

"I don't care." I hold out my hand as I lift a brow at her. "Hand it over, or tell me what you were doing."

She presses her lips together and sighs. "Please don't hate me."

I take a deep breath and sit taller as if preparing for her words. "I'll try my best."

Alex adjusts in his spot, facing Avery as he tilts his head. "Me too."

Good, at least it's not just me here in the dark.

She chews her lip. "Fair. Okay. I was texting Jake. He mentioned about a month ago that Reece was coming for a wedding in a couple weeks, and I thought it was a coincidence with this wedding as well. But when we discussed it more, we connected that it's the same wedding and Reece would be here."

The more she explains, the more my chest caves. She knew all this time that he would be here, and she didn't tell me.

"But," she rushes to interrupt just as I go to open my mouth, "I didn't know he would come here, especially right now. I thought he was just coming for the wedding. And I thought your dad would've told you already. I didn't know that you didn't know. I thought we were just not talking about it like everything else."

"Who cares if I didn't know? Why didn't you come to me to talk about it? I would've preferred that than finding out you knew all along."

I know I'm being irrational and I shouldn't take it out on her, but my emotions feel like they've gone haywire at the moment with a repetitive cycle of questions reverberating in my mind. *How? Why? Is this real? Why now?*

She sighs. "I know. I'm sorry. I didn't mean to keep it from you. I just didn't know how to broach the subject."

I don't blame her for that. I'd forbidden any talk about Reece since I moved, but that didn't make this all hurt any less.

God, he hasn't been here for more than five minutes, and he's already turning my world upside down and creating drama I don't need.

I rest my head in my hands as I balance my elbows on my knees and blow out a long, steady breath. "I think I just need to be alone right now."

"Dakota—" Avery starts, but I cut her off.

"Please. Just leave. We'll talk later. I just want to be alone."

It's all too much, and it makes me want to crawl out of my skin.

The hangover I'm experiencing on top of that certainly doesn't help, as my stomach begins to churn again.

Reluctantly, they both leave, but not before Avery squeezes my leg and Alex drops a kiss to the top of my head.

I sigh as the door shuts behind them. I can't blame her for not telling me. I would have done the same. I would have assumed it was known and avoided the topic as I've begged them to do for the past six years.

I didn't want to know anything related to him. I wanted to block him out like he was never a part of my life.

I wasn't expecting this all on my third day being home, and it makes me want to run back to Melbourne already.

I flop down on the bed and stare at the ceiling, wondering if I could hide in my room and pretend the interaction never happened. But i know that will make things worse. Being in this room will feed into everything. Because this room was one of the biggest reminders of who he was to me. Of the boy I once knew. Of the boy who looks eerily similar to the one I confronted downstairs.

My stomach definitely doesn't like that idea either as it rolls again. I try to get my body to cooperate so I can go get some food, but the fear of running into him again has me frozen here.

At least, until a knock sounds from the door.

Cautiously, I crawl off the bed to open the door and see Dad standing there with a tray of bacon and scrambled eggs with a cup of coffee on the side.

"Hey, Chook." He smiles hesitantly, lifting the tray. "Peace offering? I gathered you would be hungry."

I don't want to talk to anyone at the moment, with my head so busy fighting all these conflicting emotions, most of all feeling betrayed by my own family. But with the offering of food and my dad's worried expression, I reluctantly take the tray from him, leaving the door open for him to enter before I slide back under the bed covers, setting the tray beside me. Being hungover, I feel too weak to his dad-like charm, and maybe, I just want him to tell me that this was all a misunderstanding.

It's silent between us for a moment as he wanders over and sits by my legs on the edge of my bed, cautious of the tray. He turns to face me, reaching over to hold my hands between his. When he squeezes them, I look at him to see the sympathy swimming in his eyes, and I feel my heart crack, the hope that he was ignorant to the situation snuffing out as quickly as it came.

"You knew." My voice is shaky as I breathe the words.

He sighs and looks down. "She told me I should tell you, but I..." He trails off, and I remove my hands from his as I feel my eyes well.

"I can't believe you. You know what happened. You knew who he was, but you still invited him."

His gaze flicks to me again, and he shakes his head. "But that's the thing, Chook, I don't know what happened. You never talked about it." I chew my lip and avert my eyes to my hands in my lap, knowing he's right. But still, he should have told me. He saw how heartbroken I was. It might be unreasonable for me to think that, but I'm just confused and frustrated. "But yes, I knew who he was. I knew there was history between the two of you. I didn't tell you because I knew you would have cancelled and not shown up. Not until the wedding, at least, and I knew you wouldn't have stayed long for that. I needed you here."

My heart sinks as I fiddle with my fingers, the ache in my chest increasing. Once again, I know he's right. I wouldn't have come if I knew he would be here. And I hate how he knows that. I hate that he had to omit this information just to have me here and spend time with him.

But still, I'm confused.

I shake my head and look at him again. "So, why is he here right now? You have me to help prepare. Why do you need him?"

Dad takes my hands in his again, smiling cautiously. "I don't want to overstep because I know there are reasons you haven't come to visit, and I know one of them is him. But with me and Jenna getting married, you may see him more often. It may be rare since he lives in the U.S., but I didn't want you to be confronted every time you see him. He's a part of Jenna's life and, unfortunately, that makes him also a part of mine." The last sentence he says begrudgingly, which makes me smile a bit. "So, I thought, this time would give you guys a chance to work through things to at least be cordial and not make things awkward. I don't want you to be uncomfortable when he's here and run away. I want you to enjoy your time back. I want this to feel like home again. I'll be here whenever you need me, okay? I've already had talks with him, one just before you came down–threatened him a little–so I know he won't step out of line and break your heart again."

A bubble of laughter bursts past my lips as I duck my head, a tear escaping as I do. "Oh my gosh, Dad."

He moves the tray over to my other side to shuffle closer to me, then reaches up to wipe the tear away before squeezing my shoulder. "I'm sorry for not telling you. I just want you to be happy, Dakota. I want you to come back home and feel comfortable. I don't want you to feel scared to be here."

My heart aches, but I smile up at him, lip wobbling. "I love you, Dad."

He opens his arms, and I crawl up to sit before falling into their comfort as they wrap around me. "I love you, too, Chickadee."

The tears I've been trying to hold spill over as he holds me.

I've missed this. I miss being able to hug my dad whenever I need it. I miss seeing him every day. I miss being here. I just miss him. It's not the same when I only see him every six or so months.

There have been so many moments where I wanted to talk to him and hear his supportive words over the last six years, but I stopped myself mid-text. Since moving to Melbourne, I started to think I was too much. I considered myself a burden in everyone's life and didn't want to rely on anyone to cheer me up. I'd already made too much drama in my life that I didn't want to ruin anyone else's.

The couple of weeks after the move, I didn't talk to anyone. It wasn't until the night Ellie dragged me out and I ended up pouring it all out to her in a drunken ramble, turning the night into a therapy session as I cried in her arms in the middle of the bar. The morning after, she pushed me to answer all my unread texts from my friends and family. I cried that whole day on the phone to everyone as I apologised.

But it didn't quite ease the feeling. Even after multiple therapy sessions, there's still been that niggling feeling in the back of my mind, which is why I haven't told Dad the full story between Reece and me. And I won't be starting now.

Just that reminder of those months reminds me of my goal

here. That this is the past, and I can't let it affect me like that. I can't let it affect me by being home anymore.

I pull myself from Dad's arms, and he rubs my arms before standing.

"Both he and Jenna went out for the day to give us some space. They'll be back for dinner later and we're all going to have it together, okay?" He raises his brow then, his words more assertive than a question.

I begrudgingly nod. "Okay."

He tilts his head toward the door. "You want to come watch a movie like old times after you finish your breakfast?"

My lips pull up. "I do."

We spent the rest of the morning and part of the afternoon lounging on the couch and re-watching our favourite movies while he fed me greasy food and loaded me up with snacks.

The dread I felt for later tonight—having to sit at a table and have dinner with *him*—fell to the wayside as I enjoyed the company of being with Dad like old times in the comfort of familiar walls.

7

REECE

After the awkward encounter between Dakota and me, Jenna suggested I drop my things in the spare room and go out with her for the day. Although my body screamed in protest, wanting to rest for the next couple of hours after the eighteen-hour flight I was just on, I didn't object.

The last thing I wanted to do was make Dakota feel uncomfortable, and I could tell by my showing up here was as unexpected as it was for me to see her. I was meant to be staying at their house for the next three months, but that just didn't feel right anymore now that I knew she was here. It felt wrong to stay, like I was invading her space. My next option was to look for a hotel close by. Given how late of a notice this was, my luck was minimal at best, but I didn't have another choice.

We go out for breakfast, and I immediately order a coffee with a double shot before we venture around the markets and walk around the city. Jenna suggests going by the river to pass time, but I immediately decline. I'm not ready to take a trip down memory lane. I have enough of my past coming to haunt me as it is.

The rest of the morning and much of the afternoon is just

me following Jenna around while she attends errands, before ending at her bakery. I sit in the corner of the quiet shop, sipping on another mug of coffee, staring out the window in a daze. My entire body feels exhausted, every muscle aching, but my head is an entirely different story. Every thought is centred on her and how, in one morning, everything has flipped on its head.

We finally decide to make our way back to the house later in the afternoon, and I'm thankful with jetlag starting to set into my bones. Hopefully, I have time for a nap before dinner as my eyes start to droop when I sink into the passenger seat.

"There's more to the story between you and her, isn't there?" Jenna pipes up a little while into our drive back.

The question has my eyes popping open, jarring me as I stretch in the seat, rolling my right shoulder when a dull burn settles in it. I turn my head to look at her, trying to shake the sleep from my body, knowing I need the energy for this conversation. "What do you mean?"

She side-eyes me before returning her gaze to the road. "You know what I mean. Don't play dumb, boy."

I sigh, rubbing my hands along my shorts as I turn my attention out the window. I can never hide anything from her.

"Yeah," I confirm in a whisper, "a lot more."

I've never told her the full story between Dakota and me. I never had the chance to before I moved to the U.S. Then it was easy to avoid the topic with the distance between us.

It's not that I didn't want to. I wanted to talk to someone about her so badly, but it just hurt too much to bring up. I didn't need to be told how much I fucked up, I hated myself already for it. I lost the three people who meant so much to me all at once. All because I was a fucking coward I couldn't let her look at me differently like I did myself.

Jenna was the first person in my life to show me a bit of kindness, and it was the strangest concept to grasp, even at the age of seven. I'd grown accustomed to my dad's aloofness and feeling unwanted by him that I thought it had been normal, so I was taken aback when she showed interest in me and wanted to know me.

But those years before she came in, I had built this kind of wall around my heart, a defence mechanism to protect it from disappointment. I had been quiet and standoffish toward her when she first came around to look after me. A child who was afraid to do anything but sit there and be quiet. Her caring and warm nature melted a little of that armour with time, but never entirely. My usual quiet nature just slowly turned into hiding behind the smile and humour she taught me to use.

Though I never got used to the feeling of her kindness and love. It still felt like a strange concept by the time I met Dakota.

But she had been like a breath of fresh air when I felt like I had been drowning most of my life. She had somehow started to slowly stitch me back together, healing the broken and beaten parts of me that I thought were dead.

When I met her, I hadn't expected the girl who looked at the moon with rapt fascination to end up meaning so much to me. So, when I found out I was leaving, I tried to grasp onto that feeling for as long as I could. I thought I could hold onto it forever and never have to face real life.

But in the end, I just ended up hurting us both. And that was my biggest regret.

After that, I reinforced those walls and never let myself be vulnerable to anyone, even with Jenna. Because I led myself to believe my father's words. That I was made to ruin any bit of joy or happiness in everyone's life. Which also ended up with me going to therapy.

So, yeah, there was more to the story. But how the fuck was I meant to tell her that when I couldn't even face it myself until recently?

I denied it and shoved it to the back of my mind for years. It

47

wasn't until Jenna brought her up when she was telling me about her new fiancé that it all slammed me right in the chest. I hadn't heard her name in years. I was scared to utter it. Fuck, I mean, I even made up some code word when I couldn't help but ask Jake about her.

I'm a weak man when it comes to her. She's like my Achilles heel, and I have been crawling through these years with her cut from my life. I deserve every moment of this suffering, living in the darkest days since I broke her heart. I don't even know how I got out of bed most days. They all blurred together until days became months and then years. I drowned out the memories most nights in the beginning with a bottle of Jameson in my clutch or on the bathroom floor, sobbing.

But hearing her name after so many years, it was like it slapped me awake from the nightmare I had been living. It was years of pent-up emotions, bottled-up anger and frustration at myself when I finally broke on a video call with Jenna. It swallowed me whole, blurring the edges of my vision.

She had talked me out of the panic attack somehow, soothing me as she had when I was little. I'm sure I had blacked out at one point, as patches of memories come back to me, from freezing on the spot in the bathroom, to finding myself wrapped around the toilet bowl.

I felt fucking horrible for reacting like that after she announced her engagement. I apologised profusely afterward, but she waved me off.

She tried to get me to talk about it, but I refused. Not that I didn't want to, I just couldn't piece together the words to even start. And maybe that was the defence mechanism that I had developed to protect myself from being vulnerable. Because I never fucking talked about anything.

She then asked if I had thought about seeing someone I wasn't close with to talk about it all. I'd waved her off, saying I didn't need to, but she was very convincing that it might help to vent to someone I didn't have any connections with in my life.

The next week, she booked me in with a therapist close by in Arizona and told me to be there or she would fly over and I would have to deal with her.

So I went. I sat there for almost the entire first session, not saying a single word. The therapist tried to get me to open up with casual conversation, but I was short in my answers. I didn't feel ready to dive into the details of my private life with some stranger.

But then, she struck a chord. Of course, Jenna had told her what I was there for. The therapist started to mention my father and my panic attack. I bee-lined straight for the door then, feeling betrayed and like all my bottled emotions were cracking under the pressure that had been stuffed into them.

Her words had halted me from pushing through the door, though. They still feel as clear as day, echoing through my mind. She said, 'This is a safe space, Reece. You can yell, you can scream, you can vent about whatever you need. Nothing inside this room will hurt you. I am no one to you, and you are no one to me. But I will be here if you need someone to work through your feelings.'

And then I broke. Again.

I slumped against the door, my forehead resting on it as I screamed a long drawn out 'fuck'.

It was almost embarrassing, but my therapist, Susan, didn't say a word as she let me sob on the floor by the door well past the time of our session before helping me stand and offering me a pack of tissues. She didn't say a single word as I walked out of the office, which was luckily empty apart from the receptionists, but I somehow found myself back in the chair the following week that Jenna booked.

Throughout many sessions, I eventually started to open up. From my mother to my father's treatment of me, to everything about Dakota and the complete mess I made. It probably took the better half of the past year to get me to lay everything down on the floor. But it was oddly freeing, feeling the pressure ease a little off my chest with every day that passed. The feeling didn't come without guilt that I didn't have the guts to be this honest with Dakota though. That this all could have been avoided if I had just opened up to her.

She was long gone, and there was nothing I could do to bring her back. Plus, I couldn't have let her carry the weight of my baggage. She didn't deserve any type of darkness in her world, and I was slowly infecting her with it every day that I spent in her life. So, I did what I thought was best for her.

It was never my intention to hurt her, but staying with her would have hurt her more.

All I wanted for her was to chase her dreams and be happy, but I knew I would have just dragged her down with the state of mind I was in then.

With her entering my life again, I was sure she would never let me back into her life like I had been before just as easily, and I didn't expect her to. At the least, I just want to make up for what I had done to her. To heal the inner children in us who were just young and in love and didn't know a thing about anything.

My dreams would have to do if that was the only way I could have her. The way I've always wanted her.

I clear my throat and blink back the gathering tears, snapping myself back to the present where Jenna still watches with a patient, albeit expectant gaze. That's when I notice that we're already at the house, pulled into the driveway, the engine idling.

Right, she's waiting for me to elaborate on the situation with Dakota and me.

I'd like to think the therapy sessions have made me better at this, but truthfully, it's still just as hard to push words past my lips and form sentences to explain everything.

But this was a step in the healing journey, right? To be open with those you love. I mean, I owed it to Jenna to tell her the truth.

So, I tell her. It's a slow process as I try to piece all my words together, but she watches me with a soft gaze, listening intently. She gives me time as I stumble my way through the story, from the moment I met Dakota to the day I let her go, and every day that I have suffered since.

She reaches over at some point as I talk, taking my hand and folding it between hers as the tears stream down my face.

My head starts to throb and I pull a shaky breath between my lips once I finish, dropping my head back against the headrest before slowly exhaling as if that will slow the erratic beat of my heart. It's one of the ways Susan taught me to control the panic attacks. In for four, hold for four, out for four.

I peek over to Jenna, seeing the track marks on either side of her face as she stares at me with so much sorrow.

I shake my head, squeezing my eyes shut again as if to block the way she's looking at me. But it was already ingrained in my head, and seared behind my eyelids. I think that was probably worse.

"Please don't cry for me. I don't deserve that."

I feel her squeeze my hand, and my eyes snap back open.

"You're wrong, Reece. You are so wrong. You are still so young and deserve so much more than what life or your father has shown you. You have so much potential, and god, I wish I could take away some of the pain you hold because this is way too much for someone as young as you to experience. I wish I could have done something more to protect you when you were younger so you didn't have all this scarring your soul."

I swallow thickly. "It wouldn't have mattered. I was fucked up way before you came in."

"But you're not, Reece. You never were. You were always the most extraordinary kid that I had the pleasure of looking after, and my thoughts have never changed."

I peer over, searching her gaze as if trying to detect a lie. I know I won't, but still, I search. "Do you still think that after what I just told you?"

"Of course. Probably even more so. Because you are even braver and stronger than I realised."

I scoff, shaking my head as I look out the window.

"I'm being serious, Reece. There's not a single thing about you or anything you could say that could change my perspective of you. Because in my eyes, you are like one of my own. And I know you hate hearing it, but I do love you."

My chin wobbles at those words, and I look back at her as she squeezes my hand.

"You are not a horrible person. You are human."

And just like that, I fall into her embrace, wrapping my arms tightly around her while careful of the pull in my shoulder that feels a tad more annoying now. She holds me just as fiercely to her, and I know, without her holding me up and pushing me to look after myself throughout all these years, I would have lost myself.

I owe my entire life to her.

8

DAKOTA

The scraping of utensils against plates is the only noise that echoes in the dining room.

Dad cooked chicken alfredo and broccoli for dinner, and it almost felt like how it used to be, cooking together again, with laughter and happiness filling the air. But then I heard them come home, and my smile slipped, the walls inside my mind and heart building their barricade.

Jenna immediately gravitated toward Dad when she entered, greeting him and kissing him on the cheek before heading upstairs. She squeezed my shoulder on the way past, but I kept my focus on stirring the pasta. I could feel his presence lingering in the doorway behind me. Could feel the weight of his stare even as I ignored every instinct to look up.

He excused himself after a moment, mentioning something about resting before dinner was ready. As soon as he left, I set the spoon down and blew out a long exhale.

I knew this dinner was going to be hard.

And I was right.

There was little small talk between us, and an awkward

silence filled the room. At first, Dad tried to engage Reece and me in a conversation, but it fizzled out as quickly as it began.

The weight in the air feels suffocating, and it's becoming impossible to ignore. I would feel guilty for how uncomfortable it feels, but I can't keep focus on anything other than the man in front of me.

I still can't believe he's here, sitting at the dining table so casually of the childhood home his eighteen-year-old self still haunts.

I peek up at him as I spoon a piece of pasta into my mouth, tracing over him, finding pieces of the boy I knew all those years ago. The pieces I had fallen for.

His eyes are still as I remember, dark green with specks of gold that had a way of dissolving all my worries. The crease between his brows is more prominent with age, but seemingly still softer than I remember. The glimpse of his smile I saw earlier still holds the dimple I always used to search for in every smile.

But yet, a lot has changed about his appearance. He's no longer that lean boy anymore, that's for certain. And his messy curls were longer than I remember him having.

It's the tortured look that used to always shadow him when he was younger that keeps my attention, though. It lingers there still, maybe a little darker now. The part of me that still holds a soft spot for him yearns to know why. To ask if he's okay.

He looks up from his plate then, gaze colliding with mine and catching my moment of vulnerability, and damn it, I can't tear my eyes away. His soften as the seconds pass by, and it's like I've been transported into a different time.

There's so much history hanging in the space between us, and with one glimpse, all those memories and the heartache comes rushing back, pressing down on my chest.

I was so prepared to put him in the past and heal the wound that never really closed. But now, here I am, wondering how we got here, from meaning so much to each other to staring at each other like total strangers.

The clattering of plates shocks me back to the present, and I snap my gaze away to Jenna as she presses a hand to her mouth, a yawn escaping her.

"Oh," she sighs, "I'm so sorry. I had very little sleep last night, and waking up early this morning has finally caught up to me."

Dad squeezes the hand she had resting on the table and smiles, nothing but affection in his eyes as he looks at her. "Let's get you to bed then."

She shakes her head. "Not yet. I've still got to clean up here."

I wave her off. "Don't worry about that. I'll clean up." I'm happy for the distraction and a way to distance myself.

She sighs and shoots me a sleepy smile. "That would be great, thank you."

They stand together, bidding us good night as they leave to head upstairs. Dad presses a kiss to the top of my head as he passes, making me smile.

I stand and start gathering the empty plates, trying to ignore Reece's presence as he sits unbudged at the table. I can feel his eyes tracking my every movement, unnerving me as I wait for him to say or do something.

He pushes back his chair, clearing his throat as he stands. "I'll help you."

I frown, keeping my eyes down and focusing on the leftover food. "You don't need to. I've got this."

"Kody, it's fine. I want to help."

I freeze at the mention of that name. That nickname. I haven't heard it in six years, except for the echoes in the quiet of my sleepless nights.

My gaze snaps to his, watching them flick between my own,

his mouth opening before pressing in a thin line as if shocked as well for it to have passed his lips.

I shake my head, narrowing my gaze. "You do not get to call me that. Not anymore."

I can't look at him. I can't bear to be in his presence. It hurts. Everything just hurts too much. The throbbing in my heart intensifies with every second he's this close to me.

I retreat to the kitchen, carrying a stack of plates, hoping he gets the message and stays away, or even better, leaves.

"Wait," he calls from behind me, the sound of footsteps hurrying closer, and I close my eyes. I place the dishes on the bench next to the sink, just as his hand rests on my forearm, and my muscles instantly tense at the contact. It's almost funny to think that hand used to make me melt when it touched me, and now, all I want is to peel it off.

"I'm sorry. I didn't mean to upset you. It just slipped out. Old habits, I guess."

His words make me boil. Old habits. Like it hasn't been six years since we've seen each other. Like he hasn't had six years to unlearn those habits. Like he doesn't know how he's slowly killing me by the mention of that nickname and him showing up here like we'd just be old pals again.

I turn to him, straightening my shoulders as I look him dead in the eyes. Even I can feel the fire burning behind my gaze, which fills me with satisfaction when I watch the swallow work his Adam's apple.

I tilt my head. "Funny. You never seemed to have much trouble before. Although now that I think about it, it always seemed to 'slip' when we were alone, so I guess it's fitting."

I watch as his jaw clenches, and his eyes soften. "Dakota, I—"

"There you go. See, wasn't so hard, was it?" I shoot him a sarcastic smile.

He sighs, glancing down at the stack of dishes before his

gaze rises back to me. "Look," he starts, but I don't give him a chance to continue, setting things straight.

"I'm only here for my dad, and then I'm heading right back to Melbourne once this is all over. There are three months between now and then, so during that time, I think it's best we keep things civil here if you're going to be staying. But we don't need to be friends, or hash things out, or recall things of the past. Been there, done that. This is for them and nothing else. We can continue with how things have been, pretending each other doesn't exist, okay?"

I watch a flash of hurt wash over him, and for a moment, I think maybe I was too harsh. But then I remember all the nights I cried myself to sleep while my dreams were haunted by him. All the times I brought his number up, ready to call him even after I had blocked him just to hear his voice again, and when I finally broke and dialled the number, it didn't connect, and I felt my heart breaking all over again.

No amount of hurt I deliver to him will ever make up for how he broke me.

He clears his throat before nodding. "Okay," he whispers. "Just...let me at least help with the dishes, and then, I'll be out of your hair. It's the least I can do."

I glance up at him, eyeing him as he watches me in turn, pleading with me to agree. The last thing I want is to spend more time with him, especially alone. I would love to tell him to go. That he doesn't belong here. But I'm tired. Tired from the absolute roller coaster that was today. Tired of complications. I don't want to create any drama for Dad or Jenna during this time. I want them to have a smooth and perfect wedding, and if that means playing nice with Reece, then I will. I would rather pretend he never existed, but it looks like he isn't going to let that happen easily.

"Fine. I'll rinse. You can stack them in the dishwasher."

The next ten minutes are silent between us, apart from the clanging of dishes as we work together.

It's odd standing next to him like this. Someone I used to know, but a stranger all at once. Knowing everything about him, but also nothing at all. Standing here, in this domestic setting, washing dishes together as if there isn't this huge, aching wedge between us. It's a strange position to be in. One I want to be as far away from. I don't have a single interest in exploring anything to do with him. I don't want to know what he's been up to for the last six years. I don't want to know if there's a difference between eighteen and twenty-three-year-old him. I don't need to be his friend to help my dad and Jenna. But being this close to him, all those questions itch beneath my skin to be answered.

Once the dishes are loaded into the dishwasher, he puts the tablet in, closes the door and pushes start.

We awkwardly stand there as the machine rumbles in the quiet, not knowing what to do or say from here.

I turn toward him at the same time his voice cuts through the silence.

"I've already booked a hotel to stay at. I was planning on staying here in the spare room until the wedding, but that was before I knew you would be here. I didn't mean to upset you in any way. I didn't know you'd be here when I agreed to come here. But I don't want you to be uncomfortable in your own home. I'll try to stay out of your hair as much as I can until the wedding is over if that is what you prefer."

He speaks without even looking at me and I frown, the age old throb in my chest sharpening. Then he turns, disappearing down the hall to the spare room before I have a chance to speak. Not that I could. I'm too stunned to even form a thought. All I can do is stare at the spot he was standing in.

When he comes back into view with his suitcase dragging behind him, he smiles tightly and swallows. I can't help but notice the missing dimple in his smile, and I hate myself for picking up on that fact. That I still know to search for it to know it's a real smile.

"I'll see you around then."

He's out the door in the next blink, and I'm left standing there, heart hurting and soul bleeding.

Maybe I should have stayed away until the wedding.

9

REECE

It was about eight p.m. before I swiped the card through the lock of my hotel room, emotionally and physically exhausted. Searching for a decent hotel with a last-minute vacancy before dinner was hard, but I'd somehow been lucky with this one close to the house.

Pushing through the room, the weight of the day was finally starting to settle into my bones. The earlier burn in my right shoulder was now a constant throbbing ache, and I knew I needed to ice it.

I don't know how I kept my eyes open throughout the whole dinner. Even with the awkward silence keeping my muscles locked, I was fighting hard to keep awake to eat.

I drop my things by the door, grab the ice pack I asked for at the reception, and collapse on the bed, placing the pack on my shoulder with a hiss.

I could have easily fallen asleep then and there; however, my brain was still wired even with my exhaustion.

Images flash behind my eyelids of that summer six years ago. Of the week in Airlie Beach. Of reconnecting and falling for her. It wasn't anything new. It was how I fell asleep every night. Like a ritual. With her on my mind and the regrets that punch me in the gut each time I remember. But now I'm here with fresh memories of her, and it's cutting into all the crevices where she exists in my heart.

No matter how much I repeat in my head that I deserve this, it doesn't ease the pain. But like the masochist I am, I dive further into the pain. I play into the memories. To the ones of falling asleep next to her. Even going as far as imagining she was here with me now, with the fresh images of her forming, and feeling her curl into me like I was the safest place to land, like she was for me. I torture myself with that imagery because it's the only way I can fall asleep before waking and realising it isn't, and never will be real. Because for all the shit going on in my life, when I fell into her arms, it was the only time I could breathe easier. My world only becomes brighter when she steps into it. She's the break in the storm clouds that always rule the sky in my life.

I think if I hadn't met Kody by the river, I probably wouldn't be where I am today. I was so close to giving up on everything before her. During her, I began to realise I would have wasted my life giving up, but in the end, I couldn't risk bringing her down in that darkness. Everything I did was for her, even as far as letting her go.

It wasn't an easy choice that I had to make. I guess we were just doomed from the start, like my dad had warned me.

I never truly deserved her. She was the sun, where I was the moon, and as prophecies go, the two are never destined to meet. We were never meant to fall together. We were never the puzzle pieces we thought we were at eighteen. But fuck, did I wish we were. She was the only one to ever make me feel something, and without her, I was nothing. I *am* nothing.

I skim my fingers over the tattoo on my hip, the matching one we got together.

I knew I had fallen for her that day, although I was in absolute denial. I would've done everything with her; getting a tattoo together was just the start of it.

The design initially was a reminder of the week in Airlie Beach, the crashing waves under the moonlight, with a plane setting off over the mountain. But it slowly became everything about her. The first time our eyes met on the pier, the friendship that evolved from the unlikely meeting, the way she slowly sank into my veins, the feelings I began to have for her, the months of silence, and meeting her again with her dazzling smile sneaking right back into my heart. It was a tether I held onto when it all became overwhelming, as if this tattoo held a string that attached me to her, and if I pulled hard enough, I would find myself back to her.

I guess it finally worked.

Absentmindedly, my fingers begin to trail to the other piece of ink around my left side not too far from the first one before I scrub my hands over my face and roll onto my side, chucking the melted pack of ice onto the bedside table.

I know I told her I would keep my distance from her, but I don't think that would be possible. Not only under the circumstances we're in, but I don't think it would be possible for me to avoid her now that she was so close. I had to have seas between us to keep us apart, but now...I just can't let her slip through my fingers again. I needed to find a way to make it up to her. I would grovel my way back into her life if I needed to. Even if it's only to be a friend, although it would be agony to be so close to her and not have her the way I wanted to be again, I would live with that.

I just needed to find a way to gain her trust back.

There's an ache in every inch of my body when I reluctantly roll out of bed the next morning, especially in the same fucking shoulder, still burning more than ever after a restless night's sleep. Partly because of he ice having done shit to ease the pain and making it harder to ignore, but mostly because I couldn't stop thinking about *her* and the way she looked at me, sharp and guarded.

Picturing her in my arms didn't lull me to sleep like it usually did, because now I had fresh memories of her, and fuck, if they didn't haunt me. Ghosts of fingers point at me to blame for that, and I couldn't deny them. I'd hated myself for that exact reason for years now.

I sit up on the edge of the bed, rolling out my neck before moving to stretch my shoulders back, feeling the tight pull before letting go. I dig through my bag and pull out the small pack of Nurofen, popping two to take with a swig of the water resting on the table. I used to hate taking them, especially around teammates and coaches, but some days, the pain is too unbearable to grit through. I'd rather get through the day without grimacing with every movement.

I reach over to grab my phone, unlocking it to see a message from Jenna telling me she would like to talk and to come over as soon as I can this morning. I can take a shot in the dark on what she wants to talk to me about. Especially with the time of the message being sent, I guess she came to the realisation that I didn't stay the night.

Though I would love to run over there to talk to her, I also wanted to respect Dakota's boundaries.

I know that all this was unexpected, hell, I'm still shocked by seeing her for the first time in six years, but I feel like a complete stranger in that house, unwanted and isolated. And that takes a stab at the already shredded remains of my heart.

But I'm here for Jenna, after all, and the last thing I want to do is let her down.

So, I get dressed, grab my phone and hotel card before heading out the door.

Their house used to be a place where I found solace. In the beginning, I had her brother to thank for that. He took me in like I was family when I told him of my strained relationship with my dad and gave me a place to feel safe when I wasn't in my own home. But it was Dakota in the end who gave me the peace I so desperately needed with every glance and secret moment we shared.

That was the thing about the Summer's siblings, they had hearts of gold, and I, like a fucking idiot, took advantage of that. Nate gave me safety, and Dakota gave me an escape. The two were exactly what I needed, but at exactly the wrong time. Because my head was too fucked up to be saved and I thought the only way to properly escape everything was to grab hold of the opportunity dangling in front of me—to move to the U.S. and flee.

But it didn't do shit. If anything, I think it made everything worse.

And now, looking up at the house as the Uber pulls up, I feel so far removed from that place.

I get out of the car, thanking the driver before making my way up the driveway. I almost go straight for the door handle out of old habit, but I pause as my fingers graze it, thinking better and knocking. I swallow thickly, wiping my hands on my dark shorts when Jenna answers the door with a smile.

"Great, you're here. Come in." She waves me in.

I step past her, taking my shoes off by the door. My gaze lifts to the lounge room, noticing Dakota already sitting on the couch, making me pause. I don't know why. I expected her here, but I was still processing the fact that she was really here.

When Jenna joins her, Dakota glances over the couch, meeting my eyes for the briefest moment before her lips press into a thin line and she twists back around. Just like that, the distance stretches between us.

I take the space on the other side of Jenna, putting her between us, and I try to stop my gaze from drifting to Dakota.

"Okay," Jenna begins, leaning forward to grab the TV remote to turn it off before sitting back. "So, I understand there is some history between you two, and I don't want to force you guys to talk about it." At that, Dakota's eyes flick to mine, frowning slightly before tearing them away again. "But I need you two to work together. You both mean a lot to us, and we wanted you to be involved in the wedding as much as possible. Do you think you can make it work for the next three months for us?"

I look over at Dakota, meeting her gaze once again. I watch her jaw clench as her eyes flick over my face. I want to know what she's thinking. I want to know what she's feeling. Because while I'm eager to spend more time with her, I know that's far from what she's feeling. I just want to know what exactly it is.

But she doesn't give anything away. She just redirects her gaze to Jenna and smiles flatly. "It's fine, Jenna. It's all in the past anyway, right, Reece?" Her questions pointed toward me, but it's loaded underneath. I hear it in the sharp way she says my name. And I get the meaning immediately. It was all she said last night. That there's nothing left between us.

I inhale a breath, feeling my heart cracking and a heavy feeling sitting on my chest. "Sure, yeah. All in the past. We'll help with anything you need."

Jenna smiles. "Great, because I have a list for you. Some of them you can split between the two of you, but some I want both of your opinions, so you'll have to work together on those."

Dakota grabs the list first from Jenna's hand and reads through it.

She nods. "Okay, seems easy enough."

"Of course. I'll be organising the bigger things with your dad. But these are the things I need the most help with. With the bakery in the busiest time of year, I didn't have much time to prepare all these things. But I wanted you both here, so I guess I'll have to deal with that." Jenna chuckles.

After Dad had let her go from babysitting me, Jenna went all in on starting her own bakery, which took off almost immediately. Her baking was one of the top perks of her looking after me. She would bake so many things throughout my childhood and have me try them. My favourite was always her apple and cranberry pies. Then, when she finally opened her bakery, I was there almost every day after school and after baseball practice and games since it was just around the corner. It's the exact bakery I went to when I planned that picnic with Dakota.

I take the list from Dakota when she holds it out for me and skim through it.

The list is simple enough, and I notice the few things Jenna has highlighted for us both to work on, where I can spend more time with Dakota. Things like the playlist, table settings, and the suit and dress fitting.

"I can trust you guys with this, right? There won't be any drama?" Jenna asks, flicking her gaze between the two of us.

Dakota smiles at her. "Of course. Don't worry, we've got this covered."

"Good. I don't want whatever past you guys have to interfere, so if you change your mind, please just let me know. I'm grateful for you two coming to help, but I'll manage if you're not able to work together."

I shake my head. "It's fine, Jenna. I think we can be civil for a couple of months. You don't have anything to worry about."

Jenna smiles again and reaches over to squeeze my hand. "I know. I love you both. Now I have to head off to the bakery. My laptop is in the kitchen if you need it. It's got most of the wedding plans on it, so you can use it when you need."

Dakota nods. "Sure. Now go. Otherwise, you'll be late."

She checks her watch and curses. "Shit, okay. Thank you both so much. I'll see you later."

Jenna grabs her handbag and bolts out the door, leaving both Dakota and me alone with an uncomfortable silence wrapping around us.

But it's not for long when Dakota stands abruptly.

"I've got to go," she says shortly, walking around the couch.

I stand, taking a step toward her and calling her name. "Dakota, please."

She pauses, and I watch the rise and fall of her shoulders before she turns to me. Funnily, the couch acts like some kind of barrier between us this time instead of empty space. "Remember what we talked about yesterday. We don't have to be friends. We don't have to talk, catch up, or do anything past doing this for my dad and Jenna. My goal while being here was to finally get some peace over you. I'm not about to let you storming back in here ruin that."

"That's not my plan, Dakota. Please, I just..." I trail off, looking for words.

"You just what?" she snaps.

I flinch at the harsh delivery of her words before sighing. "All I wanted was to know that you were doing better than I was. That you were happy and well, and I'd hoped when I saw you at the wedding, we could clear the air and maybe even eventually be friends again. But I never wanted to interfere with your happiness. That's the absolute last thing I want."

She doesn't say anything for a moment as her brows pinch and eyes soften just slightly, but nothing gives away what she's thinking, and it just makes me feel so far away from her because I used to be able to read her like a book.

But then she clenches her jaw, eyes snapping to mine again, hard and guarded like before.

"Well, I'm not, so you can have that for your peace of mind."

67

Then she turns on her heels, grabs her keys, and storms out the door, leaving me with the echo of those words.

10

DAKOTA

I feel like a ball of fire as I slide into Dad's car, boiling with anger and frustration. Luckily for me, Dad has his work ute so I have transport to get out of the house whenever I need to escape. Especially with Reece here.

I cannot believe him. He comes in and messes with my plans, then has the nerve to say that? Like he deserves to know about me.

He lost that privilege a long time ago.

I shouldn't have said what I said, though. I should have just kept quiet and left. But my anger got the best of me, and I wanted him to know I wasn't okay. I didn't want him to have the satisfaction he craved, that breaking me was the best thing to do. But now that I'm out of that room and my head starting to clear as I drive, I know that bit of information is just going to make him try harder to talk to me.

I don't know if that should be considered a good thing or a bad thing.

Maybe I'm just in dire need of a drink.

I park in front of Alex and Avery's house and get out.

What I really need to do is push him to the back of my

mind, where he's been for all these years. So that's exactly what I do as I climb up the driveway: I push the thoughts of him right down into the deepest, darkest corner of my mind. Out of sight, out of mind.

Entering the house, I can already hear their voices echo from further inside, the familiar laughter and bickering of my friends.

I find them in the kitchen, busying around with baking our snacks before our movie marathon.

Alex cradles a bowl to his chest while vigorously mixing his chocolate paste while Avery adds flour to the dough she kneads in her own bowl.

Alex turns his head when he hears me round the corner. "Good, you're finally here. Grab a bowl and start creating. I'm making brownies, and Avery is making banana bread. You're already behind."

I roll my eyes. "So demanding."

"Damn right. We were going to wait for you, but I was getting hungry and decided to start, so hurry up."

I drop the car keys on the counter and wash my hands at the sink. "Sorry. Jenna just wanted to talk to both Reece and me before I left."

"What about?" Avery asks, flopping her dough onto the patch of the counter she covered in flour.

I pull up the recipe I had searched to make peanut butter jam drop cookies before searching their cupboard for the ingredients we'd shopped for the other day.

"Oh, just about us working together and what she wanted us to do. Wanting to make sure we were okay to work together," I reply, trying to sound dismissive of it all, so they didn't ask too many questions about it, and we didn't have to talk about it longer than needed.

"And are you okay with it?" Avery asks, turning her head to

look at me as I set all the things I need on the counter next to her.

I shrug. "I mean, I have to be. I'm not just going to *not* help them with this wedding because of him. And it seems he won't either, so I have to put up with it."

They don't say anything more about it, and I'm grateful.

I get to work, making the cookies and mixing them all in a bowl before rolling them out onto a baking tray. Alex starts licking the leftover mixture of his brownies from the bowl, and I cackle as chocolate smears onto his nose and chin, which starts a little food fight between us. Flour ends up in hair and smears of chocolate over skin.

Once our baking is in the oven, we go to clean up.

As I close the door of the bathroom, the quiet settles around me, and it's that exact moment those thoughts start to wiggle themselves back out. My mind starts to wander back to Reece and what he said, wanting to know if I was happier than he was, that I was okay.

It makes me wonder if he ever thought of me. If he ever asked about me or searched me up, though he wouldn't have gotten far with the latter, as I blocked him on all my social media. Did he ever try to call me like I did him before realising I blocked his number? Before he changed his number?

If he ever asked about me, he wouldn't have to wonder how I was, though, right? If he knew what it had been like for me for the past six years, he wouldn't have to come here to find out himself. I knew he was still friends with Jake, he'd accidentally brought him up in conversation a couple of times when he came to visit with Avery. And Jake, he was never good at keeping his mouth zipped.

No matter how much I try to stop myself, I can't help but wonder what the last six years looked like for him.

When I blocked him on social media, I also blocked his name on all search engines and everywhere he could come up, just in case. It was also a silent agreement between Alex and Avery to never bring him up. Avery had to remind Jake of the same when he would slip up.

But now, it's like I have this sudden urge to know. Maybe it's because I gave him that tidbit of information before, and now I want to be even. I don't want to be the only one who is vulnerable.

I couldn't ask him, though. I couldn't let him know I was even the slightest bit interested.

So, I went to the only source I knew.

After cleaning up, I collapse next to Avery on the lounge as the TV plays a rerun of Friends. She hands me a glass that looks like it's just cola in it, but as I take a sip, I smell the notes of whiskey.

I take a long pull of it, making her side-eye me.

"Woah, okay. You alright?" Her wary gaze scanning over me.

I set the drink down on the coffee table in front of me before turning to her and Alex on the other side.

"Tell me what he was like over the years?" I demand.

Her brows pinch. "What..." she pauses before her brows smooth and her eyes widen a little, "oh. Nope. No. We're not doing this."

"Come on, please. Just give me something," I beg, pushing aside how pathetic it feels.

"No," she snaps, turning her body toward me and folding her legs in front. "You made me promise that if you ever asked about him, I wasn't to tell you anything. I've kept that promise for the last six years, I'm not about to start now."

"Please, Avery. I need this. Even if it's something small. Just tell me something so I can know that I wasn't an idiot," I plead.

Her eyes soften as she sighs, reaching over and gathering my hands in hers. "Dakota. Stop. You're not an idiot."

"Then prove it to me. Make me believe that. Because right now, I do," I tell her, a desperate lilt to my tone.

I just want to know that I didn't spend the last six years stupidly hung up on him and ruining any chance I had of moving on.

She pauses, gaze flicking between mine as if searching, digging for something before sighing again, body slumping. "Fucking hell, I knew this was a bad idea," she mutters to herself before shaking her head and taking a deep breath. "Fine. But you can't ask anything else. What I give you is what you get and nothing else, okay?"

I nod, squeezing her hands. "Promise."

"Okay." She nods in return. "The beginning was...really rough for him. But now, he's just finished his second season in the Major Leagues."

I frown, processing those words before shaking my head. "That tells me nothing."

She gives me a pointed look. "It gives you everything you want to know."

I fall silent, the information swirling in my head before we're interrupted by the oven timer buzzing.

Alex stands. "Okay, enough of that. No more talking about he who shall not be named. Let's enjoy our baking and watch some movies."

It's not until later, after the sun sets and I'm back home, alone in the quiet of my room, that I give in to my temptation. I pull out my phone and remove my blocks before starting to search.

The minute I search his name, his photo comes up front and centre, dressed in his team's baseball fit. There are interviews and a history of him on Wikipedia. I look through the articles and notice one from five years ago. It says something about an out-of-control party, but I don't scroll through the article. I'm too locked on the photo at the top. He's not even the focal point of the photo, but he's all I see. Him and a woman draped across him while his head is tipped back in a laugh and his arms wrapped around her. I note the date and feel my heart crumble as I realise it wasn't even a few months after he left.

I don't need to read the article to see the truth. That he didn't even mourn me like I did him.

And that's all I need to know to re-cement my stance of having nothing to do with him.

That there isn't a chance in hell I will forgive him.

I sit stretched across the couch with Jenna's laptop the next morning as I go over the RSVP's to confirm numbers for her. Luckily, I had set up online invitations for them months ago to easily track, for the most part, who was coming, apart from those who needed physical invitations sent.

That's what prompted her to ask for my help after she had been stressing about designing invitations and I told her about online invitations. She said she needed me to calm her down and there was no way I could say no to her.

Jenna joins me, cradling a cup of what I assume is her regular evening tea. She's still dressed in her flour-covered jeans and T-shirt with her bakery logo on her chest, having only arrived home about ten minutes ago. She groans, kicking her feet up on the coffee table and resting her head back on the couch, looking utterly exhausted.

I press my lips together and poke my toe into her thigh, making her groan again.

"You okay?" I ask, closing the lid of the laptop.

"I'm fine. Just been a long day." She sighs and rolls her head to the side to look at me. "How are you? What have you been up to today?"

"Nothing much. I was just going through your RSVPs on the website. I've got about fifteen at the moment, but still waiting for a few more that I followed up with."

"Why can't people just RSVP on time? It's not that hard," Jenna says, exasperated.

I smile. "They probably just forgot. You've still got a couple of days before you need the final number for the venue, right?"

"Yeah, but it would be nice to know a *little* bit more in advance."

"It's okay. I'll keep pushing them, and if we don't hear back, you can un-invite them."

She rolled her eyes. "Yeah, right. I wish. They'd just turn up anyway."

I shrug. "Hey, maybe if fewer people are coming, you'll have a spare allocation in the budget to hire someone to kick them out."

She chortles. "I'm not some celebrity who needs security for a wedding. It'll be fine. I'll sort something out. Maybe I just need to anticipate them coming anyway and waste money. I don't know." She sighs loudly. "Why are weddings so stressful?"

"Hey." I nudge her again with my foot, making her look at me. "That's why I'm here. I'll sort it out for you, okay?"

She smiles then and reaches over to squeeze my calf. "Thank you. I'm so grateful for you and Reece being here."

My smile falls flat at the mention of his name, and I look away, reality slamming back into me.

I keep thinking that maybe I've been dreaming the last couple of days, but when I hear his name, it all punches straight into my gut.

Jenna must see my change in tune because she straightens and turns to face me. She gently takes the laptop from me and places it on the table, making me look at her again.

"Can I ask you a question? It's okay if you don't want to answer. I just want your perspective."

I frown before nodding. "Sure, what is it?"

She clears her throat. "What happened between you two?"

What a complicated question. One, I would have thought

she knew, but now it makes me confused and a little angry at Reece. Because, of course, he keeps me hidden even after all these years, but yet, I thought he was close to Jenna and would have at least told her.

I look down at my hands, picking at my nails, trying to piece together a simple answer to give her, but nothing about us was ever simple enough to summarise in just a few words. It was complicated and messy. Young and freeing. Everything that left me broken and yearning.

It was an inevitable heartbreak from the start, but I still fell for his unanswered promises.

"I wish I had a simple enough answer for you," I admit, a breathy laugh escaping my lips, "but it was just young love that didn't turn out the way I hoped for. And like an idiot, I fell for living for the hope of it all."

And as sick as it made me, I loved him. Not a thing I would admit then, but I knew it now for what it was. He was the best but also the worst lesson in what I learnt about love.

She leans forward and takes both my hands in hers, a gentleness that always seems to get me to open up to her, reflecting in her eyes. "I have time if you want?"

I swallow, tears pricking my eyes as she smiles softly.

If only I had her years ago in the beginning stages when I closed off on everyone. Because in the next second, I was spilling everything to her. From beginning to end.

It's easier the second time around, and with every word, the pressure in my chest eases a little more.

I think my therapist would be proud of me.

When tears start to trail down my cheek, Jenna swipes them away and pulls me into her arms. She holds me for a few moments before pulling away.

Her gaze flicks between mine. "Thank you for telling me." She squeezes my hand before sighing. "I won't try to defend him because he should not have treated you like that. But I will tell you that I think he knows how much he screwed up. I understand his thought pattern. He was a complicated boy, holding the weight of the world on his shoulders. He still is." There's a haunted flicker behind her eyes as those last words pass her lips, but it's gone just as quickly. "But god damn him for pulling you into his mess without knowing how to treat you properly. I thought I had taught him better than that. I guess his father had sunk his claws deeper than I thought."

I sniffle, wiping away the residual tears on my cheeks. "Thank you, Jenna. It's okay, this has all just been unexpected, but I'll be okay. I've moved on."

She frowns, flicking her gaze between my own as she tilts her head slightly. "Are you sure?"

I flinch, frowning at her words. "What do you mean? Of course, I am."

She shakes her head. "No, I'm sorry. I didn't mean for that to come off as judgmental or like I don't believe you. It's just that you guys do have a strong history together. I wouldn't blame you for having some conflicting feelings about this all."

I snort and shake my head. "No. Truly, I'm fine. You know, that's all it is. It's history. And I have no interest in repeating it."

Not one single bit. I know better now not to risk my heart so carelessly. Especially for a boy who can never keep his promises.

She glances at me for a moment longer, regarding me with a contemplative look before she smiles and pats my knee. "Right, I'm sorry. I don't mean to throw around assumptions. I would never want you to get hurt again."

"I know. Thank you, Jenna. For everything."

From the moment she entered our family's life, she'd spread light in all our lives. She was the one to suggest Callie to me when I was looking for a therapist. She got me to step out of my comfort zone and try new things with my photography, which led me to start sharing them with the world. She helped me discover new styles and explore more than I had been willing to do because I didn't believe in myself.

And for that, I'll always be thankful for her.

"Of course, my dear. Please let me know if you need anything. If you don't want to be anywhere near him, I can accommodate that. I'll clear my schedule as much as I can—"

I interrupt her with a shake of my head. "No, Jenna. It's fine. I can deal with working with him. I don't want you to have to leave work earlier than you wanted. That's exactly why we're here, right? You focus on your business, and we'll help you with the wedding."

She squeezes my hand back with a smile. "Please, do not hesitate to call me at whatever time during the day if you need me. I've tried to organise everything I want for this wedding, so if something doesn't work, call me and I'll deal with it."

"Of course. You can trust us."

She leans over and wraps her arms around me before standing up and heading upstairs with a parting, "I appreciate you."

I smile at the sentiment.

Jenna was the softness that this family needed in the eye of craziness. With my move to Melbourne and the tornado that was Reece that ripped me apart and left Nate losing his closest friend, she was what we needed. She was the calm that Dad needed too, and she slotted in so effortlessly into our life. She made us feel whole. It was everything we needed to mend a broken family.

But now, this dynamic has had a wrench thrown in it with the connection to Reece, and I'm trying to figure out how this little information didn't come up in the last two years.

God, I need something strong to forget the ways my life has turned upside down once again.

11

REECE

I take a moment standing at the end of the driveway upon arriving at Dakota's house, hearing the distant chatter of people gathered in the backyard before taking a deep breath to gather every ounce of courage I have in me.

I wanted to talk to her tonight. I've been trying to build myself up to try and talk to her about everything since the dinner, but as soon as I do try, her pain-filled eyes flash in my mind, making me choke up. I was so close to it the other day, but she walked away before I had the chance to spit out the words. It's hard to when she's wanting to forget about the past, and all I want is for her to know the full story like she deserves and how much I've regretted it.

It's Jenna and Tim's engagement party tonight, finally holding their celebrations after waiting for me to finish the season before doing so. They told me they wanted the whole family to be there when they did, so they held off until we were all available.

I'm kind of thankful here wasn't going to be the first time I saw Dakota, like I originally thought. That we had the initial shock of seeing each other away from an audience of strangers.

But I still feel nervous, knowing there may be a chance I will see Nate tonight. He was the second person on my list of people that hurt to lose. I hadn't heard from him since he flew down the day before I left for the States and sent a punch flying straight into my face. I knew why but he made sure I knew when he spat in my face as I held my nose, pouring with blood.

"That was for fucking with my sister when I warned you not to."

The absolute hatred in his eyes hurt more than anything.

He had been like a brother to me and when I was at my lowest, he was there to clap me on the back and pull me up. He was there for my rare panic attack, sat with me and distracted me from the swirling thoughts in my brain. He was there to give me a place when I felt I didn't have a place to go. He took me in and allowed me to stay at his when I couldn't stomach being home.

That was when I found his relation to Dakota, bumping into her at the front door to her home, eyes widening as she saw me after two weeks of me avoiding her.

I didn't mean for everything to get so fucking complicated. I wanted to create space between Dakota and me after I found out she was dating my best friend, Liam. When I realised I was developing feelings for said best friend's girlfriend. The same girl who was the stranger by the river. The girl who made that location the only place I found peace in.

But I found myself going over to Nate's house more than I needed to just to get a glimpse of her. I didn't have the guts to talk to her, though, knowing I could never have her and already having butterflies with just the sight of her made it more dangerous. I took advantage of my connection to Nate to see her, but every time she would turn to look at me as I walked through the door, I looked away because I knew I would fold under her ocean-blue gaze. It was all I allowed myself of her until Nate moved away.

I kept in contact with him, playing online with him, and catching up when we could, but I couldn't bring myself to call her.

Then that summer happened, and everything just got too messy, and all that I feared happened.

I missed Nate's friendship, but fuck I was scared to see him after the way things ended.

I take a deep breath and force one foot in front of the other up the driveway. It's mostly dark inside when I push open the door. The kitchen and hallway lights are the only things guiding my path to the backyard, where it looks like everyone is gathered.

I glance through the kitchen, where Jenna stands with a few other people. She catches my eye and calls my name, waving me over.

As soon as I'm close to her, she wraps me in a hug, squeezing me before introducing me to the other people.

"This is my family. My sister, Nora, and my parents, Elijah and Jada. Not sure if you remember, but you've met them once before when you were eight. This is Reece. The little one I looked after and raised years ago. Well, not so little anymore." She chuckles.

Jenna never really talks about her family to me, maybe with small insights in conversation now and then, but I don't remember. I don't remember meeting her parents either. I don't think I remember much from that age. Truth is, there wasn't much talk outside of baseball in my house. It was plastered on every wall, seeping into every crevasse and suffocating the air surrounding.

Sounds fucking depressing now that I think about it.

Her parents embrace me first–her mum hugging me, and her dad shaking my hand. Their smiles are soft and welcoming, and I don't know, it just makes me feel like I belong with them. Like I was a part of their family. It's...an odd feeling. "It's so nice to meet you again, Reece. We hear so much about you. Jenna always says the highest praises about you and how good you were."

I raise my brows and look at Jenna. "Really?"

She just shrugs at my scepticism.

Her sister greets me next, shaking my hand. "Really. She talked about you like you were her own."

My gaze snaps to Jenna again, and I have to swallow past the lump growing in my throat. I know she tells me all the time how proud she is of me, but it still feels so fucking strange to me when I've always been a disappointment or burden. It's always hard to believe when my own parent has never said so. But I'm beginning to believe her. Every time I hear it now, my chest swells under the praise instead of the usual skepticism and I guess I have therapy to thank for that.

She smiles at me, and there I see it, the flash of pride in her eyes as if she were confirming that when she looks at me, there was something worth being proud of.

I look away before she can see the water filling my eyes, shake my head, clear my throat, and look up at her parents again.

My smile is stiff as I suppress the emotion swelling and hide behind humour like it's my default guard. "Well, that's at least someone." I clear my throat again. "It was lovely to meet you all. I just have to look for someone."

We say our goodbyes, and just before I step out of the kitchen, Jenna calls back to me.

There's a spark of amusement in the tone of her voice as she tells me, "She's in the lounge with her friends."

I frown at first before it clicks, and I shake my head. "I wasn't—"

"Please, Reece," she scoffs. "I'm not blind."

I press my lips together and turn around. I try to force my legs to go in the absolute opposite direction from where Jenna said she was just to prove her wrong. But I can't even make it two steps before I'm cursing under my breath and backtracking. Jenna's laugh follows me as I pass the doorway and head into the lounge.

I hear her voice before I see her, and even that has my heart pounding against my chest.

But her words make me pause in my step, staying just out of sight behind the wall, standing in the middle of the hallway.

"He called earlier today. His flight got cancelled and there were no other flights he could catch. Now he can't get here until midday tomorrow. Dad reassured him that they would do something together when he got here, but I think Nate feels a little guilty since they waited to hold this party until we were all together."

I can't help but breathe a sigh of relief hearing that, but I know that I will have to confront him at some point. Maybe I can avoid him after all.

"How long's he here for?" Jake asks, and I send a silent thanks to him for asking the exact question I was just thinking.

"He's only here for the weekend. Then he'll be back for the wedding," she answers.

I have a little bit of time then, and I'm hoping by the time the wedding comes, I'll be on Dakota's good side. And that's with a lot of fucking hoping.

I make my appearance then, rounding the corner to see them all sitting on the couch, Dakota, Avery, Jake, Sage and Alex. Jake is the first one to notice me as he sits in the recliner with Avery sitting on his lap.

He holds out his hand for me to clap, greeting me.

"Hey, man. Good to see you again. It's been a while."

I clasp my hand in his and shake it as I nod at him. "Yeah. Good to see you too."

I smile at Avery before I scan my eyes over to Sage, nodding at him, which he reciprocates. Then my gaze lands on Dakota, lingering until her eyes meet mine, almost like she doesn't want to look but can't help it.

I smile softly. "Hi, Dakota."

She swallows, whispering her greeting under her breath that I almost don't hear before averting her gaze.

The silence that envelopes afterward is a little awkward, and I shuffle on my feet before deciding to take my cue to leave.

Jake stops me, though, just as I turn to leave. "Come on. Let's go grab a drink." He presses a kiss to Avery's cheek before prompting her to stand with a tap on her thigh which she follows. He tips his chin at Sage as he stands. "You coming?"

Sage nods and stands with Jake before all three of us turn to leave.

"Don't miss us too much," Jake calls back as he steps into the hall with us.

I hear Avery scoff before she calls back, "In your dreams."

The words spark a memory flashing to the forefront of my mind. Of Dakota and me in the airport, and a similar retort came from her mouth.

Keep dreaming, Fischer.

You're always in my dreams, Summers.

God, I didn't even fully comprehend the fullness of that statement then. I had still dreamed of going back to the way things were, to have the comfort of her friendship when we were a couple of nobodies finding comfort in each other.

Now, I dream of everything about her. From the softness of her gaze to the warmth of her embrace. From the way I felt so completely at peace with her to the way she felt against me.

I follow Jake down the short hall, past Jenna again to the backdoor. Walking out onto the dimly lit patio, smoke sizzles from the barbeque off to the left where Dakota's dad cooks the meat and chats to a few people. He notices me and gives me a polite nod, which I return before he turns back to his conversation.

Jake pulls out a couple of beers and a cola from an esky by the sliding door and hands them out to us, giving me the cola before taking a seat at the outdoor table. Sage and I follow suit, him taking the seat beside Jake, and I take the one opposite both of them, facing the backyard and the darkening sky.

It's Jake who cuts the silence, meeting my eyes after taking a sip of his drink. "So, how's life? How's living in the States?"

I shrug, taking a sip of my drink to give me a minute to answer. "It's okay. I mean, I'm doing what I love and that's all I care about."

"How is the MLB life?" Sage asks, eyeing me in that quiet observant way of his.

I tap my fingers against the can, pondering over his question before answering. "Tough. But like, nothing I wasn't prepared for, I guess." I reach up to scratch my jaw, before continuing. "It's a lot of training and keeping in shape, which I was used to before." An awkward pause settles between us and I hesitate to tell them more of what it's been like before shaking my head and end up adding, "The travelling is what's hitting me the most I think. Which is funny because for the last few years, I spent them sleeping in buses. You'd think that would be worse." I chuckle, only telling them half of the truth. I'm not ready to voice the reality of what I really think yet.

Because, yeah, it's tough, but I feel so numb toward it all. Like I'm going through the motions, but I'm not really there. I'm not really enjoying what I used to enjoy. And fuck, if that doesn't say a lot.

Sage hums. "Yeah. I guess that's why it's been hard for you to keep in contact with us."

I choke on my drink and look up at him. The guilt weighing on me of the times I left their texts unanswered and spent my nights drinking my pain away. When I dove into my self-destructing behaviour and tried to push them away because I thought I was meant to be alone.

I was a fucking dick to both of them, and I wouldn't be surprised if they still hate me for it even after I apologised to them. I can never tell with Sage if he ever forgave me for that, though. It was hard to read him, and I couldn't tell if he was taking a jab at me or being serious. It didn't matter though because I would never stop apologising to them for being such a shitty friend.

I smooth a hand over my jaw as I lean back in my chair. "I don't really have an excuse for how much of a shitty friend I've been. And I don't really expect you to forgive me for how I've treated you both. But I am sorry. I'm trying to be better."

One side of his mouth curves as he watches me stumble over my words before he finally cuts me off, "I'm just fucking with ya. We were just worried about you. We know you were going through some shit. But we'll always be here for you. No matter how 'shitty' you've been."

I shake my head. "I don't know how you guys have put up with my shit over the years."

It really says a lot about them for sticking by me when I was stumbling through life the first year after I moved. Especially the years after, as it repeated in my head that I didn't deserve anyone and would go silent on them for months. When I was losing the passion I held for a game I grew up playing, and started sinking into a deeper hole. When I went through surgeries I thought were pointless to keep myself in the game, but was pushed into them by my agent.

They were there, steady and unyielding in their friendship, tethering me to the ground when I thought I was going to sink through it.

And fuck, if months of therapy hasn't shown me just how grateful I am for them.

He tilts his head. "I mean, it hasn't been easy."

I smile. "Fuck you."

He grins as he takes a sip of his drink. "You wish you could."

Jake looks down at his phone as it lights up and starts typing before looking up at us. "Avery said they are planning to go out afterward if you guys want to go?"

My immediate thought is if Dakota's going, of course I'll be there, but I press my lips together to keep from agreeing too fast and blurting those exact words out.

I wait for Sage to agree first before I give my answer with a noncommittal shrug. "Sure. Could be fun."

And then I hide my smile behind my palm as I smooth it over my lips.

I wish I was more intoxicated than I am right now, which is a total of zero percent, thanks to the stupid sobriety vow I made after the countless fuck ups I committed under the influence.

At the start of the night, I would have said I was a little intoxicated, but not from alcohol. My entire body seemed to buzz to life just with her standing mere feet from me. I couldn't look away from her, magnetised to the pull of her orbit.

As soon as we got to this bar–a small Irish place along the strip and our third stop of the night–they all tossed back a few shots together. I could tell they were all pretty buzzed already, and it was kind of entertaining to be the only sober one. It was after their second shot that Dakota's friends pulled her into the mass of swaying bodies where they'd stayed since.

Jake and Sage pull me into a game of pool, and, even though I try to focus on the game, my attention always seems to drift to her. It seems as if her attention's always pulled to me as well, because when I look up from lining up my shot, her eyes are on me. I don't tear my gaze away from her as I fluke my shot and stand up straight. I don't even listen to my friends complain and poke fun beside me. Everything around me blurs except for her.

It almost feels like she's dancing for me because I notice straight away when my eyes connect with hers, she sways her hips more, the roll of her body more enticing, the exploration of her hands over her body hypnotising.

It feels as if she was made to torture me. I know better than to think that, but fuck, if it doesn't feel like that.

That's when it happens, what brought me to wishing I could drink and forget. Because with my eyes zeroed in on her as I wait my turn, the most sinister smile crossed her face. I can vaguely hear Jake and Sage call my name, but I can't do anything but watch as she turns and grabs the nearest guy, pulling him flush against her. I don't notice when my hands ball into fists until my nails start biting into my palm. But it does nothing to divert my attention from her.

She leans up to speak in his ear, and whatever she tells him makes him smile, making the fire in my chest burn fiercely. Then, she whirls around in his arms and pins her eyes on me.

And I fucking knew this was all for me. To show me how not mine she was. To show me she was not mine to laugh with, to kiss, to touch, to fall for. To show me that she was long gone from my reach.

I want nothing more than to storm right over and rip that guy's arms off her. To show her just how much she still affects me. How much of a hold she still has on me, even when not a single finger of mine touched her.

But I deserve this hit. I deserve the sinking feeling and the fire torching my veins seeing her in someone else's arms. I deserve to this torture. It's something I was prepared to see when I came for the wedding, knowing I couldn't expect her to be waiting for me.

I'm a weak fucking man when it comes to her though, so I look away, wiping my mouth before deciding I need some air. I mutter to Jake and Sage that I'm stepping out, handing them the cue I held before weaving my way through the crowd.

When I push through the front doors, I take a huge inhale of air, almost like my lungs had seized working inside. I walk a few steps down the street before leaning against the wall of the building, tilting my head back and closing my eyes.

I had no right to feel this way. To feel jealous that some random guy could touch her when I couldn't. To feel heartbroken like I was losing her all over again.

I almost laugh at myself for being so pathetic, but I'm interrupted from my self-deprecation by a soft voice calling my name.

"Reece?" she calls, and when I look over, Dakota stands feet away, back cast with the glow of the street lamp behind her.

I must be dreaming or hallucinating because she looks kind of angelic in this light.

Was something put in my drink? Why is she out here with me?

"Yeah?" My voice is thick as I croak out the word, and I clear my throat.

She steps closer, and I peel myself off the wall to stand straight.

I didn't expect anyone to follow me out here, least of all her.

She frowns as she looks at me, then tears her gaze away to focus on a spot to the left of me as she speaks.

"Sorry. I just wanted..." She fumbles over her words before she huffs, straightening her posture and meeting my gaze. "I'm sorry. What I did in there was kind of embarrassing, and to be honest, immature. I think I've had way too much to drink because I don't do that."

I shake my head, a smile tilting my lips. But it holds no humour to it as I force my words past my mouth, everything inside me rebelling against them as a sharp pinch slices my chest. "You don't have to apologise, especially not to me. You can do whatever and be with whoever you like if that's what you want."

She nods. "I know, but still, I shouldn't rub it in your face like I was."

I huff out a laugh, almost sounding self-deprecating before tilting my head side to side. "I kind of deserve it, though, don't you think?"

A smile tugs at the corner of her mouth. "Maybe a little. But still...I don't want to be that type of person."

The silence wraps around us for a heartbeat, and I realise this may be my chance to finally talk to her and say the things I've wanted to tell her.

"Dakota," I start, taking a step toward her, but pause when I realise I was reaching for her and drop my hands by my side, clenching them to stop the urge. "You have every right to hate me and torture me. To not make this situation any easier for me."

She watches me for a moment as if trying to piece me together to fit the boy she knew, but the pieces aren't matching. She watches me with a curious and hesitant gaze, and I don't blame her, but it makes my nerves prickle along my skin.

I swallow, inhaling a breath as I gain the courage to continue.

"I think I should be the one apologising. I know no amount of apologies will make up for everything that happened when we were younger, but I think you deserve a real, sincere one rather than the desperate, empty one I gave you in the moment."

She stills, but surprisingly, she doesn't walk away and I let out a slow breath.

"So...I'm sorry. So extremely sorry for ever putting you in a position where you felt unworthy or discarded. I never intended for that," I tell her, remembering when Avery had finally snapped at me during her stay at my house with Jake and she told me exactly how she felt and what I made Dakota feel.

I can see the change in Dakota's expression as she stares at me, softening the more I speak.

"I wanted to give you everything, and I really thought I could, but I was scared and I clung to you out of desperation. You were the only person to make me feel so at peace when everything else was spiralling in my life. And yes, I had Nate and I had Liam, Jake and Sage, but none of them made me feel what you did." She swallows at that and looks away from me. But I don't let her get out of this that easily.

I reach out against my earlier restraint to hold her wrist again, stepping closer so she has no choice but to look up at me again.

I lock onto those ocean-blues I used to drown in, staring into them with sincerity and intent, hoping my words sink into her and she hears me. "I should have told you I was leaving. I shouldn't have led you on the way that I did. I should have made it work and given us a chance. I should have been open to everyone about us. I should have done so many things. I was so overwhelmed, and I didn't know how to process anything. I know that my words won't prove anything, but I want to show you that I have changed. Show you I'm not that eighteen-year-old boy anymore. I just want a chance to be in your life again. In whatever way you'll have me."

The pleading in my voice is not lost on me, but I would get on my hands and knees for the rest of my life if that's what it takes, just to have her again.

The guard she's held so strong in her posture and the expression in her eyes suddenly shatters in front of me. Her shoulders slump and her eyes fill with tears as her lip begins to wobble, and my heart completely breaks at the sight.

I panic, my eyes jumping over every inch of her face as if it held some kind of answer.

I fucked up. I fucked up bad. I didn't mean to make her cry. That was the last thing I wanted.

Shit, shit, *shit*. How do I make this right?

"Dakota," I whisper pathetically, and she sniffs before stepping out of my arms.

"You have no idea how long I waited for those words," She whispers back before folding a hand over her mouth, eyes snapping to mine, looking like she didn't really want to admit that piece of information. Her other arm wraps around her waist, like she's holding herself, protecting herself. From me.

I go to reach for her again, before thinking better and clenching my fist, dropping it weakly by my side. It's as if that broke the sound barrier that had enveloped us. The music vibrates from the bar a few feet away, muffling through the doors and our existence whirling back into reality.

She shakes her head, stepping further away and closer to the door, ready to escape. "I'm sorry. I have to...I have to go. I'm sorry."

And then she's fleeing back into the bar, and I'm left standing in the middle of the sidewalk with my chest caving, pathetically watching the doors she disappeared through, wondering how I thought I could just beg for her to give me another chance.

I know I said she didn't need to make this easy for me, but I didn't want her to run away from me crying. That was the last thing I wanted. Flashes of her crying in my car the day I broke up with her run through my mind, and I know I have to make this right because I can't do that to her again.

But for now, I give her the distance she clearly wanted. Especially after I walk back into the bar and Jake tells me that she and her friends are being picked up by her dad.

I just don't want to be the person to break her heart twice.

12

REECE

I must be a masochist.

It's the only explanation for willingly bringing myself to the river that holds too many memories for my heart to handle.

Although the same memories have haunted my dreams for the past six years, so I guess it makes no difference where I am. They're just beginning to haunt my waking moments now.

Maybe it's because I used to find solitude in this place, and I thought I could take a moment to reflect and figure out how I was going to fix things by coming here. But I'm beginning to realise it was the person more than the place that made it that way, and god, does that fucking suck. I mean, it makes sense, but still.

It felt like a little bit of the weight had come off my chest when I finally apologised to Dakota the way I'd wanted to all these years. But when she ran away from me with tears filling her eyes, I felt like I was at square one again. Really, I never left.

I don't know what I thought would happen when I talked to her, but I certainly didn't think she would run away. Since then, it all feels like it weighs ten times more sitting on my chest. I thought coming here would give me a break, breathing in the fresh air and surrounding myself in the bubble that used to encapsulate the area.

But I was wrong.

It hurts. Like a continuous throb in my chest when I'm reminded of what a fucking idiot I was to let her slip through my fingers. She matched me in ways I needed but didn't realise that I did. She was the peace I craved in my dark days.

I didn't realise how much I needed her until I left. Then, with every day that passed in my first few months in the U.S., I craved to hear her voice, feel her next to me, and her lips on mine again. I held tight to the memories as those feelings started to fade from my mind. I wanted to crawl back to her, to my home, but I knew I had burned every single bridge that could make that happen.

Being here doesn't feel right without her by my side. So, I sink into the memories of the summer I had her as if that can replace the feeling of her absence. To feel how safe I felt in her arms. How she was starting to heal parts of me that shattered so long ago, I never thought they would be able to piece together again. How I started to feel what true happiness felt like. As if all those things combined could conjure her ghost to appear next to me.

It makes me realise how out of touch I was with my feelings for her until it was too late. Only registering it was love seeping through my veins and making my heart beat to its own drum again when she'd already slipped through my fingers.

My mouth surely knew before I did, though, when I had almost blurted it on our date in the city. And maybe that's why I ran. But also talking to my therapist, I identified that it was my dad's whispers in my ear that ruined everything good that ever stepped foot in my life.

Those words echo in my head now.

You don't deserve love.

You really think someone like her would love a life sucking lowlife like you?

If you're thinking about quitting now, you can forget about calling this house home. You think some girl is going to stay with you when you have nothing going for you? That's not how this life goes, kid.

You are a fucking disappointment, kid. It should have been you, not her.

He was right, though. I never deserved that kind of love. I never deserved her.

Which was why I couldn't keep her. I was just going to bring her down.

I would've loved to say I've spent the last six years being a better man for her, but truth be told, I spent most of the beginning nights in a drunken stupor, trying to forget her. Trying to forget how I made the biggest mistake of my life. Because I knew there wasn't a chance in hell I could come back into her life like that. I did the damage and made my bed.

I spent a good chunk of the first year coasting by, putting in just enough effort to keep my seat in the minors while drowning my nights in a forgetful haze. That was until one of my coaches pulled me aside and set me straight. Said if I kept up my act, I would kiss the chance to play in the Majors good-bye. That if I didn't clean up my act, he would make sure of it.

That talk is what shook me awake, and I realised that if I wasted this time here, this whole thing would be for nothing. I would have lost her for nothing. I didn't want to waste my days away, sulking and licking my wounds. It wouldn't change the outcome.

Now that we were here, in this unexpected predicament, I didn't want to watch her slip through my fingers. Not again.

I knew it wouldn't be easy. Didn't expect it to. I could tell there was a hundred-ton stone wall surrounding her heart, and

I would climb the highest mountain to find my way back to her side.

But there was still that niggling fear that I wasn't good enough, *will* never be good enough for her. That no matter how hard I try, I'm bound to screw something up.

The voice that sounds oddly like my father's comes back to me.

You don't deserve anything this world gives you. Nothing but a disappointment.

It's hard to shut them out. Not when they ricochet around my head like bullets, finding the weak spots to penetrate.

Not when they wrap around my throat like a vice.

Not when they strike like a viper when I'm at my most vulnerable.

Fuck. It sucker punches me in the chest like a freight train, constricting my lungs and making me fight for my next breath.

I haven't had this in months. I've been able to fight these consuming thoughts off before they got this far, using my therapist's strategies to ground myself again.

But this...this snuck up on me. Waiting to pounce at the right moment, when I was at my weakest.

I can hear my heart beating in my ears. I press a shaky hand to my chest as if that will stop it from bursting out.

His voice seems to whisper louder now. They aim straight at the place I was most vulnerable, subtly becoming harsher.

How do you expect to be good at anything if you can't lower your ERA stats?

You won't get into any Major League team if you're wheezing after six laps. You think they won't push you harder than I am? Think again, boy. You don't know a fucking thing.

You're a disappointment.

You will never be a son to me.

You killed her.

I close my eyes, trying to push those thoughts out and pull air into my lungs through my nose. But it's pointless because I'm practically gasping.

I don't want to draw attention to myself to the people walking by. But god, I can't. Fucking. Breathe.

I grip the edge of the planks of the pier underneath me as I gasp like a fucking fish out of water. I ignore the burn in my shoulder as I do. I welcome it, actually, as if the physical pain will distract me from every thought buzzing in my head.

My vision starts to blur, making me sway. I just hope like hell I don't take a nose dive into the water below. Although, it might shock me out of this stupid fucking panic I've gotten myself in.

What do I have to panic about?

It's my own fucking fault my life is the way it is. I have it good compared to others, so what the fuck is this all about? Why now?

This is so fucking stupid.

Just snap out of it, dude.

Maybe if I wasn't such a fuck up, this wouldn't be happening. If I hadn't been such a coward, I would still have her and Nate, and maybe even Liam.

You're a goddamn coward, Reece.

Her voice sends another sucker punch into my chest. It echoes, repeating over and over. It's so loud that it rattles and hammers in my brain.

I considered you a brother to me, and this is how you treat me? I hoped I wasn't right about you. I was trusting you would treat her right, but you're just a big fucking disappointment.

You were my best friend. But you can rot in hell for all I care.

You were the one person I trusted not to break my heart.

I know.

I know.

I fucking *know*.

"Reece?"

God, now I think I'm hallucinating. Her fucking voice is like an angel sent down to kill me and I'm just going bat shit crazy sitting on this pier.

"Reece. Look at me." Her voice turns stern as a hand ghosts over my cheek. It's like a key unlocking my lungs for oxygen to pour in, and I greedily gulp it down. Everything still feels tight and dizzying, though.

I try to listen to those words and filter them through my head before my eyes finally peel open.

I see her kneeling beside me, and instantly, it tethers me. Grounding me in ways, all the tactics my therapist tried to teach me never quite worked. Her touch breathes life into me as I lean into it. Everything she is, is everything I dream of.

I most definitely am dreaming right now. Maybe I passed out in my panic from lack of oxygen because there's no way she would be here, touching me and looking at me with worry in her gaze.

It's then that my gaze starts to wander to my surroundings while I feel myself gasping for each breath. My whole body shakes with all the pent-up anxiety as my gaze trails around the trees, the park, and the people behind us. Some casting weary glances.

Shit.

"Hey, look at me," she says again, dragging my face back to her, and my eyes snap back to hers.

"Dakota?" My voice hoarse as I say her name, as if I was somehow deluding myself that she's here.

She smiles slightly. "Yeah," she frowns as she continues, "are you okay?"

My head and heart still pound, and I can feel the start of a headache forming at the front of my head. I try to keep the shaking in my hand to a minimum as I reach up to wrap it around hers that still rests against my cheek. Her skin is warm under my chilled fingers, and my muscles loosen at the feel of her.

She's real.

She's here.

"Yeah, I think so," I say weakly. *I am now with you here.* I keep those words to myself. "What are you doing here?"

She looks around. "I...I was getting some air. Taking a walk," she says, and I know there's more to the story of her being here. But she looks at me again and frowns as she adds, "What happened?"

I shake my head, looking away, making our hands drop, and she pulls hers to her lap. "Nothing new."

And it's the truth. I've experienced enough of them in the last six years. I'm just over the feeling it leaves me with. Complete emptiness and a reminder of everything missing in my life.

"Do you..." she starts, before wiping her palms down her thighs. "Do you need anything?" she says, hesitation in her voice.

Again, I shake my head. "No. It's fine," I reply, exhaustion entering my words. "Thank you, though. For coming to check on me."

"Of course." She nods and I look over at her again as she chews her bottom lip, and I almost think it's kind of cute if I didn't see the conflict waging in her eyes. "I can give you a lift back to your hotel if you'd like?" she offers.

I hesitate, looking away as I take in her question and the way she asked it.

"It's okay. I can find my way back. I don't want to put you out."

She shakes her head. "You're not. I'm offering. Look, I know

I haven't been the nicest to you since you got here, but I'm not that heartless to know when you need someone."

My heart cracks at her words, and I look up at her as a lone tear escapes the corner of my eye. I quickly wipe it away.

"You don't need to take pity on me."

"Reece," she says my name. Then the weight of her hand smooths over my shoulder, and just the feel of her touch relaxes the muscles there. "This isn't me taking pity on you. This is me helping you."

I can almost hear the unspoken words she's holding onto. *Like I tried to all those years ago.*

My shoulders stoop as I blow out a resigned breath, accepting her help. Truth is, I want to get out of here. I can feel my skin starting to crawl with the residual effects of the lack of oxygen.

"Yeah, okay."

She stands before offering me a hand. I grab it as I stand, and when I look at her again, she stares at me with this new empathy and curiosity. Like she wants to ask what happened to me, but her lips stay closed. I'm thankful that she doesn't ask because I don't exactly know the answer. I've been in this sort of spiral all my life with no direction to take.

Her eyes flick between mine for a moment, and my hand lingers in hers before she inhales and nods for me to follow her. Her hand leaves mine, and I'm left to follow her like a lost puppy. And I do so willingly.

She walks to a car I know all too well that has saved me multiple times from being forgotten after a game or practice.

She turns to me when she realises I stopped a couple of steps away. "She's not here. I borrowed Jenna's car to come here. I didn't know you would be here, but I guess it was good I came."

My lips twitch. "Yeah, I guess so."

I climb into the passenger seat as Dakota rounds to the

driver's side and hops in. She sits there for a second before starting the car and turning to look at me. She chews on her lip, hesitating over the questions I can see floating in her head.

"Has that..." she stops before continuing again, "has that happened often before?"

I pause and hesitate on my answer as my gaze flicks between hers. It's embarrassing to admit that even now that I'm free of the shackles of my father and the cards life has dealt me, it still has an effect on me.

But in the safety of this car and her, I nod with a swallow as I admit, "Yeah, many times."

I don't say anything more, though, and as if reading my thoughts, Dakota doesn't push it.

It's a silent drive to my hotel after I give her the address, and when she pulls up in front, I hesitate to leave, afraid to be left in the silence alone.

I know none of this changes how she feels about me. I'm still the idiot who broke her heart when I promised not to. No amount of empathy for my sufferings would change that, and I hope it doesn't.

But I would be lying if I said I didn't hope she won't let me sit in this suffering alone. She pulled me out of a god damn panic attack with just her voice and touch. I didn't want that feeling to leave.

I take a deep breath and clear my throat. "Thank you."

"No matter how much I hate you for what you did to me, I would never just watch while you suffer, Reece."

A tear trails down my cheek, and I quickly wipe it away before I look up at her, which only breaks my heart further. Because I stare at the iron walls I know she's solidified because of me. She looks at me as if I am nothing more than a stranger breaking down in front of her.

It blurts out of me in a puff of air before I can stop it. "I was so stupid for letting you go."

And then those walls crack as her expression wavers and tears line her eyes.

My next action confirms that I'm still that coward, because I exit the car and leave the broken pieces of us in her lap like I did six years ago.

Then I call my therapist and break down even more.

13

DAKOTA

When I arrive home, I idle in my car for a moment, the last words Reece left me with still whirling in my mind. I want to put this morning in the back of my mind, especially with Nate's unexpected delayed arrival, but I sat there and couldn't help but agree with his words. He was an idiot for letting me go. He was an idiot for how he ended it, keeping me in the dark about what our future truly looked like.

But I hate to admit that anger I was holding over him was starting to slip from my grasp, leaving only heartache in its wake.

Truthfully, I was never mad that he was leaving—I was happy for him, ecstatic even. I can't be mad at him for chasing his dream.

It was the way he kept that information from me and let me fall for him that kept stoking the anger. I trusted him when I was about to give up on love altogether. He saw all my insecurities, and instead of giving me advice or telling me none of my thoughts were real and needed to ignore them, he lent me a shoulder to lean on while sharing a part of himself with me. And then, he washed it all away like it was nothing.

After last night and his apology, a true, meaningful one that explained everything I wanted to hear, I felt it pick at the edges of the scab, opening up everything I had tried so hard and long to smother.

I came to the river to clear my head, to think, to do something against the torrent of emotions in my head, remembering a time when it had been a place I took solace in.

When I saw him sitting there, I didn't want to intrude if he was there to be alone. I was almost about to turn around and leave, but then I saw the shake in his shoulders and the way he rocked in place, and I just knew. I knew it by the sinking feeling in my gut as I watched him that I couldn't leave him there.

I'd never seen him like that. Maybe once, in the car on New Year's, when I held him after he told me about his mother. This was more though. I could see it even from the distance I was. It was raw, spiralling, like he was losing grip.

At that moment, he wasn't someone I used to know. He was Reece. The seventeen-year-old who used to meet me by the river, where we leaned on each other for comfort. I couldn't leave him like that.

Maybe I had been a bit rough on him, giving him the cold shoulder when all he had shown me was kindness.

That didn't mean I would let him back into my circle. I just... Maybe I could hear him out. Maybe I could not be so harsh and push him out. I could still hold him at arm's length and smile at him. Couldn't I?

An hour later, even with the arrival of Nate waltzing through the door with a backpack strapped to his back, this morning still lingers in my mind.

I paste on a smile, though, welcoming the distraction as he wraps me in a hug when I meet him by the door. It's been almost six months since I last saw him. Not that I would admit it to him, but I did miss him.

"Kodaline, it's good to see you." He squeezes me once before letting me go. "Have you grown? I swear you're like an inch taller."

I shove him by his shoulder. "Oh, stop. Maybe you've just shrunk."

He gapes, but amusement shines in his eyes. "I'm perfectly the same proportions as the last time you saw me."

I snort, and he lets his grin loose.

"Where's Dad?" he asks.

I shrug. "Not sure. He was here when I left this morning, but he was gone when I came back around an hour ago."

He hums, then shrugs as well. "Well, I'll just put my bag upstairs. Want to order food and watch a movie? I'm starved."

We sat on the couch, ordering ramen while Nate searched for a movie to watch.

It was after the food had arrived and we were halfway through the movie that I couldn't hold in the information anymore regarding Reece.

I decide to ease into it and tiptoe around the subject, not knowing how he'll react when I tell him.

"Hey, so, you've met Jenna, right?"

He glances at me with a strange look, and for a good reason, because what kind of question is that?

"Yeah," he drawls.

I swallow. "Did Dad tell you, you know, about who she used to look after?"

The crease between his brow relaxes as realisation hits him. He pauses the movie before turning to face me.

His gaze roams my face as if trying to gather his own information from reading my face. "He did," he replies.

I nod, trying to push down the hurt that I was probably the only one kept in the dark, looking down at my hands as I clean under my nails. "How do you feel about it?"

There's a long beat of silence, making me look back at him. A frown mars his face as he watches me before throwing the question back at me.

"How do *you* feel?"

I reel back, not expecting this to point back at me when I was trying to gather how he feels.

I open my mouth before closing it again, slumping back into the couch cushion as I work a swallow.

"I'm not sure. I was angry at first, maybe I still am a little. But I wanted to finally move on from that part of my life being here. I just, I don't know how I should feel..." I trail off.

He releases a long sigh then. "Well, I'm not exactly excited to see him at the wedding, but at least it won't be for too long. You won't need to see him for very long."

I narrow my eyes and tilt my head, questioning if he actually knows that he's here already.

"Nate, he's already here," I tell him slowly.

He frowns. "What?"

"He's here. He's staying at a hotel nearby. He'll be here for the next few months."

His anger deepens the crease between his brows as he straightens in his seat. "What the fuck?" He shook his head, meeting my eyes. "Why didn't anyone tell me? I would have been here earlier if I'd known."

"That makes two of us," I mumble.

He stares at me for a moment. "I can stay if you want? If you need someone else around for the next few months."

I shake my head. Ever the protective brother. "It's fine, Nate. I can deal with him. And maybe this is a good thing. If we talk, I can finally get the closure we didn't get back then. We can move on." I can move on.

"But what if he hurts you again? I don't want you to get hurt by him."

I shake my head. "He won't. I won't let him get that close

again," I say firmly. But I do need to be careful. This morning made me realise that. I could be there for him in a time of need, but I couldn't let him seep into the soft corner of my heart that's strangely the exact shape of him.

He watches me for a moment before nodding. "Need me to talk to him?"

I titter. "No. Definitely not. I think you did enough when everything happened."

Extremely so. It still surprised me when he told me he flew down just to confront him before he was planning to leave the country.

A laugh escapes him before he gestures me over. He wraps an arm around my shoulders in a side hug as he murmurs, "I'll always protect you, Dakota."

A soft smile curls my lips as I squeeze him a little tighter. "I know. This is a battle I need to do on my own, though."

"Understandable. I still got your back, though."

Our relationship has only strengthened over the years. After the mess of that summer, his presence was unyielding in my life. His unwavering support and friendship of sorts was something I always wished I had when I was younger. I mean, he's always been protective, but I never knew how much he was there for me. He was there in the shadows, but never quite there when I needed.

It was different now, though. There were frequent calls and visits. The bickering never left, though.

I would never admit it to him, but it's something I treasure dearly.

"I know. I appreciate that."

"Good. And I'm only a short flight away. I know this weekend was a bit of a dud, but if you need me, I'll jump straight onto the next plane."

A burst of laughter escapes me as I shove away from him. "Don't go all soft on me. It's a weird sight."

He scoffs before dropping his smile again, pinning me with his serious gaze. "I'm being serious. I don't care if it's the middle of the night," he pauses, then, before retracting his words. "Okay, no. Maybe I will care. But anytime during the day...past nine a.m., I'll answer."

I snort. "Okay, okay. I get it. But I'll be okay. I can handle this. But if I need you, I'll call."

He smiles and nods. "Good. Now stop talking. We have a movie to watch."

I roll my eyes, but sit back on the couch as he presses play on this new murder mystery movie, and enjoy the familiarity and nostalgia of being here with my brother like we used to as kids.

Luckily, there were no run-in's with Reece over the weekend while Nate was here. I would get another couple of months before that confrontation.

Dad and Nate had a night out together that night, which they hit pretty hard. Dad was trying to keep up with Nate, which only resulted in spending most of the next morning hugging the toilet bowl. I decided to be gracious and cook them a greasy breakfast just like Dad had for me the past week.

We spent his last night with us out as a family on Eat Street, trying and sharing different foods, chatting and laughing like an actual family again. Normal and without anything straining between us. It was nice.

But I still couldn't get Reece's words out of my head. Having Nate around was a welcome distraction, but in the quiet moments when I was alone, especially as I was falling asleep, his words would come back to me.

I was so stupid for letting you go.

It made me wonder if I had my assumptions wrong, if maybe I jumped too much when I came across that photo of him online. I wondered if he suffered as much as I did all these years.

It was a horrible thought, but I kind of hoped he did. It would make me feel better for all those failed dates and hook-ups I went through while I compared every single one to him. And at the end of it all, I still had that gaping hole in the shape of him inside my chest.

14

REECE

Since the morning by the river, I'd been hesitant to set foot in Dakota's house. One, because when I decided I should see Dakota about two hours after the river, I saw Nate entering the house and hesitated. I watched through the window, how happy he and Dakota were to see each other as they embraced each other, and I wasn't brave enough to interrupt that. I felt like an outsider. And two, because I felt...exposed and a little embarrassed. I didn't want anyone to see me like that, but especially not Dakota.

But now, I couldn't avoid the house. Not after I had Jenna pull me out of the hotel, holding the promise I gave her over my head regarding her wedding.

Since the night of the engagement party, everything between us just feels...fragile. It's the only way I can explain it. Something tells me Jenna can feel it as well, which is why I stand here alone as she pulls out of the driveway to head to the bakery.

But with my apology and her running away, then her seeing me mid-panic attack, it's like the scab has been picked and now it's slowly oozing with the things we were scared to face when we were young. I won't run away from it this time, though. I'm not going to make the same mistake twice and watch her slip through my fingers. I have a lot of work to do to make her believe my words are true. It's not going to be like when we were kids, and all I gave her were words and no action to back them up.

I was scared then. I wanted her, but I didn't know how to make it work. There was so much going against us that I didn't want to ruin. But I did that all on my own anyway.

Even now, I'm scared, but it's all for different reasons. Back then, I was scared of losing all that I had and disappointing my father. Now, I'm only scared of losing her again. I can't lose her. I've been in a six-year withdrawal from her and I'll be damned if I drown in the misery of it anymore.

So, I knock on the front door and swallow all those fears.

She appears at the door a moment later, surprise flicking over her face when her ocean-blue eyes meet mine.

A small, hesitant smile curls the corner of my lips. "Hey."

"Hi," she replies in a soft voice.

A beat of silence falls like a blanket over us as we stare at each other before I clear my throat and point a thumb over my shoulder. "Jenna just dropped me off. Apparently, some RSVPs need to be finalised and table settings to be arranged. Don't know how much help I can be, but she insisted."

She opens the door wider, a silent invitation. "Yeah. I'm going through them now. Do you know much about Jenna's family?"

I step through the threshold, looking down at her when I'm beside her. She tilts her head back a little to meet my gaze, and I feel myself fall into the depths of hers. So quickly, so easily. So naturally pulled to her.

"I don't. She didn't talk much about her family to me."

She sighs. "She gave me a few notes on who gets along with whom. You can help me decipher them."

I chuckle. "I'll do my best."

She pulls back, and it's only then that I realise how close we were standing, with the loss of her warmth from her retreat.

She leads me into the dining room, where a large mock layout of the table settings is drawn on an A3 piece of paper, and other cards and paper sprawl across the table. It's a mess, and I can't help but smile.

A laptop sits at the head of the table on the far side, where Dakota goes to sit. I take the seat on her right, my eyes drifting over the papers before landing back on her.

"Where do we start?" I ask, and then I watch the spread of her lips as she smiles at me before ordering me on what to do.

A couple of hours pass, and now, I just sit there waiting for her orders. I tried to help finalise numbers and table settings, but Dakota ended up deciding I was no help. Now she only asks me questions and my opinion or orders me to fetch her something, like scissors, paper, and even a damn drink. I don't mind, though, because when she isn't ordering me around, I get to watch her as she delicately writes names on place cards in the most intricate cursive. She reluctantly had me help her at one stage before immediately banning me after ruining two. I did it on purpose of course, just so I could sit her and have time to relearn the curve of her lips and find the freckles I had memorised while finding new ones.

"I can feel your eyes burning the top of my head," she speaks up after a long stretch of silence.

A sheepish smile stretches over my face. "Sorry," I say, but not an ounce of apology enters my voice.

She looks up after finishing the place card she was working on and raises a brow. "I'm very convinced," she deadpans.

I shrug, and she narrows her eyes when I continue to stare at her. "What's so fascinating? Do I have something on my face?"

I shake my head, smothering the smile that wants to break through. "No."

She huffs and sets her pen delicately to the side, careful not to get any ink on the empty cards.

"Then what?"

I finally look away, grabbing a random card from the pile and flipping it between my fingers. Try as I may to stop it, the corners of my lips turn up slightly.

"Nothing."

A long moment stretches as she continues to pin her glare on me while I sit there, unable to tear my attention away as I rest my head in my hand. She eventually sighs, shaking her head and going back to signing the cards, taking the one I had picked up as she mutters, "Still as annoying as ever."

I smirk. "Always."

She spares me a glance beneath her brows, short blonde strands falling in front of her eyes like a curtain.

God, she's even more beautiful than I remember.

I shake my head, focusing back on the cards in front of me.

She puts me in charge of proofing them to make sure there are no spelling mistakes and spraying them with a smudge-proof spray once the ink has dried before packing them away in a black box. There are about fifty cards altogether, and we've gotten through about twenty of them. It's probably the most boring job, but I would sit here watching Dakota for ten hours if that's how long these cards took, so I didn't mind one single bit.

The sound of pen scratches seeps through the silence that grows between us as her whole focus narrows on the cards she writes on. Although watching her has become my favourite pastime, I can't handle the silence. I want to know more about her, hear her laugh and most importantly, just hear her voice. It was a calming balm to my soul, a feeling I had been chasing for years since I left her. And I want to fix the cracks between us, to slowly peel back that band-aid and soothe the wound beneath.

"Let's play a game," I announce.

She looks up at me again. "We're a little too busy to play a game."

"We can multitask."

She narrows her gaze as she watches me for a moment, then gives in. "What kind of game?"

"Twenty-one questions. A classic. Just to get to know each other."

"But we do know each other," she drawls, acting uninterested, but she sits up a little straighter as she drops the pen to the side, giving me her full attention.

"It's been six years, Dakota. A lot can change over time."

My gaze latches onto hers as the last sentence passes my lips, and I watch a world of emotions flicker behind her eyes. I can only imagine a mirror image in mine as memories of the two of us play like a film reel in my head.

She pulls her gaze away then, and I long to have her attention back on me.

She picks her pen up again, and I think maybe she's going back to ignoring me when she speaks up. "Fine, but only if you continue working on these cards. I need to at least get these done before three this afternoon."

"Why?" I can't help but pry.

"Because I have things to do." She pauses and peers up at me. "I'm counting that as your first question. My turn."

I scoff. "Hey, we hadn't agreed to start yet."

She shrugs and focuses back on the card in her hand. "I agreed to play, so that's close enough."

I narrow my gaze at her, but my lip twitches as I lean forward on the table, resting my forearms on the edge and lacing my fingers together. I don't miss the way her gaze drew toward my arms as I did so before quickly averting, and I can't stop the grin from spreading before I smother it.

"Okay, fine. Go ahead. I'm an open book." She lifts a brow at that and I almost go to add *only for you,* but I press my lips together instead.

She doesn't say anything for a moment as she mulls over a question to ask me.

"Favourite colour?"

I raise a brow. "Really?"

"I'm just going easy on you. Saving the tough ones for last." She smirks.

"Whatever you say," I trail off, pressing my lips together to fight the smile from rising.

I meet her eyes as she waits for my answer. The answer comes so naturally to me, though, one I've never thought much of, but it's in every haunting dream I've had when I close my eyes.

"Blue."

"Blue?" she asks with a quiet curiosity.

"Yeah."

"Huh," she ponders, "I never pictured you as a blue kind of person."

"What kind of person did you think I was?"

She hums, pondering it over as her eyes scan me in a slow sweep, and I feel it burn a path in its wake.

"Burgundy."

I smirk. "That's an awfully specific colour."

She shrugs. "You're dark and mysterious. But not so mysterious that people wonder what you're hiding. You can tell you have passion and a thoughtfulness that everyone craves."

I rest my head on my palm as I lean further toward her, magnetised toward her, and she tracks my movement like a hawk.

"I didn't think a colour told you what kind of person I am."

She shrugs. "That's my theory. Of why we gravitate toward a specific colour. It's like we relate to the emotion of the colour. Every colour evokes an emotion. Like green makes us think of life, growth, renewal or even jealousy. Pink makes us think of femininity, love and compassion. Red, in retrospect, makes us think of power and confidence. And blue," she meets my gaze then, "makes us think—"

I cut her off as I breathe the word, "Peace."

She nods, eyes flicking between mine. "Yeah," she whispers before clearing her throat and looking back down at the card in her hands. "Calm, peace, security. Even wisdom or success, depending on the shade."

I pause as I let her words sink into me, thinking of what I always knew the colour meant to me, but never knew the depth of it.

The exact colour stares right into me now. I feel my heart thud against my chest the longer she stares.

Peace.

It's exactly what I feel when I look at her. It's exactly what I feel when I'm around her. Even after the years of separation. She's always been the place I find peace in, especially when all I had of her was in my dreams.

She clears her throat, breaking the tension building and suffocating the room between us, and I reluctantly sit back in my chair to give her that bit of distance.

"Okay, your turn," she states, picking up her pen and another card.

I think for a moment before I turn to her, and rest my head on my hand again. "Do you have a boyfriend?"

She scoffs and looks up with a raised brow. "Seriously?"

I shrug. "It's a simple question." And one I've desperately wanted to know over the years, if she's ever moved on.

She looks back down and for a moment she doesn't answer, but I see her chew on the side of her lip. My heart pounds as I wait, hoping to god that her hesitation isn't what I think it is.

But then she finally answers with a whispered, "No."

And I blow out a heavy breath.

"Have you dated anyone in the last six years?" I can't help but add.

She tsks. "Uh-uh, my turn to ask the question now."

The side of my lip turns up before I wave my hand toward her. "Ask away."

She leans back in her chair as she pins me with her stare. It's piercing, and I brace as much as I can for her question, knowing it's going to bulldoze me.

"What's your biggest regret?"

My heart thuds in reaction, but I hide it under the smirk I send her. "Thought you were going easy on me first?"

She tilts her head. "I was, but then I thought, why waste time?"

I don't break eye contact with her as a sharp ache radiates through my chest, the question rolls around in my head. It's such a simple question, but loaded with so much unsaid.

I know what she's searching for. The answer is the only one that fills my head. But I hesitate to answer because I'm not sure if she's ready to hear it. Not sure if she'll run away again.

Fuck it, I'm just going to say it.

"Leaving you. That's my biggest regret." I pause as I push those words past my lips, hearing her sharp inhale and wonder if I should continue. Because I want to say so much more than that. To make her understand.

My tongue makes the decision first, though, as words begin to tumble from my mouth before my brain can comprehend.

"I think about it almost every day. How I treated you and left you like you weren't the most important person in my life. I was an idiot for doing that and for caring what anyone thought. You were there when I needed someone, and I took that for granted. I was just scared and felt like I had no control over my life. It's no excuse and I wish I had dealt with it better so I didn't lose anyone in the process of figuring it out."

Her eyes soften with every word that spills from my lips, and I don't know what to do with that. I don't know what it means or what she's thinking for her to look at me like that. I nervously thrum my fingers against my thigh while my leg bounces, but I don't look away from her. I take in every change in her expression, wondering what's going on in her mind.

And I guess I'll never know because she clears her throat and presses her lips together in a flat smile before saying, "Your turn now."

My eyes flick between hers, hoping my plea comes through in that one look, but she doesn't pay in any mind as she looks down again.

I sigh and concede to playing this little game I've roped myself into.

"Okay then. Have you dated anyone in the last six years?"

"You already asked that question."

"Yes, but you never answered. So." I wave a hand toward her in a gesture for her to fill in the answer.

I don't know whether I wanted to torture myself by asking that question, both wanting and not wanting to know the answer.

She crosses her arms as she thinks on her answer, and my heart thuds loudly in my chest in anticipation of the answer.

"Yes," she starts, and my heart breaks a little, "but not seriously. It just never worked out that way."

Her eyes meet mine as the last sentence passes her lips, and the sentiment behind them hits me square in the chest as the fog clouds the space between us. It's years worth of missing and mourning things we never got the chance to have. It's memories of the two kids who never knew how to navigate the situation they were put in for the chance to feel something, but ended up obliterating it. It's wishing things could have been different if we–*I*–had just done things differently.

But the fog dissipates with the sound of the front door opening and shattering the quiet we have been absorbed in.

Jenna enters the kitchen and spots us at the dining table with all the cards spread on top.

She smiles, completely oblivious to what she walked in on and the lingering tension suffocating the room.

"I'm glad to see you guys in a room together and behaving well. Oh, you started on the name cards? They look fantastic." She picks one up and flips it over between her fingers. "You have such beautiful writing, Dakota. I love them. Thank you."

She walks over, wrapping her free arm around Dakota and squeezing her for a quick second before her gaze flicks to me.

"I hope you haven't ruined any." She lifts a brow.

I place a hand over my chest and open my mouth to defend myself, but Dakota pipes in.

"I stopped him at two."

Her eyes sparkle with mischief, and I can't even defend myself as I transfix over that look.

I don't even pay attention to what Jenna says next and don't care.

Even as Dakota's gaze leaves mine and she laughs at whatever Jenna says, I can't move my gaze from her.

I'm just as obsessed with her as I was when I was seventeen, and no time has changed that.

15

DAKOTA

All these years I've spent building a steel cage around my heart, going around in circles with the same repetitive dates that end in the same result, leaving me unsatisfied and empty before all the doubts set in. That I'll never find something as real and true as what I had with him.

And now here he is, only taking a couple of weeks to start chipping away at that armour like it's his soul purpose in life. It's frustrating as hell.

But is it? Because even I don't believe that's true.

He'd always been able to sink so deep into my heart without an ounce of effort. Like he belonged there. Like it was his home. And maybe it was.

I may have been trying to fill the space he left with strangers I'd picked up from bars or dating apps, but I think deep down I always knew it was only ever going to be him who could fill that space.

Truth be told, I really did miss our friendship. Everything we built was based on the friendship we sought in each other. He was my friend first before the mess that became us.

And now, here I am holding my thawing heart, wondering if

I'm stupid for considering opening myself up to the possibility of him in my life again. That twenty-one-question game gave me a glimpse of the truth he spoke. Of how much he changed and the sincerity in every word he spoke. Of how open he's been, right off the bat.

But it's the memory of how he scorched the trust I had in him that has me hesitating.

His answer to the question that has always burned in the back of my mind whirls in its place, the one of his regrets. It's the answer I hoped he'd give, but it still shocked me to hear it.

A week has passed, and still, we've carried on with the game, picking it back up where we left off. But the questions have been surface level, and I know that's my fault because I'm afraid to dive into what we need to and he's been following at my pace. I can see it in his eyes, pleading with me to dig deeper. But I just hesitate.

I know there are a lot of things we need to talk about. A lot of hurdles that need to be overcome to let the past fade behind us. But I'm still afraid to jump into that with him again. I'm afraid to hear what he has to say.

I don't want any more apologies. I don't want to keep reliving the past. It's haunted me in every corner of my life for the last six years and, as I've said to Callie, I'm ready to move on.

I wonder what she'll say now that my original fear has become a reality with Reece being here. I wonder what she'll say when she hears I'm actually considering giving him a chance. God, how everything has changed in the short span of almost one month.

Even as I set up my laptop in front of me in bed and nervously chew my nails as I wait for eleven o'clock for our scheduled appointment, I don't know how exactly to explain everything.

I expected this first session to be for me telling her about my healing and what I'd done to get over everything, but instead, my life had done a complete U-turn.

Maybe I could avoid telling her anything. Maybe I could avoid telling her he was here, just like I feared. That I hadn't done a single thing I aimed to do to move on entirely.

It's like as soon as he entered my life again, my entire orbit paused in his presence.

It's frustrating how much of an impact he has on me still.

Then again, it isn't.

An incoming call comes, and I take a breath before answering the Zoom.

Once it connects, Callie's face pops up in the frame, a soft smile making its way on her face as she sees me, and I muster a smile of my own as I wring my fingers together off camera.

I know she can immediately tell my tense posture, but she eases into the session just as she usually does.

"Hi, Dakota. How have you been?"

I tilt my head from side to side as I tuck my hands under my legs to keep them from fidgeting.

"Yeah, I've been okay. You?"

An amused smile twists at her lips. "I've been good. How has being home been this past month?"

I nod and bite down on my lip before I piece together an answer that won't sound like I'm avoiding.

"It's been okay so far. It's been good to be close to Dad again. Wedding prep is well underway, so it's been a good distraction."

She tilts her head. "Distraction from what?"

I press my lips into a thin line, hating that she can see straight through my words.

"From everything I don't want to focus on," I vaguely say.

"And what is that?" She pushes for me to elaborate more, and I sigh.

"I can never hide anything from you," I mumble, looking down at my hands as I pull them back to my lap.

"Why do you want to hide?"

I groan. "Because it's confusing and I don't know how to feel about it. I don't even know if I'm ready to confront any of it."

She doesn't say anything for a moment; she just waits for me, letting me take the floor as I mull over my words.

I must take too long because she speaks up. "What makes you think you're not ready to know how you feel?"

I choke on a laugh as I hold back the tears already trying to pool in my eyes.

"Because then I can't pretend I'm stronger than I am."

She pinches her brows together. "You are strong, Dakota. Much stronger than you think. You need to give yourself some credit. Look at how brave you were moving states, fresh out of high school, where you knew no one. Look at your rebuilt relationship with your mother. Look at the life you've built all by yourself with your photography career, your friends."

I can't keep the tears from flowing over as she lists all those things, making me realise all I have accomplished. I guess I've never really looked at it individually. I just felt like I was barely surviving. And yeah, things are looking better each day, but it still feels like I'm struggling to pull through. Maybe I've built the life I've been dreaming of by myself, but still, I struggled so much to pick up the pieces to get here that it clouds my mind to see the strength she talks about.

So, with her words of wisdom, I summon that little bit of strength she believes I have with a slow and steady inhale before the words tumble from my lips. "Jenna, the woman my dad is marrying, happens to be the same woman who looked after Reece when he was younger and practically raised him. And in a cruel twist of fate, he also agreed to help Jenna in the months leading up to the wedding, so he's here. He's been here for the past month, and as much as I was dreading walking down memory lane, I don't think I was a hundred percent ready to run into him. Like yeah, I was scared of running into him on the off chance he was visiting his friends, but there was that big possibility that I wouldn't."

She takes in the information, sitting back in her chair, and I can see the wheels turning in her head. I can practically see her analysing my words, my facial expressions, and everything I'm hiding. I almost want to hold my breath against the anticipation of her reply.

She leans forward in her chair again, leaning her chin on her hand.

"Have you talked to him?"

I blink, not expecting such a simple question. I was waiting for her psychological analysis on all the emotions I'm afraid I'm not exactly hiding very well here.

"Well, yeah. It's kind of hard not to when we're forced together like this."

"What I meant was, have you talked to him? Have you had an open discussion about the two of you and the things you've been holding on to?"

I swallow. I know that's what she meant, I just don't want to answer.

I sigh. "No. Not really."

"What does 'not really' mean?"

"He's...tried. But I completely avoid the conversation when he does and may have yelled at him once for it." I wince.

"I think it would be good to have that discussion with him and lay it all out in the open. It will help give you that closure you've been seeking over the situation in a different way. This way, you'll get his side of the story. To see where he was coming from."

I pick at my nails as I rest them in my lap, not looking up as I speak. "I am beginning to see that. His side, that is. The little bits that he's opened up to me about before I steer the conversation away, I do realise that maybe I was a bit quick to blame him and push my anger toward him."

"I think what you've been searching for is forgiveness. Everything happens for a reason, and maybe that is why he is here. Exactly for your purpose of closure. To do that, you need to lay the situation out there and forgive him. It doesn't mean you need to forget, but to understand the situation and let it be. That's what real closure is, in my opinion. To understand and let it be."

Her words are like a punch to the gut as they land right in the sensitive corner of my heart. My chest hollows as tears prick and slide down my cheeks.

I know she's right. Everything does happen for a reason, and I know it's exactly what I need to do.

But I'm scared.

I've been holding onto the memory of him for so long that it's been ingrained in a part of me, and it feels as if I were to seek the closure I was originally so desperate for, I'll lose that. If I let go of that string for good, I'll lose him and be left cold and alone.

It's like when you're a kid and you're given a balloon and it becomes your most prized possession. You hold on tight because no matter what, you want to keep it forever, and the memory of that time. But then the wind picks up, and suddenly the string slips from your fingers. You jump to try and catch it again, but it floats away too fast to grasp it. It's gone forever.

That's what losing him will feel like. I just know it.

No matter how many times I've said I was over him, I know I never truly was. I was still holding on tight to the string of our memories. I thought telling myself that I was over him, that over time, I would start to believe it. But that's not how it worked.

Maybe Callie was right. Maybe this was what I needed to move on. I needed to let go of my anger toward him and let the past be the past.

But feeling my chest cave in at the thought, is that normal?

16

REECE

I have to admit, this is a beautiful place to get married. Even as rain dribbles down the gazebo I wait under, the scene around me has a romantic air. With the vast lavender fields spanning far into the backdrop of mountainous ranges, and the lake that sits behind me, raindrops rippling the calm water, I see why Jenna picked it. It's quiet and calm, and the crisp, damp air adds to the feeling.

She's always loved places hidden away from the chaotic rush of the city. She would always take me away to places like this when everything got too loud at home. When my dad would yell and scream at me for all the wrongs I did or would want me out of his sight, she would take me out, buy me an ice cream, and we would just sit and listen to the wildlife around us. We wouldn't say a single word, and I would close my eyes, my ears pricking at every whistle of birds in the trees, the wind rustling the leaves, and the buzz of insects hiding in the bushes. It was like she knew exactly what I needed. Exactly what quietened the noise that threatened to make my head burst.

I close my eyes as I lean against one of the pillars, hearing it all now, the rain speckling the ground drowning out their sounds. It's almost peaceful, though it feels like something is missing.

Slowly opening my eyes, I spot someone with an umbrella making their way toward me, and it's like the missing piece clicking into place, the one thing that was missing.

Dakota looks up when she nears, smiling a little when her eyes meet mine, and all the sounds drown away. The noise around us and inside my head disappears. All I see is her.

I didn't for one second expect her message yesterday, inviting me here to come with her so she can scout photograph spots for the wedding. She mentioned having never been here, and as the appointed photographer for the wedding, she wanted to be prepared, which led to her asking me to join since Jenna told her she'd taken me here a few times.

The way my heart thumped so wildly in my chest, seeing her message. I didn't know who it was when the number popped up, but then I saw the beginning of her message, the 'hi, it's Dakota' had the widest smile stretching across my face, until I realised I hadn't had her number. Didn't have it because she had blocked me on my old phone, causing me to smash it against the floor when I attempted to call her. Didn't have it because there was no way I could reach her when I finally got a new phone and had to start all over again. Because I was on a different continent and a different phone service. Even if I did, I wouldn't have the guts to call her again. I'd already been shot down once by her answering machine.

I didn't even think of getting her number again. Doubt she would have given it if I had asked anyway. But god am I glad she has mine now, however she got it. Most likely Jenna. I'll have to hug her next time I see her.

Once she's under the safety of the gazebo, she closes the umbrella before climbing the small step to stand in front of me, still a few inches away. The rain falls heavier around us, and she steps a little closer so I can hear her over the downpour.

"Well, this is kind of pointless now."

Her hand comes to rest on the camera she hung around her neck, eyes assessing the dark sky.

I shrug. "It's not meant to last very long."

"Let's hope not."

She doesn't say anything more as she watches the rain, and I just watch her. I can't help it.

Her eyes flick around the area, and as if she can't stop herself, she clicks a button on her camera, powering it on before holding it up to her eyes. She clicks a few buttons, and then the camera snaps as she takes a couple of photos.

It reminds me of the trip to Airlie Beach when we went hiking and I watched her exactly as I am now, taking photos of everything around her. She's lost in the life around her. It's like she sees something everyone else doesn't, as her eyes light up, taking notice of every little thing and finding something beautiful in it. Or maybe it's just me. Maybe I'm the one who doesn't see it.

But she eventually showed me.

Every moment I spent with her, she showed me the beautiful moments in life.

I've been without it for so long now that I've forgotten what it feels like.

The rain slowly begins to ease, and she turns to look at me, finding me already looking at her, and I don't shy away. She can know that I was watching her, admiring her. Because I would never stop.

With the rain becoming a slow sprinkle, I jerk my head out toward the grounds.

"Want to go exploring?"

She folds her arms across her chest. "It's still sprinkling. I'll get wet."

I lift a brow. "So?"

She gives me an incredulous look. "So... We can't go out there."

"You have an umbrella."

"But you don't have one," she says exasperatedly, looking pointedly at my empty hands.

My lips twitch, my chest warming a little at her concern. "I don't need one. Plus, I can just take shelter under yours."

"Not quite. I need you as a prop."

My smile drops as I frown. "A prop?"

Amusement shines in her eyes. I would be lying if I said I didn't miss that sight. Miss the back and forth between us. "Yes, so I can get a clear visual of the best photo vantages."

I smirk as the immediate instinct to tease her comes back to me. "You're gonna take photos of me?"

She lifts her chin, narrowing her gaze on me and making my smile deepen. It's then that I realise how close we were. In the time since she arrived, I had pushed myself off the pillar and taken a step closer to her. I was just thankful she hadn't noticed yet and stepped away. Or maybe she didn't mind. That was the hopeful part of me that she was warming to me.

"Yes. You have a problem with that?"

I chuckle. "Oh, definitely not. I love having your eyes on me."

She rolls her eyes. "God, you're so full of yourself."

I grin now, wide and full, showing my teeth, loving to rile her up. "You love it though."

She shoves me. "Just get out there."

"Oh, so now you want to do this?"

She shakes her head, but I see her fighting a little smile that wants to pull at her lips. "You're so annoying."

Laughing again, I take a step back. "And I've missed annoying you."

The smile drops from her eyes, and I realise I've ruined the illusion around us. Me teasing her like I used to, her acting like she's sick of me, and then I go and remind her that I screwed that all up.

She pastes on a tight smile, mask falling into place. "Let's go. I don't want to be out here too long, and I want to get as many locations as possible in mind for Jenna and see inside the chapel."

So, I follow her, the light sprinkles catching my hair and trailing down my skin. But I didn't care about the rain; I only cared about getting Dakota to smile again because it filled me with more oxygen than the air I breathed.

She orders me around and tells me where to stand. She's stiff in her movements, though, guarded in the way she talks and looks at me. And the more photos she attempts, the more frustrated she gets as she looks down at the screen of her camera, flicking through the photos and muttering something about there not being any sun and it not helping.

I can't help myself, I want to see that smile back on her face.

"Give me your phone," I order.

She looks up from her camera, frowning as she regards me. "Why?"

"Just trust me."

I walk over to her, meeting her steady gaze as she stands still, not moving an inch.

Stopping in front of her, I wait, holding her stare for as long as she will. I take in the splattering of freckles I used to trace lazily when she was in my arms, watching me in the same way I was. The swirling blues and yellows in her irises like the ocean crashing into the sand. The curve of her cupid's bow and how goddamn kissable her full lips were.

I wait until she finally moves, reaching around to grab her phone from her back pocket and holding it out to me. My smile grows as I take it from her, a little piece of me acknowledging that her handing it to me was like a silent agreement that she did trust me. To some extent.

I click a few buttons before 'Say It Right' by Nelly Furtado begins to filter through her phone's speaker.

Her frown deepens as she looks down at her phone in my hand. I hand it back to her, and she slowly grasps it in her free hand as I back away.

I roll my shoulders in a steady rhythm with the beat of the song, knowing I'm probably going to look like an idiot here, but I just wanted her to smile.

"What are you doing?" she blurts, watching me in confusion.

I spread my arms wide, grin still in place. "Isn't this what people do at a photoshoot?"

She rolls her eyes. "This isn't a photoshoot."

I furrow my brows, feigning confusion. "No? I could have sworn, what with you and your camera and me as your model."

I don't miss the side of her lip quirking, and I know I've almost got her.

So I sink in further and start to circle my hips and raise my arms above me.

And she snorts before slapping a hand over her mouth.

"Come on, Dakota. Indulge me. You know you'll want photo evidence of this," I croon, spinning in a slow circle as the rain soaks my skin.

"You're an idiot."

I don't remember the last time I smiled this wide. It's been so long. "I know."

Always an idiot for her.

She shakes her head, gnawing at her bottom lip to hide the rising smile that pulls at the sides. Then, she raises her camera, and my lips part as my grin splits my face. The shutter goes off and I don't think there would be a person in the entire world I would do this for than her. That I would be out here in the drizzling rain, my clothes slowly becoming drenched, dancing just to make her smile and loosen up around me.

Only around her am I like this, able to smile, laugh, and feel genuinely happy without restraint. It feels nice not to force a smile or laugh. It feels nice to have this bubbly feeling in my stomach while my heart thuds along with it, something I learnt to recognise as happiness. A feeling I only came to know from being around her.

Before, I had always pretended to be happy. It was a mask that slipped into place when I was around people. It was something I couldn't help but do. I wanted to make the people around me just as happy as I wished to be, like that would fill some sort of metaphorical self-gratifying cup within me. But all it did was make me more miserable. Because what I really wanted was for people to see how much I was suffering inside. For someone to see right through the façade I tried to keep up.

And then, Dakota happened.

She walked up that pier, and when our eyes finally met, it was like she looked through me, not just at me. She was the first person to see me and see what really laid beneath me.

I may have had friends and Liam, who was my best friend since pre-school, but none of them saw me like she did. Liam may have known about my home life but never really noticed how it affected me.

Only her. And it felt so good to have someone like that.

Maybe it was the Summers' effect, too, with Nate walking in and becoming the brother I'd always wanted and needed. All the things I always thought Liam was to me.

But I was too much like my father, self-destructing and damaged.

I didn't want to be that person anymore. I didn't want to be my father, bitter and unhappy because of the choices I made, blaming everyone but myself.

So, I danced, pulling out the most awful moves, and posed for her, making her smile, her laugh like my heart's favourite song, while she got the photos she needed to make her dad's day special and memorable.

I couldn't take my eyes off her. She was so fucking beautiful in this light, her hair sticking to the side of her face as the rain clung to her and her smile so broad, it was blinding. It was like she should be in front of the camera, the way she burned so brightly, but I knew it was behind the camera that she became radiant. It was where she soared, capturing the world in her eyes. And in her eyes, the world looked so damn beautiful. It only made me hopeful that I could see it like that one day. Maybe around her, I would relearn the way she began to do all those years ago.

"Okay, I think I've got enough. You can stop embarrassing yourself now," she finally cuts in. Her words shake with the laughter she tries to suppress.

"Who said I was embarrassing myself? I'm having fun."

"With those moves? You should be embarrassed."

I hold my hand over my heart. "You wound me, K-Dakota." I catch myself before I blurt out the nickname I had been fond of calling her, hoping she doesn't notice.

And she didn't. That, or she ignored it as her smile stayed in place. "I'm sure you'll get over it."

I picked up my rain jacket that I had tossed off at some stage while she took photos and hooked it over my shoulder. She stood under the gazebo again, flicking through the photos with a ghost of a smile still playing on her lips.

I wasn't ready for this thing between us to end just yet. I wanted to continue feeling like this. Exactly what we felt when we were younger.

So, I take a chance that she feels the same, nibbling on my bottom lip as I hesitate for a second. Just in case, I fold my arms behind my back and cross my fingers.

"Do you want to go somewhere? Grab something to eat, go for a walk, and adventure a little? The night is still young."

133

She looked up at me then, eyes flicking between mine, a hint of hesitation of her own in them.

"I don't know if that's a good idea." She mumbles.

I step a little closer, prepared to beg if I have to. "No pressure at all. Totally casual and nothing serious. Just a couple of people reminiscing on how foolish one of them was when they were younger. An opportunity for him to apologise. He'd also pay for everything, as well. Whatever you're in the mood to eat. He'd pay the price of anything to be able to gain your forgiveness and move forward."

Her lips tug at the side. "Well, if he's willing to pay for anything, then who am I to deny? But just a little warning, my tastes have gotten more expensive with time."

A slow grin spreads across my face. I try not to seem so happy with her response, but I can't help it.

"Anything you want is yours. As you deserve."

17

DAKOTA

I'm meant to hate him.

I'm meant to keep hating him for all the hurt he put me through when we were younger. To keep hating him so I can find someone who isn't him. Or like him.

But the more I spend time with him, the less that's even possible.

God, he makes it impossible to hate him. And I'm impossibly weak to his charm. No time has changed that, apparently.

I've been feeling all that bottled anger and frustration I've held on to for six years start to slip thread by thread the more I'm around him and his intoxicating presence. Now, all I want is to put it all behind me. As Callie said, coming to understand his side may be the thing I need.

Being in his company this afternoon gave me a flashback to how things were in the beginning with us: fun and carefree. I felt eighteen again, waiting for someone to see and love me, hopelessly praying for someone to break my beliefs.

But I know it can never be real. And this little snippet in time will only live for a short moment between us. It's all we

135

were destined for. For short spaces in time to feel and lose ourselves in the raw feelings we brought to each other.

So, by the time we pull into a small restaurant with the most delicious and expensive food, the feeling I felt just moments ago at the wedding venue in the rain starts to fade away, replaced by the reality of him and me. All that's swirling in my head is how to start the conversation between us because I have absolutely no clue. I didn't think about that when I messaged him to come with me to the lavender fields.

I'm anxious, my heart beating erratically in my chest the further we weave through the restaurant. Anxious to talk to him, anxious to hear the answers to all the questions that swam in my head, anxious from being around him.

Our clothes have mostly dried in the fifteen-minute drive here, but still cling to us like a second skin. I try not to notice that with him and how his T-shirt stuck to his chest and stomach. I try so hard not to notice how much bigger he is and the muscles that have most definitely grown through the years.

I'm sure I look like a mess compared to him, with my still-damp hair sticking to the sides of my face haphazardly. I didn't care to fix any of it on the drive here. Haven't had time to think about my appearance. That is, until stepping inside the restaurant and realising my disarray. I start to fidget with my appearance, brushing my fingers through my hair and fixing my clothes as a waitress leads us toward the back to a table for two. We slide into the chairs opposite each other as she hands us both menus. We thank her before she promises to be back to take orders and leaves.

I prop the menu up in front of me as I search through the options, creating a kind of barrier between him and me so I can gather some semblance of thoughts.

Since leaving the wedding venue, the silence has stretched thin between us. I can feel the multiple questions we're holding back thicken the air we breathe, but we're both hesitating for some reason.

I know I need to air everything that has been sitting on my chest like Callie said, but something in me is still clawing for the comfort of how things have been between us. All the careful, simple questions we ask, never digging deep and keeping a safe distance between us.

I don't know why he's hesitating, though.

Since bursting back into my life, he has been a persistent force of nature, pushing to explain and talk about us when I was too scared to. His silence is throwing me off, though.

I feel his eyes sear through the top of my head, piercing me from across the table, and I bite my bottom lip as I try to ignore that feeling.

"What are you thinking?" His question finally breaks the still silence, and my gaze pulls to meet his as I lower the menu. He watches me with curiosity, and I'm unable to stop the way my cheeks heat under his attention. It's the way it's so heavy and intense, piercing through me, as if he wanted to climb inside my head and see the thoughts swirling in my head.

I look back at the menu, pulling myself out of his hypnotising gaze. "I'm not sure. I might get pasta, or even the lamb sounds good."

When I glance back up at him, he tilts his head as his eyes pierce straight through me, narrowing just slightly. "That's not what I meant, and you know it."

I swallow, hating that he sees straight through me, even now.

I sigh in relief as I spot the waitress over his shoulder on her way over. She smiles and takes down our orders on a notepad. Hopefully, this interruption takes his unyielding gaze away from trying to bury under the many walls I built because of him and turn to much lighter topics.

I need to slowly build to that stage, to gain the courage first, because if I don't, I know I'll say the wrong thing or mess up somehow. Or, just run away like I had countless times already.

Unluckily for me, though, the interruption doesn't dissuade Reece from resuming the conversation. He folds his hands under his chin, pinning me with those dark green eyes of his.

"I know you have something swirling in that mind of yours, Dakota. Don't hold back on my account. I can take whatever you have to deliver."

I can't help but bite out, "I'm not holding back because of you. I just don't want to lose my head in this restaurant."

A slow smirk lifts one corner of his lips as he leans back in his chair and lifts a brow. "Lose your head? You hate me that much?"

I huff. "I never said that. I just have a lot of things I'm mad at you about."

His smile grew. "So, you don't hate me?"

I shake my head. God, how is he still this infuriating? But still, even as I think that, I feel a slight tug at the corner of my lips before I smother it. "Seriously?"

He shrugs, his eyes bright as he watches me. "I don't mind you biting my head off here. As long as we talk, I don't care what happens."

I sigh and massage my temples. "You're relentless. I think we should eat and then talk after."

He leans in, resting his head on his hand, his smile still in place. "You still want to be around me after dinner?"

I wipe my hand across my lips as my smile becomes uncontrollable. I don't know how he can make me smile so easily in a time I'm trying to be serious. "Can you stop being annoying for like two seconds?"

He grins. "Sorry. It's default. Especially around you."

I shake my head again. "We'll talk after dinner."

"Okay, that's fair." He concurs with a slight tilt of his chin.

I watch as he leans back, relaxing in his seat, before raising a hand to his right shoulder, pressing a thumb there, and massaging it. I narrow my gaze at the action, noticing him doing that a lot.

I nod at his shoulder. "Is something wrong with your shoulder?"

He freezes and drops his hand before shrugging. "Just an ache. It's nothing though. I've had it for a while. Just years of repetitive movement with pitching."

My brows pinch, worry flooding through me. I'm not sure if I believe that it's just nothing going off the pained expression he just wore, but I nod and let it go for now.

The rest of dinner is silent except for the scraping of utensils and murmurs of others dining around us. I can feel his gaze on me again as he watches me eat, and I glance up once to meet his stare at the same time I take a bite of the pasta. He smiles and then looks back down at his meal. I frown and shake my head before subtly wiping the corner of my lips, wondering if maybe I had something on my face, causing him to stare this much.

We finish our meals soon before Reece clears his throat.

"Let me take you somewhere."

When I look up at him, his eyes shine with a softness and a hint of melancholy that makes my chest thud in warning, like a defense mechanism to steer me away from the temptation of that look, the exact one that pulled me in when we were younger.

Maybe I should be listening to my heart more, because it looks like that exact one that brought me here, sitting across an almost lover, the ghosts of our past spinning around us in a heart-aching memory.

But I can't bring myself to walk away. Not when I know that's where I lose. I'll lose my fight with finding the closure I've been swimming toward.

Which is why I take his hand despite everything in me

screaming to walk away and do this another time. When his charm and wit haven't worn down my heart.

"Let's go."

It feels like we've done a full one-eighty coming back here to where it all started, walking down the river after so many years separating us and the shift in dynamics from the last time we found ourselves here.

There's a whole mix of emotions unravelling and twisting in my stomach, with nerves and uncertainty taking centre stage.

Reece hadn't spoken at all in the short walk here. I hadn't either. I guess the whole pending conversation looming over our heads has us absorbed in the calm before the storm. Before all the bottles cracked and we spilled everything unsaid. The years of pushing it all aside, thinking we could overcome it on our own.

This would have happened eventually. I should have known that since the moment I saw him standing in the doorway a month ago. But I wanted to believe we could sweep it under the rug and ignore it. I thought it would be easier since it would only be three months before I was back in Melbourne, and it would be like this never happened.

Reece had been pushing for this since the first day he walked back into my life, and I hate that he was right. Hate that I can see he's not the same eighteen-year-old avoiding anything real. Hate that I can't say the same for myself.

It made me grieve what we had lost all that little bit more because this is all I asked for then. To talk and be open. But I also feel proud of him for having grown from his self-destruct-ing, closed-off ways.

As we make our way down our pier, all that invades my senses is the smell that I had always referred to as warmth and freedom. It wraps around us like it always had, surrounding us in the comforting bubble where it was just him and me.

Sitting on the edge, Reece follows suit, allowing a few inches of space between us.

It's almost amusing at how metaphorical it is to us. The space between us is what allowed this wedge to split us. The space he always held me at, so close yet so far away at the same time.

He leans forward slightly over the water and stares at the reflection rippling off the water, his hand resting between, almost tempting me to do the same and let our pinkies just barely brush together. Maybe it was just my need for some kind of connection, seeking comfort to ease the whirling thoughts and emotions. Or maybe it was just this place and his presence together.

I keep my hands folded in my lap as I try to find the words to start this conversation.

But he beats me to it as he speaks in a low voice. "I know I have a lot of things to make up for with everything that happened six years ago, but I want you to know that I will never regret anything more than how I treated and left you." He turns his head to look at me then. "I can only hope for a chance to show you that."

My lips part as a long, shaky sigh escapes me, my gaze locked on the swirling depths of his, reading all the open emotions he's laying right in front of me, a vast contrast from the eighteen-year-old kid I met here. The vulnerability of that sends a shiver down my spine before I look away, trying to gather my muddled thoughts together. It's harder to open up about this with him than it was with my therapist, admitting to him how much he hurt me. But I focus on the water beneath my feet, swallowing down the lump in my throat and forcing words to pass my lips.

"I moved states because of you. It was a photography course

that gave me that olive branch but ultimately, it was you who made me grasp it and bolt so abruptly and impulsively. I couldn't handle driving these streets, walking this river, being in my own home, because it all reminded me of you."

From the corner of my eye, I see him flinch a little as I tell him this and I almost stop because, despite everything, I still hate seeing him hurt. But I need to get this out, the words flowing now that I've cracked it open.

"I started going to therapy because I couldn't cope with everything in the months after. I closed myself off and I hardly ever left my room. It was embarrassing how one boy could make me feel like that. But even when I started therapy, I couldn't talk about you. Because I couldn't let you go. I talked about my family and my fear of love, even when I hopelessly romanticised everything. I talked about how I could never trust myself to fall for anyone because I'd already been burned once. But never you. Not a single word until last month when it all spilled out in a single session and I realised after that I never really healed from you."

I trail off for a moment, staring off through the water as I lose myself in the pain of my younger self. Reece is quiet as he listens, letting me take charge of this conversation and I was thankful for that.

"I've resented you for a long time, but now, I'm just exhausted from holding onto all that. But I can't just let go of that anger. I need a reason to. I need explanations of why." I meet his eyes again over my shoulder, feeling parts of myself finally crack under the weight I've been carrying, asking the questions I've mentally screamed for him to answer. "Why me? Why did you leave like you did? Why couldn't we work? Why did you give me so much hope just to break me?"

His brow creases together as a flash of pain crosses his eyes, deepening as he listens to me list all these questions and I could only imagine mine reflected the same.

A puff of air escapes his lips as he drops his head, keeping it lowered for a couple moments before lifting, looking at me again but this time with a sheen in his eyes.

As he begins to talk, not once does he tear his gaze away from me. Not even when tears start to trace down his face.

"I hate how much I hurt you. I knew it then when I drove away from you. But hearing it come from your mouth...I feel like such a fucking idiot. There's nothing I want more than to turn back time and right every single one of my wrongs involving you. It will always haunt me, and I will gladly take that on because I fucking deserve that pain. But not you. God, the last thing I wanted was to hurt you. I wanted to believe I could be someone who made you as happy as you made me." His Adam's apple bobbed before adding, "I still find it hard to communicate all the fucked up things in my head, but I want to explain. I want to give you those answers, even if it takes all night. Just please don't leave."

That lump in my throat from earlier grows with his last words as I hold back the tears that blur my vision. The tiny niggling feeling of fear hits low in my heart and even though I've finally told my side and faced it, there's still a part of me that's still afraid to hear his answers. Like I can still hide behind the protective wall I'd built for the last six years.

But I don't. Instead, I let myself get absorbed into the vulnerable bubble that always found us here and moved my hand off my lap, resting it in the space next to us, my pinky just barely grazing his as if offering him a sign of acceptance.

I watch as he exhales, closing his eyes at the contact before he glances down at our hands before bringing them back to me. A reflection of our history bouncing between our connected gazes.

"I've told you some things about my past, but I never told you everything. I guess that was obvious, but I want to be open with you about everything because that's probably the only way

I know how to explain everything. With my choices and my reluctance to open up. Anyway, umm," he sniffles and wipes his free hand across both cheeks, wiping away the dried tears staining them, "I guess, growing up, I never really had a good definition of what family meant. You know my mother died in childbirth and my father was never present in my life. So I never had a good representation of what family was. Truthfully, it never felt like I had a family. I had no one. My dad was my only true family, but even then, not really. I don't remember a time he was even around longer than five minutes when baseball wasn't involved." He shakes his head before continuing.

"I had many babysitters over the years, from the moment I was born to when I was six or seven. None of them stuck around for more than a month, from what I'd been told. I don't remember any of them and I don't know why none of them stayed, but Dad always blamed it on me. But then Jenna came in and everything changed.

"Even at seven, I was waiting for her to leave. I knew the routine. I was counting the days that she would inevitably leave from the moment I met her. I was a very aloof kid at that age. I was just used to having no one but myself and everyone around me leaving. But once the month came and went and she was still there, I took it into my own hands to drive her away. I started acting out and trying to make myself too hard for her to handle so she would be forced to leave. I thought it was inevitable anyway, so the sooner the better. No matter what I did though, she stayed. She was patient and kind and didn't at all deserve the wreck I made. She was too nice and I thought I didn't deserve that because no one had shown me the kindness she had shown me."

I watch as a tear trails down his cheek and my heart breaks for him, seeing the pain deepen the groove between his brows. I want to reach across and hold his hand, but I refrain, tightening my grip on the edge of the wooden plank of the pier.

He continues, ignoring the trail of tears down his cheek as if he doesn't notice. "Then one evening, when I locked myself in my room, she had found a way in and saw me curled in my bed, sobbing as I held a photo I had found of my mother. My dad had thrown everything of hers out, including every picture of her. I'd never seen her before so I never knew what she looked like but I just knew when I found this picture. Just something in me knew it was her. It was the first time I had truly cried over her. Jenna came over and sat next to my bed. I tried to crawl away and pretended like I wasn't crying. But she stopped me. And I still remember what she told me. It still feels so vivid to me. 'You are not alone. I'm here. And I will always be here'. She stayed by my side for a long time, well into the late hours of the night, while I sobbed beside her."

He chuckles, but there's something broken and empty about it that pulls at every single heart string. "I guess from that point, I changed. Or she changed me. She taught me how to have fun and smile and laugh. My dad thought she was softening me. He tried to fire her, but I heard them arguing one evening and I don't know what was said but she just never left."

He swallows and clears his throat. "When I went to school, it took a while for me to make friends. I'd always been a loner, but Jenna pushed me and brought me to playgrounds for me to socialise, like it would help. That's how I met Liam. I began to realise that the more I socialised and joked around with other kids, it took away the questions of what was wrong with me and why I was so quiet. But I guess that instinct of keeping people at arm's length never went away. I never truly let people get close to me. Not even Liam. And I know that doesn't excuse everything, but I guess I only really realised this...habit when I went to therapy. I'm trying not to be like that, but I guess it explains a lot."

When he finishes, he looks over at me, finally, seeing the tears streaming down my face and his face crumbles.

"Dakota," he whispers.

I wipe one side of my face with my thumb and sniffle. "It's okay, I'm fine. I'm sorry. It's just..." I trail off before giving in to the urge to fold my hand over the one he has resting beside mine. "I don't know why I'm crying. I guess I'm glad you had Jenna in all that. And I kind of wish I was there for you more."

All those evenings by the river, all those times I pleaded with him to open up to me, and this is what he was holding in? What he was bottling up and pushing people away for? Maybe I should have pushed more. Maybe I should have been more persistent in getting him to open up. I should have held him longer. Told him how much he meant to me. Maybe I didn't do that enough for him to trust me with being open with him.

But I guess that doesn't matter now. It's in the past. I can't change it. And here he is now, cutting open his heart for me to see the dark, messy side of him. The side of him that I always wanted him to trust me to see.

"I'm glad I had Jenna too." He smiles, but it's a broken kind of smile that wobbles. "And you were there for me. More than you'll ever know."

He reaches up and swipes softly at the tears against my cheek. I feel as though I should be the one doing that, but I can't find it in me to move, frozen in the feel of his skin against mine. "Please don't cry for me. I don't deserve any more of your tears."

Slowly, his smile falls, followed by the hand against my cheek as it drops back to his lap. But his other hand never moves out of my hold, he only laces our fingers together. I hold tighter, wanting him to know I'm here. That I've got him.

His gaze never wavers from mine as he continues. "You were the first person I didn't want to push away. If anything, I felt gravitated to you. I just wanted to indulge in that. And with every evening we met by the river, I felt parts of me clicking into place."

He inhales deeply and my heart starts to thump heavier. "But when I saw you and Liam together, I felt I had to push you away because I knew I was falling for you, and it scared me. I missed you every day of those seven months. I missed the light you burned into my soul when you were around, and the complete ease you surrounded us in." He pauses, swallowing. "In that time, I found out I had been offered a minor league contract after Dad sent them clips of my games, and they came to a few of my games with the ABL team. I had so much pressure put on me to take the deal that I felt I had no choice. It was my duty to make it up to Dad for ruining his life, you know. That's what had been drilled into me for all my life. I just wanted to have a break. I wanted to shove all that pressure and the impending move to the back of my mind and just...relax."

He squeezes my hand, a small smile ticking the side of his lips while my heart cracks so deeply for him. "I wanted *you*. I wanted to run to you and indulge in your peace. I needed you back because I felt like I was diving into a dark hole without you. But coming back to you, I didn't realise would have dragged you deeper into that dark hole with me. I just wanted to pretend like my life was mine for a little while. I wanted to pretend that I wasn't leaving and that I could have everything I ever wanted. But it was selfish of me to think that while I was slowly breaking you in the process. And for that, I will always carry that. I will never not be sorry for how selfish I was when I had you."

He says all this while looking right into my eyes, pouring every desperate emotion into me, and slowly breaking me in the process. I cry more, and I can tell he's trying hard not to wipe them away for me as his fingers twitch in my hands.

I didn't realise closure would feel like this. Like it was shredding my heart to bits while lifting a whole weight off my chest at the same time.

Before, I didn't think talking to him would give me the

147

closure I needed. But with his hands in mine and the mirroring tears that track both our cheeks, I feel the anger, grief, and sadness loosen their grips around my heart, and it's like taking my first gulp of fresh air for the first time in six years.

I should have asked for this a long time ago. But maybe this came at the exact right time that I needed it.

I squeeze his hand and it's like that is the jumpstart he needs, setting him in motion as his hand finally reaches over to my cheek, wiping the tears.

My brain finally connects to my lips, slipping two words into the air between us. "Thank you."

He frowns, pausing before looking up at me. "Why are you thanking me?"

I shake my head as I huff a laugh, dropping my gaze to our connected hands. I should probably pull away, but I can't find it in me to move. If anything, my hold tightens.

"For being honest with me. For being open with me. It's all I ever wanted from you."

We don't move from the pier for a long while, and eventually, my head makes its way to his shoulder as my hands stay in his.

We don't move, and it almost feels like puzzle pieces snapping back together.

But I shake the thought almost as fast as it comes.

Almost, I say, because for a moment, I let myself indulge in that feeling again. Like I'm eighteen again, and he came back right where he left me.

18

REECE

I huff an exaggerated groan, dropping my head onto the back of the couch as I stretch my legs further to sink into my seat.

"I'm *bored*," I draw out the word, tilting my head to the side to look at Dakota.

She sits on the other side of the couch, her legs curled underneath as she balances Jenna's laptop on her lap. We've been organising the playlist for the wedding reception for the last hour, but all I want to do is talk to her. The twenty-one question game we played a few weeks ago now has me starving for information about her.

I want the friendship we used to have, the way we used to know everything about each other so deeply. I've spent the last twenty minutes talking about anything other than music, and asking her questions about her life. She doesn't let me stray off topic for very long, though, always pulling me back to the purpose of us being here.

I could feel something shift between us after that evening by the river. Where I finally told her the whole story. Where I could give her the apology and explanation that she deserved. But I still felt and heard the hesitation in her demeanour to every question I asked, no matter how surface-level they were. She's still keeping me at arm's length.

I know everything won't be fixed or erased magically with just one night. That night was just the start of me weaving back into her world and rebuilding the blocks of the bridge between us. Now, all I can do is try. Show her I mean every word I said, every promise I made. It'll take time to regain her broken trust in me, but I have nothing but time for her.

My charm, though, still has an effect on her as her lips curve the slightest at my dramatics before she presses them together. I was still able to make her smile, which was confirmed, but maybe I could even make her laugh again. I just needed to melt the stone surrounding her heart a little more. Getting to know her again, showing her I was still the same charming guy she knew, was how I would do that. And I knew it was working, going by every tiny reaction I caught when I asked her questions about her life in Melbourne, avoiding her dating life.

She sighs, closing the laptop before setting it on the coffee table, and I grin, knowing I won. "Okay. What do you recommend we do then?"

Shit. I didn't really think that far ahead.

Didn't think of anything other than wanting her attention.

I buy myself some time to think as I smirk at her. "Oh, I could recommend so many things," I drawl, laying it on thick and teasing her, watching the slow rise of pink staining her cheeks.

She rolls her eyes. "Savoury answers only."

I let out a disappointing sigh. "Fine." Then I remember something Jenna mentioned about a farmers market down the street today, having nice food and entertainment. "You know, I've never been to one of those farmers' markets. You know the ones all those healthy, rich people go to? I kinda wanna see what all the fuss is about."

She lifts a brow, as if not believing what I suggested we do. "You want to go to a farmers' market?"

I shrug. "Why not? It's early enough."

I watch her as she chews her lip, waiting with bated breath for her to agree. Not so much that I was excited to go to this market, more so that I wanted her to agree to spend time with me alone, outside of obligation, just like she did after we visited the venue. I wanted her to want to spend time with me as much as I did her.

Then she says those magic words. "Fine, okay. Let's go."

I pop up in my seat. "Really?"

She frowns, obviously shocked at my reaction. "Why do you seem so surprised about my answer?"

"I..." I start to explain, but pause, not wanting to admit how hopeful I was for her to agree. Thinking about it makes it seem like I'm obsessed with her. Which I am. But she doesn't need to know that. Not yet, anyway. "Nothing. Never mind. Do you want me to drive?"

She shrugs. "Sure. Let me get my purse. I'll meet you at the car."

I nod before pushing up from the couch. "No problem."

While she ducks upstairs, I grab the car keys by the entrance and make my way to the car, waiting for her as I lean against the passenger door. I absentmindedly spin the keys around my fingers, eyes cast down the quiet street, while flashes of the past come back to me. Of us walking this street hand in hand after we spent most of the night by the river, lost in each other and deep conversations of life and dreams. Those thoughts seem so trivial now, with how much time has passed and all that's happened. I wish I could reach across and transport myself back to that time. A time when we were still naive about the world, but a world where I still had her trust and friendship. Where I hadn't screwed everything up yet, and I could shake myself out of making that mistake.

I know I lost a piece of myself the night I dropped her back home after telling her I was leaving. But every time I've looked at her over the last month, I've found myself feeling like I've found that part again. Like coming home. And all I want to do is reach out and grab hold of it.

I look up as I hear the front door shut, seeing her emerge with her purse strapped across her body, dressed in an over-sized T-shirt I wish was one of mine and three-quarter length pants.

When she reaches me, I open the car door for her and she slips in past me with a quiet thanks before I shut her door.

I hop into the driver's seat and pull out of the driveway shortly after.

She's quiet, turned away from me as she looks out her window at the passing houses and buildings. I keep glancing at her, checking on her, and wondering why she is so silent. Wondering if I did something, or what was on her mind. The music from the radio cuts through the silence, but it does nothing to dissolve the thickness building in the cab of the ute.

I finally decide to break the silence as I turn the music down, shooting a glance at her when she catches my movement before returning to the road.

"Why are you so quiet?"

She frowns, lifting her head from the window to look at me. "Me? You're quiet, too."

I chew my bottom lip briefly, catching her look of confusion. "Did I do something?"

She shakes her head. "Why would you ask that?"

"Because I feel you being distant. I know nothing will magically go back instantly, but I thought we were making slow progress," I state, fingers tapping in a sporadic pattern against the steering wheel.

There's a pause before she replies, "We are."

"So...did I do something?" I ask, my voice quiet, shooting another glance at her.

She rests her head back against the seat before letting out a sigh. "It's just... Is it really just that easy to go back to normal with everything that happened? I just don't know how to go from here and to trust you again."

Bobbing my head, I press my lips together as I absorb her words and let them sink to the bottom of my stomach.

She had every right to question that. I know it won't be as easy as saying the word go and her trust to repair itself. I wish it were, but I don't want that for her. I want her to have a reason to trust me again. I want her to make me work for the trust she deserves.

Everything between us came so easily when we were younger, and the way we fell into each other.

But that's exactly what we don't want. I want things between us to be different. And I know that starts with me and my candidness to her, opening myself up to everything I was always scared to confront. The main thing being my feelings for her and my intentions. I don't want her to ever question my true intentions here. I want her to know that even in the six-year absence, she was all I thought about, never leaving the occupancy she rooted in my heart when we were younger.

I pull up in the car park and switch the car off, letting us sit in complete silence for a moment before turning to her. Her hesitant gaze flickers over to me while mine stays unwavering. Everything outside the car blurs to the point that she's the centre of my vision.

"I don't want easy with you. I don't want that for *you*. I want to work for your trust. I want this to be fifty-fifty, give and take. Honesty and openness between both of us. I want you to have what you deserve in this friendship. That means not going back to how things used to be. We're building something new here.

We're going to fight and frustrate the hell out of each other, but we stick together no matter how hard it gets."

I swallow before admitting, "I thought I was doing what was best for you by letting you go after everything and letting you live your life without me. But I know now you know what is best for you, so where we go from here is wherever you steer us." The corner of my lips curves. "That being said, I want you to know there wasn't a single moment you weren't on my mind in the last six years. From the moment I opened my eyes to the second I fell asleep and beyond that, you were here." I tap my temple twice. "So I hope I do earn your trust back. I hope I earn more of you like I've ached for all these years."

The crease between her brows deepens at my last words. "Really? Because from the photos I saw online, it looked like you forgot about me pretty quickly and moved on just fine."

I frown, trying to think of the photos she's referencing before it finally clicks what she said, and a smirk pulls at my lips as my head tilts. "Did you look me up?"

Her face falls flat. "Reece..."

I hold my hands up, unable to help myself from teasing. It's a default around her. "I'm sorry, it's just nice to know you were still thinking of me and wanting to keep up with me. I couldn't get a single thing about you online and had to coerce Jake into giving me information throughout the years."

"I didn't," she says a bit too quickly, and my amusement fades like a slap to the face. "I mean...I kind of blocked you from all of my searches until a month ago when I saw you again," she sheepishly adds.

My gaze drops as I stare at the centre console, my stomach sinking as I slowly nod. "Oh."

I know I shouldn't be upset. I wouldn't want to know about me either after what I did. I'd want to block out the reminder of the person who hurt me, too. But fuck, if it doesn't send fuel to the ever-present guilt swirling in my stomach. I keep pretending that what I did was all in the past and that we can move on from this, but maybe I did too much damage between us.

She shakes her head. "I'm sorry. That sounded so rude. I just couldn't face hearing about you-"

"No, I get it," I interrupt, choking on a snicker that rises at the back of my throat. "I deserve that."

Silence falls upon us again, and I finally pull my gaze to her, hating the concern swirling in them when she looks at me. I smile at her, trying my best to reassure her that all is okay. That she shouldn't feel guilty for anything. That this is all my burden to carry.

I clear my throat, turning back to the subject she brought up. "About the photos or articles you saw, I was a real mess then. Leaving you and everything I knew tore me apart. I drowned myself those nights, trying to distract myself from jumping on the first flight I could and coming right back to you. I guess in those photos, that was me trying to... I don't know..." I try to find the words to explain what was going through my mind back then that resulted in me partying my nights away and letting faceless women drape themselves over me. I could hardly even stomach bringing them home with me. "I guess it was to forget you somehow? It was useless since you were always there, though. The articles might make it look that way, but I rarely ever made it out of my home when I was in that state. No matter how hard I tried, you would still find a way into my head, and I knew then there wasn't a chance in hell I would rid myself of you."

She watches me for a long moment, a conflicting war of emotions flickering in her gaze as they jump between mine. It's the perfect example of everything between us, raw and conflicting, and I want nothing more than to decipher and understand them. I catch a few of them, glimpses of longing, anguish, and a second of confusion. They pass so fast through her eyes before she flattens her expression, blocking me out and leaving me yearning for more. For her to tell me what she was thinking.

I swallow hard, leaning back in my seat, not knowing I had started to move closer to her, and tilt my head toward the farmers' market. I want to escape the thick and heavy cloud that's enveloped us, and show her that this can be something different. Something lighter, easier.

"Shall we get going?"

She glances out the front window, the muffled music coming from the busy street coming into focus before she nods. "Yeah."

As we wander through the market, I can still feel the tension pulled taut. Her words are short, and she barely looks at me. I can tell she's still lost in her head, and I want nothing more than to pull her out of it, to talk to me, to yell or snap at me. Anything to evaporate the distance I know I keep causing between us.

I try my hardest, though, checking on her now and then as I send a smile her way. Everything that she shows even the smallest interest in, I buy for her. She tries to stop me the first few times, but it's no use. I want to spoil her and make her happy with everything she wants. I grin the third time, noticing how she stops trying to fight me and hides a smile of her own.

Then I aim for a laugh as I pull her toward the caricature artist, and we sit still and patiently together. I think it was pretty successful when she snorts as the drawing is revealed, seeing our exaggerated features. But I can't help but notice how the drawing of me is turned, watching her, heart eyes replacing my eyes, and I join her round of laughter. I didn't notice I was doing that, but I think it's the most accurate drawing they could have done.

By the time we decide to take a break from walking around to grab a coffee and a few pastries from the bakery van, that tension has slowly evaporated. It's in the way she smiles and laughs more with me, throwing back the teasing I send her way.

We find our way to a free bench near the live music and start to pick at the pastries while sipping our coffees, watching the people who walk by as silence draws between us.

It feels oddly normal and strangely coupley sitting here with her like this. Freeing, the most relaxed I've been in a long time.

"I'm sorry," she breaks the silence, and I snap my attention to her at the same time she does.

Confusion pinches my brows. "Why are you apologising?"

She swallows, fiddling with the paper wrapping from her pastry that's long gone now. "I made everything awkward again. After we'd talked, I wanted to put it all in the past and try being friends. But I guess it's not as easy as that."

It hurts my heart seeing her distraught over this. I don't want her to carry that.

I reach across her, folding my hands in hers and loosening a breath from my lungs when hers curl around them. My gaze flickers between hers for a moment as I brush my thumb across her hand in slow strokes. "It's okay. It's okay for it not to be easy. I don't expect my words to be the thing that fixes us. I'll be here waiting, showing you that I am worthy of your trust again. We don't need to rush this. You take as much time as you need, and I'll keep proving that to you, okay? And please don't apologise for anything."

She watches me for a second before she lightly squeezes my hand in a show of agreement.

I look over to the musicians as they begin to play a cover of 'Anchor' and I see a few couples sway in front of them, looking sweetly and lovingly at each other.

When I return my gaze to her, I get an idea and stand in front of her, dropping our rubbish in the bin next to the bench. I take her hand, and she frowns up at me, while I grin.

"Come on. Let's join." I flick my head to the group, and she widens her eyes.

"You're kidding."

"I'd never joke. Come on. Have fun with me," I coax, pulling a little on her hand to see if she'll come with.

She withdraws, shaking her head. "I don't think that's a good idea."

I shrug, teasing her a little. "Call it practice for the wedding. I've seen you dance, and I wouldn't want you to fumble over the dance floor."

It's not true at all. She was mesmerising when I watched her dance at the bar weeks ago. I just want to get a rise out of her.

And I do just that as she narrows her eyes at me and lets me tug her up before leading her over.

When I turn back to her, her hands wrap around my shoulders, resting there like they were always made to be there. I hesitate as I reach for her, placing my hands by her waist before subtly dragging her closer until she's mere inches away. I hear her intake of breath, and it shouldn't fill me with such satisfaction to hear how I affect her, even in such a small way.

I start a slow sway, never tearing my eyes off her as hers stay latched on mine as well.

A crease forms in her brow. "So, what exactly are we practising for? Shouldn't it be the bride and groom for this sort of thing?"

I grin. "You're right. But this is practice for when I ask you to dance. And I wanted to see something."

She gaffaws, and I'm caught in the view of her blooming smile. "Pretty presumptuous of you. What did you want to see?"

"I wanted to see if we still fit together like we used to. Like puzzle pieces."

She laughs. A full, head-thrown-back cackle that catches me by surprise. My grin stretches, full and wide at the sound of it, magical and unrestrained. Something I never thought I'd be able to hear again.

When she tilts her head back to look at me, her eyes light with amusement and something else I can't quite capture. But the more she looks at me, the more they fall from her as she flicks her gaze between mine, her breath catching.

"And? What are your findings?" She whispers the words for only me to hear, not that anyone else was listening, but the intimacy of it pulls me closer to her.

I tuck a strand of hair behind her ear and whisper back, "Exactly what I already knew."

That we were made for each other.

19

DAKOTA

A week later, I'm sitting in Mum's kitchen, swirling a glass of wine, lost in my thoughts and the last week.

It feels like the dynamics have shifted, and it's weird how in a short space of time, he's begun to weasel his way back into my life.

I found myself smiling and laughing more whenever he was around, as he took every moment he could to tease me. Though I still felt myself hesitating around him, waiting for this all to be just my imagination and he would be gone in the next second, I felt as though we were getting back into the rhythm of how we used to be.

He came over more often, hiding behind the guise of helping Jenna, but then he would take me out for food, to the botanic gardens, or pull me in to dance whenever he came to help me with the playlist like we did at the farmers' market.

I'd spent many years trying to forget what it felt like to be around him, it all felt oddly nostalgic now, spending so much time with him.

But this thing with him...it feels too good to be true. It's been just over a month since he bounced back into my life, and yet, in that time frame, so much has changed. I don't know if that's a good thing or a bad thing.

In terms of the wedding, I would say it is good. It makes things easier for Dad and Jenna not to worry about us. But in terms of my heart, I didn't know.

Mum joins me at the kitchen counter, our takeout that just arrived in one hand and her own glass of wine in her other.

"I'm still surprised you haven't ventured into cooking. It's been years," I muse as she deposits containers of a variety of noodles in the space in front of us, while she takes the seat to my right.

Dad was always the cook in the family and made it a whole experience together as a family. Mum never joined, though. As kids, she would just sit at the bench and watch before slowly fading from the family image when she left.

But even after the divorce, cooking never interested her. She preferred eating out at a restaurant, predominantly because she spent most of her nights at work dinners.

For me, though, for the last six years, she's blocked off every second Tuesday of the month to sit down and have dinner with me over FaceTime. We both ordered food and it became a tradition.

I always suggested cooking when her visits fell on those days, but she always declined, and today was no different.

She shrugs. "Just not a fan of it. Plus, I don't think it's wise for me to be in the kitchen. Your dad tried when we first got together, but all I did was burn food or make it too salty. You're lucky you take after your father in that respect."

"You know I could have cooked too?"

She waves me off, passing me a fork and a plate as she starts taking off the lids. "Then I would just be sitting here, doing nothing, and I would hate feeling useless."

I chuckle as I scoop some noodles onto my plate and Mum follows suit. Silence envelopes us for a moment as we start to eat, but it doesn't last for long as her question pierces me.

"So, your dad tells me that boy is back. How are you feeling?"

I flick my eyes up to her as I fight the smile twitching the corner of my lips. "That boy?"

She rolls her eyes and kisses her teeth. "You know what I mean."

I avert my focus back to the noodles as I try to piece together an answer.

"It's been okay. It was weird at the start but it's better now. We've talked and it's not as tense, I guess."

When I look back at her, she gives me a pointed look. "You're worse than me at avoiding the real question. I asked, how are you *feeling*, like *really* feeling?"

I swallow, knowing she was right but wishing she would overlook it like she used to. But that's also a lie, because it made me feel warm knowing she knew me enough to point that out now.

"I was angry at first. I didn't want anything to do with him because I still held a lot of the hurt he caused. But he has a very persistent nature and didn't give up trying to insert himself back in my life. I saw glimpses of that boy that I fell in love with and also more. A man who was determined to be different. Then we talked, and now," I trail off with a sigh, searching the space over her shoulder for words but failing, "I don't know. I don't know how to feel about it. All I know is that I don't want to get hurt again."

She reaches over to gasp my hand that rests in my lap, squeezing it as she presses her lips together in a smile. "You have a heart of gold, Dakota. It is strong and forgiving and fierce in its ability to love. It's something I admire most about you. You believe the best in people, especially when they don't deserve it. It's what brought us here, to this relationship we have now. And I'm so grateful for that. But I also know it took us time to get here. And from that, I know if someone wants to make an effort to do better, they will do all they can to prove it." She pats my hand, then lets go, reaching for her wine and taking a sip before continuing. "I never want you to have your heart broken again, and I want nothing more than to protect you from those who have hurt you. But I know you know what is best for you. You know who deserves a place in your heart and that's a great attribute."

I didn't even know tears started trailing down my cheeks until Mum reaches up to swipe one away with a soft smile.

I let out a half-heart snicker before dropping my fork to my plate and bringing the heels of my palms to my cheeks, wiping away the remaining tear stains.

I looked at her again, then threw my arms around her, catching her off-guard as she let out a surprised gasp. But almost immediately, she wraps her arms around me in return.

Slowly, over the years, she has shown small acts of affection toward me, but I know she isn't the most fond of physical affection. She will squeeze or pat my hand every so often, but hugs are rare, and that's okay. After our many talks and understanding her acts of love more, I never feel like I'm lacking in feeling her love. I just feel overwhelmed by her words right now and need her hug.

"Sorry, I just..." I choke on my words before whispering. "Thank you."

She squeezes me a little tighter. "Don't be sorry. And I should be the one to thank you."

I pull back from her, sitting back on my chair. "What do you mean?"

"Because of the chance you took on me, I get to sit here and have you open up to me like this. So, thank you."

My chin wobbles as I take a deep breath and look up at the ceiling. "Stop, you're going to make me cry again."

She laughs softly. "Sorry."

I look back down at her and smile. "Love you, Mum."

She smiles back. "I love you, too."

And then we go back to eating our noodles and drinking our wine while I absorb her words into the crevasse of my heart, which has just started to slowly stitch back together.

20

REECE

I can feel the ease start to settle between us, lightening the distance that pushed us apart for far too long. I don't know what did it, the evening by the river or the morning at the farmers' market, but fuck am I glad for it.

I feel relieved, feel lighter with the air cleared, especially when I'm in her vicinity. I'm able to break down that barrier she's pushed between us. I'm able to see her eyes soften when she looks at me instead of harden. She smiles at me more. She laughs at my jokes and gives me back that banter that was between us when we were younger. I don't think that would ever change, the way we were able to joke with each other. It's the familiarity, the comfort of it all.

I know nothing would go back to how it used to be, but it feels like we were coming back together with the friendship we both clung to. We were each other's comfort years ago, and it feels like coming back home.

For the past couple of weeks, we've been organising the joint bachelor and bachelorette party. Both Jenna nor Dakota's dad wanted anything fancy or traditional. They just wanted a night out to celebrate being one month out from their wedding before everything got too busy and chaotic. It's been fun working with her to make it a special night for both of them. Truthfully, just working with her on anything for this wedding has been fun. I just enjoyed being with her. I'd missed her presence and everything she made me feel.

I walk up the stairs to Dakota's house with a skip in my step before rapping my knuckles against the dark wooden door, waiting for someone to answer. The wind picks up, rustling the bushes next to the steps and easing the heat of the sun beaming down, making my hands sweat that little bit more.

I wipe my hands down my thighs like I'm nervous or something. It's weird. I've only ever been like this once before walking up to this house, and that was when I was picking Dakota up for a date. The only date we'd ever officially been on. I don't know what's making me nervous today.

I received a text from Jenna telling me that Dakota and I needed to get our suit and dress fitted since we missed the first appointment. Everyone had gone to the first one, and now, it was just us left, which I'm glad for. It was another reason to be around her alone.

Maybe it just felt intimate, this dress fitting, and that's why I feel my heart pounding in my chest. Or maybe it's the thought of seeing her in her dress, and my delusional thoughts leading to what the future looked like with us.

The door opens, and I meet Dakota's eyes as she leans against the door with a smile on her face. A smile just for me. A smile that sang straight to my heart.

I'm totally gone for her. Always have been.

My eyes track down from her short blonde hair, curling the soft curve of her jaw, before falling along her silhouette, fitted in a cropped sleeveless T-shirt and a denim skirt that hugs her hips, cut off at mid-thigh. The warm sunlight casts through the door, somewhat illuminating her, brightening her features, and reflecting in her eyes.

She's so beautiful that sometimes it hurts to look. But I've already accepted the fact that I'm a masochist. There wouldn't be a chance I would ever look away from her. I would gladly fall at her mercy.

I have a feeling that's going to be the theme for today.

"Hi," she greets.

"Hi," I breathe before clearing my throat and throwing a thumb over my shoulder. "You ready?"

She nods, lips spreading as she turns to grab her purse. "Yeah, let's go."

She hooks the strap of her bag over her shoulder before breezing past me toward my car, the sweet smell of her perfume like a lasso, wrapping around me to follow after her.

I unlock the door to Jenna's car as soon as she steps up to it, and then she slides into the passenger side before I get in the driver's side. When I turn the car on, the beginning chords of *I Remember Everything* pour through the speakers, and I relax into the seat as I pull away from the driveway.

I see her turn her head toward me from the corner of my eye, and I can't help but cut a glance at her as she does. "What?" I probe.

She shrugs. "I just didn't take you for a country music person."

I lift a brow as I glance at her again. "What kind of music did you think I was into?"

She thought about it for a while before answering. "Honestly, I don't know."

I puff a breath through my nose in the form of a laugh. "I don't have a preference really, I like everything. Except for classical. That's boring as fuck."

She lets out a light laugh and bites her lip as she lets the music wash over us.

Truth is, this song is on my playlist because it reminds me of us. I first heard it listening to a random playlist on a bus to an

Albuquerque game, and it's been on repeat ever since. That first year, I didn't want to remember anything about us because it hurt too much to remember. But when I heard that song, I felt it all. Because no matter what I did, I always remembered everything.

It's impossible to forget a woman like Dakota.

I wish I weren't so broken when I met her. Because in that state of mind, I took and took all that I could grab my hands on, breaking her in the process.

I may have tainted her memories of us, but to me, she will always be the light of my fucking life.

The difference between younger me and the me that sits beside her now is that I want her to know I can be that to her as well. That I can be her light. I don't want to take. All I want to do is give. And I will give my whole life to her.

It's about a half-hour drive when we pull up in the parking lot and start the short walk to the dress shop.

Walking beside her in the busy streets of the city brings me back to our first—and last—date that we went on. When we wandered the city and visited the art museum, and ate ice cream. When the realisation that I had loved her punched me straight through the centre of my chest, and like a fucking idiot, I shut it down.

It's funny how full circle this has come, and we landed right back to where it all fell apart. Maybe it was fate giving us a second chance. I'd like to think it was that than the alternative, that it was teaching me a lesson of what I had lost. Because I already know what I lost, and now, I'm trying my best to get her back.

Walking into the shop, the bell above the door rings through the small showroom. Wedding dresses line the racks on the right, with a couple of mannequins wearing flowing dresses and suits lining the other side with mannequins alike.

We stroll through the aisle as the store attendant peeks out from a door behind the counter.

She smiles as she spots us. "Hi. Welcome. Can I help you two with anything?"

Dakota smiles politely as she steps forward, taking the lead. "Hi, yes. We have a fitting booked in. It should be under Jenna Baard."

She searches through the book on top of the desk to today's date and taps her finger atop it as she looks up at us. "Right here. I've set up a room for you to try on the outfits chosen. There's a complimentary glass of champagne in there. Let me know if you need anything or need any adjustments made. Jenna gave us your measurements, but it's not the same as visualising the adjustments on the first try. I'll show you guys upstairs."

She says it so casually and with no judgment, but I don't miss the guilt flashing in Dakota's eyes before she turns to follow the shop attendant. I didn't have the option to come here when they first went shopping for suits; my team was in a Wild Card game at the time. But her guilt is misplaced. It's mine to carry because it's my fault she couldn't set foot back home, going by what Avery has told me and berated me about. It's my own damn fault for casting her home in a cloak of shadows, haunted by the ghosts of my mistakes.

Climbing up the stairs, the woman brings us down a short hall of rooms before stopping in the door frame of one on the right and ushering us in.

"This is you guys. Now, I'm the only one in the store today, so I'll be downstairs if you guys need me, but I'll come back in about ten minutes to see how you guys are."

We thank her, and then she disappears back down the hall, leaving us alone.

I turn to Dakota as she walks toward a set of two lounge chairs in the centre of the room that sit in front of a small platform and a wall of mirrors. She plops down on one of them, grabbing one of the flutes of champagne before turning her chin over her shoulder to look at me, where I'm still lingering by the doorway.

"Your turn first," she says, turning back around and catching my gaze again in the mirror, a flicker of mischief in her eyes as she sips her drink. I might have fallen to my knees if I didn't know she'd have laughed at me.

"Me? I thought we were doing this together?"

"We are. But there is also only one dressing room, so..." She trails off, and my gaze drifts toward the left side of the room, realising there is, in fact, only one curtained-off area.

"Okay, fine."

I grab the suit hanging next to the room and close the curtain behind me.

I've been to a lot of suit-fittings these past two years, more than I ever have since being called up to the Major for off-field appearances and interviews. I've never had so many cameras stuffed in my face as I have since everyone wants to know how an Australian went from the small leagues in Australia to the MLB, like it's some kind of legacy. It's not that special, though, in my opinion, many people put in the same blood, sweat, and tears that I've had to, and no one's paying as much attention to them.

I quickly shrug on the shirt and jacket before zipping up the slacks and buckling them in place. I slide the curtain back as I fix the tie around my neck, tightening it to fit snugly before looking up at Dakota.

The flute of half-filled champagne pauses at her lips like she's about to take a drink while her smoky eyes bore into me. I try my hardest to hold back the grin, fighting the pull at my lips before puffing out my chest, putting it on for her. My body has changed a lot and it feels nice for her to take notice of that. I'm no longer the lean boy she knew. I'm in no means large, but

I'm broader, muscles replacing the slim adolescent figure I had.

Her gaze rakes down my frame as I make my way to the platform in front of the mirror. I don't face them, though; I direct my attention straight to Dakota. I can't hold my grin back anymore as her eyes snap back to mine when she realises.

"How do I look?" I ask, but even I can tell the smugness in my tone.

She rolls her eyes. "Take that ego somewhere else, Fischer. The room is too small as it is."

"Oh, last name basis now?" My smile grows as she lifts a brow. "When you're looking at me like you are, you can't expect anything less."

Her eyes lock with mine, a challenging glint in her eyes, and I tilt my head slightly as I try to figure out what she was thinking.

Her chin lifts then before she pushes off the chair without breaking our gaze. She glides herself closer until she's climbing onto the platform with me. I don't dare move a muscle, scared that if I do, she may run away, pushing me back to keep me at arm's length.

Her eyes scan down to my chest before her hands come up to wrap around my tie. This time, it's my breathing that ceases in my lungs, like even that would break the bubble surrounding us.

She fiddles with the tie, loosening it as she fixes it. Then her eyes flutter up to meet mine. Innocent and oh so daring. She's fucking intoxicating, this woman.

Her voice comes as a whisper as she says, "And how do I look at you?"

Jesus, *fuck*.

Scratch that, she's fucking wicked and I don't doubt that she knows it.

I narrow my eyes as I try to read what game she's playing at.

"You know how," I drawl.

And then she grins, tightening the tie so fast, I choke on a breath. But it's not tight, she just caught me by surprise, and it definitely was no accident.

She tilts her chin up, her breath mingling with mine, and I can feel my heart stuttering in my chest with every brush of air against my lips.

She has me so weak in the palm of her hand, and she doesn't even have to do much. Just breathe on me, or *fuck*, even be near me, and I'm putty.

"I want you to tell me," she says in a sultry tone.

I clench my fists beside me, keeping myself from reaching for her and pulling her into me.

And despite my better judgment of falling into her little game, I answer her. "You're looking at me like you want me. Like you've forgotten all those years apart, and you want to make up for lost time. That you're considering forgetting what I did to you for one little taste."

She pauses for a moment, eyes flicking between each of my own before slowly lowering to my lips. I think I stop breathing altogether again.

I thought that admission would have stumped her and pulled her out of this game. But by this look alone, I almost think she's considering it, and it makes me ache all over.

She hums, and then her heat disappears as she steps off the platform with a playful smirk tilting her lips.

Oh, she knows exactly what she's doing to me.

"Is that right?" she drawls, backing further away from me as she hitches a thumb over her shoulder. "Well, I better try my dress on so I'll be back."

A chuckle breaks through my lips as I watch her grab her dress and head into the dressing room. I stop her, though, before she closes the curtain behind her.

"You never denied it," I point out, trying to gain some semblance of reality back.

She just grins and slides the curtain closed without answering.

I internally groan as I tilt my head back to the ceiling, closing my eyes, and taking a deep breath while trying to tamp down the overwhelming arousal that's made my dick so hard with just her close proximity.

Shaking my head, I turn to get a look at the suit on me. I was too caught up in Dakota to actually look at how it looked on me.

It fits nice and snug but has enough mobility that I can move my arms around without restriction. It's a nice colour too. There's not a lot of variety in colours when it comes to suits, and black is a classic, but this slate grey could be a top contender.

I take a seat on the couch next to the one Dakota had been sitting on and wait. I relax back and kick a foot up to rest on my opposite knee, pulling out my phone to distract myself from the aching semi I still have.

She still knows exactly how to lure me in, to have me on my knees and begging. And I was so willing to dive in, tossing aside caution and restraint as soon as she pulled an inch of the string she had wrapped around me. I don't know if I was imagining the lust in her eyes or if that was just a game to her, to rile me up, but I needed to get a handle on myself. Find some sort of control. I can't have her running away from me because I read her wrong when I just got her back.

She finally emerges from the dressing area, pulling my attention straight to her, and I suddenly lose the ability to breathe again.

I was right before, that the theme for today would be me at her mercy.

She is... God, all the words have evaporated from my vocabulary. I don't think a single word in the English dictionary can describe just how fucking breathtaking she is.

Standing in front of the changing room, her bright blue eyes met mine, a small smile forming on her lips, but this time, instead of the confident, sultry one she wore moments before, it was a little shy. I don't know why. She must know how she illuminates the space she takes up.

My gaze trails down her slim figure, taking in the dusky pink dress with off-the-shoulder straps, hugging every inch of her skin until her hips, and then flowing out. The satin material accentuates every bit of her small curves and hugs her body like I yearned to do since the moment I laid eyes on her again.

She looks angelic. I don't know, maybe it was the light coming from behind her or maybe it was simply her. She's my type of angel, sent to me to bring me to my knees. And I'd gladly kneel before her.

I stare at her with my mouth slightly agape, trying to piece together any semblance of a coherent thought through my lips.

Her shy smile transforms to a slight smirk at my dumbfounded look, and when I start to stumble over my words.

"Holy—wow—you—" I stop and just stare at her, a rushed breath escaping me as I give up talking.

She makes her way to the small platform in front of me, and when she steps up to it, she does a small spin in front of the mirror, smiling as she looks at herself in the mirror.

Finally, I was able to piece together words.

"You look so beautiful, Kod—" I breathe before cutting myself off and clearing my throat. "Dakota."

Her smile widens as she meets my eyes through the mirror, before shifting her gaze back to her reflection, running her hands down the sides of her body, and for some reason, to me, it was the sexiest move I've seen. She's so unintentionally sexy without trying and I fucking love that about her. It's always so subtle, but I notice it all.

She shifts, turning her back on the mirror and looking over her shoulder at the drooping back that shows most of her back. Then she turns her gaze back to me, but I can't stop mine from dropping again, taking in every inch of the dress made to fit her so perfectly.

I don't even notice her fidgeting as she interlocks her fingers in front of her until she speaks in a low voice, "You know, you can call me Kody. I don't mind."

My eyes immediately snap back to meet her hesitant ones as she chews her lip before she adds quickly, "Only if you want to. You don't have to."

I can't help the growing smile stretching across my face as my heart leaps with the meaning of those words. Of the knowledge that this is her offering me a bridge toward her trust because of the role that nickname played between us. Of the intimacy of that nickname between us.

I pop up from the seat and walk the couple of feet to reach her until I'm standing on the platform with her inches away, just as she did moments ago with me.

I look down at her, fighting the urge to reach up and caress her face. But I don't fight it enough as my fingers graze her waist, nudging her to turn. She follows my silent request before I find her gaze again in the mirror.

Maybe I wasn't imagining it in the end. Because I see it right here, in the depths of her ocean blue gaze, as I fall into the pull of them, like crashing waves pulling me to sea. The heat flickers, igniting with a spark the more I stare.

My hand rests on her waist, feeling the soft fabric under my fingertips shift, and I can't stop myself from breathing this moment in. The fucking magnitude of it is digging its claws deep under my skin.

I don't tear my attention away from her as I lean down to graze her ear with my lips. Her breath hitches, and I keep the smirk that's fighting to be freed in check.

"You look absolutely stunning in this dress, Kody," I whisper and then watch a path of goosebumps rise down her arm before a little shiver shakes her shoulders.

Little by little, I can see her changing how she reacts to me, and this...this just ignites a little light on the hope in my heart that I will have her in my arms again.

Because she doesn't pull away from me. She melts a little further into my arms as a smile blossoms on her face, creasing her cheeks in the cutest way, and I fall a little more in love.

21

DAKOTA

I lean over the bathroom counter to add a subtle wing to my eye as the door flies open and Alex and Avery burst through with their bags of makeup and clothes.

I don't flinch at their sudden arrival, only cutting them a sideways glance, having heard them moments ago with the slam of the front door, their loud voices and footsteps echoing as they made their way upstairs. I focus on the smoky eyeliner I'm trying to create, cleaning under my eye as Avery sidles up beside me and starts on her makeup.

It was the bachelor-slash-bachelorette party tonight, and though I was excited to go out and have fun with Dad and Jenna and my friends, my stomach swirled at the thought of seeing Reece.

After the dress fitting, I hadn't seen him for the rest of the week. Maybe that was a good thing because I was beginning to think that being with him every day was doing something to my brain and softening the hard-formed walls around my heart. Friends was risky, because it was only a step closer to falling for his charm and stupid dimple again. And after telling him it was okay to call me Kody, it was like opening myself up to doing just that.

Mum's words of reassurance come back to me, telling me that I know what's best for my heart. And despite everything I told myself before, I know giving him the chance he's desperately clawed for since coming back into my life is the start of something new between us.

That nickname was the start of everything. Because he only ever called me it when we were alone, and if he really did mean everything he said, this was the chance for him to prove it. No more hiding. No more holding back.

I didn't know what to expect tonight, how we would act together. It was much easier to hate him and avoid him, but now it was getting complicated, and I wasn't sure if this was a risk worth taking, or if I would end up in flames like I did last time. It was scary because even now, I knew he still had the ability to break me, and I was giving him that chance again, hoping he wouldn't this time.

It was fun for the short time we were in that room together. Where we could pretend like we were young again and tease each other. But we weren't eighteen anymore and we couldn't surround ourselves in that bubble where only he and I existed.

So much has changed.

I have changed.

Maybe this is all just a bad idea.

I paste a fake smile on for my friends as they laugh and joke beside me, but I have a feeling they can see through it. It's hard to fake the way I drift off in my head, thinking about the stirring feelings I felt in that dress fitting. Like I was eighteen again, and I could take the chance to be happy. It's all that's been circulating in my head this past week and I wish I could shake it off. Tell myself I'm just overreacting.

"Dakota?" Avery waves a hand in front of my face, snapping me back to the present, realising I was staring at my reflection.

Avery touches my shoulder and I drop my eyes to her. "Everything okay?"

I strain a smile. "Yeah, everything is good. Sorry, I zoned out there for a bit."

She frowns and nods. "Yeah, for a little bit."

Alex pipes up behind me. "You sure everything is okay?"

I wave them both off as I step back from Avery and run my fingers through my hair. "Yeah, I'm sure. I think I just need to have this night and have fun with the two of you."

Alex grins. "We will make it the best night, not only for you, but for your dad and Jenna."

"I'll have a drink to that," Avery says, pulling out a bottle of tequila and shot glasses. She sets them in a line on the counter before pouring the clear liquid in, spilling most over the countertop.

We each pick up a shot and hold it out to one another.

"Sorry, I didn't bring up a chaser or salt and lime. But fuck it, we can raw dog it. I'll get some after."

I grin and shake my head, knowing this will be bad but throwing out logical thinking.

"To my dad and Jenna, and to have the best night of our lives while we're together."

Our glasses click before we throw back the drink, and I immediately grimace, wanting to spit it out. But I grit my teeth and swallow it down.

"Fuck, Avery. That was a terrible idea. You're meant to be the logical thinker in this group."

She smiles widely. "Tonight, there is no room for that."

And then Alex groans. "We're completely fucked."

We were indeed completely fucked.

After downing three of Avery's shots, we caught an Uber to

179

the bar, and when we arrived at the private room we rented out, drinks were shoved into mine and Alex's hands within the first five minutes by Avery.

She's on a mission, I fear.

But fuck it, I want to have fun. I want this to be the best night for Dad and Jenna, but I also want to let loose and forget about how overwhelming life feels at the moment.

I feel like I missed out on the 'party' phase everyone had when they turned legal. I never had that. Most of those years, I spent heartbroken and trying to piece together those parts again. But tonight is about drinking, dancing and spending it with the people I love.

Dad is not a dancer, but luckily, Jenna loves to, and I'm always in favour of embarrassing my dad and making him dance. Although he will do anything Jenna wants, so he never complains when she pulls him out and makes him dance with her.

Close friends and family start to arrive, and I greet everyone as they enter. But I can't help when every fifteen minutes, my attention starts to drift toward the door, waiting for a specific someone to walk through. Avery and Alex notice though, keeping me distracted by refilling the drink in my hand and turning me away. But the thing is, they don't know. They don't know how things have changed. They don't know that what I feel toward him is no longer hostile. It's no where close to it anymore. And somehow, that makes my anxiety grow. But I want to see him first, to know this isn't all in my head. That it isn't the situation we are in.

It's when everyone starts to take a seat at the long table in the middle of the room that I feel a tap on my shoulder. I turn my head over my shoulder to see Reece standing there, dressed in a fitted suit like many of the men in the room, but on him, it's different. To me, he stands out in every single crowd.

I turn to face him, unable to contain the smile lifting my cheeks as he looks down at me. His slow perusal of my frame heats my skin as they slide over the tube top and crocheted skirt I wore before slowly trailing back up. I instantly feel warm under his gaze.

"Hi, Reece," I greet in an almost whisper.

His eyes flick up, and one side of his cheek twitches as his lip pulls up. "Hi, Kody."

My heart stumbles over itself hearing the nickname in the open air, and it's like I'm transported back in time to when he first called me that on the beach at Airlie Beach. I feel my lips part as I watch the way he looks at me when he says it, bright and soft, his grin widening.

Before we can say anything more, I hear my name being called from across the room, and I turn to see Daniel and Ellie enter. Instantly, I beam before glancing back at Reece to apologise but he interjects before I have a chance to.

"Go. I'll catch you later."

I smile and reach over to squeeze his hand. "Promise."

I don't give him a chance to reply before I run straight to my friends as they both wrap me in a hug.

"You made it. I was worried you wouldn't. Why didn't you let me know you were here?" I push away to look at both of them.

"We wanted to surprise you. Plus, I wasn't sure I was going to get this much time off until yesterday, so it was all very last-minute."

I pull her into a hug, squeezing her. "I'm glad you made it."

And then I turn to Daniel and wrap my arms around him. "I'm glad you're here, too."

He snickers. "Gee, thanks." He pulls away, resting his hands on my shoulders, brows furrowed as he stares at me, then over my shoulder. "Is he here?" he asks in a soft voice. I know exactly who he's talking about, and now I regret telling them I'd run into him.

"Yeah, I want to meet that motherfucker. Teach him a little lesson," Ellie voices, folding her arms across her chest. I wince, knowing there's a lot I still haven't told them since I informed them he was here. I haven't talked to them since that evening I spent by the river with Reece, and I know this is going to be hard to explain. They've only known my hate for him. They didn't know me before, like Alex and Avery did. They never saw our friendship.

"Guys," I try to interrupt, but Daniel talks again.

"Never mind, think I found him. Oh, he looks very angry. Think he might be jealous." Daniel grins down at me.

Ellie rolls her eyes. "He has no right to be jealous. He lost his chance." Then she gazes around. "Which one is he?"

"Guys," I say more firmly, and their gaze snaps back to me. "It's okay. We're fine. We've talked, and we're...working things out."

Ellie narrows her eyes at me. "What do you mean by 'working things out'?"

I sigh, chewing on my lip as they continue to stare at me expectantly. "It's...it's complicated. Things have been different after we talked. Please don't pester me about it because I don't fully know what's going on between us either. Just can you promise to be nice?"

For a moment, they just watch me with sceptical gazes and I shift nervously.

Ellie is the first one to crack as she releases a sigh and holds her hands up in surrender. "Okay, fine. I'll be on my best behaviour."

My shoulders drop in relief. "Thank you."

Then I look to Daniel, who shrugs with a mischievous grin.

"Hey, I can't promise anything. Especially when I can feel

his gaze burning the side of my face right now. I could make this very interesting, if you wanted?"

I frown and look over my shoulder to see, sure enough, Reece's piercing gaze aimed right above me to Daniel. He drops his gaze to meet mine and immediately they soften before he tunes back into the conversation in front of him with his friends, Jake and Sage, who I didn't see come in.

I turn back to Daniel and point at him. "No funny business."

I ignore his pout and turn to find a seat at the table. Daniel immediately takes the seat beside me, which makes me roll my eyes. Ellie takes the other side of Daniel, while Avery and Alex, after greeting the other two, sit on the other side of me, almost like a protective cage to prevent a certain someone from sitting close. But they never thought about the seats across from us, which is exactly the seat Reece takes. His eyes lock with mine as he lowers himself into the chair, a slight tilt to his head as he studies me. His attention then flicks to the people next to me, narrowing just slightly as they skim over Daniel that I almost miss it before looking back at me.

He leans closer over the table to tell me, "I didn't get a chance to tell you before, but you look beautiful tonight, Kody."

One side of my lip twitches at the compliment before I press my lips together.

Before I can say anything in return though, Ellie leans in over the table with her narrowed gaze on him. "Just because you're sitting in front of us, doesn't mean you can talk to her."

My head snaps in her direction as I stare wide-eyed at her. I hear Alex choke on his drink and Daniel snickers in his seat beside me.

"Ellie! What the fuck?"

Her gaze flicks to mine as she shrugs and sits back. "What?" There's an innocent lilt to her tone.

I lift a brow as if to say *seriously?*

She crosses her arms, her shoulders dropping as she huffs. "Right. Fine. Best behaviour."

I sigh and look back at Reece whose eyes are alight with amusement as they flick between me and Ellie.

"I'm sorry about her."

He smiles. "It's fine. I get it. No hard feelings."

I smile, vaguely hearing Ellie mumble 'very hard feelings' but I ignore her.

The rest of the dinner goes fairly well with no more side comments from my friends aimed at Reece.

Though, throughout the dinner, I can't help stealing looks across the table at him. It's like there was something tugging at me, dragging my attention straight to him every time. It probably doesn't help that whenever I do look, he's either already watching me or moments later will look my way like he can feel me. Like he feels the same tether.

After a couple speeches from Dad's and Jenna's best friends and then both Dad and Jenna themselves, we wrap up the dinner and move the festivities down a couple blocks.

Most of us have had a few drinks with dinner and were pretty tipsy as we make our way down the street. Linking my arms through Alex and Avery's arms as Ellie and Daniel lead in front, I can't help the giggles that pass my lips. Alex and Avery shoot me amused looks as Ellie looks over her shoulder, her brows creasing.

"What's so funny?" Ellie asks.

I shake my head before another burst of giggles bubble up.

Once I calm a little, I start, "You guys are acting like my guard dogs. Have been all night. It's just funny."

Ellie rolls her eyes but her lips tug up in amusement as she turns her head forward again. And then, in the most deadpanned voice, she replies, "Woof."

That makes the rest of our group start cackling while the rest of the group turn their heads in question.

I catch Reece's curious gaze and they immediately soften under my stare as his eyes roam my face, catching momentarily at the tug of my lips. It immediately starts a flurry of butterflies in my stomach. I can't help it, it's like an automatic response as blood flushes my cheeks pink.

We all head into the nightclub and find a free booth before Alex drags me onto the floor to dance while Avery goes to order drinks. It's pretty early in the night, around nine o'clock, so there aren't very many people on the floor or in the nightclub for that matter. But still, the music pumps through the speakers and Alex and I start swaying our hips to the beat and singing songs we knew to each other. Avery saunters over with our drinks in hand, passing them out to us and we form our little group. Jenna starts to pull her friends up and onto the floor with us and I get lost in the music and the people around me, having fun and just enjoying the moment.

I don't know how much time passes, my tipsy mind losing track by being absorbed in the freeing feeling, but it's when I turn and my eyes collide with Reece again, that time comes back to focus and slows at the same time. The heat of his gaze rolls down my body as my hips sway before they flick back up again.

I'm entranced and that string that has always seemed to tether us together pulls taut now. He must feel it too because the next minute, he's making his way to me, weaving his way through the crowd I didn't realise had grown around us. Every step toward me has my heart pounding against my chest and the heat of his gaze keeping my skin flushed so I have to look away. I turn so my back is to him, trying to catch my breath and my heart to calm down.

But then, it happens before I can get any semblance of control of my emotions. I feel heat cover my back and the tickle of his breath hitting my hair and I can't contain the shiver that shakes my shoulders.

I know it's him, my body too familiar with the feel of him. His hands slide over the fabric against my hips, confident and possessive. I close my eyes at the feeling, but force myself not to lean into him like I had too easily at the dress fitting.

But it doesn't matter, because it's him that I feel leaning closer this time, lips pressing against the shell of my ear as he speaks loud enough for me to hear over the music. "This okay?"

I let out a shaky breath, melting into him and losing grip of my restraint toward him in an instant. With a couple simple words, I fall into his embrace.

"Yes," I answer back, my voice almost like a whimper, a plea because I'm desperate for more. Then one of his arms wraps around my waist as the other rests on my hip, like a comforting blanket surrounding me in its warmth and safety.

I don't move at first, I just bask in his embrace, the feeling just as I remember wrapping around me as he steps into me, his body flush against the back of mine. His breath hits the skin of my neck as he rests his head against my temple. I can't help but close my eyes.

"You look so fucking beautiful tonight. You always do," he murmurs into the skin behind my ear and my skin pebbles.

He begins to move our bodies together in sync, a slow subtle sway. Then the hand that rests on my hip begins to move. His fingertips run alongside my ribs before slowly descending down my arm. It's like my entire body has surrendered to him because I can't get myself to move even an inch on its own. He's in full control here and I don't do anything but let him.

His fingers lace with mine before he lifts it until it's wrapped around his neck. I flutter my eyes open and it's then that I notice I my head had been resting against his chest. I flick my eyes up to see his hooded as he watches every one of my reactions with rapt attention. On their own accord, the hand he just wrapped around his neck starts to drift, curling through the ringlets at the nape of his neck. An action I've been dying to do since seeing him again. It's still just as soft and perfectly curling around my fingers just as they used to. More so now with the length curling over his ears.

His shuddering breath hits my neck. "You know," his gravelly voice in my ear sends another shiver down my arms, "when that guy had wrapped his arms around you at dinner, my chest burned so fiercely. I'd never felt that way before. I'd wanted to march up to you, rip his arms off you and wipe the smirk off his face. I've never been a violent person, never felt so intensely."

My lips twist into a smile. "Is that why you looked like you wanted to murder Daniel?"

He puffs out a laugh. "Yeah, I guess so." Our bodies still sway to the music as people around us move and push closer into the confined space as it grows more crowded. My fingers sink deeper into his hair as I close my eyes. He continues to talk though. "I've never let go of you over the years, Kody. You're all I've ever thought and dreamed about. It was always going to be you for me. No one else could ever make me feel the way you made me feel. But if you've moved on, I can accept that. It'll hurt like hell, but I can deal with it. All I want is to have you in my life. I don't care how, just that you are part of it."

My eyes pop open, blinking slowly the more I listen and absorb his words. Words that only confuse me.

I turn in his arms, his fingers skimming my body as they rest at my waist now. I look up at him, his gaze burning in the way he only could make me feel with one look. His gaze held so much emotion: longing, pleading, heat. It all wrapped into one and that string pulled once again between us, but this time it was more like a tug.

Fuck, there goes my stomach again, roaring with butterflies like they never went away.

"Daniel and I, we've never... I mean, we're not—" I shake

my head and the relief in his eyes is instant that I can't help but smile and reach up to rest my hand on his cheek.

Something I'm beginning to realise though, with every moment I'm near him, the feelings I held for Reece never truly went away. It's the tiny corner of my heart shaped like him that I lock under bolts and chains where they live dormant, and as soon as he re-entered my life, they banged on the door, fighting to be freed again. All this time, I think, I was just fighting it, thinking I was just afraid to be hurt like that again. Fighting the truth that I never really let him go and there was a small part of me that held onto the hope that he would come back to me.

And now, here he was, back in my embrace, fighting to have me back like I always wanted.

In my half-intoxicated mind, I can't see past that. But like they always say, a drunk person's words are a sober person's thoughts. So, I can't hold back as I tell him, "I've never moved on, Reece. I tried so hard to forget you, but it was impossible. You were too ingrained in my soul, remember? And all these years and hours in therapy could never scrub you clean from me. And I'm grateful that it didn't because all that time spent trying to rid you from me, I never stopped missing you and hoping you came back to me."

His throat works as he stares at me, eyes softening as he touches his forehead against mine, breathing in the close proximity of us just as I was.

"Good. Because I've missed you. So fucking much, you have no idea."

My arms up to wrap around his shoulders as I let my smile escape. "I might have some idea."

He smiles in return. "Yeah?"

I lean in just a fraction, but before I can respond, I'm ripped out of his hold and spun around until I'm facing Ellie.

"What the fuck, Elle?" I exclaim, but then I take a second to look at her and I frown. She looks pale and just generally unwell. "Are you okay?"

"I think I had too much. I do not feel well. At all," she drawls, staggering a bit in spot before I hold either side of her arms.

"Okay. Home time?" I speak above the music.

She nods before paling further. She holds a hand to her lips for a moment, breathing deeply, then exhaling and looking back to me. "Home time. Definitely."

I lace my fingers with her, then turn back to where she pulled me from Reece, which I'm sure was half on purpose and half in desperation.

Reece still stands there watching us. I lean in, reaching up to speak in his ear, my free hand curling around his neck just to feel him a moment longer. In return, he places his hand on my waist in a feather-light touch. The complete opposite of before when it was like he was clinging to me.

"I'm sorry, I have to take her home."

He leans down to reply in my ear. "It's okay. Do you need me to come with you?"

I shake my head slightly. "You don't have to."

"But I want to. I want to help. Please let me."

I pull back to look at him, meeting his pleading gaze, like he doesn't want to let go of me just yet tonight. And to be honest, neither do I.

So, I nod and shout back, "Thank you."

He smiles before shifting his gaze to Ellie and leaning down to talk to her. Her eyes shift to me as she listens to him, widening before turning questioning toward me, like a silent question whether she should trust him. I smile and give the smallest nod before she looks back at him.

Her shoulders drop dramatically and she draws out a long sigh. "Fine," she shouts back.

He turns his head to look at me and grins.

"You guys make your way outside and wait. I'll go get your friends."

I shoot him a grateful look before I loop Ellie's arm over my shoulder. Before I leave though, Reece leans down again to speak, "I'm on a mission to win back your friends. I mean it when I said I want you back in my life. I don't plan on leaving again and I have a lot of patching up to do."

And then he turns and weaves through the crowd and I'm left melting in a puddle at his words.

22

REECE

The noise echoing throughout the car is obnoxiously loud with the four drunken people babbling in the cramped backseat. But I didn't mind one bit as long as I had Dakota sitting next to me as she was, casually flicking her eyes to me every now and then, watching me as I drove them to her house. I can't help the grin that pulls at my lips every time I feel her gaze on me until I quickly glance over at her, and she looks away with a flush.

It almost makes me giddy having her attention on me like that. Much different than the one she used to give me a month ago, where she watched me like a hawk, almost waiting for me to screw up. It's curiosity that I see now, mixed with a warmth that I can only guess is like familiarity, which only builds on the flickering embers of hope I cradle so close, feeling the difference in the way she looks at me.

Though I never want to tear my eyes off her, I focus on driving and keeping an eye on Ellie through the mirror. She's passed out with her head leaning on the guy's—Daniel, as I learnt from Dakota—shoulder. She fell asleep almost immediately when we piled her in the car, and I'm thankful for that since I thought she would be throwing up all the way home.

Pulling up in the driveway, Daniel rouses Ellie, nudging her with his shoulder, making her jolt awake. She blinks rapidly as she takes in where we are and yawns.

We all climb out of the car, and I round to the opposite side to help Ellie out. Daniel stands in the way, though, and attempts to help her, but wobbles in his place.

"It's okay, I'll help her out," I tell him.

He turns his head, raising a brow. The movement has him slumping against the open door, and then it's my turn to lift a brow at him.

He huffs as if mad that I was right to cut in because he was too drunk himself to help before stumbling toward the house when Dakota, who stands behind me, hands him the keys.

"I'm fine. I don't need help. Especially not yours," Ellie slurs from her seat, jabbing a finger at me as she narrows her eyes.

Dakota rounds to her other side. "It's okay, Elle. He's just going to make sure you don't fall over. You're way too drunk to walk on your own and he's sober."

"I'm not that drunk."

As she says this, she stands, pushing me out of the way, which only makes her stumble to the side and knock into Dakota, almost taking her down to the ground in her stubbornness. I manage to catch them before they go down, though, as Dakota pulls Ellie up on her feet again.

She huffs, pushing her hair back as she leans back against the car. "Fine," she eyes me cautiously, "but I don't like you."

My brow rises as I glance over at Dakota. She presses her lips together to hide her smile.

"I don't expect you to. I'm just trying to make sure you get safely inside."

Ellie eyes me for a few moments before sighing and sloppily hanging her arm over my shoulders. I catch Dakota's eyes from the other side of Ellie, and she mouths a silent thank you to me as we slowly walk up to the house.

We don't even make it to the steps before Ellie stops suddenly, and with unusual accuracy for being drunk, she b-lines for the garden, her knees meeting the ground before she's hunched over and spilling all her night's consumption.

Dakota rushes to her side and holds her hair back, sending me an apologetic look over her shoulder.

I was used to this, though, but more so in the position Ellie's currently in for the whole of my first year overseas. I was often found hunched over bushes because I'd drunk too much. Not my proudest moments and one of the reasons why I don't drink anymore.

When she finally feels well enough, I help her up to her feet and we carry on through the house. The others have started to raid Dakota's kitchen for food, but we pass them as she directs me up to the bathroom.

I sit Ellie down on the closed toilet seat when we enter before backing away, hoping she doesn't topple over. She leans against the counter next to her.

"Can you grab some clothes from my cupboard? A pair of pyjamas. You can check the third drawer," Dakota asks as she sifts through the drawers, pulling out a pack of wipes, a hair-brush, and a toothbrush.

I nod and turn, making my way toward her room.

When I open her door, I pause in my step, nostalgia smacking me straight in my chest.

I realise I haven't been in her room since that summer, and it looks exactly the same as it did then. The same curtains, the same bedspread, the same bookshelf, the same collage of photos on her wall of her friends and family. It's like walking back in time.

I wanted to sit down and absorb myself in this snapshot of the past, but I think that would be a bit creepy, plus I don't have the time right now to take a walk down memory lane.

So I head straight to the cupboard like Dakota instructed

and open the third drawer. I sift through, plucking a random shirt and pants. Just as I'm about to close the drawer, though, my eyes catch on a piece of crumbled paper that peeks through the pile of clothes, like it was hidden under there. I hesitate, knowing I definitely shouldn't snoop through her drawers. She only permitted me to grab some clothes and nothing else. It feels like I'd be invading her privacy. But...for some reason, I feel pulled toward it.

Because I catch the first line. A simple line that packs a punch.

To the one who hurt me.

I know instantly that this was about me. That it's addressed to me, the one who hurt her, and my chest aches.

"Reece?" Dakota's voice floats down the hall, and I instantly tuck that note underneath the clothes again and shut the drawer, hiding the evidence that I ever read it.

I take a few deep breaths, calming my thumping heart and the ache behind it, before replying. "Yep. I'm coming."

I pad down the hall, trying to shove what I saw to the back of my mind as I return to the bathroom where Dakota is kneeling in front of Ellie, cleaning her face with a wet wipe. I lay the clothes beside them and step back into the hall.

Dakota meets my gaze over her shoulder, a smile playing at her lips and softening the corners of her eyes. "Thank you."

My lips twitch. "I'll wait out here."

I close the door behind me and lean against it, head tilting back, eyes closing. My brain whirls a million miles a minute as it goes over the note I just saw.

I could only assume what that note consumed, and it breaks my heart imagining her heartbroken figure bent over a page, scribbling words aimed at me. All the guilt and regret I felt over that summer came to a head, and I pressed a palm over my chest as if to ease it.

I tried to focus on other things to pull myself out of my

head and all my mistakes. Focusing on senses, shifting my thoughts to nicer ones, and mind exercises my therapist taught me. But my ears grasp onto the whispers instead, behind the closed door.

"Maybe he's not as bad as we thought he was," I hear Ellie say, and my eyes flutter open as I strain my ears for a reply, distracting me entirely and quieting the pound in my head.

"Who?" Dakota replies, almost absentmindedly, as I hear the tap turn on, muffling their words, but I still catch them.

Ellie scoffs. "You know who. Who else but the man who watches you like you created his entire world?"

"He does not," Dakota says defensively, making me smile. Oh, she has no idea. I *so* do. At least I'm self-aware of it.

"Did you not see him tonight? The whole time during dinner and while you were dancing, he watched you like you were the only person in the room. That man only has eyes for you. And as much as it is painful to admit, maybe he has changed."

There was a long pause between Dakota's answer, and the ache started returning. But then her voice came in a whisper that I almost didn't catch.

"I think so, too."

Before I can let my grin fully unleash, the door starts to open, and I rush to the side and try to act as casually as possible to not look like I was eavesdropping.

Dakota steps out of the door and looks at me, tossing a thumb over her shoulder.

"Can you help me take her to the spare room?" she asks.

I do nothing but nod before stepping past her to Ellie.

She looks a little more refreshed and less pale now, which was a good sign, though she looks two seconds from passing out again.

I help her stand with Dakota on her other side as she leans on me while we walk. We bring her to the spare room and place her on the bed. Dakota tucks her in, and as soon as her head hits the pillow, she's fast asleep, quiet snores coming from her mouth. We sneak out of the room and close the door softly behind us.

Dakota turns to me, her hand curling around mine as she squeezes it. My lips part at the contact as I look down at our joint hands, but her hand retreats as fast as it came.

"Thank you for that. You didn't have to," she mutters.

I shake my head and look back at her. "I don't mind. I'm pretty sure she would have ended up hurting herself at the end."

She giggles, and warmth spreads through my chest at the sound. "From experience, probably."

Her shoulders droop, and it's then that I take her in; the exhaustion set in her face and the hunch in her posture as concern floods through me. A need to take care of her taking over me.

I step toward her, and to my relief, she doesn't pull away. So, I take another chance at my luck, tentatively reaching up to tuck a strand of hair behind her ear. I watch her eyes flutter shut in response, making my heart swell.

My hand drops to hers, her eyes snapping back to me as I nod my head in the direction behind me.

"Come with me."

Her brows furrow as I lead her back to the bathroom. "What are you doing?"

"You're about to fall asleep here, and you just helped your friend who was way too drunk, so I want to do the same for you. I want to take care of you."

She shakes her head, but she still allows me to lead her into the bathroom and sit her on the toilet seat as Ellie did before. "You don't need to. I'm fine."

I kneel in front of her, meeting her gaze with a pointed stare. "But I want to. Please let me."

When the plea passes my lips, her gaze softens as they flick between mine, reading me and feeling the need in them.

I don't know if she's too tired to fight me or if she really is opening up to me when she whispers her agreement. "Okay."

My lips lift as I reach over to the packet of wipes she left on the counter and pull one out. She holds my stare as I reach up, tucking my fingers underneath her chin before taking my other hand to gently drag the wipe over her face, removing her makeup.

She doesn't once remove her eyes from me, even as I finish taking her makeup off and move to stand, grabbing the brush next.

I smile at her, beckoning her up. She stands, moving to stand right in front of me, her back to me, and my breath hitches. I don't know why, because it's right where I wanted her, but maybe it still surprises me at her willingness to be close to me, no snipes or quips.

"You can brush your teeth while I do this," I suggest.

She doesn't say anything, just grabs her toothbrush without question. I didn't realise how bright her eyes had become, but they sparkle under the glow of the bathroom light now as she watches me through the mirror. There's no sign of the exhaustion I saw before, but I ignore it. Ignore the flutter that starts in my chest at the way she looks at me. I don't want to push this too far, especially with how much she has drunk tonight.

It's silent as she brushes her teeth while I focus on her hair. She melts into my arms, and it feels strangely domestic and extremely intimate as I run the brush through the tangles, but I don't want to be anywhere else. Don't want to do this for anyone other than her. I take my time with every strand like it's my day job.

Once we finish, I lead her to her room. She sits on the edge of the bed while I go to her cupboard. I hesitate for a second before quickly pulling a random top and bottoms from it, ignoring the flash of the paper beneath as I shut the drawer.

I lay the clothes beside her and kneel in front of her again as she fiddles with her fingers. She looks up at me, still no signs of that exhaustion, like it's been wiped from her. But I know she must still be tired.

My eyes flick between hers before I weave my fingers between hers, squeezing like she did with me moments ago.

"Good night, Kody."

When I start to pull away to stand, she tightens her hold around my hand, drawing my attention back.

"Wait, I," she pauses, swallowing before continuing, "I don't feel as tired anymore."

My head tilts as I watch her and the nervous energy swirling in those blue eyes before she diverts her attention to our intertwined hands.

"Okay," I reply and then wait for her to tell me what she wants. By the flush in her, I have an inkling, but I wait, wanting her to say it, praying that I wasn't reading her wrong.

"Can you..." she trails off, but then huffs and eyes locking with mine again with purpose, heat flooding them. "I want you to stay."

Both her stare and words almost knock me off my feet as a breath rushes from me.

"Yeah?" I say, gruffly.

"Yeah," she breathes, and I lean a little closer to her.

"And why do you want me to stay?" I ask, teasing her a little.

Her gaze turns pointed. "You know why."

My lips tilt up, moving closer, just inches away from her, feeling her breath ghost over me and breathing life into me. "Do I?"

She huffs. "Don't make me beg."

I lift a brow. "I wouldn't dare." My other hand reaches up to smooth over the outside of her thigh, and her breath hitches at the contact. "It would be me who would be the one to beg." Something flashes in her gaze and I grin at that as my voice deepens, thickening in the lust-filled haze she's entrapped me in. "You'd like that, wouldn't you? Is that what you want? What you need? To see me on my knees and beg? Because I would gladly and happily do that for you."

God, she's fucking beautiful, especially as she watches me with that half-lidded look in her eyes. She leans closer, and then her lips are grazing my ear as she whispers, her own voice thick. "Maybe I do."

I shudder, and she leans back a few inches until she's nose to nose with me, her free hand coming up to touch the side of my face as if holding me close.

"Kody," I draw out her name, groaning as I try to hold onto whatever restraint I could find in me. "How drunk are you?"

"Not at all. The drive home sobered me."

I swallow, taking her face in my hands. "And you want this? Want me?"

She touches her forehead to mine, and god, I feel that connection down to my toes, pumping life into my heart. And then she voices those magical words.

"I don't think I ever stopped."

This raw and desperate need overtakes me when our lips finally meet. Every nerve ending in my body lights with a flame, burning underneath my flesh so fiercely that I forget how to breath. I don't know how I ever functioned without this feeling for so long. Because in this moment, I feel more alive than I have ever felt.

I want to stay like this forever, something I don't fear anymore like I did when I was younger. I'm at her mercy, destined to live a life where she rules my world.

It's just as Ellie said, I did see her as the sole person who created my world. Because she is the one who spread light and colour through my formerly dark and bland world. She reached places in me that I thought were hollow and empty, and filled them with hope and love.

After everything, I was the luckiest god damn person for her to even give me the chance to touch her like this again. To kiss her like this and swallow her whimpers as she kisses me back, just as starved as I was.

I move closer to her, crawling over top of her until she's lying flat on the bed as she digs her nails into my back, pulling me closer. I groan at the feeling, nudging her knees apart with mine so I can fit between them, all while never parting from her lips.

She tasted divine, a mix of peppermint toothpaste and a hint of the sweet drinks she was sipping all night. I want to drown in the taste, drown in the tongue that swirls with mine.

I feel her tilt her hips, rocking against me, sending a jolt of pleasure through my body, and I moan against her lips. I part from them, kissing her cheek, then her jaw, before meeting her eyes.

"Tonight is just about you. Because you may say you're not tired now, but when I'm done with you, you won't be able to keep your eyes open."

Her eyes widen, and she chokes on a breath. I dive into the curve of her neck, kissing her there before lowering down the length until her chest.

"Awfully confident there." The breathy way she speaks brings a smile to my lips as it wars with her incredulous words.

I look up at her, watching her head tip back and eyes close, her chest rising and falling with shallow breaths. I feel the way her heart thunders beneath her chest, every single response from her screams anticipation, and god, I'd spend all my days delivering it to her.

"Very."

I pull away just enough to pull her top over her head, and then I still, breath catching at the absolute beauty of her underneath me. It's utterly mesmerising the way her hair fans around her, her blue eyes hooded and lust-filled, blinking up at me, and her back arching toward me while my hand travels down the side of her body, skimming the side of her breasts, eliciting a shiver from her.

I crawl down the length of her again until my knees hit the floor, and she's sitting up with a curious look. I just grin at her.

"See? You don't even have to ask, and I'd kneel before you. Now lift your hips for me."

Her lips part with a gasp, but she does what I tell her, and I peel her skirt along with her underwear down her legs. My gaze latches onto the glistening lips between her thighs, and my mouth practically waters at the sight.

My eyes meet hers again before I push her down on the bed with a light press on her stomach. "Relax, baby."

I grasp under her knees and pull her to the edge of the bed before my lips immediately latch on to the bundle of nerves that has her arching for me.

I don't go slow, fuck, I feel too starved to go slow on her because the way she writhes against me has me desperate to hear all the noise I can elicit from her mouth. Fuck her friends, I just need her.

I swirl and flick my tongue against her before adding a single finger in her, curling it against her, making her bow off the bed and whimper with restraint, like she's trying to hold in her noises. Fuck, I desperately want to hear those uncontrollable moans, but I know she probably wouldn't want that with the people here, so I let her bite her lip and restrain those noises.

God, now I just want to take her to my hotel or tell everyone to fuck off while I devour her, but I don't think it would be possible to tear my lips from her for long enough.

Because that's exactly what I do, I devour her, pumping my finger into her while flicking my tongue until she's screaming into the palm of her hand, and I feel her pulse around my finger. It makes me wish it was my cock with how tight she squeezed me that I had to readjust myself while I lapped all she gave me.

When I pull out and away from her, she whines, fluttering her eyes open before giving me the most devastating, sated smile.

"You have no idea how beautiful you are right now," I mutter to her, leaning up to kiss her, the taste of her still lingering on my lips.

"Why? Because I'm naked underneath you?" She says, amused as I stand in front of her.

I shake my head. "No. Because of that smile. You could bring me down with that smile and I'd thank you."

Her laugh breaks off with a yawn, and I smirk. She catches it and rolls her eyes. Before whatever comeback can roll off her tongue like I know she's seconds from doing, I hold my hand out to her. She closes her mouth, her eyes bouncing from me to my hand before folding her hand in it.

I pull her up to stand as I tell her, "Let's get you dressed and in bed."

As I unfold the shirt, still neatly placed on the bed next to us, she snatches it from my hands. "I can do it myself."

I bite my lip to tamp down the rising grin as I watch her pull the shirt and shorts on before getting underneath the covers.

I lean down, curling her hair behind her ear and pressing a kiss to her temple before pulling away. She snatches my hand, her brows furrow as she looks up at me.

"Where are you going?" she questions, and I let my grin free.

"I'll be back. I'm just going to check on your friends to make sure they haven't burnt anything."

She pauses, eyes softening as they flick between mine before she squeezes my hand.

"Thank you."

I lean down to press another kiss to her cheek and squeeze her hand back. I don't know what kind of luck I was bestowed with, but I'm thanking my lucky stars that I get to have this with her again.

"Good night, Kody."

23

DAKOTA

I squeeze my eyes shut against the piercing stream of sunlight peaking through the billowing curtains, making my head throb. As I turn to the warm body next to me, I nuzzle my face into his chest, blocking out the light as much as possible while an arm pulls me in tighter.

It takes me a while to piece together where I am and how I got here as the fog of sleep clings to the edges of my brain. Images of the night flash through my mind from the dinner to dancing to almost kissing Reece to...having him put me to bed. To me, curling up to him as he slid back into bed.

My head throbs as I slowly peel my eyes open, a frown creasing between my brows as I come to face a wall of skin I know so familiarly and intimately. The solid muscles under the smooth, soft plains of tanned skin are a lot different from the lean muscles that I remember, but it still brings me, if not more, warmth being in his arms.

He brings a hand up to my face, trailing down the side to tuck a piece of hair behind my ear, and I sigh into his chest.

"Morning," he says, his voice raspy and deep, the sound rumbling his chest where my forehead is pressed.

"Morning," I reply, sleep thickening my voice as I press further into him, making him chuckle and wrap me tighter in his arms.

He tugs a light blanket over us, covering my head and blocking out more sun in the process. It all feels so domesticated and nice until the sleep fades from my brain and I realise who this is and what we are.

I pull away from his hold, rolling onto my back and trying not to make it obvious I'm rolling away from him. His hand disappears from my waist, and he pulls the blanket down until our faces are visible. I peek over at him, meeting his vibrant green eyes swirling with curiosity and a hint of disappointment that tells me he knows exactly why I pulled away, and it wasn't to stretch.

Without the liquid courage and the realisation of our actions last night, all my confusing feelings toward him came to the front. It felt so good to be wrapped in his arms last night and swaying in the middle of the club that everything fell to the wayside. I wanted to feel. But with the morning light, it all came back to me.

I just don't want to jump too fast into the comfort of his arms. It might be a bit late for that line to be put down now with what we did last night, but waking in his arms, curling into him, I just don't know what I should be doing. What are the rules here in this kind of situation? Was it reckless of me to jump right into bed with him? Should I be taking this slow since we dived too deep the last time?

All I know for sure is that I never stopped wanting and waiting for him. Is that enough to forgive and forget? To give this another shot?

He clears his throat, breaking me out of his thoughts as he starts to move to sit up, shoving his shirt over his head and covering the wide span of his back. I see a small glimpse of ink on the left side of his back but it's gone before I can register what it is. He looks over his shoulder at me, bracing himself on the edge of the bed as he smiles, but it doesn't meet his eyes.

"I'm just going to the bathroom. I'll see you downstairs?" he asks quietly, and I feel bad for all this push and pull I keep giving him because I know what it's like being on the receiving end.

"Yeah, I'll see you downstairs," I reply.

He stands and starts to walk toward the door. Before I can stop myself, I call his name, making him halt in the middle of my room.

I can't leave it like this. I don't want to push him away. I don't want to confuse us anymore. I want simple, straightforward, no bullshit. I just want him, if I'm being honest with myself.

So, I sit up and start to shuffle toward the side he just got out of as he turns toward me.

He frowns as he watches me kneel on the edge of the bed, forgetting all about the throb in my head as I move. "What are you—"

"Kiss me. Please," I plead, breaking through the anxious swirling in my stomach and giving in to everything I've been holding myself back from.

His shoulders sag, and then he's right in front of me in a few strides, cupping my face gently as he angles my head back and pressing his lips firmly against mine.

It's bliss, butterflies, and everything I've been chasing for the last six years. I should have known I would never find it anywhere else than right here. In his passion, in his persistence, in his entire soul.

He pulls away too quickly, pressing his forehead against mine before then replacing it with his lips, soft and gentle.

When I open my eyes, he's staring directly at me and smiles, this time it meets his eyes.

"I'll meet you downstairs," he says again, and all I can do is nod before he walks out the door and down the hall.

My jaw starts to ache and I realise how widely I'm smiling. It's uncontrollable and I don't know when the last time I've smiled like this was.

I press my lips flat and scrub my hands over my face, attempting to pull myself together as I crawl out of bed. I pad down stairs to the kitchen, feeling like I'm walking on cloud nine when I stop in the doorway, the sound of popping fills my ears, and the smell of bacon hits my nose.

Looking up, I spot my brother in front of the stove, turning over bacon in the fry pan, before he looks over to me and grins. Me? Well, my stomach drops as shock and panic shoot through my chest.

"Funny seeing you here," he greets and waves me over.

I swallow down the pit forming, letting a smile stretch across my face and indulging in the fact that my brother is here as I race over to him, wrapping my arms around him.

"Hey, Kodaline." He wraps an arm around my head and kisses the top of it while stirring the bacon.

I keep my arm around him as I ask, "What are you doing here? I didn't think I would see you until the wedding."

Shit, how am I going to avoid this interaction between Reece and Nate? I can't just run upstairs and hide Reece in my room, Nate will know something is up. And Reece, I don't know how he will feel with Nate here. Last I heard from Avery, the last time they saw each other was when Nate flew down to confront Reece and punched him. They haven't talked since and I know Nate holds a lot of resentment toward Reece.

He chuckles, taking me away from the panic. "Thought I'd come to surprise everyone."

"Well, surprise you did."

All the questions and thinking about how to escape this makes my head throb in tandem with my heart. I head to the cupboard for the Advil and pour a glass of water, popping two tablets and sipping the water.

I turn back to him, playing it off like it's just a hangover. "Sorry, my brain feels like it might burst out of my head."

He grins. "That's why I've prepared all this. From what I've heard, I knew everyone would be a bit worse for wear this morning."

I shake my head. "I don't even want to know how the others are. They went way harder than me." Especially Ellie.

He snorts and goes back to cooking while I peer over my shoulder at the kitchen doorway, relieved no one is here yet. Maybe I can go upstairs and act as if I'm waking everyone. That'll give me time to warn Reece.

But they take that exact moment to show face, trudging through the kitchen and taking a seat at the bench. Ellie looks like a complete zombie as she shuffles in, still wrapped in a blanket and as pale as ever.

Alex and Avery both greet Nate before shooting me wide glances, knowing they're on the same thought pattern as me.

It all happened so fast, and my brain is trying to catch up with the panic of trying to keep them separate, and now, with apprehension. It was too late to avoid the drama now.

My wide eyes snap to Nate just as Reece appears in the doorway and stops almost abruptly.

Nate looks over my shoulder, smile slowly melting off his face and hardening with every second that passes. His jaw tenses and I chance a look over my shoulder to Reece, a blank expression on his face as his eyes never waver from Nate.

"What the fuck is he doing here?" Nate snaps and I look back at him, his eyes glowering as he glances at me for an answer. But just as I'm about to open my mouth to answer, Reece speaks up.

"Dakota asked me to."

I want to slap my hand against my forehead. Is he stupid?

"Like fuck she would want you anywhere near her after the

shit you pulled," Nate spits, taking a step closer, jabbing a finger toward him.

"I don't want any trouble. But it's been years, Nate. I'm not that person anymore."

"Nah, fuck that. I don't believe you. And no one's answered my question. Why. The fuck. Are you here?"

I step up to stand in front of Nate when I notice him taking another step forward. "Nate, please."

He looks down at me, eyes softening a little, but still anger lingers in them. "What's going on? You told me he was staying at a hotel, staying far away from you as necessary."

I swallow. "He was, but...I told him he could stay here last night."

His eyes narrow. "Why?"

I sigh, shoulders dropping as I explain. "It's been six years, Nate. We've talked, and now we're moving on," I tell him.

"So you've forgiven him? After everything he made you feel?" He scoffs and steps back from me, running his fingers through his hair. I just stand there and watch him as he turns, facing away from me and pulling at his hair.

"Nate, look, I—" Reece tries to explain and calm the situation, but Nate spins and points at him, eyes sharp as stone on him.

"Don't you dare talk to me. Better yet, leave the fucking house. I don't want to talk to you. I don't want to see you."

"Nate, come on. Just let me at least explain—"

"No. You had plenty of time to explain. I gave you chances to explain why you decided it was a good idea to fuck with my sister, but you just stood there in silence. I took you in and gave you a place to go when you had nowhere. I protected you when it came to your dad, like you were my own fucking brother, and in return, you go behind my back with my sister. But I wasn't mad about that because I could see the connection between the two of you when I connected the dots on your birthday. That wasn't the worst of it. The worst was you breaking her heart. Because you didn't just lose her, you lost me and all the trust I had in you that you wouldn't. Now, you want to come back in here and ruin everything again? Think again."

Nate stands there, seething as he stares down Reece, and when I peek over at Reece, my chest caves. His eyes are glassy as he stares back at Nate, a world of pain and grief in his gaze, but the tears don't fall.

"You *were* my brother," Reece whispers.

Nate scoffs, tears welling in his eyes now. "You sure fucking acted like it."

Reece drops his head, shaking it. "I'm sorry."

He walks out of the kitchen, and my heart aches. Before I know it, I'm following after him, calling his name.

"Dakota," Nate calls and I turn to him.

"Just...just wait. I'll be back and I'll explain."

I don't give him time to reply as I turn back and follow Reece up to my room.

When I enter, he's pulling on a shirt and wiping at his eyes. He must hear me at the door because he looks up, his eyes still glistening with unshed tears as he sniffs.

"Reece," I breathe his name and walk toward him, wrapping my arms around his neck. He responds immediately, wrapping his hands around my waist, holding me to him as his face drops to my shoulder. "I'm so sorry. I didn't know he'd be here."

"Please don't apologise. You have nothing to be sorry for," he mumbles into my shoulder before pulling back, meeting my eyes. "But I think I should probably go."

"No. Please, don't. I'll talk to him."

He shakes his head. "It's okay, Kody. I think you guys have a few things to talk about. I'll find another time to talk to him, where it isn't such a surprise to see me. I know I won't be able to talk to him like this. Plus, I have to go back to the hotel anyway."

I press my lips together, wiping my thumb across his cheek, making his eyes flutter. "He can be such a dick."

His lips twitch. "He's just protecting his sister."

He leans down and ghosts his lips over mine. "I'll see you later."

"You'll be back here, right? When I told you to stay, I meant you didn't have to go back to the hotel either."

He pulls back to look at me, a smile forming on his lips. "I'll be back."

A wide smile takes over my face in return, before he kisses me and then grabs a set of keys and walks out the door.

I take a deep breath before going back to the dining room, noticing my friends have made themselves scarce and taken their plates of food with them.

Nate's eyes find mine immediately as I enter, wiping a hand across his mouth. "Explain."

I sigh, slumping into one of the dining chairs as Nate does the same. "I didn't want anything to do with him at first, you know that. But truthfully," I admit, swallowing before continuing. "I never truly got over him, and that's why I came here months early for the wedding. Not only to help with the wedding, but so I could find closure. But with him being here, that threw a spanner in the works. I wanted to ignore him but it's been impossible to. I knew that I needed to talk to him, that it would help heal that wound from the summer. So when we talked, it gave me an understanding of his side and I told him how I felt. And I guess that allowed us to understand and move on from it."

"So you've forgiven him?" Nate probes.

I don't know if I've forgiven him yet. I understand why he did what he did, but I don't agree with how he went about it. I don't agree with how he hid that he was moving away for months, all the while making me fall in love with him. But...I get it. I truly do.

So, I answer, "Not entirely."

"Fuck," he mumbles, folding his arms across his chest and looking up at the ceiling. After a moment, he looks back down. "I'm still so fucking mad at him. I thought I was over it, but seeing him here, it's just brought it all up again."

I smile in understanding. "I know what you mean." It's exactly what I felt.

I don't know how much the break in their friendship affected Nate, but I know how close they were, and I never bothered to ask, too stuck in my own grief to see anyone else's. I refused to bring Reece up or hear his name. But Nate never seemed to mind, and since then, our relationship has only gotten closer, with him becoming much more protective of me, that is.

During the first few months I moved to Melbourne, he called me almost every day to check up on me. It was sweet at first, but then I got frustrated and asked why he was so protective all of a sudden. That's when he told me, "I should have been protecting you from the start. Should have stood up for you much more than I did. With Reece, with Mum. I feel like I've failed as a brother."

My heart broke at that, and I feel like we've clung to each other since then, to be there for each other and make up for all the years we barely knew each other.

I just hope that with Reece being here, it doesn't mess it all up. Because I was just starting to open up to him, and it feels really good to be in this place with him.

Maybe, in time, Nate will understand Reece the same way I do.

24

REECE

Seeing Nate was much harder than I thought it would be.

Just like seeing Dakota again, all those emotions of losing him sucker punched me in the gut when I saw him in the dining room yesterday.

In the short time I got to know him, he became my brother. Someone who took me under his wing and invited me into his home. He saw me in the midst of a breakdown and knew I needed somewhere to feel less lonely. To have someone on my side.

I had lost Dakota at that time, and consequently, Liam as well, all by my own doing when I separated myself from them. I'd already begun to attach myself to Dakota and couldn't allow that to evolve when I found out she was dating him. I was alone, I had no one to confide in, and I could blame no one but myself.

Having Nate swoop in when I was at my lowest felt like some kind of blessing in disguise. No matter how many times I told him to fuck off, he laughed it off and sat beside me like it was just your regular Tuesday evening. I don't even know how he did it, but by the end, he had me shaking my head and calling him a fucking idiot while making me laugh.

He somehow drew me to tell him every single detail of my life from birth to then, and all the fucked up things in my life. Afterward, he pulled me up and brought me to his home to play video games together until it was late at night. It all gave me fucking whiplash, but it worked in distracting me from the panic attack he found me in.

That whole night spun me, though, when she walked through that front door as I was about to leave, her wide, puffy eyes meeting mine as Nate came down and introduced her as his sister. It was like fate intervening, bringing me right back to her again.

That's why I'll always deserve every fucking thing Nate throws at me, because after the kindness he had shown me, I turned around and used it to be close to her again. Used him to see her, pretending to be there for him. Used him so I had an excuse to be around her when I promised to stay away from her and the feelings she brought out in me, even when I never talked to her at that time.

I ignored his warnings when he inevitably noticed my growing feelings for her. He warned me away from getting involved with his sister before he left for Noosa, not wanting me to hurt her. He warned me again after that Airlie Beach trip when I told him I was moving away. But like an idiot, I didn't listen, even though I knew I should have. And then I fell for her, before leaving her torn heart at her feet. Exactly what he warned me not to.

I wasn't surprised when he came down the day before my flight. I was prepared for it because I knew how protective he was of her. So, when I answered the knock at the front door, I wasn't shocked to see him, nor did it shock me when he sent a left hook across my jaw. I didn't stop the two other fists he delivered, one right after the other, before he grabbed me by the collar and hauled me to him so we were nose to nose.

But the words he sneered at me are what still haunt me and clutch at my chest.

I considered you a brother to me and this is how you treat me? I hoped I wasn't right about you. I was trusting you would treat her right, but you're just a big fucking disappointment.

He knew what that last word did to me. How that word reverberated in my head twenty-four-fucking-seven. So, when he let go of me, pushing me away, I collapsed to the ground, my heart caving in as he slammed the door behind me.

That was the last time I saw him.

I would have loved to talk to him earlier and tell him my side, that this wouldn't be like last time. But that's where the Summers siblings are similar: with the shock of my presence so sudden and out of the blue, they retreat into themselves behind their walls, and there's no reasoning beyond that.

So, I take my time packing my things around the hotel room, not sure if it's a good idea to check out of this hotel just yet. I don't know how long Nate is in town for again, and I don't want to create any rifts in the house with my presence.

But...all I can focus on is Dakota's words, her wanting me to be close to her. And there's not a single bone in my body that can resist that request, wanting nothing more than to wake up in the morning and her being the first person I see.

Just as I zip my suitcase, I receive a text from an unknown number, but I immediately know who it is when I read the context.

> I think it's time we talked. Dakota made me promise not to punch you, so you better be on your best behaviour.

My lips twitch at that before I text back.

> Promise. I'll be there in ten.

It feels like the shortest drive I've taken, and I wish it had taken longer as my palms sweat, gripping onto the steering wheel as I exhale slowly. I don't know what to expect from this, but I have so much to say to him that it all feels like it's jumbling in my head, and I can't make sense of it all, never mind putting it into words.

I just have to hope and pray for the best.

I pull Jenna's car up in front of the house and go to pull out the suitcase before thinking better of it and leaving it in the backseat. I don't want to set him off before even starting because I just know if I walk in with my suitcase, he's going to explode with the knowledge that I'm staying here.

When I approach the front door, I hesitate before deciding to knock instead of walking in like I had been the past couple of weeks.

Dakota answers the door with a smirk playing at her lips, and I blow out a slow breath at the sight of her.

"Did you just knock?" she asks incredulously.

I nod once. "I did. I thought it might not be appropriate to look so comfortable to just walk into your house like it was my own."

She mulls over my words before agreeing. "You're probably right. He's a little sensitive right now."

A muffled voice yells back from the direction of the lounge. "I heard that."

Dakota tries to hide her smile as she presses her lips together, and I have the sudden urge to lean down and kiss her, to feel that smile grow against mine, to taste the full extent of the sunshine and sweetness it exudes. But I hold back, especially when my attention strays over to the lounge and I find Nate watching like a hawk from his sprawled position on the couch.

216

I swallow and make my way over to him, feeling Dakota follow close behind.

It's so quiet that the thud of my footsteps is the only thing that reverberates in the mostly empty house as I take a seat in the recliner to his left. His cold gaze tracks me the whole way, but I don't back down from it as I lift my chin before Dakota interrupts.

"Okay, I think that's enough testosterone for me for the year."

But just as she turns to leave, Nate stops her.

"Stay. You're just as involved in this as we are. And if we need to be somewhat civil, then I need you here to explain how you've forgiven him so quickly."

She sighs, shoulders drooping. "Nate, come on."

"No, I want to know, Kods," he pushes, and my eyes narrow at his tone. "Because it has me absolutely baffled when all I remember is hearing you sobbing over the phone, and I couldn't do anything to help you. All because of him. So tell me."

I see her wince, and I feel it deep in my chest, especially at the mention of her sobbing on the phone. I don't want her here if she doesn't want to, if she's uncomfortable. We've relived the past between us for long enough.

"Maybe we should leave her out of this," I begin to say, but then he turns his glare back on me.

"I didn't ask for your opinion."

My head snaps back before a scowl makes its way on my face.

"You better watch your fucking mouth. This may have started with her and the reason you hate me so much, but she does not have to be in the middle of this now. This is between you and me."

With his glare locked on me, he begins to stand from the

couch, taking a step toward me, and I tense, readying myself for the inevitable connection of his fist against my face.

But then Dakota steps in front, pushing him back as he stumbles back into the couch, and his wide eyes meet hers. Not going to lie, that shocks me too. Turns me on a little as well, seeing her stern face directed at her brother, protecting me against him.

"Will you stop acting like such an alpha male?" she snaps. "People change, Nate. It's been six years. I can't hold it against him for chasing his dreams. Especially because you know the relationship he had with his dad."

I flinch a little at the mention of my dad, but then she looks back at me, and I fall a little under her spell when she sends me a small, apologetic smile. A smile just for me. A smile I want to pluck and stuff into the depths of my heart where only she belongs.

I look back at Nate, who stares at Dakota for a moment, processing her words before meeting my gaze again.

He crosses his arms over his chest, appearing to look bigger to most likely intimidate me, but I sink deeper into the recliner, relaxed and not at all phased. I'll take whatever he has to deliver.

"What are your intentions being here? Apart from the wedding."

"Nate," Dakota berates.

"What?" He shrugs. "I'm asking a genuine question. I don't want you to get fucked over again. Especially not by him."

"I've got no other intentions other than trying to fix everything I've broken. I thought I owed that to Dakota first because, like you said, I fucked her over and she deserves more than that."

Nate nods, then stares straight into my eyes. "And what about me?"

"You were second on my list."

"I feel honoured," he says, faux appreciation entering his tone, but keeping a straight face, making my lips twitch in reaction.

"You should be."

He rolls his eyes. "So, how are you going to fix it? Your words don't mean shit to me, so don't think just an apology will suffice."

I nod, knowing he's right. "I know. But it's a start, right? I want to earn back your trust. Most of all, I want my best friend back. I want to do this right this time."

"What do you mean 'do this right'?"

My eyes shoot to Dakota's on instinct. I take in every inch of her face. Every little detail that I've loved and dreamed of for the last six years, even beyond that.

My eyes transfix on the way her lips part as I punctuate the one word. "Everything."

I want everything she has to offer to me. I want every little thing that I've missed over the years. I just want her.

Nate scoffs. "Fuck off."

I look over at him again. "I'm serious. I fucked up six years ago. I self-sabotaged because I didn't deserve the good you guys brought into my life, only to realise how much I lost by doing so. I spent the last six years losing myself in that regret and self-deprecation, before realising my mistakes and working through everything, making sure that when I did ask for your forgiveness, it would be worth it."

I pause in my speech as I let him process before I continue. "You were my brother. But she meant everything to me before we became friends. And though I would love for you to forgive me and have you trust me again, you should know I've never stopped loving your sister since the evening I met her by the river. All I want is a chance to be hers again. And ultimately, it is her choice, but I want your support too because I respect you. I know I won't get it right away, and I don't expect it to be easy, but I just want you to know that."

I meet her glassy eyes again while aiming my words toward Nate, still, but wanting her to hear the conviction in my voice as I take a shuddering breath. "She is the reason I breathe. She's the reason my dreams have come true. And I've loved her since the day I met her."

I don't take my eyes away from her, even as a tear stains a line down my cheek, a racing match against the ones streaking down hers, before she lightly dabs under her eyes to not smudge her makeup.

Nate clears his throat, making my attention snap back to him.

"You still haven't apologised."

I almost grin at that, but I hold his gaze as I tell him. "I'm sorry. I'm so fucking sorry, man. I broke your trust, and I had no intention to hurt anyone like I did. I just got scared, and I know that's no excuse, but there were too many things changing around me. I was scared that I was losing everything that I just ran before I could get hurt. I never had anyone care for me like you two did." I swallowed before lowering my voice on the last sentence. "I didn't want to ruin anyone else's life."

Silently, he sat there, watching me through narrowed slits and arms still tightly crossed over his chest, as if trying to pick up even the slightest hint that I was lying to him. But not a single thing that poured from my mouth was a lie. I just hope it didn't frighten her in response.

I didn't mean for this to be where I told her that I loved her; it kind of just tumbled out, but I also needed Nate to know that I was serious about coming back into their lives.

Fuck, that was the first time I'd said those words to her. To anyone, for that matter. They had been on the tip of my tongue when I took her on that date around the city six years ago, but that had been when my fight-or-flight kicked in and I had been scared off by the vulnerability of those words.

But not now. I'm not scared of those words anymore when it comes to her. Not when they have run so deep for the last six years that they've ingrained so deep in my beliefs.

"I don't trust you," he says after a while, not budging an inch.

"I don't expect you to."

"I'll be watching you closely, breathing down your neck if even your pinky steps over the line."

My lips twitch. "I expect nothing less."

He leans forward in his seat toward me. "Even if I'm hundreds of kilometres away, I'll hunt you down if I even receive one phone call from her crying because you hurt her again."

"I think he gets it, Nate," Dakota interrupts exasperatedly.

He shrugs, leaning back again. "Just making sure. I don't want to be put in that position again. It fucking killed me hearing you like that over the phone. It still haunts me."

A sharp pain shoots through my chest as he admits that. "I will do my best to make sure that doesn't happen again. I want the absolute opposite of that."

He points to me. "You better."

I draw a cross over my heart, and a hint of a smile peeks from his lips, making the tension in my shoulders ease a little at the reaction.

His gaze flicks between us before he audibly sighs and walks away from us. I frown, but before I can ask where he was going, he tosses over his shoulder, "I need a drink. I'll be back later, have some friends to see."

The front door closes behind him, and silence stretches through the house. I turn back to Dakota, the dried tear streaks on her face, making me want to reach over and wipe them away. But I hold myself back, waiting for her to break the silence, because I'm afraid that if I do, I'll just pounce on her, and after the admission I just spoke, I wanted to ease into this.

"Do you really mean what you said?" she asks, her voice quiet, and I have to ask her to repeat what she said to hear her, making her finally meet my eyes.

When she does, I take my chances, unable to resist as I stand, stepping up to her. I tuck a stray strand of hair behind her ear once I'm close enough, cupping her jaw as my eyes bounce between her ocean blue ones. God, they're the most gorgeous eyes I've ever had the pleasure of looking upon. My favourite colour to drown in, my favourite place to escape in, and my favourite vision to dream of.

"I mean. Every. Single. Word," I tell her, punctuating every word.

She reaches up, wrapping her hand around my wrist, the one that caresses her cheek, to hold it there as she leans into it.

"Tell me again," she demands in a whisper.

Slowly, I release a breath, taking a step closer like I can't get close enough. Toe to toe, chest to chest.

"I love you."

She closes her eyes as two tears race down her cheeks out of each eye, and I reach my other hand up to swipe them away as panic rises to my throat.

"I really hope these are happy tears. Was it too much? Should I have waited? Fuck, I'm sorry."

She shakes her head, opening her eyes again, flicking between my own as she clasps onto my other arm. "No. No, it wasn't too much. It's just..." she pulls her lip between her teeth before continuing, "I prayed to hear those words coming from your mouth before you left. I dreamt of them months later. And now, hearing them now..." She swallows before ending in a whisper, "I just don't want to be hurt again."

I rest my forehead against hers, closing my eyes and breathing her in. "I know. And I don't expect you to say anything right now. I want to earn those words from you. I'm bound to fuck up somewhere, but I will never hurt you. Never again. I am all in on this. On us."

She pulls my hands away from her face, intertwining them and holding them between us. Her gaze holds mine as we hold each other like that, breathing in each other's air, and slowly, I feel that bit of peace seep back into my heart.

Her eyes seem to darken before she starts pulling me to follow her, and my brows crease.

"Where are we going?" I question.

Over her shoulder, she says, "I need you."

And when I see the heat and longing swirling in those ocean depths of hers, my cock instantly stirs to life, and I'm suddenly all too eager to let her drag me anywhere as long as I get to have her.

25

REECE

We don't quite make it out of the lounge when I break out of my trance. I pounce on her, too eager to have her in my arms as I scoop her in, spinning her around and pinning her against the wall.

She looks up at me, and I feel entranced, fixated on the fact that she's looking at me, not with hurt or disdain, but with desire. Like I'm the only one who can help satiate her. Like this is all she needs, right here with me.

We stand here, her in my arms, watching each other for a time that felt like minutes, but could have extended to hours as time seemed not to even exist in this moment. It was just me and Dakota. Us—intertwined. Us—colliding, like we were meant to happen this way.

She makes the first move, reaching up to touch my cheek, which I subconsciously lean into, drawn in by her. I can't stop myself from exploring with my hands at her waist, travelling up. I hesitate, though, not wanting to fuck up. Which seems like a ridiculous thought when I ate her out only two nights ago, but still, I don't want to overstep and scare her away when I have her here, where I've craved for her to be.

"Is this okay?" I whisper.

She nods before verbalising her answer in a whisper, "Yes."

She tilts her head up, and I take her nonverbal cue, slowly dropping my forehead against hers again. Just like moments before, I breathe her in, the vanilla of her hair and the floral fragrance of her perfume, feeling her beneath my fingertips as they rest on her ribcage, barely touching the underside of her breasts.

Her fingers dance over my right shoulder as her other hand that holds my face leaves, following the same path to wrap around my neck, raking her nails through my hair. I almost groan at the sensation, closing my eyes as her touch sends prickles of pleasure through my whole body.

"All I wanted was for you to trust me to love you. I wanted it so bad when we were younger." Her voice is breathy as her lips brush over mine.

"I know. And I know it may take a while for you to trust me again, but I will wait forever for you if I have to. This won't be like when we were younger because there's not a single ounce of fear in me now. Not when it comes to you. I will be here, loving you, bleeding for you every day for the rest of my life. Even the space between us over the last six years didn't stop me from doing just that. And I'll wait, if and when you're ready to give me your heart in return."

I open my eyes to look at her again as she does the same. The usual light blue of her eyes deepens with the lust and longing swirling in them.

"I have always been yours, Kody. Always. No amount of time or space diminished that."

She moves closer, arching her back so her body presses into mine, and it feels so fucking good and right, like the perfect fit.

"Can you say it one more time?" she whispers, lips grazing mine, and my knees almost buckle with the feeling, teasing me with just a taste of her lips.

And I know exactly what she wants. My lips move against hers as the words form, teasing her back as my tongue brushes her top lip. "I love you."

As soon as the words come out, her lips meet mine in a bruising kiss.

I make a promise to myself that I'll tell her a million times a day if this is the way she kisses me.

I meet her kiss just as urgently, the years of yearning, grieving, and missing her pouring out. Her nails rake against my scalp and I finally let out that groan I wanted to earlier.

I part her lips with my tongue as I push her flush against the wall, every inch of my body pressed to hers, earning me a whimper from her. When her tongue meets mine, I feel it all the way down to my toes.

My hands start to drift, my right travelling down over her hip to hook her thigh while my left curves around her side, pulling her further into me. She responds to me, hooking her leg around my ass, pulling me against her, making my dick rest right at the spot between her thighs. I'm already hard as fuck and when I roll into her, we sigh in sync at the feeling.

My lips leave hers to trail across her jaw, under her ear, and down the slope of her neck. All I hear are her pants, and god, does it sound heavenly to me.

"I've missed this feeling. Having you in my arms. Being able to touch you. You don't know how much I've restrained myself over these past months to keep my hands to myself."

She whimpers and then rocks against me, seeking the friction that both of us need. I curse under my breath, my eyes falling to watch her continue to meet my thrusts, both of us turning into horny teenagers dry fucking each other in the middle of the hallway. And I couldn't care less, I just wanted—needed—more of her.

The thin straps of her dress have fallen from her shoulders, and the vision, her hair and clothes disarray as she grinds on me, drives me fucking wild. I drag my lips across her chest, peppering kisses as her nails scrape against my scalp, sending shivers down my spine.

"Reece," she breathes my name, and it sounds like a prayer falling from her lips. But it should be me praying to her, worshiping her as the only religion I know.

So I do just that.

Slowly, I descend to my knees, keeping my eyes locked on her, watching the way her pupils dilate. A grin tilts the side of my mouth.

"Is this okay?" I question, letting my fingers graze the outsides of her calves, and her shoulders shake with a shiver.

I can still taste the remnants of her from the night before, and it only makes me starving for more, eager to die a happy man between her thighs, just to hear the noises she makes, like symphonies in my ear.

She nods aggressively, fingers gripping onto the shelves behind her. "Please, I need you."

"You need me, huh?" My fingers reach her thighs, and she lets out a sigh, tilting her head back. "Uh-uh. Eyes on me, baby. I want you to watch everything I'm about to do to you."

She whimpers but obliges, lifting her head again and dropping her gaze to me, hooded and feral. Exactly how I feel.

My fingers keep tracing a path up the outside of her thighs before I introduce my lips to her skin as well, leaving a trail of kisses to the inside of her right thigh before doing the same to her left. She squirms the more I tease her, letting loose a whimper when my nose grazes just beside the dampness gathering on her panties.

I snigger at her response before dragging my teeth over her hip. At the feeling, her wide eyes meet mine, before I tug the fabric of her panties between my teeth to her mid-thigh and hook my fingers in them, pulling down the rest of the way.

Does it make me evil that I enjoy teasing her? Having her unravel at my hands, all too eager just to have me? Probably.

But Dakota, with her eyes set on mine, her chest heaving in anticipation, her dress bunched to her waist, and her leg wrapped around me, ready for me to worship and devour her like I was made for this, is a sight to see. And maybe I am made solely for this. Maybe I am just made for anything when it comes to her. And her pleasure is high on my list at this moment.

I send her a devilish grin before I lean in, letting my mouth just barely touch her, so she could only feel my breath. She whines at the feeling, hips seeking to meet my lips, but I pull away.

"Reece, please," she pleads, her hand finding my hair, nails scraping my scalp in a way I'm learning I love. She clasps my hair before arching her hips to bring me close to her. And because I can never resist her for very long, if ever, I give her what she needs, my lips covering her clit, making her buck into me. I groan at the same time she blesses me with a deep moan.

I hold her against me, her weight almost entirely supported by me, as I grab her ass. She makes these little movements, grinding against my face, and it unravels me as I moan against her.

"Fuck, that's it. Ride my face, Kody."

She moans again, her head hitting the cupboard as she closes her eyes. "When did you get so vocal?"

I run my tongue over her, lifting a brow. "It's been a long time, Kody. Maybe your mind was clouded while I was fucking you but I was vocal then."

She shakes her head. "Maybe, but it's different."

I stop and look at her. "Do you not like it?"

Again, she shakes her head, this time more vigorously. "God, yes. Please do not stop talking."

I grin. "Good to know. Now, look at me. Don't take your eyes off me."

She listens, and then my mouth is back on her, continuing to work her, watching how she responds to every flick and swirl, listening to the symphony of whimpers and moans falling from her lips. It's almost fucking torture how hard those noises and the taste of her are making me, but I resist the urge to palm myself to ease the ache.

When I insert a finger and curl it against her, her back instantly bows, and I can't help but grin against her. It's when her moans start to quiet that I speed up, knowing she's so close, tightening around my fingers as I fuck her with them.

She quivers, and I watch the devastating view of her falling apart under my tongue as she releases a strangled noise as she tries to keep quiet. And fuck, this is the most beautiful sight that I've seen.

With one final swipe of my tongue, I pull back, slowly slipping my fingers from her, and because I can't help myself, I suck her taste off my fingers as she watches me under a heavy-lidded gaze. I smirk up at her as she slumps against the wall behind her, and I carefully unwrap her leg and stand to hold her in my arms.

I can feel her heart pounding against her chest as she leans into me, and if this is all I will have of her, all she will let me have, I will gladly lay myself at her feet.

I am nothing, if not hers.

Always.

26

DAKOTA

He loved me.

That would have been an inconceivable notion at one point in my life. Hell, two months ago it would have. But hearing them now, after wanting to have heard them so many years ago, filled me with mixed feelings.

After everything that I've seen and the ways he's shown me he has changed, I know the man he is now is much different from the boy I fell for when I was younger. I still get glimpses of the old him in the way he teases and jokes around, the tender way he touches me and looks at me, it's all the same. But the way he speaks so openly of his feelings and the way he's always right beside me when I need him fills that previously empty space in my heart that he created. It's the way he acts like he has no intention of ever leaving my side that reassures a part of me that's preparing for him to run away.

How everything has changed in the short span of two months is crazy. I hate to admit how right Callie was in the session we had before I left. She told me three months was a long time for things to change, and look where I am now.

Back then, I feared walking through the ghosts of my

memories that I wanted nothing more than to smother and die. I feared the possibility of running into him because of the close relations with Avery dating Jake, and the end of the baseball season lining up with me being here. My wild imagination conjured so many scenarios of bumping into him with them. I knew it wouldn't happen, I knew Avery would tell me if he were to be there. But I never pictured bumping into him in my own home.

I tried so hard to ignore him and hate him, just as I had successfully done for the last six years, but I should have known that would be hard to do. It had always been hard to ignore his presence, an all-consuming entity that draws me in. And though I fought it at the start, there wasn't a resistant bone in my body now. I was a willing captive in his hold.

But a tiny part of me still wondered how long this would last. Because when things felt like it was good between us, something always broke that spell. It was like we were too good to be true. That it was some kind of fantasy to dream that we were meant to be. And after shielding a part of my heart for so long to now slowly letting him into that place again, I feared it would slip out of reach again.

But today was my birthday, and I didn't want to think about what the future would or wouldn't hold. I didn't want to think about the fear that still held onto my heart.

I wake to consecutive knocks on my door, and drowsily, I call for them to enter, thinking it was Dad or Nate.

I was wrong, though. The door squeaks open as I peel my eyes open to see Reece stroll in with a tray in his grasp and a beaming smile.

I sit up immediately, yawning and wiping the sleep from my eyes before blinking them open.

"Morning," he greets, his vibrant green eyes meeting mine as he sets the tray on the space next to my right hip before he sits behind.

It's then that I notice the contents on the tray, the aroma hitting me at once. It's an array of scrambled eggs, bacon, and toast with a cup of coffee steaming beside the plate. My eyes then drift to the small cup-slash-make-shift vase with a single white lily placed in it.

My attention drifts up to him as he starts to talk. "There's a whole bouquet for you downstairs, but I thought I would wait until you woke to give them to you. Then I got impatient and decided to make this for you."

I choke out a laugh before reaching over to check my phone. A few messages pop up on the screen, but I ignore them for now, focusing on the time.

My wide eyes meet his again. "It's seven-thirty."

He sheepishly grins. "Yeah."

"How long have you been up waiting?"

He rubs the back of his neck as he looks away. "I may have woken up around five this morning. Went to the store to grab all this."

"Reece," I breathe his name, and he snaps his eyes back to me, softening as they bounce between mine. "You didn't have to do that. But thank you."

"Happy birthday, Kody," he says softly, and I feel myself slowly melt and mould to fit into the palm of his hand. Right where he had me all those years ago.

My smile is soft as I lean toward him, grabbing onto the collar of his shirt to pull him closer. He gets the message, carefully leaning over the tray of food to reach me.

When I brush my lips to his, it's soft and gentle and everything that makes my heart beat faster for something that only lasts for a short caress. He pulls away slowly, reluctantly, and rests his forehead against mine.

"You should eat breakfast before it gets cold," he murmurs and starts to pull away, but I pull him in again, pressing my lips against his again in a desperate plea for more.

232

He chuckles against my lips but doesn't deny me the pleasure as he teases my lips with his tongue. I gladly welcome it, opening for him and tangling mine with his, tasting the peppermint on his tongue. It's a mix of tenderness, longing, and so much love, both spoken and unspoken. It's an intimacy that I've lacked for the last six years and haven't allowed myself to indulge in.

But with him, it comes so naturally.

He stops again, chest heaving as he meets my gaze and grins. "Eat."

And this time, when he pulls away, I reluctantly let him, tucking my hands underneath my thighs.

I look down at the food, my stomach grumbling at the wide aroma assaulting me.

He lingers by the door, turning back to me. "I'll come back for you once you're finished for our date."

I lift a brow, chewing and swallowing the bite of scrambled eggs I took. "Date?"

He beams then and taps a finger on the wall. "Yeah, Kody. A date."

My smile is uncontrolled as I watch him. "Okay."

He nods, drumming his fingers on the door frame before turning to leave. "I'll see you soon."

"Wait," I call, and he stops and turns back, "why are you leaving? You don't have to go."

Even from a distance, I can see the way his pupils darken. "If I stay, I won't be able to keep my hands off you, and you won't eat."

My breath hitches. "Oh."

He smirks. "Yeah. Oh. I promise I'll be back."

Then he disappears down the hall, and I press my hands to my cheeks, feeling the heat gathering there, like I'm eighteen again with the butterflies running rampant in my stomach around him.

Once I've eaten and changed out of my pyjamas into a mid-length white skirt and a baby blue corset-style top, I meet Reece downstairs.

He's sprawled casually across the lounge, an arm spread across the back while he scrolls through his phone, a pair of sunglasses sitting on top of his head, looking like he just walked out of a photoshoot. With his linen shirt thrown over his shoulders, the top buttons undone, and cream shorts hugging his thighs as he rests one ankle over his knee, I itch to take a photo of him just like this. But with my phone's crappy quality, I know it won't properly depict every detail that I want pictured and my camera is back in my room.

He looks up as I round the couch, and his lips start to rise before falling as his eyes roam down my body.

I swallow under his unwavering attention and shift. "I wasn't sure what to wear. You never really said what to prepare for."

He stands and makes his way to me, his hand coming to rest on my upper arms as his eyes pierce mine. "You look beautiful. I'm a very big fan of this fit."

"Yeah?"

"Hell yeah. Don't worry, this is the perfect outfit for what I have planned."

My cheeks ache from how wide I smile. "Good."

"Just make sure to bring your camera."

"My camera?"

He smiles softly down at me, tucking a strand of hair behind my ear. "Yeah. I want to remember this day for years to come and for it to come through your eyes."

I press my lips together to tamp down my aching grin. "I'll go grab it then."

I race upstairs to my camera bag and pull out the camera before hanging it around my neck.

When I meet him back downstairs, he's leaning by the front door with his hands in his pockets as he looks up at me. I can't help it then, I power on the camera and hold it up to my face. I watch a grin spread across his lips through the lens and the camera shutters as I capture that moment.

Lowering the camera, he rolls his eyes, but I notice the colour change in his cheeks.

"Come on. We don't want to be late."

My lips tilt up, but I climb down the stairs as he leads me out the door with a hand ghosting over the small of my back. He opens the door to the car for me, and I hop in before he rounds to the driver's side.

Driving down the street, I don't bother to ask where we are heading, welcoming the surprise he has planned.

It makes me feel a little special, after spending the last five birthdays by myself before getting a call from my parents and Nate, as well as Avery and Alex. Ellie and Daniel took me out for my nineteenth, but after that, I refused. Because my birthday never quite felt the same. It lost its spark like everything else, until I found my own little tradition for myself.

It's something I've never told or shown anyone. Every year, I pull out a box I keep hidden under my bed, a time capsule of sorts. I would place a photo and a letter I wrote from that year, shove it into that box, and never read it again. I guess that's why I forgot about that letter I wrote about him, because it was lost in the pile of the other letters I wrote, and they all blended together.

My therapist had recommended it, but she also told me to read them every year. I never did. Just like the letter I wrote before I moved to Melbourne, they all got stuffed into the box and ignored.

Except for when I started to get distracted while packing to come here. Then I read all the letters until I got to that one.

The raw emotions that bled onto that piece of paper still haunt me.

But when I look over to Reece, the subject of that letter and subsequently all the goals that were printed in the ones following, I realise I was never going to get that part of me back because it was always and forever meant for him. Always and forever belonging to him.

He glances over at me, lips curving when he sees my attention already on him before his hand reaches over to rest on my mid-thigh, fingers curling between.

We're in the car for a while, and I know the direction that he's heading, but still, the destination unknown. But I enjoy the ride as I wind down the window, the salt in the air becoming more potent until the vast horizon of water becomes visible. The music becomes a peaceful lull until a song catches our attention enough for us to start singing along.

The day hasn't even started, and this is quickly becoming one of my favourite birthdays.

It's about twenty minutes later before he pulls into a mini-golf place along the water.

I look over to him and he smiles. "Ready for me to kick your ass?"

I lift a brow, the competitive side coming out automatically. "You wish."

His smile widens to a grin, and I follow him into the course.

It's easy to fit back into the easy banter that came so naturally between us. In these types of situations, that is, where there was no real talk or deep topics, just our competitive natures and pushing each other's buttons.

And that's how the next hour went as we tried to sabotage each other's game. Still, as I predicted, I won. But I knew it was because he let me. There were a few shots he fluked that were easy, and when I pin him with a disbelieving look, he would innocently shrug and nod for me to take my turn.

We return our putters, laughing as we walk out of the building, as I try to tell him how I know he let me win, though he keeps denying it.

"You are so annoying," I say while laughing.

His grin is so wide that I'm sure it matches my own. "What can I say? I love getting under your skin."

"I don't think you need to try that hard to do just that."

His smile fades a little as he meets my eyes. "And what does that mean?"

I look away, frowning as I try to tamp down what I want to say, but they force themselves past my lips. "You're already so ingrained in my skin, like a tattoo on my soul."

He stops me with a hand holding my wrist while his other gently grabs my chin to pull my face to his. He stops when our noses are just mere centimetres from each other.

"And you are in mine. There isn't a moment that I don't feel the grooves you've wedged in my heart."

Then, he covers his lips over mine, and I sink into the warmth that seeps through the scars of my heart.

When he pulls away, he cradles my face between his hands, and I don't think I've been handled with such gentleness. Not a single time in the years I tried to replace the feel of his hands. He'd always had the most gentle touch around me, whether to hold my hand or, as he was now, holding my face like it was the most precious to him.

"I have another surprise for you," he tells me.

"You do?" I wrap my hands around his forearms as if to hold him there while I peer up at him.

He nods. "Yeah. Come on. We'd better leave now or we'll be late."

We drive away from the coastal views and back to the city. Golden rays of what's left of the setting sun disappear behind buildings and pierce through the car's window while the sky darkens behind us, swirling in a mix of pinks and purples. And Reece, well, he never untangles our intertwined hands the whole drive. Even when he has to shift gears, he takes my hand, guiding my hand with the motions.

Arriving home, he pulls up in the driveway, where I notice my friends and Dad's car parked on the street and the spare space in the driveway.

I look over at him expectantly, wanting to know what secret he has stored. But he just smiles and hops out of the car. He rounds the front to my side and opens the door for me, offering a hand to help me out, which I take.

He walks me to the front door of the house with a hand pressed against my lower back, but I stop him as he reaches for the door, wanting just one more moment alone with him before being swamped by my family and friends.

I pull his lips down to mine again, breathing him in as his hand lands on my waist, drawing me in closer, reading into exactly what I need without saying anything. I kiss him and all those little sparks that lay dormant come alive again, buzzing under every inch of skin he touches. A fuse to every nerve ending in my body.

I'm the one to pull away this time, and he chases the feel of my lips, stepping closer to me as I fall back into the door frame, snickering at his antics as he presses his forehead to mine.

"I can't get enough of you," he whispers a hairsbreadth away from my lips, his eyes closed, and I almost give in to another taste. "Can you be addicted to the way someone tastes? Because I'm sure I am."

A banging against the window beside us has us pulling apart, before a peel of muffled laughter ensues and I roll my eyes at the obvious sound of my friends' voices.

Then Dad opens the door, narrowing his eyes at our position, making Reece immediately take two steps away, clearing his throat as he meets Dad's watchful gaze.

Dad flicks his gaze to me, nodding in the direction of the kitchen. "Hurry up and get inside, your dinner is going cold."

Before he turns away, though, he sends me a quick wink, leaving the door open as he disappears through the kitchen.

I look at Reece, who peers down at me, a rising smirk on his lips as he laces our fingers together again. "You're a bad influence, Summers."

I grin. "Didn't you know? Only the bad can be influenced, Fischer."

He throws his head back in a laugh as we join everyone at the dining table.

My friends immediately wrap me in their arms, separating Reece from me as they wish me happy birthday. When I catch his gaze over Ellie's shoulder, I mouth an apology to him. But all he does is smile as he watches me interact with them. Not quite so much when Daniel hugs me, though.

We sit around the table, and Reece manages to snag the seat beside me as we do, looking triumphant as he does.

Dad serves the dinner and the conversation buzzing around the table bounces from our day to the wedding. I can't help but keep glancing at Reece throughout the whole dinner, watching as my family and friends interact with him like he just slips so easily into our lives. Like he never left and has always been a part of this family all along.

It makes my heart beat a little faster thinking about how this is my life. That this was how it was always meant to be, with him here next to me, caressing my hand with sweeping motions of his thumb. How he looks at me like this might be where he was meant to be as well.

Even when we were younger, he fit so effortlessly into this family. With my brother, with my friends, with the little communication he had with my dad. It's all I've ever needed.

All I've yearned for these last six years. And I have it, right here, right now. I don't think my heart has ever felt as full as it is now.

When we finish eating, they pass around my gifts and I open them one by one, thanking each of them as I do. Reece rests his arm on the back of my chair as I do, twisting strands of hair around his finger. I notice Alex and Avery watching this happen before sharing secretive smiles. Daniel and Ellie, though, look at me in confusion, but they don't say anything.

Reece digs into his pocket, pulling out a small box before passing it to me, locking eyes with me as he does. "For you."

I take the box from him, flipping it open to reveal a small necklace with a star pendant. There's a black circle in the middle of it and I know immediately what it is. When I look back at Reece, he smiles, nodding down at the necklace.

"Take a look. Hold it up to your eyes and look through it." He points to it and I immediately do so.

What I see takes my breath away. It's the photo he snapped of us in Airlie Beach. When he stole my camera and went crazy photographing everything around us.

He leans in then, whispering for only me to hear. "I've had this for years. I was meant to give it to you on our date, but we know how I screwed that one up. So I held onto it, and now, it's yours."

He pulls away slightly to meet my gaze and my heart skips once, twice, as I hold the necklace to my chest.

"I love it. Thank you."

He smiles before twirling his finger. "Spin. I'll put it on for you."

I hand him the necklace before turning, facing Avery, who sits beside me. She lifts a brow, a small smirk on her face as Reece reaches around, resting the pendant on my chest before clasping it at the back of my neck while I hold my hair away.

I blush as I look at her, but I think she must see the turmoil flickering in my gaze, no matter how much I try to push my thoughts away, because her head tilts. But I focus back on the rest of the gifts before she can say anything.

Once I receive all their gifts, I pack everything up as Avery offers to clean up. That's when she meets my gaze, piercing straight into me. "Can we talk? In private?"

I nod, frowning a little at what she would want to talk about. "Of course."

I look over to Reece, who smiles and kisses my cheek before whispering in my ear. "I just have to talk to Jenna. I'll see you soon."

He walks away, and I trail after Avery as she brings the stack of dishes to the sink.

She turns the water on, letting it fill the bottom of the sink and drown the continuing chatter in the dining room before she spins to look at me, analysing me as her gaze roams my face. Then she cocks her head.

"You look happier," she states her observations, and my brows crease.

"Thank you?" I don't mean for it to but it comes out as a question, emotions warring with each other in my head.

"I just mean, I haven't seen you look like this in a long while, only for a rare second when you're behind the camera," she pauses as a slight tilt of her lips grows. "It's him, isn't it?"

"What do you mean?"

She tsks. "Don't play dumb. I mean, I already know. It's hard not to see how close you guys were outside. Even before then, it was noticeable."

"Before tonight? Nothing was going on before tonight," I tell her. But it's not quite true, is it? I mean, look at us at the bachelor party, and that was only a week ago.

"I saw you guys at the farmers' market a while ago. I was far away from you guys and didn't want to interrupt, but I could just tell there was something there. I mean, there always was, wasn't there? It's why you never wanted us to mention a word about him. Why you never wanted to come back. Why any date you forced yourself on or one we tried to set you up with never worked. There was always a piece of you that was his."

Tears blur my vision as I turn my head away, blinking them back before they have a chance to fall.

"You're way too observant, Avery."

I see her shrug in my peripheral vision. "It's why I'm good at my job. It's why I'm such a good friend to you. Because I can tell when you need me."

I look at her again, and she smiles softly before reaching for my hand to squeeze.

"So, ask me what I know is floating in that head of yours and I'll tell you straight," she coaches.

I shake my head, letting out a huff of a laugh. She really is good at her job.

But I feel she is the only one who can answer this honestly for me. Because no one else has seen it from all sides but her. Because she is the only one with all the answers.

I sigh. "Am I crazy for falling into this again? You saw us together a few times when we were younger. You saw the damage we made. You even saw both of us in the years after everything. Is it too good to be true? Or will I just be chasing something out of reach again?"

She doesn't say anything for a moment, just holds my hand tightly in hers as she watches me.

Then she says, "Girl, that boy has been so head over heels gone for you the second you guys met." She chortles. "He never stopped asking about you every time we saw him, and I had the great pleasure of denying him that information all these years, because I knew you wouldn't want that. But that didn't stop him from asking every chance he got. I think you guys have put yourselves through enough misery and mistakes to deny this. Because I do believe he's honestly a hundred percent about you and will do everything for you. To be with you. To make you happy. To make sure he doesn't let you slip through his fingers again."

I feel a wet drop trail down my cheek, and I quickly wipe it away, sniffling and blinking back the rest before they can fall. It's the answer I wanted and the reassurance I needed, filling my chest with relief.

"But what about the distance? Is that not going to factor once again in how this thing between us will go?"

She chews on her lip, her gaze flicking between mine with so much conflict. "That's the one question I can't answer for you. That, you should ask Reece."

I squeeze her hand. "But you know something?"

She steps closer, staring straight at me. "I don't know everything going on. Which is why you need to ask Reece."

My gaze flicks between hers, as if I could see some kind of answer in them. But then, I hear footsteps behind us, and her hand slips from mine as she busies herself with the dishes.

A hand ghosts down the side of my arm, and I turn my head over my shoulder, seeing Reece.

"Everything okay?" he asks, eyes bouncing between mine.

All the questions fall to the back of my mind when he steps closer to me, hand brushing the short strands back off my shoulder.

"Yeah, everything's okay," I reassure him.

But I'm not sure if it's for him or for me.

Because just as I thought all my questions were answered, more resurface.

27

DAKOTA

The beige-toned material of the dress I wore was light in weight, as it clung to my chest and waist before falling loosely to my shins. But it did nothing to relieve the heat sinking into my skin as the warm breeze kissed my skin. I thought that being higher up on the rooftop of a high-rise would make the temperature a little more bearable, but it appears not.

Multiple shades of green from the plants adorning the area were woven throughout the area, accenting the white balloons and tablecloths decorated throughout. Fairy lights hung above, twisting along the wooden beams of the ceiling, casting a small portion of the tables in a soft, warm glow. The rest of the tables were in the open air, sitting under the moonlit sky, with the only other light coming from other skyscrapers.

It has a romantic air that tightens my chest as my eyes coast over the guests. Many of Jenna and Dad's family and friends mill about, nibbling at the finger food sprawled across a table to my right and chatting away with each other.

I try not to, but of their own accord, my eyes search out for his, wondering if he was already here and doing the same as I was. But I didn't get the chance to look for long as Daniel bumps my shoulder, bringing my attention back to my friends beside me.

"Let's go find a table, yeah?" he asks, searching my gaze in curiosity, probably wondering why I paused abruptly at the door.

Looking back at my friends, I saw they all had varying degrees of curiosity or questioning glances. Ellie raises a brow at me while I notice Avery trying to hide her smile behind her hand as she rests her elbow against the arm she wraps around her waist.

I clear my throat, turning to face the party before nodding. "Yeah, let's find a table."

We weave our way through people while I throw quick greetings to family members I vaguely remember meeting throughout the years, and friends of Dad's who always visit for beer and a barbecue feast.

We find a free table under the star-speckled sky, and my friends take their seats, but then I finally spot Dad and Jenna.

I place my bag on the table in the spare seat next to Avery and Daniel before I excuse myself.

"I'll be back, just going to say hi to Dad. Someone order me a drink?"

Daniel nods with a smile before I turn away, meeting Dad and Jenna while they're engrossed in conversation with someone I don't recognise. Dad notices me approach, and his smile brightens before he scoops me up into a hug. I wrap my arms around his neck as he crushes me against him.

"Hi, Chook," he greets softly in my ear, and I smell the whiskey on his breath instantly before placing me back on my feet.

I pull back, but he still holds me close at arm's length with his hands on my shoulders.

I grin, amused at the glassy look in his eyes. "You act like you haven't seen me in a while."

It's almost true though, it's been a few days since my birthday, which is when I last spoke to him properly, except for the odd hello in the mornings as he passes by on his way out for work. He's been busy tying up everything like Jenna before the wedding and his honeymoon, so he's been gone at all hours of the day, only arriving back home late when I'm already tucked in bed—or Reece's.

His hands squeeze my shoulders before dropping by his side. "It feels like it has been, and I miss you. I'm sorry for not being around the last few days." He points the apology to me before glancing up at Jenna, his eyes softening as he does. "But I am a free man for the next couple of weeks and I am all yours."

My nose scrunches, but amusement fills me as I watch the drunken curve of his lips while his eyes never leave Jenna, love and adoration entering his eyes. I wonder how much he's had to drink already to be this over-the-top affectionate. "Gross, Dad."

His attention flicks back to me before an apologetic smile morphs on his face. "Sorry," he says, but not an ounce of remorse enters his tone.

"Don't mind him," Jenna pipes in, her face alight with amusement. "He's drunk a lot already, which has turned him into a love-sick fool."

Dad grins at that. "Only for you."

Jenna rolls her eyes with a smile playing on her lips.

"I have a lot to be happy for right now, and one of them is you. So, why can't I express that?" Dad pouts—actually pouts. I have to press my lips together to smother my laughter.

"Tim, everyone already knows how much you love me. They don't need to hear it every five seconds. You're marrying me," Jenna says, exasperatedly.

He hums. "Don't I know it."

I back away from them, gagging slightly. "Alright, I'm out of here."

Jenna turns to me before I walk away and squeezes my hand. "Thank you for coming. And thank you for everything these past months."

I smile at her. "Of course."

I turn around before I see or hear anything more in my dad's drunken state.

I spot Nate immediately, a few steps away, making his way over, and I beeline toward him to intercept, saving him from Dad's remarks.

When I reach him, I pull him aside and tell him, "You may want to give him a little time to sober up unless you want to hear Dad hopelessly hit on Jenna."

He pauses in his stride and screws up his nose. "Yeah, nah. That's not for me." He turns to me, lips ticking up as he pats my back. "Thanks for the save, sis."

"A pleasure. Though I also don't see him getting sober any time soon. I fear if he keeps it up, he may marry her tonight."

Though amusement flashes in his eyes, he winces. "I almost want to see him try just to see Jenna smack him down, but I also don't want to be scarred."

One side of my lips twitches as I catch movement to my right, seeing Daniel waving me down and pointing to a drink in his hand. I go to excuse myself, however, Nate interrupts me.

"Have you seen him yet?" he asks, and when I look at him, he's staring at something over my shoulder.

I frown. "Who?"

Just as I turn my head to see what or who has captured his attention, he says his name.

"Reece."

My gaze connects with his almost immediately across the rooftop as he leans against a wall, a glass held to his lips. He smiles behind the glass before taking a sip from it, all while his gaze never wavers from mine, and I think I feel my heart skip a beat.

"Since I arrived about five minutes ago, his eyes have never strayed far from you. Especially after seeing me, he just nodded and returned to watching you."

The more he talks, the faster my heart picks up its rate. It's as if we were under the same spell now from the moment my eyes fell on his, because I couldn't tear them away from him.

"Do you know when he got here?" I ask Nate.

I see him shake his head from the corner of my eye. "Not sure." There's a pause before he continues with an exasperated tone, "Go talk to him."

My attention snaps back to Nate. "What? No, it's fine. I'll see him later."

He raises a brow. "Really? You'd put me first? I should feel honoured."

He touches a hand to his chest with his words, and I roll my eyes at his dramatics. But I press my lips together as I focus my gaze on his, feeling a divot form between my brows.

"I put him first before. I don't want to do that again when everything feels good with us."

His eyes soften as he tilts his head. He steps closer and holds either side of my upper arms. "Nothing will ever come between us, you know that. Not again. You're my sister, and I will always be here for you and protect you. But I see the way you both look at each other. Even in the couple of times I've seen you both together. It's as if none of those years have passed between you. It's kind of disgusting to watch if I'm being honest."

I roll my eyes at him again. "You're exaggerating."

He shakes his head. "I'm really not. You saw how he was looking at you. It's absolutely pathetic and lovesick. And it hasn't once changed since you looked away. Well, maybe he looks a bit curious now because I keep looking at him. But he's absolutely smitten with you, Kodaline. I may hate him for everything, but after hearing how he talked about you, I may agree with you about how people can change."

My eyes water as I stare at him before I wrap my arms around him. His arms stay limp by his side for a second in shock before he finally returns the hug. Hugs between us are always rare, but I think this one is needed.

When I pull away, I look up at him with a shaky smile, voicing words that have always been a rare combination to pass my lips. "Love you, Nate."

He grins. "Love you too, sis." He nods over my head. "Go, before he combusts from patiently waiting."

A burst of laughter escapes me before I finally turn back to Reece. But he might be right as I notice the way his fingers drum against the glass he holds between his folded arms. His foot taps in a slow rhythm as well, almost in sync with each drum of his fingers. My smile widens at that, and his eyes brighten.

I make my way toward him, and, as if he couldn't wait or hold himself back, he pushes off the wall and meets my stride. Like two bodies lurching toward each other, the string pulling taut between us.

He stops just in front of me, and it's almost as if he had been holding his breath until he was right in front of me, because a rush of air passes his lips, and his body visibly relaxes from the drop in his shoulders.

"Hi," I greet, my voice coming soft and a little breathy.

"Hi, Kody." The smooth drawl of my nickname has my heart thumping wildly.

His eyes drop down my frame, taking in every inch of me from my shoulders to my toes and back up again to the strands of my hair. When his eyes meet mine again, they appear darker, heating the very blood under my skin in an instant. "I really don't have anything appropriate to describe

ZOE GRACE DOUGLAS

how I feel about you in this dress with so many people around us."

I immediately flush at his words as my lips part in shock. Any words that form in my mind evaporate before they can land on my tongue.

Then he steps toward me, invading my space and wrapping me in his warmth, making my already warm skin overheat. He takes a strand of my hair between his fingers before tucking it behind my ear, his lips following.

"But for your ears only," he whispers against my ear, and I shudder at the feel of his breath skating across my skin. "I don't know whether I want to strip you out of this dress or keep it on while I fuck you. Because it moulds to every single curve and dip I love and makes you look absolutely divine."

It feels entirely too hot between the limited space of our bodies. Even when he pulls back to meet my eyes again, it only gives it room to rise and enter my lungs, making it hard to breathe.

But I can't find it in me to pull away or look away from him. Because it's addicting. *He* is addicting. And every single cell in my body knows exactly what keeps it alive.

"What makes you think you get the chance to fuck me tonight?" My voice is full of smoke and lust, and I don't think I've ever heard myself speak like that. Not for a very long time.

It's the Reece effect. It always comes to him.

From the way his lip curls in the most wicked and sexiest way, I know he knows exactly how much he's drawn me in. How much he affects me.

"Oh, I know. Because we both know we can never take our hands off each other when we are in the same room."

He turns a pointed glance down his chest, where I realise I have a tight grip on his shirt, like I'm ready to pull him close or push him away. I feel him twirl my hair between his fingers, and I know I can't even deny his statement now.

250

I look up at him again, peeling my hand from his shirt and taking a step back, making his grin widen.

"You are just wicked." I shake my head.

He smirks now, and I want to smack it from his face. He's getting too cocky now.

"I know. I can show you just how much if you want?"

I shove him back, but he doesn't even budge, just laughs.

I go to retort, but the call of my name pulls me from the bubble we'd been pulled into.

I swing my head to see a vaguely familiar person coming toward me with surprise etched into their face and a wide smile. I think one of my dad's cousins? He has a way too big a family to keep track of.

I glance at Reece, sending him an apologetic look. But he just presses a lingering kiss to my cheek, shocking me on the spot.

"I'll find you later, yeah?" he says, reaching down to squeeze my hand. He doesn't give me a chance to reply before he's blending into the crowd, and I'm being swamped by questions from Dad's cousin about who that cute boy was.

It was about twenty minutes of being pulled left and right, catching up with family and trying to dodge the questions about me and Reece to the best of my ability.

I finally collapse in my seat next to Daniel and Avery, finding the drink Daniel had gotten me was already gone, the glass empty sitting in front of me. Glancing over everyone, my eyes meet Alex's as he sends me an apologetic smile and shrugs.

"Sorry. Didn't want the drink to go to waste."

My eyes narrow on him before I reach over and snatch his half-empty drink in return, and take a big gulp of it, needing something to quench my parched throat from all that talking.

When I hand the drink back, Alex eyes me. "Go ahead, I guess."

I smile. "Thanks."

Daniel nudges my shoulder, and my attention snaps to him. His brow creases as he looks down at me with concern. "You okay?"

I sigh, slumping in the chair a little. "Yeah. My family knows how to talk your ear off, though. Every time I tried to leave, there was someone else waiting in line to talk to me."

Alex snorts. "Seemed like it. Ellie was going to save you, but we feared we would all be sucked into the never-ending loop of trying to save each other and being dragged into conversation with how it looked around you."

I sent him a dry look. "Gee, thanks."

Daniel clears his throat, his brows still pinched, but this time with what looks to be confusion. "We saw your interaction with Reece..." He trails off and all I think is...*shit*.

I know exactly where this conversation was heading, and it filled me with dread. I've been avoiding it for a few days now, since I've spent them trying to help calm Jenna while she freaks over every single detail to make sure it's all ready for the wedding.

He continues. "What's going on there? Because last we heard, you hated him."

I swallow against the rush of emotions tightening around my throat as I feel all my friends' attention directed at me. I planned to talk to them about this. I've only spoken to Avery about this. Mainly because I feel she understands, having been in the middle of all this with her relationship with Jake. Alex most likely knows from Avery as well, given their secretive smiles anytime I catch them watching me and Reece.

I feel Avery fold her hand around mine under the table, a sign of her reassuring me and being on my side, facing this. Because I know they will have a lot of opinions about this. From my suffering to my avoidance of him to now, being wrapped in his arms, I can only imagine their confusion.

I take a deep breath before speaking. "We were young. There were things I didn't know and things we both could have handled better. But having been around each other for the last couple of months allowed us to talk and put the past behind us. I guess it was the closure I was searching for. But once we did, I think we realised that our feelings for each other never really went away. Even in the years I thought I would never see him again, I think I knew it would always be him for me."

It was Daniel who spoke first once I finished explaining. "How do you know he's not just going to leave you like he did last time? Because look what he did the last time he promised not to leave you. How can you just trust him so blindly? He's not good for you, Dakota. You deserve so much better than a man who can't keep his promises."

I look at him, his pinched expression still in place as if he still didn't understand. But I didn't need him to understand; I just needed him to support me as a friend.

"I get where you're coming from and appreciate your concern, but this is different. We're different. You didn't know us back then. You didn't get to see the side of him I did. You don't know him like I do. There's so much between us that you don't know about. We've told each other things we've never told anyone. I know him more than anyone. He knows me better than even you guys. That's not something I can throw away like I thought I could. But I'm not just throwing my trust blindly back at him, I'm still building that. And if that blows up in my face again, then that's on me. But...I know this time is different. We're not kids this time."

He presses his lips together. "I don't like this. I still don't trust him."

"You don't have to. You just have to support me and let me do the rest."

Avery squeezes my hand again, bringing my attention to her. "I support you. And we're always here for you."

I smile as Alex and Ellie parrot their agreement.

I meet Daniel's gaze again, waiting for his response. His eyes bounce between mine before he sighs and slumps back in his chair. "You know I support you, too. I just don't want you to get hurt again. I don't want you to go down the hole you went down when you came to Melbourne."

I reach over to squeeze his hand, and his gaze softens on me.

"I know. And I won't."

God, I hope I won't.

28

REECE

I lean against the railings of the rooftop, sipping on my glass of water while I watch Dakota interact with her friends from afar.

I've been wrangled into a thirty-minute conversation with Jenna's family, and I'm beginning to zone out, wanting so bad to go over to her and talk to her again. Is it bad that I want to spend all my time with her? To be addicted to how alive she makes me feel?

Maybe, but I just can't help it.

I don't like that Daniel guy, though, and the way he looks at her makes every siren sound because I recognise that soft, attentive look. It's exactly how I look at her.

So, I watch them. I watch how he leans closer to her to speak to her, and how he reaches to touch her hand.

I try to give him the benefit of the doubt because I know Dakota, and she wouldn't be friends with someone who blatantly flirts with her.

But then he takes his suit jacket off and throws it over her shoulders, wrapping his arm around her in the process. I can't help it, fire fills my veins, and before I know it, I'm excusing myself from Jenna's family and bee-lining for them.

I vaguely see Avery's wide gaze and subtle shake of her head, but I ignore it, too focused on him.

Then, someone intercepts me, wrapping their arm around me and turning me away. I go to shrug them off, but Nate's voice whispers in my ear. "Let's go cool off, yeah?"

My attention snaps to him as I glare at him. "I don't need to cool off. I just want to talk to him."

He lifts a brow. "Yeah...Dakota can handle herself. Look," he guides, nodding his head back, and I look over my shoulder. I watch as she shrugs him off and hands his jacket back, waving him off and laughing.

I turn back around, letting Nate guide us through the crowd. "I don't like him."

"Yeah, but he was there when you weren't. Plus, nothing is going on with them, and never has. They're just friends."

I should feel reassured by that, but all I feel is a heaviness on my chest.

When we're a few more feet away by the door, Nate turns to me, keeping my back to them as he does.

He watches me for a moment before sighing. "Look, for what it's worth, I would rather you than him. And that says a lot."

I frown. "Really?"

He folds his arms across his chest. "What you said about Dakota. It got me thinking, and I do get where you were coming from. I get that you were doing what you thought was best for Dakota. But I hope you know where you went wrong in that and why everyone is a bit mad at you—me specifically. I really hope you have learnt from that and I can trust you won't do that to her again."

I shake my head. "I have definitely learnt from it. I'm not going to keep secrets from her intentionally. I'm not going to up and leave her without notice. The last thing I want to do is leave her like that again."

"But you will have to leave. You're an MLB player, you have responsibilities, and you'll be travelling most of the year. Is that really a realistic scenario for you guys?"

I have thought about this. It's been on my mind for a while about how to tell her. But with the legalities behind my contract negotiations at the moment, I'm forced to keep quiet about it, waiting for the final meeting. Not that I don't trust her or Nate to keep it to themselves if I did tell them, despite it all. I just don't want to jeopardise it, especially with how smooth it's all been.

"I will have to go back," I tell him, swallowing and trying to piece my words together to explain. "It's all a bit complicated at the moment, but I'm sorting it out."

He narrows his gaze. "What do you mean 'sorting it out'?"

Jesus, how did I find this so easy when I was younger?

"I'm in the middle of contract negotiations at the moment. I can't divulge much information about it."

He analyses me before throwing another question at me, and I almost give up.

"How will they even know? I'm a quiet guy, I can keep a secret. If not me, it then Dakota should definitely know. Or are you going to omit these details once again from her?"

I drag a hand down my face.

"Look, all I'll tell you is that this is something I've been meaning to do for a while. And this is the complete opposite of last time. I really wish I could tell you more. But know that I really am serious about Dakota. I want nothing more than to be the person to make her happy. I love her more than anything I've ever had in my life."

He cocks his head to the side as if he was cycling over my words and reading into them. Maybe deep inside, I wish he would figure it out, but I also hope he doesn't because I know my agent will jump down my throat.

The muscle in his jaw ticks, and then he straightens his posture. "Okay."

"Okay?" I raise a brow.

He nods. "Yeah."

Then he holds out his hand for me to shake, which I reluctantly take, giving him the opportunity to pull me close into a hug, and I tense.

"But just know, Dad and I will be breathing down your neck if you step even a pinky over the line until all this has been 'sorted out' as you say," he speaks lowly in my ear before pulling back, pasting an innocent smile on his face.

I snigger. "I give you free rein. But you may be waiting a while."

His lip twitches. "I fucking hope so."

It's silent between us for a moment as I watch him before I clear my throat.

"Are—" I stop, shoving my hands in my pockets. "Are we okay?"

He looks away, squinting while he ponders his answer.

"I guess? I mean, if you're asking if I'm still mad at you, the answer would be not really." He looks back at me. "But if you're asking if I trust you, then the answer would be not at all. But I want to. We've only seen each other twice in the two months you've been here, after six years, so I think there's a long way to go."

I nod, twisting my lips as I look over my shoulder, zoning onto Dakota's table again, seeing her already watching us. She tilts her head and I give her a small smile of reassurance that she returns.

When I turn back to Nate, he watches me contemplatively.

"She loves you."

I frown. "What?"

He shakes his head. "It's so obvious, but I think she's always held onto that love for you."

"I don't know about that."

"You'd be a true idiot if you didn't believe that. The thing with Dakota is, she loves hard, but she never lets herself believe it. No matter how much she tries to hide how much she cares, she shows it so brightly in everything she does. She thinks no one notices, but I do. Because she used to look at our mum for that validation all the time. Because I noticed it in the way she used to take photos of every sunset and landscape, which is why I gave her that camera before she went away to Airlie Beach. It's how I know she's still in love with you, because I saw it in her eyes on your birthday that summer and I see it now."

I stay silent, his words sinking deep under my skin and bones. I knew she had to care for me. How would she forgive me so easily if that weren't the case? But love? I never gave myself enough time to think about it. Still, with these therapy sessions, I'm still learning how to receive that feeling. To realise that I do, in fact, deserve that feeling.

But with everything I've done, I didn't expect to feel it anytime soon.

Could he be telling the truth?

He pats my arm, snapping me out of my head. "I'll leave you with that to ponder over. But I'm never wrong about these things."

He walks away and my gaze snaps to Dakota, watching her head fall back in a laugh as I lean back against the building wall, hearing the lilt of it sing to me like a melody.

I won't make the same mistake as last time by not accepting her love.

I want to welcome it with open arms when she's ready to hand it over.

29

DAKOTA

I knock on my dad's suite door a couple of days later, T-minus three hours until the wedding, after his vague text to help him with something.

When he opens the door, he appears a bit frazzled, wiping his forehead in distress. Instant relief floods his features when he sees me.

"Oh, thank god. Thank you so much," he greets before walking back into his room, leaving the door open for me to come in as he continues talking. "I thought I would be okay leaving this until the last minute, you know, like all the raw emotions would make it more authentic, but every time I try, it just doesn't sound right."

I close the door behind me and meet him where he stands by the small desk sitting against the left wall, just before entering the living space. Dozens of crumpled-up paper litters the surface with scribbled writing on them.

"Wait, what? Slow down. What's going on?"

Wiping at his forehead again, he points to the blank paper sitting in the middle of the mess.

"I'm trying to write my vows, but nothing seems like enough

to articulate my feelings. It all feels too simple or too little. I've never done this before. Your mum and I just did your generic vows. But I want Jenna to know how dedicated I am to this. To us. I want this to be perfect for her. I want what I say to be perfect."

I rest a hand on his shoulder, smothering the smile trying to emerge on my face at how cute it is that he's frazzled about this.

"Okay. It's okay. Just take a deep breath."

He does as I say, scrubbing his hands down his face.

"I shouldn't have left this until now." He shakes his head.

"It's okay. We'll work through it, okay? You're just thinking too much."

He nods and slumps down on the chair. "Yeah, you're probably right. I just... I want this to be perfect, you know?"

I smile. "I know, and it will be. Because it's you and Jenna. You just need to speak from the heart. Like it's just you and her and nobody else."

"Okay. But what exactly do I tell her? Aren't I meant to promise her things?"

I press my lips together as I shake my head. "Not necessarily. Just tell her your favourite memory, how she made you feel, and promise not to stop bringing that feeling or those moments to the relationship. To never stop bringing fun and laughter to each other because you love making her feel safe enough to feel that enjoyment in life."

Dad looks up at me. "Maybe you should write it for me. You'd be better at forming words than I would be."

I shake my head. "Nope. This is all you. But I'll help you make it all flow."

He combs his hand through his hair and picks up the pen.

"First, just think of a memory. Any memory that sticks out in your mind. Like when you first knew that you loved her, or when you wanted to marry her. Something special between you and her."

He chews on the top of his pen, thinking for a moment, then leans back in the chair. "It was when I first brought her into my home and cooked for her for our date. It was maybe a month into us dating. Like usual, I put on the CD you burned for me. She was just sitting at the counter with her glass of wine, watching me as we chatted. My favourite song came on–you know the one–and I didn't notice at first, but she giggled at me dancing. I was embarrassed, which was ridiculous because I'm never embarrassed; I do embarrassing things on the daily. But then she joined me, rounding the counter and turning me away from the stove. She grabbed my hand, lifting my arm as she spun under it and grinned at me. She danced with me there, in the kitchen, like a couple of idiots. Like we were young again. That's when I knew she was the one. That I loved her and I never wanted to let her go."

Tears prick my eyes as he tells me the memory, and I watch the fondness enter his eyes, like he's transporting himself back to that time.

My chest aches when I remember that I almost had that. That I had that feeling within arm's reach before it all slipped away. All the memories we danced, only for them to disappear like a cloud of dust.

And now here he is, giving me all that I dreamed when we were younger, and it just feels too good to be true. Even after talking to Avery about this, I still can't help but think that. I can practically feel the ticking clock above our heads like it was our fate to only have moments in time together. That nothing between us will ever last. And I guess, that's why I hesitate to verbalise those three words that have haunted me for way too long. Because I fear that if I give those words life, the clock will tick to its end and he will fade away again.

I don't know when I start to cry, but I feel a tear drop down my cheek, and I quickly swipe it away and sniffle.

Dad looks up at me from the daze he had been in and frowns.

"Why are you crying?"

I shake my head. "I don't know. It just sounded so sweet, and I'm just so happy for you."

His eyes soften, and he stands, wrapping me in those comforting arms of his.

"You'll find the same, Dakota. I know you will. I want you to find someone who makes you happy because you deserve it." He pulls back, holding my face between his hands and tucking my hair behind my ear. "Even if it's a second chance."

I narrow my eyes. "What do you mean?"

He gives me a knowing look. "You don't think I didn't notice the way you looked at each other at the welcome party. Hell, even in the last month. Even a blind man could see the pull you two have to each other," he pauses, hesitating before continuing in a whisper, "I just don't want you to get hurt again. I don't want you to feel what you did before you moved."

My eyes water again.

"You're my little girl, and I want to protect you from any hurt. But I trust you know what you're doing. And you can always come to me to talk about anything, you know that, right?"

I nod, a few tears escaping. "I know. I just," I sniffle and look down, "I don't know what I'm doing either. There's so much history there. I'm just scared to trust he won't leave me again."

He sighs and sits me down in the chair he was just in and kneels before me, clasping my hands in his. His eyes bounce between mine before he asks, "How does he make you feel?"

I blow out a breath as I think.

God, what doesn't he make me feel?

"I feel instantly happy when I see him. He makes me laugh. Even when I'm upset, he finds a way to make me smile. He makes me feel safe and free to be myself. He was the one who pushed my interest in photography when I thought it was just some hobby, and I was going nowhere in life. He pushes me to live. He makes me feel...loved, especially when I thought I was incapable of feeling it."

He smiles. "That's the kind of feeling you should hold onto. I know it's scary. I know trusting him again is hard when he's broken it already. Even for us, your brother and I, it'll take a while for us to trust him not to break your heart. But the truth is, I can see how much love he has for you. How much he wants to be with you. Sometimes, people do change for the better. It's just about giving them a chance to prove it."

I don't know how he thinks he doesn't have a way with words when he spews this.

I sniffle, absorbing his wise words as they pound against my heart. It warms my heart to know that he can see it, the way that Reece loves me. That it's visible to those around me. And I know he's right, that I just need to give him a chance to prove that giving him my love won't blow back on me. Truth is, he's already showing me that. But it doesn't make it less scary. It's terrifying when I've never loved anyone like I have him.

I wipe under my eyes again. "This was meant to be about you and Jenna. How did this turn into being about me?"

Chuckling, he stands, pulling me up with him. "You're right. But you needed me, and you'll always be my number one."

My lips twitch. "Don't let Nate hear you say that."

"I wouldn't dare."

I snort before focusing back on the blank paper in front of him. "Come on. Let's write your vows."

30

REECE

It's the day of the wedding, and though it's not my wedding, nerves still buzz in my stomach.

I haven't seen Jenna since she banished all men from coming near her room unless it was the hotel service bringing more drinks to them. Which also means I haven't seen Dakota since the Welcome dinner.

Is it bad that I already miss her? It's only been a day, but I miss the sound of her voice and the feel of her touch.

The girls stayed in the hotel at the venue while I drove Dakota's dad and Nate to the venue this morning from their house. Nate was put in charge of photographing all of us getting ready, and he took that job very seriously. He had the camera pointed mostly at his dad, but it was awkward as hell when he started telling me how to pose, putting my dress shirt, jacket, and shoes on. Especially when he started buttoning my shirt and adjusting it. I swatted him off as fast as he started before laughing at him. He just shrugged and told me that it wasn't him that I would be answering to for the bad photos, and I knew exactly what he meant. I kept my mouth shut on the retort teetering on the tip of my tongue that I would rather have his sister's hands on me, but I knew the outcome wouldn't be nice for me.

I can almost feel the ghost of them now, skating down my chest and stomach. Can almost taste her on my tongue, feel the way she squirmed beneath me as I brought pleasure to her.

Fuck, now I'm getting hard just remembering it. I shift in my seat and discreetly adjust myself, trying to turn my attention back to the wedding about to start.

I look up at Nate and Dakota's dad standing at the front, awaiting the arrival of Dakota and Jenna to walk down the aisle, knowing this is probably not the best time to think about that moment.

The heat has eased, giving us a reprieve for today, as a slight breeze weaves through the wooden beams of the open-structured chapel. It's kind of beautiful the way they've constructed it, leaving the structure of the chapel with its polished wood exposed to the view of vast lavender fields and mountainous terrain, with a tin roof protecting overhead. It's very rustic and very...Jenna.

Soft music fills the noise as everyone waits and chats silently with each other while I keep to myself, observing the family and friends gathered around, nervously tapping my foot, waiting to finally see Dakota.

As I turn to the front again, my gaze snags on Nate's, and I still. He stares at me for a moment, and I wait to see how he greets me first. I still feel like I'm walking on eggshells around him, waiting for his initial greeting first, as if for some sort of validation. Was I in a good place or toeing the line? Were we cordial, on our way to friendship? Or have I broken that trust forever? Would he ever stop hating me?

But then, he nods before turning back around. The tightness in my chest that was beginning to grow eases a little as I slump back in the chair.

Everyone begins to quiet as the music grows louder through

the speakers. I take a deep breath and turn my head to look toward the end of the aisle just as the doors open.

Dakota stands there holding a small bouquet, and I think I lose the ability to hold oxygen in my lungs as it all disperses from them.

She's the most stunning woman I've ever met.

Her hair falls in waves, tucked neatly behind her ears. The makeup she wears is subtle but makes her eyes pop in a way that sucks me in, drawing me into that never-ending orbit I've never been able to escape.

My gaze falls down her frame, taking in the dusky pink silk dress she wears, almost similar to the one from yesterday. This one, however, shows off the expanse of her shoulders and the top of her chest as the sleeves fall off her shoulders. I know I've seen her in this dress before at the fitting, but today, it feels different.

I can't take my eyes off her, not that I ever want to, as she starts to slowly walk down the aisle.

I watch as she casts small, greeting smiles down at her family and Jenna's as she passes them, her gait slow and in time with the music. Rhythmic and practiced.

Then, her eyes fall on me as she nears the front. Her smile never wavers, but I see the subtle change in it as it softens the edges, her eyes doing the same. And fuck, if that doesn't make me the giddiest person here. More than Jenna and Dakota's dad, and they're the ones getting married. Just because of that subtle change, the softness in the way she looks at me, a look made just for me.

She breaks eye contact, stepping up to her dad and kissing him on the cheek before taking her place on Jenna's side. She salutes Nate, then focuses down the aisle again, but not before flicking her chin at me, giving me a silent instruction to turn my attention back to the doors when she notices I haven't torn my gaze from her. I grin, watching her for a moment longer until everyone begins to stand, and I follow suit, finally bringing my attention to where Jenna stood.

Her dress was simple, accentuated by the lace sleeves ending at her wrists. She looks beautiful in it, radiating happiness as she begins her walk down the aisle holding a billowing mass of flowers. Because, of course, she had a mountain of flowers.

She used to decorate our house with thousands of flowers and plants to liven up the place when I grew up. My dad hated it and would always tell her to throw them out, but she never listened and he stopped bringing it up. I didn't mind it, though; it did seem to make the place less...empty. Without them–and her–the house always felt empty and lonely.

When she meets Dakota's dad at the end of the aisle, she smiles at him while a lone tear tracks down his face before another races against it. She turns to me and dumps the overzealous plant in my hands to free hers to wipe the tears from her soon-to-be husband's face. They whisper to each other, beaming at one another, until someone clears their throat, bringing their attention back to the ceremony. Jenna throws a glare at whoever it was behind me before taking his hand, and they both join the officiant under the vine-covered arch.

As the ceremony goes on, my gaze begins to drift back to Dakota. I try to keep my attention on her dad and Jenna, but I give up after the fourth attempt, watching her watch her dad get married. She sneaks glances at me every now and then, and when she catches my attention already on her, she blushes, shakes her head, and looks away. One of the times, she silently tells me to pay attention, which I grin at and feign bringing my attention back, but in the end, it always snaps back to her. It's cute that she thought I could focus on anything when she's standing right in front of me, looking like that. Relaxed and happy. It's like I wanted to etch that look into my memory.

Whistles ring out, snapping me out of my daze, and I realise the ceremony has finished as I finally bring my gaze back to the newlyweds just as Dakota's dad dips Jenna, kissing her.

They begin to make their way down the aisle together, Jenna grabbing the bouquet as she passes. Dakota and Nate both follow, and before I can catch up to her, people have pushed through before me, putting distance between us.

Even through the photos, I could hardly talk to her as we're pulled left and right into photos with different family members. Especially since she was the one taking the photos and bossing everyone around. It's amusing to watch her, turned me on more when she turned that tone on me to get in position. I tried to offer help when she started to set up timed photos for her to be included. But she's stubborn as hell, though I couldn't blame her. She was in her element.

It's just that I didn't realise how systematic these things were until now.

Even as we enter the reception part of the night, I've barely said more than two words to her.

And I'm desperate to have her in my arms again.

31

DAKOTA

I'm pretty impressed with the playlist Reece and I had created for tonight.

Looking around the room, I smile at the people dancing and having a good time, drinking and laughing. The romantic air might have something more to do with it, but I'm glad I could help add to the atmosphere.

I make my way over to the speaker and pick up the microphone, lowering the volume of the music before turning the mic on.

I swallow and wipe a sweaty hand along the silk dress I'm wearing. "Hi, everyone. Sorry to interrupt the fun, but it has come to that part of the night where I will ask everyone to clear the floor and invite the newlyweds to join together for their first dance. I politely ask everyone to wait until invited to join them to allow them this intimate moment together."

I turn the mic off as Dad stands from the table and holds his hand out to Jenna beside me. She smiles up at him and slides her hand in his before following him out to the empty floor. I can't help but smile at them as I watch them hold each other as

I press play and the first chords of a cover of *Iris* strum through the speakers.

They sway together at first, subtle as they get swept up in the moment, whispering and smiling secretly to each other like they could just stay forever like that.

I want that. I want to have that with Reece. To have something permanent and lasting, not short and sweet and shattering. But so many questions keep entering my mind since I spoke to Avery, and doubt grows. I keep trying to push it to the back of my mind to deal with later and just focus on today, focus on Dad and Jenna, but I can't ignore the most probing question in all this.

I want to trust him when he says he won't leave like he did last time. God, do I want to. But how do I trust him when he'll be living miles away in another country and I'll be here? We'll be in the same predicament as we were before. Maybe Daniel was right. How do I trust he won't just break my heart again because he thinks it's what's best for me? That he won't run away as soon as things become too difficult?

How would anything work when I'm in Melbourne and he's back in the States once the wedding is over? I'm due to go back to Melbourne in a few days, and I imagine he's flying back sometime soon as well. There's training and all that kind of stuff in his profession, right? He would need to be with his team.

I snap myself back to the present to announce that guests can join on the floor, but I feel so detached, thoughts running a million miles a minute as I process what this means.

It's history repeating. It's walking around in the same circle with the same result.

Just as I let myself be vulnerable, it crumbles to dust. Just as my fingers graze the possibility that this is a second chance given to us, it disintegrates at my feet.

Just as I let myself hope, the truth of the situation rears its ugly face. The truth that I neglected to think of before, because I was so focused on ignoring him at the start. It was too quick, the way I fell right back into him for my head to catch up.

A tap on my shoulder brings my attention to the man standing beside me, and just like that, like he always had the ability to do, my thoughts and fears flee from my head.

Dressed in a fitted tux, hair neatly combed back, and looking like he'd just stepped out of a magazine, Reece stands there, a curve to his lips and hand outstretched in invitation.

"May I?"

My eyes flick to the dance floor, seeing Dad and Jenna in the middle of the other couples who have joined them, before returning my gaze to Reece.

I know I need to talk to him, to figure out all the shit that had whirled around in my head moments before. To pull ourselves out of the bubble we absorb ourselves in and into real life. To keep ourselves away from repeating history.

But...I also just wanted one moment. One more moment between us before I let it all wash away. To hold tight to him and feel his sturdy arms around me. Just once more.

Fucking history. I remember being desperate for the same before he pulled away from me.

Despite my better judgment, I slip my hand into his, and his grin splits his face like I'd just given him a prize.

We find our way onto the floor, slipping between other couples before Reece spins me under his arm and pulls me to him, my free arm automatically finding its place on his shoulder. We laugh, smiling like fools at each other.

I can't tear my eyes away from his, entranced by the green and gold flecks in them, remembering how I used to do the same when we were younger. He doesn't look away either, pulling me closer so our chests are flush together as his hand rests on my waist, our other hands intertwining.

He starts to sway us as the song lulls, slowly spinning in a circle. He smiles down at me, eyes full of love and adoration, and it all floods straight to my heart. It's overwhelming, and I almost break right then.

I drop my head onto his chest, the familiar scent of sandalwood and vanilla wrapping around me as the song picks up again.

I just want to belong. Right here, in his arms. I want the universe to align for once in its goddamn existence and give me this little bit of happiness that I desperately crave. The happiness that he had always been able to give me when everything was good. To give me back the warmth of his embrace to fall into when I felt like I was falling apart.

God, here I am again, clinging to him like I need him more than breathing when I have worked for the past six years to breathe on my own. I have worked on forgetting him and my past self, who couldn't stand on her own because she was desperate for love. When she couldn't see that she had all that she needed right in front of her. Her dad, her brother, and her best friends, who she didn't deserve. All because of the overwhelming weight that had been pushed down on me of expectations to have my life together when all I wanted was freedom.

And he was my freedom, my safety.

He grabbed a hold of my hand and gave me the freedom to be myself, away from the expectations and demands. He was the safe space I found to voice my darkest thoughts and not fear being told I was wrong to feel the way I was.

It was hard to separate the boy I fell in love with at seventeen and the man who held me in his secure arms now. I don't know how to let myself just live in the moment when I'm so fucking scared of drowning again.

The song changes to a slow ballad. A cover I added to continue the romantic dance for those couples joining late. An acoustic version of *Can't Help Falling In Love* strums, and I close my eyes at the unwanted tears pooling in my eyes, everything pressing down on me all at once.

I feel Reece's head rest on top of mine, and I sigh as we continue swaying back and forth. There's nothing but the song intertwining us, making me feel like we're the only two people in the room. Making me feel like I can just stay here in his arms, under the spell of this music, and never wake up.

It's a few moments before his chest rumbles against my face as he speaks quietly, making me think that he can somehow hear my thoughts. Like he can read me like a fucking book that I don't even need to speak for him to know everything.

It's unnerving. It's...relieving.

"I know we have a lot of things to talk about after all this, and how we will work with everything. It's all I can think about, and I know it's on your mind, too. But I'm right here with you. There isn't a single thing that can tear me away from you now. I know what it was like to lose you, and I'm not making that mistake again. I know I fucked everything up when we were younger, and it took me this long to come back to you, but I just wanted you to have the best version of myself. It's what you deserve. Because it would always be you for me, Kody. No one else could ever give me that soul-deep peace that you make me feel."

I swallow down the sob lodged in my throat as I pull my head off his chest and look up at him. His face crumbles as he sees the water gathering in my eyes, and I try my hardest to swallow them back. His hands come up to cup my face, gaze pin-balling all over my face like it could give him all the answers.

"Kody. Baby. Fuck, please don't cry. Did I do something wrong? Say something wrong?"

I shake my head, pulling away from him, and though he reaches out to pull me into him again, he senses that's not what

I need and clenches his hand together before letting it drop to his side.

"No. No, you didn't do anything wrong. It's just I..." I pause to gather myself, feeling the first tear escape against my fight. "I can't do this. I can't," I choke.

He frowns, shaking his head in confusion. "What? What do you mean?"

I swallow, glancing around the room of people, only a few glances point my way, seeing my impending panic settle in.

I meet his gaze again, shaking my head. "I'm sorry. I just need to get air."

And then, I turn and rush through the tables toward the door opening into the hall leading to the toilets, hearing him call my name.

I burst through the doors, slowing my gait as the fresh, rain-scented air hits my skin through the open door at the end of the hall. I take a deep breath, gulping down the crisp breeze as I close my eyes. I didn't realise how stuffy it became in there. How hot and clammy my skin had become. But it still does nothing to slow down the spinning in my head and ease the burn in my lungs.

The doors open again, my pause giving Reece enough time to catch up as his gaze immediately latches onto mine.

"I told you I wasn't letting us go easily this time. If you have any thoughts or fears, we talk about them. No more hiding. No more running away. I am here, and I'm not going anywhere until you tell me you don't want me anymore. Is that what you want?"

I release a shaky breath. "Reece," I beg, but he cuts me off.

"Give me an honest answer, Kody. Do you want me to leave?"

I press my lips together, the crease deepening in my brow, seeing the plea in his eyes. The desperate look on his face tells me not to let him go. But I know if that's what I wanted, he'd let

275

me go. The thought of that cuts a deep, agonising pain through my stomach.

There lies my answer.

Slowly, I shake my head, my answer coming out in a breath. "No."

He blows out a deep breath as relief loosens his shoulders and smoothes out the groove between his brow. He takes two strides to meet me and cups my face. "Then, tell me. What's going on? Talk me through the thoughts in that pretty little head of yours."

I don't bother stopping the tears now that we're outside, away from others. The fight slowly drains from me as I lean back on the wall behind me, Reece following my movements as he keeps his hands cradling my cheeks.

"I'm scared," I mutter.

He swipes under my eyes with his thumbs as his eyes ping between each of mine. "What are you scared of?" he asks softly.

I exhale, looking up at the ceiling before returning my gaze to him, but looking at him has my throat closing up, so I settle for focusing on a spot on his chest, the creasing in his shirt. "The last time I listened to you weaving all these sweet words, I was left heartbroken and a complete mess, Reece. You left me, and I was sure nothing could break me quite like you did. But now here you are again, and I think you could possibly do worse damage than you did then. Because you're going to leave again and I'm going to have to watch you walk away again in a couple of days, and I don't want to do that. I don't think I can survive this time."

He brushes my hair away from my face. "I'm scared too. It's fucking terrifying how much I feel for you and the fear of losing you again. But you don't have to survive this because I'm right here. I've got you, and I'm not leaving you. Not like I did." He bends his head so he's eye level with me, catching my eyes again. "I can't undo the things I did. I didn't know how important you were to me when I had you in my arms. And I've regretted it every day since. But I know what I have now, and as selfish as it may be, I don't want to let you go again. So, if I'm not letting go, please don't let me go either. We'll figure it out together, okay?"

"How? We're going to be in different countries, Reece. That never ends well in relationships." I saw it happen with Ellie with her last relationship, and how contact slowly diminished between the two before it inevitably ended. I don't want the same thing to happen to us.

He shakes his head. "Let me figure that out, okay. I'm not going to let anything come between us again."

I scoff. "How are you going to do that? It's impossible. My assignments are unpredictable, and you're in the U.S. You're living your dream."

"*You* are my dream, Dakota. Nothing in the world matters if I don't have you by my side. Do you know how many times I have wished that you were in the stands watching me? Nearly all of my games, I have deluded myself into thinking you were watching them in some capacity. I played some of my best games when I imagined you cheering me on. You have plagued my mind since the day that I met you. The only reason I am standing where I am is because of you. Because you make me want to be better. Because I couldn't stand the thought of failing and having let you go being all for nothing. But in the end, I was always going to come back to you. No mountain could stand in my way from crawling back to you."

I stare at him, tear stains drying on my cheeks as his words leave me speechless.

They spin like a record around my head as I ruminate over them. Eventually, they travel down to my heart, wrapping around and infiltrating it until it opens that little pocket I keep tightly hidden. The little pocket only he has been able to reach.

My heart bleeds again, pumping at a wild rate as it lurches

for Reece, like it wants to leap from my chest into the palm of his hand where I had laid it all those years ago. Like it's jumping at its chance to go home. Like he is where my heart calls home instead of in my chest.

And so I relinquish my last thread of restraint toward him. I give him all I have just like I did when we were younger and hope to god he doesn't crush it again.

"Okay," I whisper before inhaling a deep breath. "I trust you."

He leans his forehead against mine. "I've got you. I love you, Dakota, with every fibre in me. And I will tell you that every day until you believe me. Even beyond that. Every day for a lifetime."

I don't hold back as I clasp the front of his dress shirt, pulling him into me at the same time I bring my lips to his, kissing him with a mix of desperation and longing...and love.

32

DAKOTA

The muffled sound of the wedding still raving inside spills through the crack underneath the door. But even as close as we are to the door, it sounds like distant noise as the air clouds around us until all we know, see, and feel is each other. And god, do I feel him everywhere.

His body cocoons me against the wall as he devours my lips, taking control as his strong hand cups the side of my neck, using his thumbs to tilt my chin up to him.

His tongue slides into my mouth, caressing mine in the most delicious and intoxicating way, making my hands tighten their grip on his shirt, pulling him impossibly close like he isn't already melded to me. Every inch of him presses into me.

One of his hands starts to wander, sliding down my shoulder and around my waist until it drifts over my ass, gripping me as he grinds himself into me, hitting the spot that makes me see stars. He lifts my leg over his hip as he repeats, and I moan into his mouth.

His lips hover over mine as he speaks. "I know, baby. But your family doesn't need to know how good I make you feel, so I need you to be quiet for me. You think you can do that?"

Fuck. A bright white flash of heat strikes right to my core at his words, and I swallow back the whimper that wants to rise, rebelling against his request.

I open my eyes to meet his, and the hunger in them almost makes me combust. God, I fucking need him so much.

He consumes me, and I want to drown in him, missing the way I could float in the current of him.

Silently, I nod, and then the hand that held my face threads through my hair to the back of my head, and I instantly relax in his touch.

"You trust me?" He questions, eyes boreing into mine, searching and I know this is for an entirely different situation, but still my answer never wavers.

Again, I nod, and with my answer, the sexiest, wicked grin climbs on his face before he pulls me into the closest bathroom, locking the door before descending upon me.

It's heat and history repeating, colliding into each other and exploding right in front of us, giving us the chance to change it for the better. I grab it with both hands, wanting to ride the wave only Reece has been able to give me.

I think my heart always knew it was always going to be him because I could feel it singing with every sweep of his tongue against mine, screaming *finally* through every vein in my body.

After kissing me breathless, he pulls away just enough for his lips to brush the top of mine as he whispers against them, "Turn around, face the mirror, and lean over the counter."

My breath hitches, and my eyes pop open to collide with his. Dark pools of forest green stare back, hungry and waiting, causing a shiver to rock my shoulders.

I peel away from the door, body brushing Reece's as I step around him, and his eyes track each of my movements. I turn away from him, facing the mirror, meeting his gaze again through it. When I start lowering my chest to the counter, his eyes turn molten, fixed on me as I bend to ninety degrees, my arms resting on the bench to hold me up.

His lips twitch before he comes up behind me. His hand slides up from my sacral to between my shoulders, and then, meeting my eyes again, a devilish spark swirling in them.

"All the way down, baby," he rasps, pressing lightly on my back until I oblige him, leaning further down until my chest meets cool marble. He hums in satisfaction, seeing me bend to his will with my ass poking out for him and I won't lie that a flash of heat zips right to my core, making me press my thighs together.

His palms slide over my hips, bunching my dress just a little before his eyes flash to mine. "Is this okay?" he asks.

I nod, choking out my words as anticipation clogs my throat. "Yes. Please," I beg.

Again, he grins at my answer before slowly working the dress up inch by inch, bunching at my hips as the satin material glides over my skin. It was fucking torturous how slow he was going and I bet he knew too how impatient I was getting with the way a smirk played on his lips.

When he finally has all the material in his hands, he pushes them over my hips until my ass is bare. I watch as his brows raise in the mirror as he realises I'm wearing no underwear.

"Fuck," he moans, drawing out the word. "You're going to be the death of me, Summers."

Then his hands smooth over the skin, squeezing both sides as he watches intently.

I spread my legs, stepping a few inches apart, making his attention snap to me.

His smirk grows as he tuts. "Impatient woman."

His fingers graze my inner thighs, just out of reach where I desperately need him, making me whimper. "I wanted to take my time with you when I finally got to fuck you again, but with where we are, I realise I can't quite do that. But I am going to admire the shit out of you while I do so."

Then, without warning, he drops to his knees behind me. I don't even have time to form a coherent thought before he swipes his tongue from my clit to my entrance and I whine at the feeling.

"Careful now, Kody. Remember, you've got to be quiet."

Fuck. How am I meant to keep any semblance of logical thinking when he's talking to me and touching me the way that he is? He drives me fucking wild as his tongue swirls around my clit before he sucks it into his mouth and flicks his tongue.

God, I'm close already as my legs start to tremble with how wound up he's already made me. I suck my bottom lip into my mouth, biting down as I swallow down the moans that are fighting their way out. He hooks his arm through my thighs and rests on my lower back, pulling me further against me as I feel every fibre of my nerve endings start to tingle. It's when he flattens his tongue to lick me right to my entrance, thrusting into me before his fingers join him to rub my clit that I combust. I fold my hand over my mouth as my legs almost give out with every wave he coaxes out of me. He moans against me, adding to the pleasure rocketing through my body with the vibrations.

I slump against the counter, dropping my forehead on the cool surface, completely spent and take a moment to catch my breath. But he doesn't allow that. Instead, he wraps an arm around me, lifting me against his chest. I meet his eyes in the mirror, dark and hungry to my dazed and sated ones, and I catch the way his lips glisten with my arousal as they skim my ear.

"I'm not nearly done with you yet," he whispers against my ear, and I can feel the fire build within me again.

He spins me around and lifts me onto the counter. My legs immediately part for him to step in between before his lips demand mine in a bruising kiss. He tastes like me, and it fills me with an intense satisfaction, like staking my claim on him. All I can do is weave my hands into his hair and let him take my weight as he pulls me to him, grinding into me. He takes all control, and I revel in the desperate need that rolls off him with the way his hands roam over me, not missing a single inch of skin before his lips join his mapping of my body.

It's like he was imprinting every inch of my body to his memory, learning the new curves and textures underneath his fingertips like he has all the time in the world. And god, do I never want it to stop. His touch and every drag of his lips ignite every single nerve ending in my body until I'm panting and writhing under him, desperate and needing him, all of him.

He pulls his lips away from my neck, as if reading my mind and rests his forehead against mine. He reaches behind him, and when his hand reemerges, the foil packet comes into our line of sight.

I smirk. "Ambitious?"

He meets my gaze as he takes the edge of the packet between his teeth and tears it.

Then his grin turns wicked, causing my breath to cease. "I'd like to call it prepared."

Leaning back, he unzips his pants, pulling out his hard cock, precum already leaking from his tip and I swallow, resisting the urge to lean down and run my tongue along him as I lean my weight back on my palms.

He rolls the condom on, then looks up, looking satisfied at what I know is the visceral need painted over my face as my eyes trail up his frame, his button-up hiding most of his body from vision except for the slip that peeks through the unbuttoned half, showing the broad span of his muscular chest.

My eyes snap to his as his hand curls around the back of my neck, pulling me to him until his lips hover just above mine, brushing when he speaks.

"God, do I fucking love you. I've dreamt of this moment for

years, wanting to feel you this close again, and I'm going to enjoy having every inch of you wrapped around me like you were always made for me. Because you are, Kody. My mind, body, my fucking soul calls to you. And I am at your mercy because of it."

He punctuates his last sentence by sliding inside me, stretching me in the most delicious way that my eyes roll back. A small bite of pain mixes with the insurmountable pleasure rolling through me.

It's been...a long time since I've been intimate with someone, almost a year, and never once has it come close to how it feels when I'm with Reece.

But this, right here, fuck, it tops any pleasure I have ever experienced, by myself, even with Reece when we were younger.

When we were younger, it felt as if we had intertwined as one. There wasn't just him and I, it was us. Now, it feels like our souls are binding, snapping back into place like two halves of one whole. This wasn't just some bodily experience, this went so much deeper. It always has been between us.

He sets a steady pace, sliding in and out, the friction and fullness that I feel making me groan as my head falls back.

Reece's head falls to my shoulder as he mumbles against my skin, "Shh, baby, I've got you. God, you feel fucking incredible. You feel... Fuck, just like I remember."

"Yeah? And what did I feel like?" I breathe, sweat clinging to my temple.

He moans into my neck before lifting his head, repositioning me as he lifts my left foot onto the counter, stretching me wider, and somehow, I feel him deeper. God, so deep.

He slaps his hips against mine, and I gasp before he lifts my head so I'm looking at him when he says, "Like mine." Then, punctuates them with each thrust of his hips. "So." Thrust. "Fucking." Thrust. "Mine."

His lips collide with mine, a mess of tongues, teeth, and lips, as our control slips, losing ourselves in each other, and muffling moans with every swipe of tongue and nip of teeth.

My muscles tighten, coiling like the pressure low in my stomach, ready to snap with every pump of his hips, while my moans fall to whimpers.

Reece pulls back, gaze locking with mine, conveying so much love and lust.

"Come on, Kody, come for me. Let me see my favourite sight."

And fuck, if that doesn't push me over the edge as I spasm around him, my back arching.

He doesn't last much longer either as his thrusts become more desperate before he's groaning my name into my shoulder, and I can feel each pulse of his orgasm.

We stay like that for a moment, wrapped in each other, Reece supporting my weight as my arms come around him, holding him close.

I can almost hear it in the silence of this room, the murmurs of our hearts calling out 'home' with so much relief and peace, surrendering to the feeling.

And it's then that my heart finally breaks free of its restraints, the reluctance and fear of those three little words, like it was just waiting for this moment. For us to fall back together.

They fall from my lips without hesitation as I press them into the skin of his shoulder like a brand.

"I love you."

God, it feels so relieving to say those words after being bottled up for way too long, and if it's even possible, I can feel my heart grow two sizes bigger.

He pulls back slowly, eyes pinballing between mine as if trying to figure out if he heard me correctly.

I smile up at him, hoping to show that he definitely did as

my hands cup his face. He melts into my touch, eyes softening, and I feel it through to my soul, my heart thumping against my chest as the feeling spreads from the top of my head to the point of my toes.

"Say it again. Say it so I know that it was real," he says in a desperate plea.

His eyes fall to my lips like he wants to see the words form, and my smile widens as I lean my forehead against his, wanting nothing more than to say them over and over again.

"I. Love. You," I punctuate, and my words take immediate effect on him, feeling every muscle in his body lose all its tension, and he grows lax against me.

He kisses me then, deep and unyielding, and I let it take me under, wanting to stay in this kind of dreamland with him forever. Just him and me.

Always, him and me.

33

REECE

She *loves* me.

She loves *me*.

I couldn't quite believe it, but hearing her say those three little words to me, the utter conviction and adoration in her eyes as she said them, flooded through my veins and breathed light into my heart.

Even now, as I walk down the bustling street with her hand in mine, that feeling remains, and I never want it to end. Never want it to disappear or fade away. I want it to stay alive and ignite, to spread through every inch of me until every single piece of me is made of her love. Of our love. Of the future we'll share and the memories we'll make together.

Every step I take feels lighter, and I can't get rid of the smile on my face. I'm a giddy man, finally having the girl of my dreams in my arms.

I feel her watching me from the corner of my eye, and I turn to her, her perplexed expression amusing me.

"Why are you smiling so much?" she asks.

I shake my head because it's unreal to believe she doesn't know. "Because of you."

Her frown deepens. "Because of me?"

"Yeah, you. I'm smiling because of you. You make me happy. Don't cramp my happiness now."

She feigns offence as she presses a hand to her chest. "I would never."

I knew she was being serious, though, because the same smile graces her lips, mirroring mine. We probably looked like two idiots smiling about nothing, walking down the street, but we were in love.

Two idiots in love.

So openly in love and, god, does that warm every inch of my heart. It's everything I ever wanted, to be entirely hers, and in return, I get to call her mine.

We left the wedding moments after our...escapades, bidding farewell to her dad and Jenna before strolling through the lavender fields in the dark, talking and kissing and, well, I just couldn't keep my hands off her. We laid in that field for a very long time, stargazing and being wrapped in each other's arms.

It was well into the early morning now, with the sun about to rise. I had driven us into the city, both of us having only one place in mind that we wanted to go.

We had only ever watched sunsets here, so it almost felt like a new beginning for us to watch the sunrise here.

Making our way through the park and down the pier, we sit at the end just like we always used to do. It's mostly quiet where we are, with the waking city noises in the background.

A moment passes before I turn my body to face her, one leg resting behind her, bent, while I dangle the other off the edge of the pier.

I watch her as she watches the river and city in front of her before bringing her gaze to me.

She smiles, the corners tugging softly at the corners, and I think that's one of my favourite things about her. The way she smiles, like she can see something good in me. "What?"

I shake my head. "I just love you."

Her smile brightens, and I reach over to tuck a piece of hair behind her ear before pulling her to me, tracing my lips over hers. It's a gentle caress, and my heart beats a little faster having her in my arms like this.

When she pulls back, her lashes flutter before looking up at me. I want her looking at me like this forever. I will do everything possible to make that happen. If we're this close or a whole country away, I don't want a life without her in it.

And I'll try my damnedest to figure this out with her.

"I love you, too," she whispers back, and I hold her a little tighter, keeping her there as she rests her body into mine until the sun has risen over the buildings and she almost falls asleep in my arms.

I wake her then, and sleepily we make our way to the car.

She reaches over to squeeze my arm in the passenger seat as she curls herself onto her side to face me.

"Are you okay to drive?"

I nod. "I'll be okay, it's a short drive."

She nods back, and almost instantly, she falls asleep.

I'm used to sleepless nights and staying awake during the day for practice. And though my lids droop and the trip feels like it takes forever, I get us to her house safely.

After putting the car in park, I reach over to brush her hair out of her face. The small touch makes her squirm, and she flutters her eyes open, sending me a sleepy smile.

"Hi," she whispers, and god, it was the cutest way to be greeted when waking.

"Hi," I whisper back before nodding my head toward the house in front of us. "We're here."

She looks over her shoulder, then stretches in her seat.

I get out of the car before rounding to her side and opening her door. I offer my hand to help her, and she takes it, her soft hand folding into mine, just like it did when I offered her to dance.

Quietly, we enter the house, aware that Nate will be asleep upstairs, and I lead her to the spare room down the hall beside the media room, the one I have been staying in the past couple of weeks.

She walks over to the bed, plopping down on the edge of the bed. She goes to lie down, but I catch her before she does as I stand in front of her, my hands holding her arms.

"Hold on now. You gotta change first."

She whines, blinking her eyes up. "I have to go upstairs to get my clothes."

"You can borrow something of mine."

She sighs, her shoulders dropping as her posture slumps. "Can you help me?"

I smirk, pinching her chin between my forefinger and thumb to tilt her head back to look at me. "You want me to help you change?"

Her gaze heats as they flick between mine before sucking her lower lip between her teeth. The action almost makes me groan.

"Please," she says in a breathy voice that has me almost instantly dropping to my knees in front of her.

I shake my head, knowing how tired she must be and wanting her to get some rest. I've got time to explore her and every way she responds to me for the rest of my life.

I go to my suitcase and pull out a clean shirt before returning to her. She looks up at me as I stand in front of her. I grab her arms, pulling her up to stand, and she groans, slumping against me.

I chuckle. "I know. But it'll be quick. You'll be more comfortable."

She watches me, but curls her fingers under the straps of

her dress and pulls them down her arms. The dress pools at her feet, but I keep my gaze locked on hers, ignoring the instinct to drop them to scan the body I absolutely adore.

I grab the shirt and pull it over her head before tucking her hair behind her ears. She closes her eyes and leans into my hands.

"Let's get you into bed," I tell her, and she nods, turning around before dropping onto the bed. She slides under the covers, nuzzling in and releasing a sigh.

I smile at how cute she is when she's tired, before slipping out of my suit, neatly folding it away along with her dress, and sliding into bed beside her.

I wrap my arm around her waist, snuggling just as she had into her, inhaling the rich vanilla scent of her shampoo. I press a kiss to the back of her head before mumbling, "Good night, Kody."

Her response comes a moment later, her voice laced with sleep. "Good night, Reece."

And then I fall asleep, getting the most peaceful and undisturbed sleep I've had in a very long while.

34

REECE

I wake with her wrapped around me, her blonde hair fanning across my shoulder, her shampoo invading my nose, an arm and leg draped across me as I hold her tight against me. It's like all the puzzle pieces have fallen back into place, and this is right where I'm meant to be.

It's probably late in the afternoon, going by how the sky is melting into a blend of orange and blue through the window. After being out all night last night and only falling into bed about five this morning, it wouldn't surprise me.

I didn't want to stop talking to her last night as we found ourselves back at our old spot by the river, watching the sunrise together. I almost want to wake her now just to hear her voice, but I don't dare move from the position we're in, wanting to keep her close with her clinging to me.

I trace my finger down the side of her face, tucking her hair away and out of her face so I can see her. She's sound asleep with the soft rise and fall of her shoulders and the small puffs of air hitting my chest. But even with how deeply she sleeps, she still clings to me as tightly as I'm clinging to her, like we never want to let go of one another.

God, she looks like an angel, sent down solely to bring me back to life, infusing her light to dull my darkness.

Being back in her arms brought me the peace I had been searching for on my own for so long. I searched for that feeling in everything I touched. People, places, hobbies. Even baseball, a thing I thought I could teach myself to love again. I mean, it gave me some sort of escape, but nothing ever felt the same as her presence and the effect it had on me.

I rest my chin atop her head, tracing my fingers up and down her back as I revel in the feeling of holding her close and her not pulling away.

She's my home. A place I can confide in and feel safe when she holds me in her arms. It's all I ever need in this life, and I feel like a lucky son of a bitch to have this chance with her again. Because now that I feel what it's like to lose her, I know how much she's worth to me, and I'm not losing that again. I was stupid for not realising that sooner.

She shifts in my arms, stretching and sighing until her head tilts back. Those bright, ocean blue eyes flutter open, locking straight onto me. I feel the way just the mere sight of her looking at me makes my heart race, as a sleepy smile makes its way on her face. It's such a beautiful sight to see. For her to wake up, see me, and fucking smile that breathtaking smile I always dreamed of, sleepy and heavenly. I wouldn't have believed it was possible to be in this position with her three months ago.

I cup her cheek, combing my fingers through her hair before resting them there again, thumbing under her eye as I stare down at her, mesmerised by her existence.

"Good morning," I rasp.

She hums, moving her arm on top of me to fold over my chest as she rests her chin on it. "Good morning."

My hand weaves through the back of her head to pull her

closer as I bring my lips to hers, but she pulls back before they touch.

"Wait," she presses a finger to my lips. "I have morning breath; it probably isn't the best idea to kiss me right now."

I roll my eyes. "Don't be ridiculous. I don't care about that. Just come here. I need to feel your lips."

She relents easily, letting me guide her until my lips brush hers in a slow, explorative manner, learning and mapping all the ways that made her press herself deeper into me and clawing for more. I gladly give it to her, my self-restraint nonexistent around her, and I don't want it any other way.

Anything of mine was hers. I was hers. It was written in the stars, I'm sure. Because if anything were to tear us apart again, there wasn't a doubt in my mind that I would find myself crawling back to her again and again.

I take my time with her, lazily dragging my lips and skimming my tongue along hers. It's familiar but new, this feeling inside me. Familiar because it's her, and nothing I ever felt for her back then ever went away. New because we are new and things are different. We've changed, grown, and learnt new patterns. But time hasn't changed our feelings. Hasn't changed the connection between us like a tether binding us together.

When we finally pull away, her lips swollen and pink, I almost want to dive back in for more.

She sighs, relaxing back into her pillow as she looks up at me. "I don't want to leave this bed."

I smile because yeah, neither do I. I'm perfectly content with staying right here until the day I die.

I hear movement outside the room, likely Nate in the kitchen or media room, and I groan, rolling into Dakota's body. She cradles my head to her chest and giggles before letting out a groan herself, hearing the same as I did.

"I can't go out there in your clothes. I can just imagine how he'll react," she whines.

I pull back from her, grinning at the thought. "I wouldn't mind—"

She cuts me off with a smack to my upper arm, and my lips curve further.

"This isn't funny. I need clothes."

I chuckle and kiss her cheek before climbing out of bed. "I'll go get some for you."

When I stand, I stretch my arms above, fingers brushing the roof before looking over my shoulder at her, catching her gaze trained on a single part of my back, right near my left hip. I almost ask what she's looking at, having forgotten all about it until now, but I freeze when I do, and she immediately notices, flicking her attention up to me.

"When did you get that?" she whispers, her voice thick.

I swallow and lean down to grab a shirt to pull on, nervous about how she will react to it.

I sit back on the side of the bed, running my sweaty palms down my thighs. The bed dips behind me, and I feel her presence come closer.

"Just after I moved. Probably a couple of months after being in the U.S."

She lifts my shirt, and I stiffen as she runs her fingers over it. Over the tattoo. A tattoo I used to look at religiously every morning to remind me of what I loved and lost. Of what she had meant to me.

My north star.

She had guided me out of the darkness and cloaked me in her light. She had guided me out of the sinking pool I had been in, only for her to slip out of my reach because of my own damn stubbornness.

I'd gotten it tattooed as if reminding me of what she had done, and what I'd hoped I could find again.

The north star inked into my skin was nothing as simple as that, though. I had her name tattooed on the north position.

295

Not her full name, just her initials, but I knew she knew. It was impossible to look past it.

"Why?" she asks in a soft voice that I almost miss.

I look over my shoulder at her, meeting her gaze again.

"Because you are my true north. I knew with you, I would find my way out of whatever shit I had to go through. And because I could never physically have you again, this was my next best thing to have you guiding me."

Her eyes glisten as she flicks her eyes between mine before she smiles.

"Well, I'm here now, so you have a two-for-one. It'll be impossible to stray off track."

My chest aches with the love I have for her, an intense, all-consuming flood of emotions flowing through me.

I cup the back of her head and pull her into me, my lips pressing into hers as I pour all my gratitude into that one kiss. She gives it right back, holding me close with her hand on my cheek, gentle but present.

I lean my forehead against hers, breathing her in before pulling away and grabbing a pair of pants.

"Let me go grab you some clothes," I tell her, leaning over once I've shoved my pants on and pressing a kiss to her forehead. "I'll be back."

She smiles up at me. "I'll be waiting."

Quietly closing the door to the room behind me, I pad down the hall to the stairs, praying I don't run into Nate right now. I did not want to be stuck talking to him while I still smelled Dakota on me. Hell, with my luck, he'd just know exactly what happened between us last night with one look and give me an earful.

I spy him in the kitchen with his head in the fridge as I reach the stairs. I rush up them before he can see me and enter Dakota's room.

Now that I'm here, I probably should have asked her what

she wanted me to get before I left her. I don't even have my phone on me to do just that now.

I sigh, deciding she would have to put up with the clothing I chose for her.

I start with her closet, picking out a shirt before opening her cupboard for a pair of pants, messing up the neatly folded stacks she had.

It's then that I happen to stumble upon that note again. The same one I saw on the bachelor's night. The one addressed to the one who hurt her.

I hesitate for a moment, knowing I should probably leave it alone, but curiosity beats me as I slide the piece of paper out.

Folding it open, I begin to read, and the more I read, the more my heart completely shatters.

Some words had faded or bled into what looked like tear stains, but I got the gist of what was written and who it was meant for.

It was a goodbye letter to me.

To the one who hurt me,

I used to dream of happy ever after. Dream of the perfect ending with the perfect guy and the perfect life. But it always felt so out of reach when my life felt far from perfect. When I had all this pressure to be that perfect someone.

But you came along and that dream seemed a little less impossible. I danced through the haze and got lost in the green of your eyes and every heart-melting smile you gave me. Everything seemed clearer in the fog you created. In the world you kept me in. In the dreams we shared and the secrets whispered in each other's ears. I almost forgot that none of it was real.

We were living in a burning house from the start, and you did a damn good job at throwing a blanket over us to hide it. But just as good as you hid, you ripped it all away at the first sign of life, of everything that could have been. You left me to burn alone with your ghost, reminding me yet again, that this wasn't real.

You made it so easy to forget all of it had an expiration date when you made promises you couldn't keep. That maybe you had changed your mind and I could keep you in my heart where you so easily wedged yourself. And I hate myself for it.

But mostly, I hate you.

I hate you so much that I don't hate you at all. Three simple, but so very complex, words stuck in my throat the last time I saw you. In the fairyland we had lived in, I had thought you felt the same and I had waited for you to say it so I didn't seem like a fool. I hate you so much that I have to thank you for saving me from the embarrassment of realising you never felt the same.

It was so easy for you to say goodbye. All the little dates and sleepless nights spent in my bed. The sweet words and secret touches, gone within a blink of an eye. All that's left is the crumbling mess you left behind. The tears that stream down my face reflect the things that have gone to waste, and I don't know where to go from here.

Maybe a final goodbye will heal the broken lump of muscle I thought had been broken long before you.

So, here's my goodbye. Goodbye to the person I thought you were and our picture-perfect days we had together. Goodbye to the tears I shed for you when I could only talk to your ghost. Goodbye to waking up next to you as the morning light hit your face, making your hair look golden, and your eyes appear as green as the crisp grass in spring. Goodbye to the jarring silence you gave me when you refused to give me the answer I desperately needed.

And most of all, goodbye to my love for you. Through the time – and the distance – may that all disappear.

Dakota Summers.

. . .

It was poetic, almost in the way it spilled with so much pain and frustration and heartache that it stirred up the old guilt and anger at myself. Though it never really left me. It was always there, clinging to the corners of my mind, ready to remind me how idiotic and foolish I was to pretend I could have her when I knew there was no escaping the reality already set in place. Ready to remind me how naive I was to think I could save her from myself before anything else grew, like I didn't already know she meant the world to me.

I was selfish and cruel. Why the hell did I even deserve a second chance with her when she had this, likely a reminder that I was the worst kind of person?

I may say I have changed and want nothing more than to be better for her, but what if I'm not? What if I'm just the same screw up? What if all those months of therapy and pushing myself to prove what I lost were for something, meant nothing at all?

What if I just didn't deserve her at all, no matter the effort I put in?

I take a deep breath to calm my erratic heartbeat, pressing my palms into the cupboard in front of me before releasing the breath through my lips in a slow exhale. I follow exactly what my therapist told me to do to bring me back, to ground myself, until the heavy thump of my heart didn't feel like it was pounding through my whole body.

It's a few minutes before it slows to a normal, rhythmic beat and I can finally open my eyes without feeling dizzy as I take a deep breath.

I look at the letter again, a sharp ache pulsing through me, but a resolve settles upon me.

Like fuck, will I let my younger self make the same mistakes again. That will be my last wish.

35

DAKOTA

Reece left half an hour after making a spontaneous plan for dinner tonight to let me get ready.

I told him he could stay and we could get ready together; however, he said he wanted to do the whole experience. Like picking me up at my front door, bringing flowers, and then bringing me back home, leaving me with a kiss. He called it 'the true dating experience,' like when he took me around the city and to the art gallery when we were younger, but with a better ending.

I had two hours to get ready before he came to pick me up, so I took my time, soaking in a bath, applying a light coverage of makeup, and rifling through the limited clothes in my cupboard that I brought. I wasn't expecting to go on a date, let alone with Reece, so I didn't pack many things suitable for that. Maybe to go out to a bar, but not a date.

I start throwing my clothes out of my cupboard and onto my bed, before I stumble on my corset-style sage green dress with mesh sleeves to my wrists that falls to my shins. I vaguely remember packing it in a drunken haze after going out with Ellie and Daniel before I left, and they convinced me that I needed to bring it since I didn't know who I'd stumble across in my time here. I needed something on the off chance I met someone.

I slide the dress on and tie the strings at my back before spinning in front of the mirror and smiling to myself. After curling my hair to fall in soft waves to my shoulders, I slide a pair of short heels onto my feet just as a knock sounds at the front door. My smile widens as I grab my purse, hanging it over my shoulder before making my way down the stairs to the front door.

Another round of knocks sound as I reach it, and I open it quickly, revealing Reece in a fitting button-up and black slacks, holding a bouquet of pink lilies, making my smile widen at the memory of him gifting me the same flowers at this very door.

His grin falters slightly as his gaze falls down my frame, taking me in as I watch his eyes flare.

"Little impatient, are we?" I question with a tilt of my head, leaning against the door.

His gaze snaps to mine again. "To see you, yes. Always."

I feel my cheeks heat under his stare as I murmur, "Hi."

His lips widen again, like he knows how he's affecting me. "Hi. You look...breathtaking." Then he holds the flowers for me to take. "I hope these are still your favourite. I know I gave you some on your birthday, but I didn't even think to check."

I take the bouquet from him, inhaling the scent as I hold it to my chest. "They are. You remembered?"

"I couldn't forget a single thing about you, Kody."

A blush heats my cheeks, and I try to hide it behind the flowers as I turn to head back inside. "I'll just put these away, and we can go."

"Sure. I'll wait here."

I step away from the door and put the flowers away before coming back to him by the door. He holds his hand out for me, and I fold mine around it, letting him lead me away.

He does everything he promised on this date: he opens the door for me, makes me laugh, and holds my hand. There's no holding back from him and it makes me feel like the centre of his world. It makes me feel whole and so full of love.

The floating restaurant over the river he takes me to is intimate, and even as I sit across from him, he never stops touching me as he holds my hand or rests his foot against mine under the table. It's probably the most romantic date I have been on in a long time.

Every date I had been on in the last six years could never hold my attention for as long as Reece could. I'd tried so many times to make something work with someone else, but no one grabbed my attention or made me feel anywhere near what I felt for Reece. And I guess that was my problem, because I tried to find Reece in every person I met. Compared his banter, smile, and looks to every date. Compared our almost instant connection within the first seconds of introducing myself to someone.

He squeezes my hand from across the table, and my attention snaps to him from where it had strayed out the window to the water.

"What are you thinking about?" he questions, drawing patterns on the top of my hand with his thumb.

I shrug. "Nothing." I don't want to admit what I was actually thinking about.

He raises a brow. "It has to be something with the way you were furrowing your brows. Come on, I want to know. You can be honest with me."

I chew on the corner of my lip. I don't want to hurt him by bringing up past dates, but I did promise to always be honest with him and I don't want secrets between us. It was the thing that tore us apart. "I was thinking about the dates I've been on in the last few years." Both his brows fly up in shock before I quickly add, "Not like that. I mean, I was thinking about how when I went on dates, I think subconsciously I always compared them to you and how fast we connected within the first few minutes of meeting. I kept waiting for that spark. That ease in conversation or attraction. But it never came. And I guess that's why none of them went past the first date."

The corner of his mouth curls. "Well, I guess I should be glad about that. Because you're here now and get to have my second chance. And trust me, I'm never going to let you go. I'm staying right here by your side."

My stomach sinks. "But you're going to have to leave soon."

He frowns, his Adam's apple bobbing with a swallow. "I know."

"I mean, technically, we both have to leave soon. My flight back to Melbourne is in two days, and I imagine you have to go back to the States soon as well."

He nods, pressing his lips together. "In two days as well."

I swallow. I guess, now we're finally going to talk about this instead of avoiding it.

"We'll be in two different time zones and way too far away. It doesn't seem like this will work. And maybe we should have considered this before everything, but I don't want to lose you."

He squeezes my hand again. "And you won't. Because I meant what I said. It doesn't matter if I'm miles away or right in front of you, I will always be yours as much as you are mine."

A crease forms between my brows as my eyes flick between his. "But how will this work? We both travel a lot. What if we never get to see each other?"

He releases a long breath as he looks away for a moment before bringing his gaze back to me, a warring conflict behind them. "Look, there are some things I can't tell you right now for legal reasons. Some things that I haven't shared with anyone but my agent. But I promise you, we will see each other. I will make sure of that. Once I've sorted everything out, I'll tell you everything."

I feel my throat constrict, the feel of the storm looming behind us, and the history coming to pull us back with those words. "That's so vague, Reece. How do you expect me to trust that?"

He tilts his chin down as his eyes pierce mine. "Do you trust me?"

I exhale, the answer coming to me immediately. No hesitation. It's like after I accepted it at the wedding, there was nothing left to restrain it. "I do."

His shoulders relax with my answer, like he's relieved.

"Okay. Then trust me when I say that nothing will ever stop me from coming right back to you. Not a job, not a single mountain or ocean could."

His answer doesn't give me any reprieve from the anxious swirl developing in the pit of my stomach, but still, I nod and smile, deciding to trust him as I swallow and press down that feeling. It may all sound ominous, but I know the Reece sitting in front of me is not the same one who deliberately kept secrets from me and strung me along.

When he drives me home, he rests his hand on my thigh, rubbing small circles with his thumb through my dress material, and it just feels like the most natural thing. Domestic and relaxing.

Pulling up at the front of the house, he cuts the engine before turning to me.

"Wait there," he instructs, then exits the car and rounds the hood to my side, opening the door for me. He holds out a hand, and I try to hide my smile as I take it and climb out.

He laces our fingers together as he walks me to the door, and I think that, with how real this date felt between us, I don't want it to end. I want this moment to last forever. To continue walking with him and his hand in mine while we talk nonsense.

I don't pull out my keys just yet, turning to face him as I finally let the smile spring free.

"This was probably the best date I've been on."

"Really?" he asks with hope shining in his green eyes.

My tone turns gentle. "Yeah. I had a wonderful time."

He grins. "So did I. I always do with you."

Silence settles between us for a heartbeat as we stare at each other, eyes twinkling, matching the stars in the sky.

"So," I draw out, twisting side to side, waiting to see his next step.

His lips twitch as he draws the same, "So."

"I guess this is goodnight."

His lips twist as he nods. "I guess it is."

"You're not going to kiss me goodbye?" I narrow my eyes, suspicious because that's all I've been waiting for.

He hums gruffly. "I want to. God, do I want to. But I fear I won't be able to stop just there, and I want this to be perfect for you."

"It already is, Reece." I squeeze his hand, taking a step closer to him. "Just having you has made this night so perfect. Plus, I think we're a little past the ideal perfect date scenario, don't you think?"

"You're probably right. I'm just trying to be a gentleman."

"Just kiss me, Reece," I say, exasperated, before fisting his shirt and pulling him into me at the same time he drops his lips to mine, wrapping his hands around my waist.

Kissing him was like finding home after wandering aimlessly with no direction. Like the warmth I've craved after years of spending it in the freezing cold alone. Like breathing fresh air after being plunged underwater for too long. Like the universe aligning, at last.

Again and again. Like the very first time, all over again.

It's just him and me, and I don't ever want a life where we

don't exist like we are right now. Like we're the only people living on this planet.

Ever since he entered my life, he's made home in the smallest corner of my heart, taking residence and refusing to budge, even when I tried to scrub him free. He was a permanent scar that I learned to live with all these years, and now it's healing and slowly returning to its former state with him at the centre, blooming under his love, unrestricted and unrelenting.

I pull away, holding his face between my hands as I smile at him. He rests his forehead against mine with his eyes closed. All the creases that seem permanent between his brows relax, I notice as he leans into my hold, looking utterly at peace in my arms—no sign of stress or worry that used to be etched into his face.

When he finally opens his eyes and smiles at me, I know this is exactly where we're meant to be.

"Still holding onto that gentleman card?"

"It's hanging on very fine threads."

"Stay with me tonight, then."

"What?" He frowns.

"I don't want you to stay in the spare room. Stay with me tonight. I just want to feel your arms around me."

He cups my face and presses his lips to mine in a deep kiss before pulling away, gaze pinning between mine. "If you want me to stay, I'll stay. I'll do anything you tell me."

We end up staying awake to watch movies until two a.m., curled around each other on the couch. It's when I start falling asleep on his shoulder that Reece picks me up, an arm supporting behind my back and the other curled under my legs as he carries me to my room.

He lays me on my bed, covers me with a blanket, and presses a kiss to my temple before sliding his body in next to me and curling around me. His arm wraps around my body to keep me against him, and it just feels like two puzzle pieces fitting together.

He presses another kiss to the back of my head, then whispers those three words against it.

"I love you."

I hum, nuzzling further into him and lacing our fingers together.

"I love you, too."

36

REECE

I feel like I didn't sleep a wink last night as I sit slouched on the side of her bed while Dakota sleeps behind me.

I kept jolting awake just as I was drifting off before curling myself tighter around Dakota. It was as if I didn't want to miss a single moment with the seconds ticking by until we had to leave.

I wish I could wrap myself in that bubble, hide us away, and never come out again. We can just live our lives, just her and me, and whatever family we create. It seems pretty damn near perfect when I think about it and tempts me to pick her up and drag her away right now.

But I needed to deal with my situation in the U.S. with my contract and injury first.

I just fear that I'll screw this up. That with the distance and time between us, she'll come to realise I'm still the same fuck up I used to be.

A warm hand smooths over my back, and I close my eyes at the feeling, my muscles loosening instantly under her touch. She has an instant calming effect on me, soothing the crazed beat of my heart.

309

"Morning." Her sleep-ridden voice lilts into my ear, and her arms curl around my shoulders as she presses against my back.

"Morning." I try to sound even, but my tone comes out short and gruff, my head still far away, even with her presence.

She must notice because she cups my face and turns it to face her. My eyes meet her bright blue ones. Even drooping with sleep, they still have the ability to pull me in. My favourite pools to drown in.

"You okay?" she asks, her voice carrying concern.

I lean into her hold, closing my eyes against the swirling behind them, making me feel dizzy as I try to rid it.

I take a few deep breaths before looking at her again, pinballing between her gentle gaze.

"How do you feel about running away? Leaving everything behind and starting fresh in the middle of nowhere. Somewhere, no one knows us."

She smiles softly, but her brows pucker as she says, "I'd go anywhere with you. But that's not going to fix anything, no matter how much we want it to. So, tell me what's wrong?"

Years ago, I would have closed off and pushed her away in the name of saving her from myself. I was so scared of hurting people when it was all I had known. I didn't want to be my dad, especially when it came to her.

But I know better now. I know pushing her away won't fix anything and will only end with me hating myself and losing her.

And I know she's right as well. Running away won't fix this. It won't make this disappear. It will only chase me down even harder.

So, I take a deep breath.

"I've been getting messages from my dad for about a month now. I haven't heard from him in, god, years. I thought I had taken care of it when I blocked his number. But he's heard some rumours about my future baseball career that no one but my agent and I should know. It's just progressively getting more aggressive, and at this stage, I just feel like I have no one on my side. It's frustrating as hell because I was advised to tell no one, but it's okay for other people to."

"Is he threatening you?"

I choke on a laugh. "When has he not threatened me?"

Her brows pinch as worry coats her features. "Should you go to the police then?"

I shake my head as I comb my fingers through my hair. "No. It's fine. I just need to sort everything out when I fly back, and then it will be done."

I'll be free, I want to add, but I can't be sure of that with Dad.

I never knew my agent was in contact with him, but it cleared a few things up. On the decisions he'd made and the advice he'd given me. It made me understand the last message Dad sent me before I changed my number. That I'd never be rid of him.

It's fucking psychotic.

Her hand curls around the nape of my neck, pulling me from the thoughts whirling in my head. Her gaze is soft but purposeful as she stares up at me, and I lean my forehead against hers. Something about the action grounds me and lets me take a moment to centre my world back to her.

"I want you to know that I'm on your side. Always. Even when I don't fully understand what's going on, I'll always stand by your side."

My heart swells with her words, and I take a deep breath as if absorbing the full weight of it.

It's something I've always wanted but never allowed myself to fully grasp. To let myself lean on someone for support. Jenna had wormed her way into my life and stood strong against my stubbornness to push her away before I eventually relented. But with Dakota, it's different. It was almost instantaneous how quick my heart opened for her. How quickly we connected and she became a safe space to me. But then my stupidity made it slip through my fingers and I just never allowed myself to do that again with anyone else. Couldn't let myself do that. And for those few years, Jenna was enough.

Now though, it's more than I ever need to have her here and telling me this.

"I love you," I whisper against her lips.

"And I love you."

Our lips meet, and I find it hard to pull away, knowing our goodbye is ticking to its final minutes.

It hits me in the gut, finding how similar it feels to our last goodbye, wanting to hold onto every single moment, but feeling like we've run out of time. But this time is entirely different. Because it's not a forever goodbye. I'm not letting her go this time.

We start packing our things, getting ready to leave once again. It's mostly silent as we get ready, but every so often, when I pass, I stop her just to kiss her, and every time, she smiles against my lips. It tastes just as I thought it would, like sunshine infusing into my skin with a single touch. But it also tastes a little bittersweet, and I think that has to do with the pending goodbye.

It's when we're standing in front of each other at the front door, suitcases packed and beside us, does it really set in. The separation and walking away again.

I take a step closer to her, cupping her cheek as my gaze pierces hers.

"Always yours, remember?" I push, wanting that statement to always be in her mind. That I'll always be hers, no matter the distance or time between us. I was only ever made to be hers.

She nods. "Always you."

Nate takes us to the airport since he's the only one available, with Dakota's dad and Jenna having left yesterday for their honeymoon.

He pulls up at the domestic airport first, dropping off Dakota first, with her flight being closer.

I let Nate and her say their goodbyes first as I lean against the car away from them.

When he steps away from her, he looks at me and nods.

"I'll go park the car, let me know when you're ready and I'll come round."

I nod and pat his back as he passes. He points over the roof of the car at me with a narrowed gaze. "No funny business."

I grin as he hops back in his car and drives off.

"Why is he leaving? You've got your own flight to catch."

I shrug. "Mine isn't for a couple of hours. I've got time to walk you to your gate."

Her smile is amused as she grabs the handle of her bag. "You gonna send me off? My, you are so obsessed with me."

My lips widen as I wrap my arm around her shoulders. "You're damn right I am."

We walk silently through the airport as she checks in her suitcase before we weave our way through security.

When we check her flight on the screen, her boarding time flashes in ten minutes.

We get to her gate with a few minutes to spare, which I use to my absolute advantage as I pull her to me and press my lips to hers. She melts instantly into me, wrapping her arms around my neck.

Pulling away is even harder now, knowing this is where we part ways, but I just want a little longer.

"I have to confess something," I admit, tucking her hair behind her ear.

Her eyes flutter at my touch before meeting mine. "And that is?"

I swallow. "I read your letter."

Her brows pinch, but I see the panic swirling in her eyes, knowing immediately what I'm talking about. "My letter?"

I nod. "Yeah. The one you hid at the bottom of your drawer. 'To the one who hurt me'."

This time, her eyes widen and she goes to step back, but I hold her to me. "You shouldn't have read that."

My lips flatten as I acknowledge that. "I know. And I'm sorry for that. But I just want to let you know that saying goodbye to you was the hardest thing I've ever done in my life. And I hate that you thought that. So that's why I'm not saying goodbye to you now. It's just... I'll talk to you soon."

Her lips twitch at that, and she relaxes again in my hold. "I think I like that."

"Yeah?"

"Yeah," she says before chewing on her lip. "I'm sorry you read that. I've been meaning to throw it out."

I shake my head. "Don't be sorry. I was a real idiot then, so I don't blame you for writing a hate letter to me. And if you don't want to throw it out, you don't have to. You keep it if that's what you really want, but I promise I will do everything to never make you feel like that again. Because that's one of my biggest fears."

She touches my cheek just as her flight announces it's boarding. Her lips meet mine then, full of longing and desperation that's cut way too short for my liking.

But then she smiles at me. "I love you."

I return her smile. "I love you. I'll talk to you soon."

Both our smiles widen at that as she returns the sentiment. "I'll talk to you soon."

Then she disappears down the tunnel, and my skin itches with the need to chase after her.

But I can only watch as her plane pulls away and she's gone.

37

DAKOTA

When I land back in Melbourne, two hours after leaving Reece, I have the sudden urge to pick up the phone to call him, wanting to hear his voice. Missing the warmth of his presence.

But I know he'll be on his flight now, and I won't be able to contact him until tomorrow sometime.

God, this long-distance thing already sucks. It's been only two hours and I miss him.

I take the bus into the city before walking to our apartment. Daniel and Ellie were already there, having travelled back the day after the wedding to return to work.

It was early in the afternoon when I walked through the door and greeted them both as they sat on the couch, lounging with their feet on the coffee table, watching some TV series.

"Hey. How was your flight?" Ellie asks over Daniel's head.

I leave my bags by the door as I flop down next to her before answering. "It was okay." Then I lean my head against her shoulder with a heavy sigh.

"What's up? Is everything okay?" she asks, pausing the show and turning her attention to me as I feel her head tilt down to catch a glimpse of me.

"Yeah," I mumble before changing my answer. "No... I don't know."

She rests her head against mine in a sign of comfort. "Oh, Dakota."

"It wasn't him, was it? Did he hurt you?" Daniel demands, eyeing me from behind Ellie.

I shake my head immediately. "No. No, he didn't hurt me. We're fine. I'm just... I guess I'm just worried about him."

"Worried about what?" Ellie asks.

I sigh. "A lot of things. He was very vague about it all when we talked about it. He said for legal reasons he couldn't tell me the specifics, but he mentioned that his dad has gotten back in contact with him all of a sudden, and I'm just worried about what that means to him. Because I know how he was treated and how desperate he was to escape him. It just feels like I'm being held at arm's length again and I know that's not his fault this time. I just want to be able to help him."

Ellie brushes her fingers through my hair at a soothing pace that makes my eyelids droop.

"Sometimes, you can't help everyone; all you can do is be there for them."

I swallow as my eyes begin to sting before I squeeze them together. "I know. I just feel helpless."

"I know," Ellie sighs, "but just trust that if he's serious about wanting you, he'll come back to you."

"And if he doesn't," Daniel speaks up, "he'll have us to deal with."

I snicker. "Thanks, guys. I don't think I have to worry about that, though. There's just something I don't like about this."

I'm woken up by buzzing.

Blinking my eyes open, I notice first that it's still just barely

316

beginning to lighten outside, the muffled sounds of the city below making its way through the sealed windows.

I'd stayed up with Ellie and Daniel until late last night, only falling into bed sometime after midnight once I showered and changed. When I pick up my phone to check the time now, though, squinting at the brightness, I read that it's almost six in the morning, with an incoming call from Reece.

I answer almost immediately.

"Hey," I answer, voice coming out groggy.

"Hey." His warm voice answers back, and I relax in bed. "Sorry, did I wake you? I didn't check what time it was there. I just landed and wanted to hear your voice."

A smile spreads over my lips. "It's fine. I've been waiting to call you, too."

"I miss you." He sighs.

My heart skips. "It's only been a day."

Only a day, but still, I felt the same after only two hours.

"All the more reason to miss you. I don't want to miss a single time without being in your presence. I've been without it for way too long already."

Tears prick the corners of my eyes, and I think my sleep-ridden brain feels too emotional at this time of morning. But god, do I feel the same.

"I miss you, too, Reece."

"So fucking much. I'm going to call you every day. I don't think I told you that, but I will. And at a more appropriate time when we're both awake."

I sigh. "You can't promise that. What if you're too busy?"

I'm sure baseball will take up most of his time, and I can't wait by the phone hoping he'll call every day. Because I know that's exactly what I'll do.

"I'm never too busy for you."

"Reece," I say exasperatedly. I want to set realistic expectations because I can't trust myself with too much hope. Too much hope is too dangerous when I know how it feels to have it broken. To have built it up so much that you believe it to be true. It only makes everything worse. All the distance and gaps cleaving between us.

"Dakota," he mimics, and I swear he may be the death of me. "Okay, how about this? A text a day, just to let each other know we're alive. And once I've fixed everything here, I'll call you and tell you everything."

"That's excessive," I muse, but I like that he's making an effort to keep in contact with me. I just hope he can keep his word.

"All I want is for you to never doubt that I will ever change my mind. No matter what you hear from others, or social media, or anyone other than me, I'm in it with you."

"Of course I know that, but now you're scaring me." I chew on my thumbnail.

"Fuck, sorry. I just mean, things in the media can be blown out of proportion, and I don't want you worrying or second-guessing my intentions."

I pause as his words sink in. "And will I second-guess them when you tell me what's happening?"

"God, I hope not. But just know that I've been holding onto all this for a while. It's a decision I'm making not only for myself now, but for you. To get a clean slate."

I swallow, then exhale a heavy breath, saying the words I know he needs and mean them. "I trust you, Reece."

"And I love you."

We say our goodbyes before ending the call, and I just hope this will all be okay in the end.

38

REECE

Landing in Arizona, my stomach is a ball of dread.

This decision has been one I've been mulling over since sustaining my rotator cuff tear, putting me out for most of the season this year while I recover.

It was my own fault for not listening to my body when it screamed at me to stop throwing pitches, but I ignored it and went on. All because I couldn't get my dad's voice out of my head, yelling at me to keep going and pushing. That I was weak if I felt any pain.

Since last year, when I was called up, I'd been getting physio on my right shoulder to keep it sharp and manage the pain that had already started to flare up. Before that, I'd just been managing what I could with icing and resting it. But it wasn't enough.

Because at the beginning of the season this year, I sustained a partial tear to my rotator cuff after my first pitch of the game, and it was fucking agony.

I went in for surgery the next day and have been on the injured roster since then, watching every single game of the rest of the season on the bench.

Coach told me I didn't need to attend, but if I was being completely honest, I was just searching for a bit of spark I had lost in the game. I thought from the benches, I could see from a different perspective what fuelled my passion when I was younger.

But I found nothing.

And that...that's when I realised I was fucking relieved for my injury. Like, I had a reason to stop playing. Like I was waiting for one thing to physically pull me out of the game.

Wasn't that just fucked up?

But still, I felt myself hesitate to make the final decision to leave. Because this game had been my entire fucking life since I could walk. I had nothing else going for me. I had no other future prospects. Nothing else I dreamed of doing or being. It was just this.

Now, though, I have someone I want to live for. I don't want to survive and live someone else's dream anymore. I'm over being haunted by the blame and the responsibility to make up for something that I had no control over. That because of my mother's death, it's my responsibility to make up for everything he lost.

Deciding to hang up my cleats was a sort of bittersweet feeling, saying goodbye to one part of my life but welcoming another, one where the future was unknown.

But it's one I know I won't regret. Because though I love baseball, it was never a dream of mine to play in the big leagues. I never wanted that attention or pressure.

So, when I arrive home and trudge into my bedroom with my suitcase in tow, I flop onto the bed and fall asleep in an instant, wanting to forget all my responsibilities for just a little while longer.

I'm woken up to consistent banging on my door, and I blink my eyes open against the glaring light blasting through the windows.

I slept through the whole night, still wearing the clothes I wore on the plane. I'm surprised my shoes made it off with the way I crashed.

The banging starts again, this time followed by someone yelling to open the door, which has me snapping up in bed, blinking the sleep from my eyes, muscles stiffening.

"You better open the door now before I break it down."

It's Dad. Even after years of not hearing from him, I still recognise that voice. I hear it almost every day in my head, so it's almost impossible to forget. I just know he would love that if he knew.

I straighten my clothes and brush through my hair with my fingers, not bothering to change before going out to answer the door. Cracking it open, I face my father, a prominent frown on his face. He looks the same, the years ageing him more than I last saw him, though, with deeper grooves on his forehead and the corners of his eyes. Still the same grumpy, stoic features that I remember.

"How did you find where I live?" I ask, knowing I sure as fuck didn't tell him, wanting to keep my life as far away from his as much as I could. And it worked for the last four years. Until now, I guess.

His eyes narrow, jaw ticking. "You don't think a father deserves to know where his kid lives?"

"Not when said kid told you he wanted nothing to do with you. Wanted no contact with you."

The subtle curl of the corner of his lip sends a wave of unease through me, knowing I won't like whatever comes out of his mouth next. Knowing it will be nothing but venom and disdain.

"Well, *kid*, in this life, we don't always get what we want. Which brings me to the reason I'm here."

Then, without even asking, he kicks the door out of my grip and barges into my house. Like it isn't my house. Like he still owns everything in my life.

I feel two seconds from losing my shit.

"You better get the fuck out before you regret showing up here."

His laugh is sinister and sends a chill down my spine. "What are you going to do? Because we both know you were never man enough to take a hit at me."

I clench my fists by my side to stop myself from doing just that. I'm not the same kid he knew. I'm far from the boy he neglected. "Get. Out."

He crosses into the lounge room, plopping himself on the couch and sprawling himself there.

"Not until you explain to me why there's a rumour of you retiring early. Because I didn't raise no quitter from one small injury."

I seethe. "You have no idea what you're talking about."

He raises a brow. "No? Well, I guess your agent was lying then."

I fucking knew it. It was my dad who got me in contact with my current agent. Why wouldn't he still be? But I thought I was clear to my agent that I cut off contact with him, and I thought he got the message to do the same. Clearly, the fuck not. All the more reason to get out of this fucked up situation.

I scoff. "So you think you can slide on through, appearing when I specifically told you to stay the hell out of my life, and what? Convince me to keep playing? You don't have the upper hand here anymore, Dad. And if I want to retire after two Major League seasons, then that's my choice."

His head jerks back at my retort before a wide, sinister

smile stretches across his face. "Well," he drawls. "Look who finally decided to grow a pair."

"Oh, fuck right off." I pull the door open and wave my hand toward the front yard. "You can leave now if that was all you came here for."

He stares at me for a moment, the muscle in his jaw twitching, before he finally stands. He keeps his glare steady on mine until he's toe to toe with me. "Your mother would be so disappointed to have a son like you."

That fucking word. That word has been the very trigger to every fucked up decision, impulse, every fucking meltdown that's made my life a living hell.

I will *not* let it break me now.

I will *not* let it have power over me now.

Just like the man in front of me

My upper lip curls as I lift my chin. We're practically the same height, but at this distance, it makes it easy to look down at him.

"You know what, from my knowledge, I think it would be you who she'd be disappointed in since she was in the process of filing a divorce."

I'd found that little information when a friend of my mothers found me online a few years ago, and we met up when I came back home so she could tell me about her. It was refreshing to hear the details of the woman I never met and not have it thrown in my face. It was nice to connect things between us. Like our humour and smile. It was nice to know I inherited some things from her.

But when she told me that, I was shocked. Mum's friend told me they had been on the rocks through her whole pregnancy since Dad gave up his baseball dream to be there for her. My heart broke, knowing the last moments of her life were like that, preparing for a divorce from the father of her child and someone she thought she loved. I hated that. Hated my dad for that, because it wasn't just me he resented for my existence, it was her too.

His gaze narrows as he seethes. "What did you just say?"

My lips twist at the corners. "You heard me."

My head snaps to the right with the fist he connects to my cheek before he pins me against the wall, fisting my collar.

I tongue the edge of my lip, tasting iron, before a grin splits across my face when I bring my eyes to his.

"And that's why I'll always be the bigger person than you." I inch my face close to his until our noses almost touch. "Get the fuck out of my house, before I call the cops. And we both know you don't want that."

He huffs, staring at me before he finally lets me go, stepping back.

"Good luck finding someone who wants you in their family, because you've got none now."

I laugh, but it's empty of any humour. All I feel is numb. "I never had one to begin with."

He doesn't say anything more, just spins and walks right out of the house. I slam the door shut, and as soon as that barrier is between us, I sink down to the floor against it, gasping in a breath. It finally feels like the end of our relationship, and the rush of mixed emotions is all I feel in that ball on the floor.

Relief.

Anger.

Grief.

Hollow.

Relief.

39

DAKOTA

It's been just over two weeks now, Christmas and New Year's passing by, and Reece has stuck to his word. Every day, I wake to a text from him wishing me a good day, then always adding something he loves about me.

But it has been three days now since his check-ins have gone silent, and it makes me worry.

I stare at the last message he sent me, pretending as if it were sent today, but also begging for a new one to pop up.

> Good morning, Kody. I hope today is as beautiful as you.

> Reason number 14 why I love you: I love that you make me forget my fears, and that I am brave enough to face them. It's in the way you look at me and believe in me. And sometimes I think I don't deserve that, don't deserve you. But damn am I lucky that you chose me.

My heart clenches as I read it over again, just as I have at least fifty times already.

The day before, I sent him a message to check up on him to

see if he was okay and wished him a happy New Year, but there was no reply. I didn't want to bombard him with messages either, knowing he was most likely busy or something. But like I thought I would, I waited for those daily messages, just to know he was okay.

I'm sure it didn't help when I started going down multiple rabbit holes when I searched his name and immediately got flooded with news articles of rumours and gossip about his past. The kinds of things that made me a little sick to look at, especially with the pictures attached of him. I could tell they were from years ago, most likely from the year he moved to the States. He looked like the boy I knew, but so different. He looked strung out and not completely right in every single photo. Drugs and public indecency were written about in articles from those years, and my heart cracks, not knowing the extent of what these years looked like for him. I click out of those pages as fast as they come.

But today, the most recent article in my current doom scroll snags my attention, and my heart leaps into my throat.

Reece Fischer: Rookie relief pitcher set to hang up his cleats in an early retirement from the sport

The phone call when he landed back in the U.S comes back to me, clicking the puzzle pieces together of him mentioning the decision he has to make, one he's making for himself, but also for me. And I understand now, the way he was so disconnected when I brought up baseball. All the little signs I never picked up on racing through my mind.

I read on, my fingers slowly raising to cover my lips as I read about his shoulder injury and the true severity of it, glazing over more rumours for his early leave from the sport.

He always plays it off like an annoyance more than something that causes him pain, and I almost want to yell at him for that. For hiding how much pain he's in.

There's a video attached to the article, a clip of the game he was injured in. Taking a deep breath, I click it. I watch as he comes up to the mound, relaxed in posture. He rolls his shoulder before zeroing in on the batter. His wind-up is fluid, and you can see how natural it comes to him. It happens so fast, from the forward snap of his arm to the early release of the ball, sending it flying way to the right of the base, to the moment he crouches in front of the mound, cradling his shoulder. The video cuts off then, and I'm left sitting there, wondering why he never told me about this. I can't imagine what that was like, how much pain he must have been in.

I click out of the article before stumbling again on a different one. This one, though, is an interview, one that was posted two days ago. An exclusive tell-all interview with Reece. I read through, him telling all about his upbringing to now. He doesn't give every detail of his childhood, though, just bare details of his dad teaching him all he knew of the game. Then I catch where he begins to talk about the summer before he moved to the U.S., and my breath ceases.

"That summer changed my entire perspective on life," he says, chuckling to himself. When asked what did it, there was a long pause as he smiled to himself. "She did."

If my heart wasn't thumping against my chest before, it's damn near galloping now.

Swallowing, I scroll on, reading as he talks about loving, losing, and second chances without giving too much away, but I know. God, do I know.

I get to the end of the interview, where he officially announces his retirement and expresses his gratitude for the last six years in the league and the opportunity given to him over the last two years.

I close out of the tab and lock my phone, staring at it like I couldn't believe what I read.

I need to talk to him, wanting to call him straight away,

needing answers as my mind starts to swirl. His birthday today being even more of a reason to hear his voice.

I pull up his contact, thumb hovering over his contact before I take a deep breath and click.

It rings four times before he picks up, and his deep voice rings through the receiver, pulling a deep sigh from my lips.

"Hey, Kody," he greets, but I can hear the exhaustion in his voice.

"Are you okay?"

He huffs a laugh, but there's no humour behind it. It's tired and resigned. "Yeah, I'm okay. I'm sorry. I know I haven't talked to you in a couple of days like I promised to. I've been in and out of meetings for the last couple of days. I didn't realise all this would arise when I returned."

"You're retiring?"

There's a pause over the line before he answers. "You've heard."

My laugh was empty. "Of course I did. It's plastered all over the internet."

He sighs. "I know. I didn't expect it to be such big news since I'm still a nobody. But I guess no one has retired this early in their career before."

"You're definitely not a nobody." Going off how much everyone is talking about him. I chew on my lip before continuing. "You were injured. Why didn't you tell me what happened?"

"It's not a big deal. A lot of players get rotator cuff tears. I'm not the first one. And it's not that bad now. Just gets a bit uncomfortable sometimes," he tells me so nonchalantly that I want to reach through the phone and shake him.

"You should have told me," I whisper.

"I know," he whispers back. "I just didn't want you to pity me, especially when I was still deciding whether to stop playing."

"Why are you retiring?"

There's a long pause before he answers, "It never felt right. I thought once I finally got to the Majors, it would all be worth it. Everything I gave up, everything I worked for, I would finally have it all. But all I felt was empty. I never had that thrill I used to have while playing when I was younger," he pauses before adding, "and I never really had everything, did I? Not when I let you go."

"Reece," I begin, but there's a deep voice that interrupts through the receiver that I barely hear, calling his name. But I don't recognise the voice. Though why would I? I don't know anyone from his life there.

"Yeah, give me a moment," Reece replies.

"Are you busy?" I ask.

"No," he answers immediately. "Not for you. It's just another meeting to finalise my contract termination. Not that important right now."

"Reece," I squeak. I would've melted at that if I weren't panicking about how he just left what is most definitely an important meeting to talk to me. "How is that not important?"

"Well, to me, you're more important. And I needed the excuse to finally talk to you and get out of these stuffy rooms. I swear, anytime I picked up my phone to text you, I would get in trouble."

I smother my rising smile as I feel my cheeks heat. "You should probably get back."

"But I want to talk to you more," he whines.

"Reece," I insist, but I can't help but think about how cute his whining is.

"Fine," he resigns. "Only because finishing this meeting means I'm a step closer to seeing you again."

"Seeing me?" I ask, as hope rises in my chest.

"Yeah. As soon as I'm free of all this, you bet you're ass I'm flying my way back to you."

"Then hurry," I whisper.

I can hear the grin in his voice as he says, "Your wish is my command. I'll talk to you soon."

"Reece," I interrupt before he hangs up.

"Yes, Kody?" he drawls.

I grin. "Happy Birthday."

He's silent for a moment before replying, "Thank you."

When we end the call, I press the phone to my chest and wish for time to move faster.

40

DAKOTA

Another two weeks pass, and communication with Reece has been on and off, but every chance he has, he sends me the same message as before. Listing all the reasons he loves me. I love it when he catches up on all the days he missed as well.

This morning's message:

> Reason 28 why I love you: Your smile. Every time you smile at me, it instantly melts away everything around me until all I can focus on is you. It's quite a peaceful world to live in when that happens. I wish I could live in it all the time.

> Reason 29 why I love you: Your patience. Through this whole time, you have been nothing but patient with me, and I truly don't know how I deserve a woman like you. God, don't I know how lucky I am to have you

Just like every time before, I wake with a smile, reading the message and melting into my pillow.

It's ridiculous and so cheesy every time, but still, it fills that little corner of my heart that is purely his with love and warmth, healing every single tiny crack until it is whole.

I pull myself out of bed, padding to the kitchen, half asleep but a smile playing on my lips.

Ellie stands in the kitchen when I enter, and when she notices me, she narrows her gaze.

"What's got you smiling so early in the morning?" she interrogates.

I shrug. "Nothing."

"Liar," she counters.

I look at her as she sips on her coffee. "Can't I just be happy?"

"Yes. But this early in the morning? No one is ever this happy."

"You're dramatic." I chuckle, turning to grab a cup from the cupboard to start making my coffee.

"That may be, but still. Tell me, why are you so happy this morning?" she quizzes, folding her arms across her chest as her eyes zero in on me.

Again, I shrug. "I just am."

She groans. "You're giving me nothing. I have to get ready, but don't expect me not to let this go."

"I would never."

She disappears into her room, and once I pour some milk into my cup, I take the mug and go to sit out on the balcony off the lounge area.

Opening the sliding door, a warm breeze passes through, whipping my hair over my cheek before I brush it away.

I love to come out here in the mornings and listen to the traffic beneath and look out at the city view. It's how I've started my day for the past six years now, and no matter how minimal our view is with the other apartment buildings squeezed beside us, you can still see a part of Albert Park from here.

I curl up in the chair in the corner, mug balancing on my knee as I open my phone and click open Reece's text chain.

I click a picture of the view and send it to him with a message.

Dakota: Wish you were here with me

I close out of the messages before thinking too much about it, and open a book on my phone that I had just begun to read.

I only get a few pages in before I hear the door slide open, making me look up to Ellie, a smirk playing on her lips.

"Well, now I know why you were smiling so much."

I frown, but then she moves out of the way, and it melts right off my face as my jaw slacks with shock.

I don't move as I try to process what I'm seeing, but then my lips spread into a wide smile, one that shows teeth and all. I place my mug on the table beside me before I stand, making my way to him.

Reece.

He's here.

He's really here.

He holds out his arms, and I jump into his embrace instantly.

"Hi, Kody," he says against the top of my head, pressing a kiss there and tightening his arms around me.

"You're here," I breathe out the words like I'm in some sort of daydream.

"I'm here," he echoes, pulling away slightly to look down at me, tucking a strand of hair behind my ear, "and I'm not going anywhere."

My brows pinch, not wanting to jump to conclusions, but hope still blossoms in my chest. "What do you mean?"

He drops his forehead to mine. "It means I'm here, offering you everything I have. Wherever you are, that's where I'll go. If you're in Melbourne, so am I. If you're travelling the world, I'll

ZOE GRACE DOUGLAS

be right by your side. My heart is wherever you are, and I can't be parted from you any longer. I'm here for the long haul now. I told you there was no getting rid of me now."

"Really?"

"Really, Kody. I bought an apartment not far from here. That's why it took me a couple more weeks after that meeting you called me in the middle of. After I bought the apartment, I had to move everything over. And that was a fucking night-mare." He snorts, cradling my cheeks in both his hands. "I wanted everything to be sorted before I came to see you. I wanted everything to be final."

"Will you tell me everything?" I ask. I know he explained part of it over the phone, but I still didn't fully understand what went down. What led him to this decision, to give up every-thing he ever worked for.

"How much time you got?" he asks with a raise of his brow.

I look down at my phone. "About another hour before I have to leave for work."

He tucks another piece of hair behind my ear. "How about I pick you up from work, take you to my apartment, cook you dinner, and I'll tell you everything there?"

I smile, liking everything he just planned out. "Okay."

He grins back before leaning down to press his lips to mine, and my entire body melts into his at the relief of feeling his kiss after a month.

He pulls away all too soon, still cradling my head. "I'll take you to work. Go get ready."

When I walk out of work in the late afternoon, a smile instantly pulls at my lips as I look up. Reece stands there, leaning against a street sign, a mirroring smile on his own lips.

He wraps his arm around my shoulder, pulling me to him

334

when I'm close enough, and we start walking down the street together.

"Now, when I promised to pick you up from work. I didn't think about transport. I don't have a car yet, so we will walk. Is that okay with you?"

I chuckle. "Yeah, that's okay. I walk these streets every day anyway."

"Alone?" he queries.

"Yeah."

He's silent for a moment. "Well, you won't be alone from now on."

"What? Are you going to walk me to and from work every day?"

He shrugs. "Yeah, why not?"

"You're crazy."

He grins down at me. "For you, always."

I shake my head, cheeks heating, but I lean into him as he tightens his hold around me. The cool breeze of the late afternoon sets a chill in my bones that I'll never fully adjust to, but in his warm embrace, I feel I can brave anything.

He asks me about my day at work, what I did, and listens so intently, like he's really interested in me explaining what my job entails. Not even my friends were ever really that invested in knowing. They just think I take lots of pictures while travelling around the city and call it a day. It's exciting, getting to go into detail about the little things I get to do and see, and have him nod along and let me yap about my passion. I've never been able to do that before. Never really thought anyone was interested in my work because it's just photography.

The walk to his apartment isn't long. Maybe ten minutes through the busy streets until we reach a tall building on the main street. He pulls out a fob before buzzing the door open. He ushers me in first, a hand resting on my lower back as he follows behind.

The loud peak city noises muffle as the door closes behind us, and he leads me over to a set of elevators. The entrance interior is simple but elegant, giving a hint of what to expect in the apartments residing in this building. It looks expensive. Nothing I would ever be able to afford.

He presses the button for the twenty-fourth floor, the last level before the penthouse.

When the doors close on us, he begins to tell me about the place.

"It's a pretty private floor. Not as private as the penthouse, but there's only two apartments on the whole floor."

I side-eye him. "Expensive and fancy."

He chuckles before meeting my gaze, heat flaring behind them. "It wasn't too bad. At least now we can make as much noise as we want."

I feel the way my cheeks heat at his innuendo and avert my gaze, hiding my face as I drop my head. "Oh my gosh."

"Is that a blush I see?" he teases. "You know how much I love making you go all red."

He tilts my head up with his two fingers hooked under my chin, and I press my lips together as I look at him.

"There it is." He grins.

I roll my eyes. "You're ridiculous."

He leans close, nose barely brushing mine, at the same time the elevator doors open before he whispers, "Again, only for you."

He leads me down the quiet hall to the door on the right, then pulls out a set of keys from his front pocket to unlock the door.

Pushing the door open, I peek around him to the wide, open floor apartment with white walls and dark accents. From the kitchen to the lounge and dining area, I notice as I slowly step further in, there's not a lot of colour. Even with the furniture he has. Everything is monochrome.

"You need colour," I comment.

He rubs the back of his neck. "I haven't decided what to do with it all. I was hoping...maybe you could help me?"

I turn to face him, where he leans against the closed front door. "What do you mean?"

He shrugs. "I could use your input. Like you said, it needs colour. I don't know where to start."

I chew on my lip as I take in his suggestion, really liking the idea of helping decorate his place. To play around with decorating like this was my home. It was a silly thought, but it got me excited about the idea.

He straightens, then walks across the room to where a large frame sits against the wall in the lounge area. "I mean, I do have one item."

He spins the frame, and my breath catches in my throat.

I haven't seen that photo in years. Never really thought about it since it went on auction years ago for a charity event during my photography course.

But seeing it now, here, him holding it, it all flashes back to me. Remembering how it had sold for a few thousand dollars. I was so shocked it had gone for as much as it did. Surprised someone liked it that much.

Gaze flicking between him and the photograph, my head starts spinning in circles.

"You..." I start, but I can't even finish the thought. Can't wrap my head around it. A rush of an expelling past my lips.

A soft smile pulls the corner of his lips. "Jake heard from Avery that you were putting a few of your photographs up for auction. I bribed him to bid for me. I thought since I couldn't have you, I could have a piece of you through this photograph. I kept it in front of my bed all these years so it could be the first and last thing I saw."

My eyes snap to his as they start to waver with the emotions overwhelming me.

He bought my photograph. Even when we weren't talking, he still thought of me and checked up on me to find out about this. I know he already told me that, but maybe it's just now hitting me. That almost a year after we last saw each other, I was still in his thoughts, and then he bought my photograph to have a piece of me.

I shake my head. "Reece," I whisper, throat clogging before I swallow and take a breath. Then, I choke out the three words. "I love you."

He smiles, placing the frame against the wall again before taking a few strides to reach me. He cups my cheeks before brushing his lips over mine in a slow, intoxicating pull. Slow and torturous. Slow and powerful. Pouring all his feelings into one kiss, so that I can almost taste the words on the tip of his tongue.

I love you.

I adore you.

I am yours.

He pulls away, gaze flicking between mine before he verbalises those exact words, punctuating each with the press of his lips against my cheek, nose, and forehead.

He nods toward the kitchen. "Come on. I'll cook us some dinner and then we can sit down and talk."

I lift a brow. "You cook?"

His lips twitch. "Yes, Kody. I cook. Now, sit over here and just look pretty."

"Seriously? I can help if you want."

He shakes his head. "Nope. This is my treat. You just relax. Play some music, tell me a story. Whatever you want. But I'm doing the cooking."

When we enter the kitchen, he drags a stool over to sit at the edge of the island bench, where he starts to set up all the utensils and ingredients.

I do as he says before pulling up my Spotify and hitting shuffle on one of my playlists.

It begins with me just watching him as he chops and mixes and prepares the food. But then it turns into something that reminds me of cooking dinner at home. With singing, dancing, and laughter. He spins me around the kitchen while the food bakes in the oven to some LANY song, serenading me with the lyrics. Then he gives me small taste tests of his food, asking for my feedback before adding different spices to the mix until he's happy with my reaction.

He plates our food before guiding me over to the small four-seater dining set he has against the wall. He sits to my left, placing our plates on the table before we start to dig in.

It's delicious and I almost want to inhale it all in one go. But I savour it, wanting to enjoy it while I mull over the questions still surrounding my head to ask him.

I wanted to wait a little before bombarding him with the questions, but I've been waiting all evening so they just slip from my mouth.

"So, what led you to the decision to retire?" I question.

He laughs. "You sound like the interviewers I've been talking to." I pin him with a pointed glare, impatient to get the answers, and he sighs. "Sorry."

Then he shakes his head before continuing. "Okay. I guess I'll start from the beginning. When Dad told me he had gotten me drafted, I felt torn about the decision. I didn't want to move overseas, but I knew this was what I'd been working toward my whole life. I mean, why would I turn that opportunity down? But then everything with us happened, and this may be crazy to think, but I was considering just that. Because the more I thought about it, I realised it was never really my dream. It was my father's. But my dad already had me sign the contract, and it felt impossible to get out of. From what he made me believe, anyway."

He swallows, looking down at his plate. "So, I left, breaking your heart in the process as well as my own. And I was miserable. I had no one. No friends. No family. Yeah, I had my team, and it's been incredible playing with everyone I've met, but I've never made any true friends there. I've been so fucking lonely and miserable all these years. I mixed with the wrong crowd, trying to fill the gap that leaving you left, with whatever would make me forget the most. I was drowning, missing you and the life I left behind. I lost that spark and enjoyment in the game I loved because it felt like more of a chore than fun. And because of that, my game got sloppy."

He looks up at me again, pausing his story as his eyes flick between mine. I let the silence carry, waiting for him to gather his thoughts and tell me everything. I knew this was new for him, being so open with me. But he was trying, and it was all I ever asked for from him.

"That was the first time I tore my shoulder," he continues. "In that first year, when I didn't care how I performed or what happened to me. I was pushed to have surgery on it, and then it was about four months before I could play again. When I got out of surgery, I realised that it could be so easy to lose everything. And then it would have all been for nothing. Losing you and everyone who meant something to me."

He scoffs. "I guess that was the motivation I needed. I pushed and worked hard to accomplish the one goal I was there for, because if I had to lose you for this, then I couldn't throw it all away.

"But once I played my first game in the Majors, nothing changed. I thought maybe I would have that feeling of 'finally' or be proud of myself or *something*," he punctuates the last word, a desperate tone in his voice, breaking my heart along with it, "but there was still nothing. Don't get me wrong, I still played my heart out. But it never became the game I once felt.

The joy of throwing a good pitch, the satisfaction of teamwork, there was none of that."

I reach across the table to lace my fingers together with his. He looks down at our intertwined hands on the table, tracing his thumb in a slow circle, before smiling up at me and taking a deep breath.

"Then the second tear happened about halfway through this last season, and though it was absolute agony, when I was pulled into the medic room and they told me I would be out for the rest of the season after yet another surgery, I felt nothing more than relief."

He frowns. "That's crazy, right? Because so many people would dream about being in my position, but I wanted nothing more than to be out of it."

I squeeze his hand as I lean closer to him. "But you were unhappy. I don't think it matters what you were doing, whether playing professional baseball or being in a blue-collar job; if it was making you miserable, then it's okay to want to get out of the job. I mean, it's not great about the injury, and I'm still mad that you didn't tell me about it, but it's still the same."

He nods, watching the small circles he continues to trace on my hand as he processes my words before adding, "That was about the time Jenna told me she was getting married, and only then did I feel something awake inside me. There was anticipation and hope because I knew that I would finally get to come home. I would finally get to see you. Because this is where everything I know and love is. My friends, the family that I found here. Most of all, it had you. I knew then that I couldn't keep living life the way I was. Though I do love baseball, and I'm grateful for the opportunity to play professionally, I loved you more. And I couldn't do more years living without you. I think six years was already too much, don't you think?"

I grin. "Way too much."

He squeezes my hand. "I love you. So fucking much it hurts. I'm with you until our next life, you good with that?"

"Yeah. I'm definitely good with that."

We smile, content and at peace with where we are, together and back in each other's lives. Where we were always meant to be. Where we were always going to come back to.

He is home.

I am home.

And I wouldn't want to be anywhere else.

EPILOGUE
REECE

Two Years Later

Looking back on the years, it's kind of crazy how much and how fast things can change once things are set in motion.

From the moment I met Dakota to now, so much has happened.

Coming back to her after leaving the U.S. was the easiest thing I ever had to do—the best decision. I only wish I realised it all sooner.

Because now I have a life that I chose. A life where I get to keep choosing. Where I get to make my own decisions and build the life I want instead of whatever others want.

And in this life, my choice is always Dakota.

She came into my life with an air of ease. Like magic, she calmed every nerve in my body and every tense muscle. She was the hand that reached out and pulled me out of the drift after I was swimming aimlessly without direction.

But it was like her and me were made to drift and collide time and again. Coming into each other's lives for a moment in time before falling apart. It was stubbornness. It was hopeless.

It was time wasted as we denied what was right in front of us all along. One of us more than the other. We were like a lighthouse to a boat, finding our way back to each other in the middle of a storm. But every time we reached the shore, something dragged us out to sea until we found each other again, like some force pulling us apart.

Maybe it was just timing. Maybe we just weren't meant to find our way to each other so early. Maybe it was a reminder to me that she existed and I needed to fix myself to come back to her.

And I did. Coming back to her was inevitable, but I needed to be ready for her. To be the best version of myself for her. Because when I did find my way back to her, I wasn't letting anything pull us apart. Like hell was I going to make that mistake again.

And now, two years later, I have never been happier.

I feel like I can breathe fresh air now. Because I know this is it. This is where we're meant to be—where I was always meant to be.

And I wouldn't want to be anywhere else.

After retiring from baseball, I didn't really have a backup plan for what to do next. I was left in limbo, wondering what I wanted to do for myself. I'd been so focused on this one thing for so long that I didn't think about anything else.

But it was when Dakota's photography blog started to blow up that we decided to travel. We'd been to so many places and met so many people through the years while she built her business of travel photography.

Spending a month in different cities and countries was an experience I'd never be able to replace. Spending it all with the love of my life by my side was something I would cherish forever. Holding her hand while we tried new foods and adventured to new places was something I could only describe as freedom. No restraints. Nobody to tell us we were wrong or doing something we shouldn't. It was just us. Just love and independence and contentment.

It was exactly what I needed—what *we* needed. Space away from thoughts of baseball and family, and responsibilities. Space to let us live our lives. To start a life of our own. A life I'd dreamed of. A life that was just now starting.

I wring my hands together in front of my body, fidgeting with my thumbs and bouncing my legs. I always want time to slow down when it comes to Dakota, but at this moment, I just want it to speed up.

Nate claps my shoulder to my right, and I snap my attention to him as he sends me a lopsided smile.

"Nervous are we?"

"What do you think?" I snap. Because, fuck yeah, I'm nervous. I can't stand still for more than a couple of seconds.

"Hey, no need to get snippy with me. She'll be out soon."

I chew my lip as I meet his stare. "She hasn't changed her mind?"

He shakes his head, amusement shining in his eyes. "Sadly, no, no matter how much I tried to convince her to."

I jab him in the stomach with my elbow, and he hunches over with an *oof*.

He may be my best friend, but he's still Dakota's brother, and I wouldn't put it past him to do that.

"I'm kidding, of course," he wheezes, standing tall again as our other friends snicker behind him.

It's only our friends, Dakota's parents, and Jenna here at the moment, just as we wanted. Intimate, small, with just our inner circle and our parents.

I swallow down the knot of emotion, knowing I've only got Jenna for family here and no one else.

Yeah, Dakota's family has welcomed me with open arms, but deep down, it will never quite feel the same.

I know, and I hear it from everyone around me, that my

mother is here in spirit, but it never quite satisfies the ache in my chest.

I could almost feel her presence if I closed my eyes and blocked everything out. Or imagine it, really, because I'd never felt what she was like. But from the memories her friend has told me over the years, I do imagine it to be warm, like a blanket wrapping around me in the coldest winter in front of a fire. It felt unyielding, comforting, and like the kind of motherly love I'd always craved.

I'd met her friend a few times over the last couple of years to talk about Mum and learn what I was never allowed to know about her. It soothed a part of my soul that ached to know about her. Just simple knowledge, so I could feel close to her, to know what I inherited. And I learned so much in those coffee visits, which is all I'd ever wanted.

Fuck, I'm already crying, and Dakota hasn't even shown up yet.

I sniffle, wiping the corner of my eye quickly before opening them.

The world comes back to focus, and that feeling lingers as the music filters through my ears. I turn, realising Dakota's friends are already walking down the aisle.

Avery, Ellie, and Alex make their way to the left side of the altar, and I smile at them before snapping my gaze back to the entrance.

There she stands, looking as radiant as ever, and my skin buzzes in her presence.

Her simple, plain white dress falls down her frame, moulding to her until her waist, where the fabric dips between her chest, before falling to her feet, trailing a few inches behind her. A few strands of short blonde hair fall in front of her face as she beams at me from down the aisle.

I don't feel the first tear until Nate holds his handkerchief in front of me, and I smack him in the chest before wiping the wetness away with my palm, my gaze never wavering from her.

In an instant, I feel her love fill my veins. The realisation that I get to spend the rest of my life looking into those ocean blue eyes, spend the rest of my life being pulled into her orbit, hits me square in the chest, and I curse under my breath.

Everyone chuckles at me as I break down in front of them. I look to the ceiling to try to stop the onslaught of tears running down my cheeks, but god, I feel so damn lucky right now. As if it didn't hit me until now.

I look down again when I feel a hand wrap around my forearm. Dakota stands in front of me, a soft smile playing on her lips, one I know so intimately as mine. One filled with love, adoration, and so much fucking happiness.

She swipes her fingers underneath my eyes, then laces her fingers in mine, linking us together, a connection that I never want to be torn away from. Never want to walk this earth without her hand in mine.

"Always yours, right?" she whispers.

A sob of a laugh escapes me and I press my forehead to hers, soaking in the reality of this moment. Her, here, in front of me, dressed in white, the diamond ring I proposed to her just under a year ago on her finger.

"Always you," I reply.

She squeezes my hand before pulling me in front of the officiant. I just stare at her, barely hearing as they start to talk. All I can think as I look in her eyes is that if every single mistake and decision I made in the past had to happen to make sure I was right here, right now, then I forgive myself for all the pain and self-sabotage I put myself through.

Because in the end, I get to have her, and that is all I need in this life.

ACKNOWLEDGMENTS

And just like that, Dakota and Reece's story comes to a close. Just like the first, the feeling is just as bittersweet. Their story has been stuck in my head for so long that it doesn't feel real that I'm finally closing their chapter.

This book has made me explore so much with my writing and who I am as a writer. This is an ever learning field and I'm so grateful I get to explore this craft, to write these stories my little brain has conjured and release them into the world for you all to read.

This past year has been a struggle, with life, personal issues, and work commitments. I lost my dog near the beginning of last year, just as I was starting to draft this book. It was the hardest thing I had to decide. I grew up with her since I was 10 years old and she's been with me through so many changes and life events. I'm so thankful to have had her for as long as I did and I will miss her so dearly.

A lot of other things have happened and naturally, as I always do, I self isolated. I grew distant and really struggle with keeping up a social media presence. I kept trying to consistently post, but it was really hard to make the effort to interact.

So if you've stayed with me since book 1, I want to give you a really huge thank you for all the support you've shown and. For sticking around and showing your love through this journey. It's always so lovely to see how supportive this community is and I'm so grateful to be a part of it.

I will always be forever thankful for my boyfriend, my life

partner, the one constant in my life. You have shown me that there is nothing stronger than love. Without your constant support and rallying, I don't know where I'd be Even when life wasn't playing fair, you were there. You have been my number 1 cheerleader, recommending my books to anyone that will hear when you're playing video games when I've been too afraid to do so with anyone. I love you always.

Though they will never see this, I have to say a huge thank you to my work friends. They don't know about this part of my life, but they helped me endlessly to get me out of the cave I was in. Dragged me out might be more appropriate. To all the boat parties, lunches and dinners we've been on, to all the laughs, tears and gossip we've shared, I'm so grateful for it all. To be in a work environment that is as supportive as it is, even with all the stress and trauma we experience looking after so many people.

To my beta readers, Elicia, Nique, Zara, Chrissy, and Lara. Thank you for all your comments, reactions, and honest feedback. It has helped me build this story to a better version.

My editor, Cassidy, thank you for your sharp eye, attention to detail and for polishing off this manuscript to make it make sense.

And lastly, I could never leave this acknowledgment without a last thank you to my Dad. I have woven so much of you into Dakotas Dad almost like keeping your legacy alive. Your warmth and kindness. Your embarrassing jokes and endless charisma. But most of all, your general happiness despite all that you were going through. It was inspiring to see and I'll always be thankful for it.

ABOUT THE AUTHOR

Zoe is a romance author based in Australia, writing heartfelt, angsty romances. From her love for reading, to her wild imagination morphing into storytelling, writing has become an outlet she's clung to in the rush of her life. If she's not writing, she's either looking after the elderly as an aged care nurse, curled up on the couch with her kindle or a paperback, absorbed in another world of romance or fantasy, or passed out with her little fur babies from exhaustion. There's no in-between.

ALSO BY ZOE GRACE DOUGLAS

Lost in the Current of You - Book 1 in the Lost in Love Duet

www.ingramcontent.com/pod-product-compliance
Lightning Source LLC
Chambersburg PA
CBHW070909260626
47162CB00007B/2612